Angel

A Novel & Guide

Gregory Campisi

Published by
AWAKEN Center for Human Evolution
a 501(c)(3) Charitable Organization
Quakertown, PA

www.AwakenCHE.org

Cover design and book layout by Gregory Campisi

Written by Gregory Campisi

GregCampisi.com

ISBN: 978-1-7342299-8-1 (Paperback)
ISBN: 979-8-9871425-0-9 (Hardcover)

AngelNovel.com

*"Simply believe,
and the gates of Heaven themselves
open before you."*

Table of Contents

Author's Note

Thank you for choosing *Angel: A Novel & Guide.*

Like so many others who have chosen to read this book, simply by picking it up, you are opening a doorway and choosing to strengthen your connection with these heavenly beings of light we call Angels.

While I have included a short guide, *Connecting with Your Angel,* at the end of this book, the story itself serves as a guide. In addition to being a beautiful meta-fictional drama, the wisdom within was channeled to serve as a tool for understanding and connecting with the divine.

Allow this story to entertain as well as inspire, teach, and guide you to learn about, and connect with, your own Guardian Angel.

As you read this book, your connection to your own Angel (or Angels) will grow, and new and amazing experiences, synchronicities, and signs will manifest. Know that your Angel is always with you, loving you through every choice you make in this life. Even the times you feel most lost and alone are the times your Angel is closest to you—watching, loving, and waiting for you to intentionally acknowledge its presence and ask for its help.

Take note of any angelic experiences you have before, during, and after you've read this book. If you feel called to, please share your experiences with me, the Angel novel community, or with anyone you feel will believe and benefit from your own *Angel* story.

Thank you for believing.

Acknowledgments

First and foremost, I want to thank my wife, Susan Campisi, for supporting all my crazy, creative, and entrepreneurial endeavors, and for being so understanding of the amount of time dedicated to completing this book.

Thank you to all the amazing people in my life who have led me down the spiritual path and walked by my side, encouraged me, and taught me to trust my own inner voice above all. To Sam, Lisa, and Sheila, thank you for your invaluable suggestions, encouragement, and praise of my writing. And to my friend and copy editor, John, "your" the best.

To my father, now one of my Guardian Angels: I wish you could still be here sharing this journey in person, and I know you are sharing it with me from the other side. Thank you for all your guidance. To my brother and especially mom, my own Earth Angel who always watches over me, thank you for caring and loving me unconditionally—possibly too much :)

Lastly, and certainly not least, I am grateful for my own Angels, who consistently show me that I am not alone throughout my voyage of awakening, through the writing of this novel, and throughout this entire journey of life.

Prologue

We were a happy, loving family with a wonderful life, filled with a lot of good moments. But bad things can happen to any of us, and they did. Our happy life was ripped away because of the move. It left us in our own personal hell, asking, "What did we do to deserve this?"

The tragedy felt random and unfair, but through it all, I learned life's events seldom are. Sometimes it's the worst experiences in our lives that change us and open the doorway to better, even miraculous, experiences. Sometimes they are subtle, and sometimes they are life-altering.

In the aftermath of the tragedy, through the darkness that surrounded our family, something miraculous happened. And while it seems so long ago, the memories are just as strong today as they were when it occurred. If I told you what we saw and experienced, you'd probably think we made it up. But if you knew our story and the events leading up to that miraculous night —maybe, just maybe—you, too, will believe …

Chapter 1:

Seeds of
Doubt

*"Frustration grows from seeds of doubt
that we plant in our own gardens."*

~ o ~

"Goddamn it!" Wendi shouted.

Her left hand emerged from behind the foyer table, revealing a fresh tear in her delicate skin. She pivoted her wrist to observe the wound. Expecting to see gushing blood, she was bewildered to be met with a shallow scrape—such a superficial wound causing so much pain.

"Wendi, language!" came the voice of her husband from the other end of the hall.

"Seriously, Pete?" she fired back, tired of being reprimanded for her less than delicate expressions. "I just scraped my hand for nothing," she hollered. "The key isn't back there, so worry more about where my car key is and less about my language." She pressed her right hand against the smooth tabletop, rising to her feet. *This is a hell of a way to start the week*, she thought.

"I worry about how your language influences the kids. It hasn't been the best, you know."

"You want to talk about influencing the kids? Okay. Maybe we should talk about how your decisions have influenced this family."

"No, we shouldn't," he said with a sincere tone. "That horse has already been dead and beaten. No need to go there again for the four hundred and forty-fourth time."

"Then don't. Don't go there." She grabbed her purse, rummaging through it a third time. "Four hundred and forty-fourth time. Are you kidding?" she mumbled. "DAMN IT! It's not here. It's not anywhere. How am I supposed to get to work? And why the hell would you throw *that* number in my face?"

"Mind your language! And what are you talking about? It's just a random number that popped into my mind. I'm not throwing anything in your face."

"Jesus, you really don't pay attention to anything I tell you. 4:44? Ring any bells? I told you it happened again last night. I had the same bad dream about suffocating in some kind of cocoon, and I'm startled awake at exactly 4:44. Then I can't fall back asleep."

"I'm sorry, I didn't realize."

"Of course not, because you're sound asleep without a care in the world that your wife is sleepless right next to you."

"Wait a minute, that's not fair, I—"

"Don't start with me about fair. I told you yesterday about it and again this morning, and it doesn't even ring a goddamn bell."

"Enough with the cursing!" He shook his head in disapproval. "Faith isn't talking, but she hears just fine. Imagine she finally speaks again, and the first thing outta her mouth is 'goddamn'." He leaned over, prepping for an imaginary conversation. "Faith, do you have something you want to tell Mommy and Daddy? What? You do? What is it?" He raised the pitch of his voice, looked up at Wendi, and whispered, "Goddamn us, everyone."

"Real nice, Tiny Tim. Your timing is shit. This is not the time for jokes. If you're going to piss me off, at least say something that's actually funny. Luckily, I didn't marry you for your sense of humor."

"No? Then what *did* you marry me for?"

"I wish I knew," she snapped, slamming down her bag. "Jesus Christ, just help me find the car key so I can get out of this place."

"Jesus has better things to do. Try Saint Anthony, or better yet, let's call in an angelic locksmith." He raised his hand to his ear. "Hello? Car key Angels? We can use some help down here!"

"Goddamn it!" she snapped again, her face flush with anger. "I'm serious. This is *not* the time."

"It never is with you anymore. Fine, let's ask for help from something real. Misty, where are the keys?" Perched on the table next to Wendi, the cat was looking back and forth at them, observing the tennis match of emotions. Acknowledging her name, she tilted her head, looking at Pete.

"Just stop with all your stupid jokes. Read the room and learn when to take things seriously. The cat doesn't know where my goddamn key is!"

"Things around here are serious enough." He paused, wondering if the daily torture would ever end. *You don't always have to be so mean*, he silently commented to himself. "Just retrace your steps and we'll find your keys."

"*Key*, not keys. Don't you ever pay attention? The car key is on one of those cheap rings with the stupid yellow tag on it. We picked it up after the oil change. He also mentioned my brakes being low, and you didn't want to spend the money unless it was absolutely necessary. I mean, why would brakes be necessary? But why worry? You can just call on the brake Angels to stop my car."

"Who's got bad jokes now? We'll fix them before winter. It's not just an expense we—"

"I know. We already discussed it. Not the point right now," Wendi interrupted as she took a breath. "We got my car back last night, and I got out to grab the mail since you hadn't. I came in the front door. I put my bag down. I put the mail down, *right here*," she emphasized, smacking the pile of mail on the table, "and I put the key on top of it. I know it."

"Check your keyring again. Maybe it's on there and you missed it."

She reached into her purse. "We already covered that, Sherlock. My other keys are right here," she said, rattling them, "and it's not on there."

A small white paw stretched out toward the jingling keys. "Look at that," teased Pete. "Maybe Misty *did* steal it. We have a real *cat burglar* on the loose," he chuckled, amusing himself. "Misty, did you take the key? Where is it? Where did you put it?" Misty kept her gaze locked on the keys for a moment, then averted her attention to an empty space above Wendi's right shoulder.

Wendi glanced behind her, then back at Misty, whose gaze was still fixated on the empty space. "Great. All fluff and no brains."

A tug on her dress drew Wendi's attention away from Misty. She looked down to meet the sad, soft gaze of her daughter. "Oh, Faith. I'm didn't mean that, Angel. Mommy's frustrated and needs to get you to school and me to work. Have you seen my car key?"

Faith smiled, shifted her eyes to Misty, then followed her gaze past Wendi's shoulder. Pete, feeling like he was missing something, also stared into the same vacant space.

"Can someone tell me what the hell everyone is looking at?" Wendi demanded.

Pete threw up his hands. *Again with the language.*

Without warning, Misty leapt past Wendi. Startled, she stammered backward, tripped on the entryway rug, and fell back against the front door. Catching her balance, she peered down at her woven assailant, now crooked and rippled from the mishap. Misty's paw delved into the small opening caused by the bent rug. As she feverishly pawed at it, the corner of a small, yellow tag appeared. Wendi bent down, reached in, and victoriously emerged with her car key.

She looked at her husband. "I don't understand how it got under that heavy rug," she commented in a bewildered voice. "If I hadn't tripped, we would have never found it."

"Huh ... I guess Misty and our locksmith Angel *did* know where the key was."

"Well, I'm chalking this up to dumb luck," Wendi admitted. "But you can go ahead and give credit to the cat and invisible beings with bird wings."

"You can denounce God all you want, but there's no need to take your lack of faith out on innocent Angels ... or discredit Misty," he added, stroking the cat's head.

"Speaking of which," Wendi said, turning to Faith. "This little Angel needs to get to school. Are you ready?"

Faith didn't respond. In a daze, she stared off into space. "Faith, what are looking at?" Wendi asked. "Bobby took the bus. No one else is here. Let's go," she insisted, tugging her daughter's delicate hand and scurrying out the door.

oomph!

Scraping along the asphalt, Bobby's palms burned as they slid on its abrasive surface. His hands failed to break the fall, and his face followed. Someone's foot had deliberately caught his leg as he ran by. The pain hesitated, then slowly pulsated throughout his hands and cheek. Still lying on the blacktop, he felt a presence hovering above him.

A thick shadow fell across his body, blocking out the sun. Although no details of his assailant could be seen, he knew who it was. Laughter rang out around him as several other boys encircled him so the teachers couldn't see. He didn't care about the others. His ears were attuned to only one voice—that of Seth Baynes.

A genetic brute, Seth towered over kids his own age. Having already failed a grade, he also had the advantage of being a year older, making the other Sixth Graders look minuscule next to him.

"Have a nice trip, Boob-y?" Seth mocked. He turned to his cronies for praise, and they all laughed again. Seth was rarely alone. His crew loved to follow him around, joining him in instigating trouble and chaos.

Bobby pressed his palms against the blacktop, raising himself onto his knees. He looked down at his scraped palms, wondering if the abrasions were deep enough to bleed. "Yeah, I had a great trip. Your mom was there and said she isn't comin' home."

A large foot swiftly pressed into Bobby's spine, knocking him back to the ground. Red began to seep through the scrapes of his skin. "You think you're smart, Booby?" They all cackled some more. "You're the dumb-ass kissing the ground. It's the only action you're going to get."

The laughing and insults faded as a single word echoed in his mind. *Enough.* The burning of his face and hands conceded to the burning inside his being. Determination and anger held back the tears swelling in his eyes. Since the move, he no longer enjoyed childhood; he endured it.

"You gonna cry like your little sister does," Seth taunted. "Or maybe she can't cry, 'cause she can't talk. Or maybe she can, and she's just faking. I wouldn't talk if I had you for a brother, either. Maybe I'll call her Fake from now on. Hahaha."

He clenched his teeth. Bobby was used to the insults. They rolled off him like droplets of water on a windshield, but words about his sister triggered the monster inside. "Shut up or I'll shut you up!" Bobby shouted. He didn't blame Faith for not speaking. He often thought his life would be better if he didn't speak, either.

Seth turned to his friends and laughed, then looked at Bobby and sneered. "Awe, you gettin' mad? You gonna shut me up? You oughta take a hint from your sister and stop talking, too." The words were followed up by a foot, slamming into Bobby's ribs.

"Go to hell, loser!" Bobby yelled with what little air was left in his lungs. As he lay there, his mind flooded with uncontrollable thoughts of anger, hate, and detest—thoughts no eleven-year-old should have to bear.

A myriad of scenes ran through his head in an instant. In one, a swift kick to the groin brings Seth crippling to the ground. In another, Bobby sweeps Seth's leg, quickly rolls on top, and pummels him until he bleeds. In every scenario, Bobby's the hero, but the thoughts dancing in his mind never materialize the way he imagines. Real life tended to manifest in much harsher ways.

Bobby hated that they moved here. He hated leaving his friends. He hated being the new kid at school. And most of all, he hated Seth. He envisioned himself jumping to his feet, swinging wildly, and spinning around, knocking them to the ground one by one before they knew what hit them. "Say one more thing about my sister, and it's the last word outta your stupid mouth!"

Pushing himself to his feet, Bobby ignored the pain in his hands and lunged forward with all his might. He clenched his hand as hard as he could and flung it toward Seth's nose. It was met with a fleshy thud. To Bobby's surprise, it was not Seth's face his fist impacted. Someone else caught his punch.

The palm was too large to be Seth's or any of his friends. It was the hand of Mr. Wacher. "You're becoming a regular friend of trouble. Aren't you, Bobby Farfalla? Please come with me."

As Bobby looked up at his teacher, tears began to fall.

Pete's day was going the same as every other: slow and boring. He took the job for the money. He thought it would make life easier for his family, but things felt worse, not better. *It is good money*, he would tell himself each day, trying to ease the pain and guilt.

ring ring

He snapped out of his afternoon funk and reached over, picking up the phone.

"Hello? ... Yes, this is he .... What? ... *AGAIN!* I'm going to kick that boy's butt myself if he doesn't stop getting into trouble ... Yes, I'm sorry, I don't mean that literally. Wait, you're saying Faith was part of this? ... Now? No ... No, I can't leave right now. I'm at work. Did you call my wife? My job's a bit more important, so it's easier for her to ... You couldn't get a hold of her? ... Did you call again? ... I see. And why do they have to be picked up? We can discuss whatever disciplinary actions you advise, but I don't see a reason ... Is this a joke? This is absurd. I don't care what your policies about fighting are. You are seriously asking me to leave my job because you don't want them on the same bus? Tell the other boy's parents to get him and send my kids home on ... Oh, of course not. Of course, you can't get a hold of his parents. They're probably delinquents, too, or just too smart to answer the phone when you call. ... Well, I'm sorry if you don't appreciate my tone or accusations, but I'm not the one telling you to leave your job because someone else isn't doing theirs ... Well, I'm sorry that you don't appreciate my tone. I don't appreciate being interrupted at work."

Pete took a breath and continued. "I could lose my job if I have to keep leaving every time something happens at school ... Well, as far as I'm concerned, this is a matter the school should handle. This is a serious inconvenience ... No, I don't mean my children are an inconvenience. I mean leaving work to get them ... Fine ... Okay ... I'll come get them. Yes, they are still having a difficult time adjusting. I am *very* aware. It's been hard on all of us ... Okay. I'll leave as soon as I can ... Yes. I need about 20 minutes. Goodbye."

click

"And where exactly are you going?"

Pete flinched at the unexpected presence looming in his doorway. Pete didn't care much for his boss, Mr. Marshall, and his boss didn't seem to care much for Pete—or all the family problems he brought to the office every day.

"I'm sorry, sir. There's a problem at school. I have to go pick up the kids."

"I thought that was your wife's job?"

"She normally handles this, but they couldn't get a hold of her. I really do apologize. I'll stay later tomorrow to make up for missed time."

"And come in early while you're at it just in case there's another problem. You know, Pete, I pride myself on keeping my work in order, and not mixing it up with personal issues. That's how you get to be a productive employee, and that's how you get to be a manager. You can choose to climb the corporate ladder, or you can be the one at the bottom holding it for everyone else, letting them step on your fingers while you watch them ascend."

"Yes, sir. I'll be the first one in. Thank you for your inspiring words. I really do have to go, so please excuse me." The Marshal, which Pete liked to refer to him as, consistently found creative ways to voice his disappointment in Pete. Pete quickly learned to choose his words carefully when answering back. His boss made it very clear how expendable Pete was. He choked back his real sentiments. *I'll hold that ladder, alright, and ascend it up your—*

"And one more thing ..."

"Yes, sir?"

"We need to take another look at those reports you submitted last week. There were a few discrepancies." He nodded at Pete with a concerned look.

Pete swallowed his anger, feeling the burning inside his chest. He took a breath and nodded back. *This place is going to give me a heart attack. God help me.*

"Well, hop to it, Pete. You don't want to keep the school waiting," Mr. Marshall insisted with a touch of sarcasm.

"No, sir. I mean, yes, they are waiting for me. Apologies again. I'll see you in the morning."

"First thing."

Pete grabbed his coat and swallowed his pride. "Of course, first thing. Bright and early." Heading out the door, he mustered up a smile as he brushed past his boss. The Marshal stood there, eyeing Pete as he squeezed past.

It was days like this that made Pete lose a little more hope in returning to happiness. He couldn't risk losing his job. It would tear everything back down. As bad as things were, they were the best they had been since the move—since the accident. His job was the reason they were there, the reason they moved, the reason it all fell apart. What would be left if he lost it? *Please, God, let some light in, not just for me, but for my family.*

Pete rushed down the hall, rounded the corner, and abruptly stopped as a welcome face crossed his path.

"Is The Marshal after you again, Pete?"

"Don't I know it, Allen! That guy must have a sixth sense for always showing up at the worst time. I tell you, he has it in for me."

"The inmates get no respect around here," joked Allen.

Pete laughed. Allen was a true friend and one of the only friends Pete had made since the move. He was one of the few consolations of the job, aside from the generous pay. He had a special way of cheering up Pete and shining light on his dark times. Their conversations made the job bearable. It was Allen who started referring to Mr. Marshall as The Marshal; a little inside joke between the two of them. That alone diffused the tension.

"I don't blame ya for fleeing this place as fast as you can, but I'm guessing something's up. More trouble on the homefront?"

"Yeah, the school called. Bobby's at it again; started a fight or something. The school couldn't get a hold of Wendi, so now I gotta run over and pick up the kids. I don't know what to do with that boy, Allen. You ever hear of an eleven-year-old getting into so much trouble?"

"Give him a break, Pete. If things are still tense at home, he's coping the best he can. My guess is he misses the family life as it were, and his anger is a cry for love and attention. After all, when was the last time you really spent some father and son time together?"

"I don't know. I'm always busting my ass here. Seems like there's always some report I have to stay late for or bring home and work on over the weekend."

"Well, trust me, Pete. It's not worth trading your soul, or your family, for any amount of money."

"So, I just leave? Or risk getting fired? I need this job. I need the money. Who's going to take care of my family if I can't?"

"God, Peter. God takes care of us all. And I hear ya about the money, believe me, I do. But what good is the money if you don't have a family left to support?" He laid a hand on Pete's shoulder, pausing for a moment, then chuckled. "Glory be! What in the world am I doin' standing here holding you up when your kids are waitin' for ya? You take care of yourself first, Pete. Get your head and your heart straight and the rest will fall into place, God willing."

"You're a miracle, Allen, and a blessing. Thank you, my friend. See you tomorrow ... God willing."

~~~ O ~~~

The door flung open and with it, a sigh of relief. Wendi shuffled out of the meeting and back to her desk. *Well, that was a waste of time. Imagine how much more work would get done if we didn't keep meeting about work.* There were meetings about too much work, meetings about not enough work, and even meetings to schedule meetings.

She flopped down at her desk and a red flashing light caught her attention. "Why is it I don't get a call all day, and every time I have a meeting, there are messages waiting?" she mumbled to herself. Wendi lifted the receiver and dialed her voicemail ...

"You have four new messages. First message, received at 2:22 p.m."

Imagine that. 2:22. That's when I walked into the meeting room and Miguel commented I was eight minutes early. She brushed it off as a coincidence and shifted her attention back to the voicemail. It was the school calling. She pressed the phone to her ear, listening intently. Another issue with Bobby. They needed to speak with her immediately. Second message ... silence, followed by a click. Third message ... same voice as the first ...

"It's Sandy over at the school, calling about your son again. We don't feel it's prudent to send him home on the bus with the boy he had the confrontation with, and we need him picked up, plus the principal would like a word about the incident. Now, I understand I'm not to bother Mr. Farfalla at work, but this is the third time I've called and can't get a hold of you. I'm going to ring him and ask that he handles this situation." Wendi glanced at the time. 3:33. *Damn it. Pete's probably at the school by now.* "We'll call back if we can't reach him. Thank you. Goodbye."

Wendi hung up and swiftly dialed the school. *Just great. I can hear him now. Wendi, how many times do I have to tell you I can't be interrupted at work? My job's too important ... Well, too bad. He has to learn that being a good father is occasionally more important than being a good employee.*

No answer at the school. *Ugh, voicemail ...* "Hello, this is Wendi Farfalla. I'm assuming you got a hold of my husband since I didn't hear back. I wanted to confirm. Thank you." *God forbid she makes an extra call to let me know.* Wendi planted the receiver.

"Why can't the school just send him home on the goddamn bus? Christ almighty," she blurted aloud.

"Well, I'll be," came a voice from the next cubicle. "Don't go having yourself a hissy fit," insisted Patty, as her big, red, curly hair popped up over the cubicle wall faster than a curious meerkat.

Patty never missed a beat or a single note of gossip; she lived and breathed it. If there was drama to be uncovered, Patty would find it, or she'd make it. "Now I know things still aren't well at home, and Lord knows you were in a tizzy when you started here, but you never used to cuss or use the Lord's name in vain like this before. So tell me, how bad is it?"

"I swear your ears are radars, Patty. I'm sorry to tell you, but the only difference between then and now is that I don't hold it in anymore. I—" Wendi paused as the small, red blinking light seized her attention. "Hold on, Patty. I missed the last message." She swiftly lifted the receiver and dialed back into voicemail. *Maybe the school didn't get a hold of Pete.*

"Wendi, where the hell are you? The school called me." *No such luck.* "I have to pick up the kids. Something about Bobby getting into in a fight. They said they tried you three times and you're still MIA, so I'm heading over. How many times do I have to tell you? I can't be interrupted at work, not unless it's an emergency. No one is bleeding, nothing is broken, and no one is dead. That school doesn't seem to understand. I can't just leave work every time Bobby has an attitude problem. You know how much stress and pressure I'm under as-is. We'll talk about this when you get home."

She let out a grunt and put down the phone with just enough force to satisfy her urge to slam it. Feeling a lingering presence, Wendi looked to her right, expecting to see Patty still eavesdropping, but she had popped back into her hole. An unfamiliar voice from over her shoulder caught her off-guard.

"Now, now, Deary. Don't get yourself in a tizzy. Can't be all that bad."

Wendi flinched, embarrassed to see who else caught her vexing. Standing behind her was the new temp, Angie. She was a short, adorably pudgy woman. Curvy, but not quite large, as Patty and her catty girls would describe some of the other co-workers. Angie had youthful skin and wonderfully round, rosy cheeks. She could easily pass herself off as Mrs. Claus, and just as well, as no one was sure exactly how old she was.

"Sorry," Wendi responded. "I didn't even ... How long ... I didn't notice you were—"

"Don't worry 'bout that. Most people 'round here don't pay me any mind, especially being a temp and all," Angie responded in her subtle Southern twang. She leaned in and whispered, "Oddly enough, though, they seem to have plenty to say behind my back. But that don't bother me none. If someone ever has somethin' to say behind your back, Deary, that's just their own insecurity talkin'," she added with a chuckle. "Oh, my goodness. I'm already gettin' sidetracked. But don't you worry. If you ever need an ear, I can listen just as well as I can talk. Oh, and I know we were chattin' the other day, but in case you forgot, the name is Angie, Dear." She reached her hand out, giving Wendi a gentle, yet firm handshake.

"I was passin' by and felt all that frustration pouring out of you, and I just *had* to stop and check in." She leaned in, lowering her voice again. "But to be honest, I would've felt you from across the room, Dear, with the aura you were givin' off. Everything okay?"

Lost in a fog of Angie's quick and mesmerizing tone, Wendi mumbled a quick reply. "Uh, yes. Just a little issue with my son at school."

"Well, I hope it all works out. But you be careful, now. Frustration grows from seeds of doubt that we plant in our own gardens. If you let it flourish into fear and anger, you eventually forget what the root of it all was. And then you're left in the dark with only your anger," Angie blurted out in her typical sweet tone. "And mind that nasty scrape on the back of your hand, Deary. The longer your wounds go without proper healin', the deeper they'll get."

Planting seeds? Deeper wounds? What in the world is this woman talking about? Wendi barely knew Angie, but already felt like she needed an interpreter to decipher her mysterious anecdotes. "Um, Okay. Thank you so much, Angie." *Where's Patty when you need her?* Wendi turned her head, hoping Patty would jump in to save her, but no such luck. She turned back, and

Angie had disappeared. Wendi peered down the aisle, but there was no sign of her.

"What was that about?" Patty's head popped up over the cubicle like a whack-a-mole. "Weeds of doubt? Plantin' gardens? That woman is sooo odd."

"She sure is. I never know what she's trying to say. Hopefully, she won't be here long."

"So, what happened with Bobby this time that has you slammin' down the phone? You plantin' your anger garden, hun?"

"I got an anger tree, Patty," Wendi said sarcastically. "They called Pete to pick up the kids. Now, I know it doesn't sound like a big deal. But God forbid he got laid off because of leaving work early. I'd never hear the end of it. They say happiness doesn't come from money. But let me tell you, we're sure as hell not living off what I make around here," Wendi jeered as they both laughed.

"Amen to that, sister! Well, alrighty, then. I guess we know what you're afraid of ... afraid of not payin' the bills!" They chuckled again.

"Yeah," Wendi sighed. "I never used to get angry like this. Neither of us did. We never even fought." She paused as tears began to swell in the corner of her eyes. "That was our thing, you know. We were that couple who never fights. Finishes each other's sentences. And now look at us. I don't know how—" Losing her voice, Wendi closed her eyes and let the world fade out for a moment, then wiped her tears. "Well, shit, Patty. I guess Angie was right. I'm angry and miserable, and I'm afraid of staying this way."

"Well, if you're so unhappy, just leave him already. I got a list of half a dozen eligible bachelors right here in this office," she announced with a wink.

Wendi allowed a smile to break through. "This may sound crazy, but as unhappy as I am, I just can't leave. I can't tear my family apart like that. It doesn't feel right. Something's still holding us together ... just barely."

"Well, if you're not going to be leavin', then ya better stop using the Lord's name in vain and start prayin' to him instead," Patty insisted.

"God doesn't want to hear my prayers," Wendi mournfully replied. "Not anymore."

"Now, why would ya say a thing like that?"

"I ... I'd rather not talk about it. I can't believe I'm standing here crying about my life because the office whackadoo came out of nowhere and blurted out some cryptic message that I need a decoder ring to understand. Then she disappears like a damn magician. And how does she know how I feel?"

"Magician? More like a witch! You've been victim to a fly-by bewitchin'! She does 'em all the time. I tell ya, that woman is odd, with a capital O. I just avoid her. That way she can't be brainwashin' me with her crazy spells," Patty laughed, waving her arms over her head.

"Come on. She's not that bad. I feel bad for judging her myself."

"Uh-oh, It's too late! She's already brainwashed ya. Ya didn't drink her Kool-Aid, did ya? I mean, have ya seen her desk? She's a witch, I tell ya. Probably has a voodoo doll of me in her drawer. I think I'm feelin' a pain in my neck right now!" She plucked an invisible needle from her neck, cracking herself up. "So anywho, enough about office witchcraft. All those messages for ya ... Bobby gettin' in trouble at school again?"

"Yes, he got into some kind of a fight again. Not sure of the details, but I gotta get home to do some damage control. Pete was not happy about leaving work early. I'll see you tomorrow, Patty."

"Sure as sugar, sweetness. And you can fill me in on all the details in the mornin'."

"Glad to know you're looking forward to the drama," Wendi nudged, "because I'm certainly not."

~~~ O ~~~

"What the hell is it this time, Bobby?" Pete felt his chest tighten as his gaze fixated on the reflection of his son in the rearview mirror, ignoring the road. *This kid's going to be the death of me.* As much as Pete was afraid of losing his family, he allowed the fear of losing his job to overrule the consequences of his words. Negative thoughts had marinated in his mind the entire ride, and he was ready to burst. "Why can't you manage to make it through *one day* without trouble? Is that so difficult?"

Bobby sat, arms crossed, staring out the window, avoiding his father's eyes. "I got through yesterday just fine," he mumbled.

"Real nice response, smart ass. Yesterday was Sunday."

"I didn't start any trouble. It wasn't my fault."

Pete held his stare on Bobby's reflection a moment longer before replying. "Of course, it's not your fault. You had nothing to do with it. Things are hard enough on this family right now and on me. How am I supposed to get my work done if I'm driving to school to pick you up? Do you want me to lose my job?"

"I don't care."

"Of course, you don't care. Well, you better start caring. You think you have such a rough life? See how rough it is when we don't have money to live on!"

Bobby's eyes stayed fixed on the passing landscape, but he felt his father's stare. "I hope you lose your stupid job," he breathed, still mumbling, "Then I never have to see this dumb place again, and we can move back home."

Sadness overwhelmed Pete's anger. Even if he lost his job, they couldn't afford to move back up north. One way or another, even if it killed him, they were staying. His tone drastically shifted. "I'm sorry you feel that way, Bud. This *is* our home, and it's going to be for a while. I need you to understand that and stop all this fighting. Stop fighting me, stop fighting at school, stop fighting whatever it is you think you're fighting. I need to be at work right now, but I'm here, driving you. So, go ahead and tell me. What happened this time that apparently wasn't your fault?"

silence

"HEY!" Pete yelled, as anger flooded back into his veins like a bursting dam. Bobby snapped out of his trance, connecting eyes with his dad for the first time since he got in the car. "Answer me when I speak to you! Why did I have to pick you up from school?"

"I don't know. Why did you? Where's mom?"

"Great question. I don't know why she couldn't get you, but she couldn't. So now I'm the one you need to answer to. What happened?"

"It wasn't my fault."

"Of course, it wasn't. It never is. The other kid made you mouth off, and he asked you to hit him, right?"

"They started it. I was jus—"

"Let me guess. You were an innocent bystander? You're a little Angel, and everyone starts fights with you for no reason?"

"YES! Seth start—"

"NO!" Pete shouted, cutting off Bobby's words again. "Whoever it was, I'm sure you did your share to provoke things and keep it going. The school told me you were fighting with this boy. Luckily, they stopped you before anyone got hurt, or worse."

"*I* got hurt!" yelled Bobby. "But it wasn't until he ... I was going to bash his face—" His throat clenched up, forcing him to pause as tears welled up in his eyes. "Forget it." He took an unsteady breath of air, fighting back the emotion. "You don't care who started it. You don't care about me. You don't care about our family. You only care about your stupid work." Bobby turned his head back to the window, watching the trees glide by.

Sadness engulfed Peter's heart again. "That's not true, Bud. Do you hear me? That's not true. I care about you and this family very much. More than you know. I work so much because I care. But we're talking about you right now, not me. No action goes without reaction. What if you get kicked out of school? Then what? Do we have to send you to a private school? Do you know how much that costs? It's time you started taking responsibility for your actions." Pete took in a long breath. "Jesus, how many times do I have to pray to end to all this?"

"If we didn't move to stupid North Carolina for your stupid job, everything would be fine. Mom wouldn't have gotten hurt, Faith would be talking, and I'd have—"

"You watch yourself, young man," he interjected with a stern voice, flopping between anger and regret like a fish out of water. "Don't blame everything else for your bad attitude. You control your own reactions. You're the only one getting yourself in trouble."

"I'm not! It's those stupid kids. And that stupid school. And this stupid place. I wish we never moved here! I wish none of this ever happened! NONE OF IT!"

Silence filled the car. Pete wished for the same thing. Hopelessness weighed down his heart. "We all wish we never moved, Bud, especially me. Believe me, I'm sorry. I'm sorry for everything. I'm sorry your sister won't talk. I'm sorry you're having a tough time at school. I'm sorry you're not happy here. None of us are happy here." Pete paused and took a breath. "I've been praying every day for things to change. I'm even looking for a new job, but there aren't any good opportunities without a big pay cut. We need the money right now."

Pete looked into the rearview mirror again, focusing on Faith. "And how many times do I have to pray for you, Little Angel? How many prayers before you'll speak to us again?"

silence

"We know you can talk, Angel. We've heard you whispering to your invisible friend. Do you think it's time to break your silence? Maybe tell us how you feel about all this?"

silence

"Why should she talk? You don't listen," muttered Bobby.

Faith looked over at Bobby, smiled, then returned to her typical peaceful trance, staring into space. Sullenness filled the remainder of the ride. Pete and Bobby sat quietly, their hearts longing for peace, while their minds filled with cries of anguish. Only Faith seemed content. Nothing bothered her as long as she remained in her own world.

Pete rounded the corner of their street. *Home at last. Thank God.* He sped into the driveway, clicked the garage door opener, and abruptly stopped. The door remained shut. He impatiently clicked it again and again. *I just changed these batteries!* The door began to open, stopped, then slowly shut. *I can open the damn thing faster myself.* He cautiously clicked the button one more time and waited for the door to re-open.

~~~ O ~~~

As Wendi raced home, her mind raced with her. *It's going to be one of those nights. Not like it's my fault. I have a job, too. He's not the only one supporting this family. It doesn't pay as much, but I'm still important to the business.* Her grip tightened around the steering wheel. The world around her phased into nothingness as her thoughts suffocated her mind. *Ugh, who am I kidding? They would replace me in an instant. Pete needs his job. He'll say he'll get canned, but he'll be fine. But then again, he works for a real asshole who would fire him over any stupid issue. What if he really does get fired? Jesus, what the hell would we do then? Tell me that, God. What the hell would we do then?* She shook her head, tightening her grip on the wheel. *Why am I asking you? It's not like you're listening. Not when we really need you.*

Her mind continued, oblivious to her foot weighing down the gas pedal. Trees and signs whizzed past her as she gained momentum. *Jesus, what a mess we are. Pete's angry. Bobby's angry. I'm angry. And my little Angel, my Faith, is still silent. Maybe we should all stop talking. Just live like ghosts.* Tears started flowing. *How did we get here? This can't be my life. This isn't me. This isn't—*

The bright red glow of taillights in front of her snapped her back to reality. "Shit!" Her foot reacted, thrusting hard on the brake. The car wailed to an abrupt stop, jerking her body forward. The seat belt locked, restraining her torso, whipping her head forward, then back. Her heart pounded. *I need to pay more attention to the road or it's going to get me killed.* As she surveyed her surroundings, her eyes focused on the rearview mirror, witnessing the vehicle behind skidding toward her. She tensed up, bracing herself. The driver reacted, stomping on the brakes and halting inches from her bumper.

A jolt of adrenaline triggered her dark memories. The storm. The plane rocking back and forth. Faith's crying. The flight attendant yelling. Feeling so overwhelmed. Her whole body began to relive it. The pounding of her heart reverberated throughout her being. The stress. The rage. The sudden jolt—

honk! honk!

Wendi snapped back to the present. The light was green and the three cars in front of her were already through the intersection. Her foot shifted off the brake and she hit the gas. She continued her journey home on autopilot, allowing happy memories of the past to creep in. She thought about all the adorable things Faith used to say and what a kind, gentle soul her boy used to be—before it all changed. Time has a way of playing tricks when caught in the spider webs of the mind. Hours seem like minutes and minutes seem like hours. It wasn't until she turned the corner of the neighborhood that she noticed the time. 4:44.

She glanced at the clock again. 4:44. *Triple digits again? How's this possible? I got to the meeting at 2:22 and the first voicemail was also left at 2:22, which alone is nuts.* She turned down the first street.

Then it was 3:33 when I listened to them. I heard the message exactly an hour and eleven minutes later. She turned another corner onto her street.

And now I'm home at 4:44, the same time I've woken up the past three nights. This can't be real. A streak of white whisked overhead, pulling her out of her mind.

Is that a dove? Barely watching the road, she dodged her head back and forth, trying not to lose sight of it in the late afternoon sun. It looked like it had landed on her house, but the hedges were in the way. *There are no doves around here. And it's not a seagull. I'm losing my mind.* The glare of the sun dazzled her eyes. She flinched as she turned into the driveway.

As Pete was waiting for the garage door to open, he peered back at the children in the rearview mirror. Bobby was still ignoring him, and Faith was looking out of her window. Her head pivoted as she followed something overhead. He followed her gaze, tracking a pair of white wings soaring through the air. As it flew out of his field of view, something in the mirror caught his eye—a familiar car whipping into the driveway behind him.

The only reaction he could muster was bracing himself while yelling out, "Whoa! WHOA!"

screeeech!

The seat belts locked as the car jolted forward. Everyone's wide eyes stared at each other in shock.

"OH, COME ON!" Pete yelled, throwing his arms up toward the sky. "This is quite the icing on my afternoon cake!" He shook his head. "Kids, you okay?"

Bobby looked over at his little sister, who was nodding her head. "Yeah, it was just a bump. We're fine."

Each respective car door opened, and Pete and Wendi jumped out onto the driveway. Pete swiftly approached her, jerking his arms up in his infamous "what the hell" expression.

"I ... I didn't see you," she stammered, knowing the day was already bad enough. "I didn't expect you to be sitting in the driveway. Luckily, it was just a tap."

"A tap? A second longer on the gas and you would have rammed me and the kids right through."

The kids are okay, right?"

"Yeah, Mom," Bobby replied as he grabbed Faith's hand, gently escorting her out of the car. His other hand held tight to the strap of his backpack, hiding his scraped palm from his mother's keen eyes. Pete hadn't noticed the abrasions on his hands, but physical marks seldom get past Wendi. He swiftly led Faith into the house before the yelling started.

Outside, Pete continued his rant. "Where the hell was your mind? How can you turn into a driveway and not see my car sitting right here?"

"It's those damn hedges. I told you before. They're too tall. I can't see the driveway until I turn into it. Plus, I was … I was following a dove, I think. I came around the corner, and there was this pure white bird that came out of nowhere, flying toward the house, but disappeared into the sun."

"Seriously? That's really what you're going with? You almost smashed into the car your children were in because you were watching a bird?"

"I can't explain it. The dove seemed important, and I saw the numbers and—"

"There are no doves around here, and no bird, dove or not, is that important," he interrupted. "We are your family. We're important. Stop daydreaming, pay attention to the road, and you won't run us over. Got it? Great." He sighed. "You're going to end up in a serious accident if you don't pay more attention when you drive. I saw a bird, too, but that didn't mean I stepped on the gas and rammed into the garage, did it?"

"Jesus. Don't be so dramatic. You're always overreacting."

"Jesus, indeed. It's funny how often you say the name of someone you have no faith in. And I'm not overreacting. This time was just a tap, but what if Faith was playing in the driveway and you hit her instead? What then?"

Wendi's eyes welled up. "*That* is not fair. Why would you say that? Why the hell would you say something like that, Pete?"

Pete's expression, along with his entire body, went catatonic, like a deer in headlights. He knew he had gone too far.

Wendi didn't let up. "I told you before to cut those damn hedges so I can see the damn driveway before I pull into it! God forbid the horrific scene you just painted for us were to actually happen. That would be on you! What a family we would be then. You'd have two dead children to blame me for."

Her words cut deep into his heart. Pete softened his voice. He had already lost the fight. "I keep them that way so we have some privacy from our nosey neighbor, who, by the way, is listening to this whole fight. And I don't blame you. I never have. It was an accident ... And please stop saying 'damn'." He shook his head again. "You damn everything you hate. Maybe try blessing a few things instead."

"A blessing isn't going to change the hedges," Wendi mumbled as she reached into the car, grabbing her purse. She stood up and looked her husband dead in the eye. "Just cut the DAMN things down and I won't have to worry about running over my own daughter." She slammed her car door.

Without another word, she walked away, retreating from the daylight into the shadow of the garage. She left her car right where it was, along with her husband, alone in the chill of the dimming sunlight.

Solemnly, Pete pulled each car into their respective spots and closed the garage door. He sat there for a moment in the darkness of his thoughts. The cold, dim loneliness of the garage felt more welcoming than his own home.

~ o ~

Chapter 2:

Losing
Faith

*"Where are you when
I need you most, God?"*

~ o ~

clink clink

Wendi tapped the spatula on the side of the pan, grabbed the handle, and headed for the table. She felt like slamming it down on the hot plate, but placed it down gently instead. *Deep breath. It's not the food you're mad it.*

Whenever she was frustrated or upset, she took solace in creating a delicious meal to distract her from the demands of her thoughts. Cooking carried her back to childhood when dinnertime was a safe and happy place.

As a toddler, Wendi loved assisting her mom in the kitchen—although she would often make more of a mess than actually help. Her mom, however, had the perfect solution when she bought Wendi an Easy-Bake Oven. While her mom prepared dinner, Wendi would experiment with her own recipes. She liked getting her hands dirty mixing the ingredients, but she'd still end up making a mess. Despite that, her mom adored having her little girl beside her in the kitchen, and Wendi grew up with a love for cooking.

As a young adult, cooking became an outlet for Wendi. Anytime she was upset, especially about a boy, she would go crazy in the kitchen. She'd cook up a storm, making more food than she needed for a week. It was a great excuse to invite friends over for a big dinner. They were happy to indulge in a free meal, and it gave Wendi the space to spill out her emotions while they ate.

Tradition was important in Wendi's family, and Sundays were a special time. Every Sunday, the family would come together over a big meal that her mom and grandmom had prepared. Wendi would awaken to a buffet of aromas filling the home from sunrise to sunset. Sunday dinners were a time for togetherness and being present with family. No matter how bad anyone's week was, negativity was left at the door.

She had learned a lot about cooking—and life—from both her mom and grandmom. She would listen to them talk as they made meals together. Her grandmom would always spout tidbits of wisdom while seasoning and cooking each dish. "The kitchen is the heart of the home," she would emphasize. "And dinnertime is where family comes together."

Her grandmother was a very traditional housewife. She would serve the men first, insisting that they were the heads of the household. Then she'd serve the children, and finally, herself. "It's a joy to serve others," she would say, pausing to taste whatever delightful dish she was stirring. "It keeps you humble in your heart and in God's eyes." But the most important lesson Wendi held onto was this: dinnertime was about sharing love, not just eating a meal. Those words were often her salvation.

"Dinnertime!" Wendi called out as she placed the last dish on the table. "Pour yourself a drink and have a seat."

No matter how bad anyone's day was, she did her best to make dinner a time for togetherness and being present with each other. Tonight, however, cooking dinner wasn't about feeding her family; it was her therapy. And it wasn't working. Cooking had helped to center her, but resentment was still coursing through her body.

Wendi smiled at Faith, picked up her plate first, and gently placed some chicken on her dish. It was accompanied by a few pieces of asparagus, a scoop of mashed potatoes, and a spoonful of peas—which she then mixed into the potatoes. She made sure she had plenty of vegetables at every meal. As a child, she would complain about having to eat her veggies, but her mother's words eventually got to her. "You can't have too much green on the scene. Now eat up, Pumpkin, so you can sprout!"

She cut up Faith's chicken, then served Bobby, and then herself. She left Pete's plate lying in front of him, empty. She sat down, and cut into the tender, juicy meat. As her fork approached her lips, Peter cleared his throat. Her hand paused just before the fork entered her mouth and glanced over.

"Aren't you forgetting something?" he questioned.

"You can serve your—"

"Grace," he interrupted. "Since when do we start eating without saying grace?"

She lowered the fork. "I didn't think anyone would mind," she responded. "I'm not feeling very gracious tonight."

"It's days like this we need it most. We may not go to church anymore, but faith is still part of the rest of this family," he affirmed, winking at Faith as he typically did when using her namesake in a sentence. He continued, "You don't have to join the prayer. Just don't stop it for the rest of us."

She looked at her children, who were both patiently waiting to begin their meal. "Okay," she agreed, resting her fork on her plate and clasping her hands together. "Go on."

"Okay, then." He nodded to his children, waiting for them to close their eyes. He bowed his head and began. "Thank you, Lord, for this wonderful meal you have provided us. We thank you for your blessings, and pray for your help: to keep this family from falling apart, to prevent our son from acting on his inner demons, to allow our little Angel to find her voice again, and to help my wife keep her eyes on the road." Pete peered over at Wendi, who hadn't bothered to close her eyes, and was not amused. "Amen," he ended, unfolding his fingers and grabbing his fork and knife.

Wendi parted her mouth, about to reply, and thought better of it. She turned her attention to her son instead. "Bobby, why do you keep getting into trouble at school? Do you care to explain what happened today?"

"No, I don't care to explain. I'd like some privacy," he replied with a sarcastic grin.

"Is that so, Mr. Smart-ass?" she asked.

"Wendi," Pete interjected. "Enough already with the potty mouth around Faith."

"Fine," Wendi sighed with exasperation and shifted her glance back at Bobby. "I am your mother, Robert Jonathan Farfalla. There are certain things you may keep private, and *this* is not one of them. And don't think I hadn't noticed your scraped hands. Now explain to me what happened at school today. Thank you."

"It was nothing, Mom."

"If it was nothing," Pete refuted, "the school wouldn't have called, and I wouldn't have left work early to get you."

"This is serious," interjected Wendi. "We need to know what really happened. Now you can tell us, or we can look up this Seth kid's phone number and call his parents to learn more."

A myriad of emotions overtook Bobby's expression, from anxiety and fear to worry and shame. His lips parted, but no words came out.

Wendi watched her son struggling and softened her tone. "I know it hasn't been an easy adjustment for you, and it may be difficult to talk about, but we already have one child not talking. I can't handle you not talking either. Please, tell me what happened. I want to hear your side of it."

Bobby took a breath and tried to push his words past the rising wall of emotions. "Seth and his friends … They're all … They're a bunch of jerks … He tripped me, and—"

"And that does not mean you get to punch him in return," interrupted Pete.

"I wasn't done!" Bobby burst out. "I don't care what he does to me. He started picking on Faith, and," Bobby looked at his innocent little sister with sympathetic eyes. "I won't let him pick on her. Even if I have to shut him up."

"And where did that get you? Punching someone is *not* the answer to *any* situation, no matter how hurt your feelings are," Pete reprimanded.

Before Bobby could respond again, Wendi jumped in with a surprising reply. "Your dad is right," she said with a sigh, adding, "but he doesn't have to be an ass about how he says it." She continued on, ignoring Pete's reaction. "We understand why you would want to hit him. If I saw him hurting you, I'd punch the little sh—" she caught herself, feeling Pete's stare intensifying, "uh, little son of a gun, myself."

"Nice parenting, Hun. Maybe I should take it from here," Pete jabbed. "It's very noble of you to stand up for your sister. But you need to be better than Seth. He's making fun of your sister not to hurt her, but to hurt you. He knows it riles you up. As long as you let his words get under your skin, he'll keep at it. Bullies like Seth like to torment people because they are the ones who are really hurting. For him to treat you that way, who knows what his family is like. Hurt people hurt people. Do you understand?"

"Yeah, I guess," mumbled Bobby. *And I don't care. He's still an ass.*

"Good," continued Pete. "It's not going to do you or this family any good if you get suspended, even for your sister's sake. Sometimes you have to bite your tongue," he advised, inadvertently glancing at his wife.

She looked Pete dead in the eyes. "Why are you looking at me when you say that? Maybe you should bite your own tongue, Mr. You're Going to Kill Another Child!"

"I didn't say that!"

"You may as well have said it. It's what you were thinking!"

Bobby sunk into his seat and quietly kept eating. The attention was off of him, but the conversation got worse—much worse. He hastily shoveled down the remainder of his dinner to get away from the table as quickly as he could.

"That's not what I said, and that's not what I meant," Pete fired back. "Don't put words into my mouth. If you watched where you were going, my bumper wouldn't have a dent in it!"

"Well, maybe some people get what they deserve!"

"Oh, I see. So it's okay to react and lose your temper when someone deserves it? That's the brilliant lesson you have for our son? Is it also okay to blame others for the mistakes you make, too? It's my fault, even though I wasn't even on the goddam plane?" Pete's expression quickly changed. The words had fallen out of his mouth before he realized it. There was no putting them back; he had gone too far—again. The anguish was palpable.

Wendi's heart dropped. *He didn't need to go there.* She wasn't sure if the tears forming in the corners of her eyes were from sadness or hate. She was torn between the pain of self-loathing and the bitterness of blame that she so often crucified her husband with.

No matter her response, there would never be a winner in this fight. Quietly, she arose from her chair and began clearing the table. She grabbed Bobby's plate, which was now empty, and her own, with an unfinished dinner still upon it, and walked into the kitchen. Pete wished he had taken his own advice and bit his tongue. He placed his hands on the table, about to rise, but the disheartening look in his son's eyes gave him pause.

Pete glanced at Faith, then back to Bobby. "I'm really sorry you had to hear all that, kiddos. Apparently, it's not the best day for any of us."

"Yeah," he said softly, looking down.

Pete nodded, rose from his seat, and walked away in silence.

Bobby peered over at his sister who also sat in silence, but hers was the only one not invoked by tonight's squabble. "You okay?" he asked.

The worry faded from her eyes as she managed a slight smile and nodded. Bobby smiled in return, stood, and followed his parents' lead, walking away in silence. Wendi watched from the kitchen as the boys abandoned their seats, leaving Faith alone. Sitting there in her chair, she turned her head and whispered something into the stillness beside her. A broad smile swept across her face, as if she had received a whimsical reply, and she finished her dinner in happy solitude.

squiiish

A glob of toothpaste engulfed the bristles of his toothbrush as Pete clenched the tube. He looked up, staring into his reflection in the bathroom mirror. *What a day. I can't wait to see what tomorrow will bring.* There were always good days and bad days, but the bad days were winning as of late. What had life become when his favorite part of the day was its end? Pete simply tolerated each day, looking forward to a good night's sleep and the hope of happy dreams.

He looked at the tired man staring back at him and sighed. *What happened to happiness?* He leaned closer to the mirror, staring deep into his own eyes. He looked for a hint of joy, just a spark of anything other than sadness. He was trying to recognize even a hint of the man he used to know.

He raised his toothbrush and slowly began to scrub. The past year had taken its toll. He was worn out and bitter. He was stressed and tired. He leaned back away from his own empty reflection and shook his head.

Wendi leaned over and peered into the bathroom. Pete had just started brushing his teeth. She quickly slid off her pants, pulled off her shirt, unhooked her bra, and slid on her nightgown, shamefully hiding her body from her husband. Despite how many arguments they had in a day, Peter was always quick to forgive when bedtime rolled around. He never liked going to bed upset. For Wendi, she couldn't handle even the thought of intimacy when she was upset. Going to bed with a heavy heart had become part of her nightly ritual.

She wasn't like him. She couldn't just erase her memory and feelings and let something dissolve into thin air. Until it was resolved completely in her mind, it ate away at her for weeks, months, or years, if it had to.

What a day, he thought to himself again, rehashing the conversation with his boss, the driveway incident, and topping it off with their dinner argument. *What am I supposed to do? Quit? Move back? That won't fix what's already broken.* Giving up on the job felt like giving up on everything. It was like throwing in the towel and saying, "Sorry. We went through it all for nothing." *Marshal will probably fire me before I have a chance to quit, anyway.* He didn't want to think about it anymore. He rinsed his toothbrush, put it in its holder, and paused. *God, what am I supposed to do? How do we fix this?*

He reached for the bar of face soap and hesitated as he picked it up, noticing his thumb covering the arch of the D in Dove.

There across its smooth surface was his answer: *Love.* His heart sank. *I wish it were that easy. Maybe it is for you, Lord, but we humans seem to have a limited supply of love. This family is just about out of our rations.* He shook his head, covering and uncovering the arch of the D. Love. Dove. Love. *Huh. What a strange coincidence.* He shifted his thumb again. *Dove. She said she saw a dove?*

Wendi crawled into bed, reached over, and turned off the light. She didn't care that it would leave Peter in the dark as soon as he turned off the bathroom light. She didn't want to see him, and she didn't want him looking at her.

Pete finished up and flicked off the bathroom light, allowing pure darkness to engulf him. There were degrees to Wendi's mood upon bedtime, and when the light was out before he was done washing up, he knew it was bad. He turned the bathroom light back on for a moment, checking for shoes or random items on the floor he might trip over. He took a mental snapshot of his pathway to the bed, flipped the switch, and made his way through the darkness.

Wendi lay there, staring into the blackness, wrestling with her thoughts. *I'm tired of feeling this way. I'm tired of being angry. Tired of being bitter. Tired of being unhappy. God, make it stop.* She laughed to herself. *He doesn't hear you, anyway. Why bother?* Her heart was already broken, and now what was left of it was crumbling.

With nothing left to lose and nowhere else to turn, she breathed in and silently began. *Fuck it. God, if you're there, if you hear me and you're actually listening, I'm asking you one last time. Please help this family. Maybe things will never be the same, but I can't live like this. I'll end up killing myself. Help us find a way back to the light.*

She wiped away the trickle of tears slinking down her face and closed her eyes. Memories of a happier time began to dance in her mind. She remembered her family like it used to be. Dinnertime was one of the highlights of her day. After whipping up another creation in the kitchen, they would all happily share stories about their day. Bobby was always in a good mood, excited about something he did in school, and Faith consistently had something absolutely adorable to add.

While she lay there drifting off to sleep, a smile slowly crept across her face. Her mind continued to drift backward in time, remembering Faith as a baby, the birth of their first little boy, and back to their wedding day. She had so many happy memories in her mind. During her waking hours, however, she kept them locked in a vault, prisoner to the pain she held onto. Life had turned upside-down in an instant for her, but it felt like the aftermath and misery had lingered for an eternity.

~~~ O ~~~

bong

Wendi's fingers froze on the keyboard. She nervously looked up from her desk, unsure of what she had heard. The familiar tone was not a sound she ever expected to hear at work—not the typing of keys, phones ringing, or even the constant beeping of a line on hold. She turned her head, peering around the room, intently listening for the sound to repeat itself. *Great. Now I'm hearing things.* Her fingers resumed their typing.

bong

Her head shot up again as her muscles tensed, certain of what she had heard. The last time that particular tone echoed in her ears was the day her life, and her family, fell apart. Her body went into shock as her eyes glazed over. The sound sent her mind hurdling into the past. A familiar phrase echoed in the air. "This is your captain speaking ..."

~~~

"We're heading toward a rough patch of weather. Nothing we can't handle, but we're going to turn on the seat belt sign and ask that you remain seated until further notice. Thank you."

The familiar *bong* rang out as the sign lit up.

Faith looked up and giggled. "Bong," she repeated in her adorable tone. It was her first flight, and everything caught her attention and delighted her. "Bong, bong," she continued, echoing her new favorite sound.

To Wendi, it was the sound of unease. Too many rough plane rides had negatively conditioned her to fear the thought of oncoming turbulence. Hearing the familiar ding of the seat belt sign caused every cell in her body to tense up. She began to pray for the best and braced herself for the worst. *Jesus, not now. Not in this condition. Not without my husband here.*

"Bong." Faith mimicked again, her eyes glistening and playful as she looked up at her mother.

Wendi's lips extended as she mustered up an uneasy smile. "I guess you like that sound, huh, Sweetie?"

"Bong," she repeated as her eyes lit up.

"Okay, Angel, I think that's enough. Do you see that picture of the seat belt glowing?" She pointed at the sign, hoping to distract her daughter. "When the captain makes an announcement, and you hear the bong, and the—"

"Bong!" She giggled, wide-eyed, making a funny face.

"Faith, *enough.* I need you to listen right now. When you hear the sound, and the picture lights up, it means the plane can get bumpy and bouncy, and we have to make sure you're buckled in tight to stay safe."

"Bow-cy, bow-cy, bow-cy," she repeated, bobbing up and down in her loose restraint. Wendi reached over, grabbed hold of the end of Faith's belt strap, and pulled. The seat belt tightened, snuggling up around Faith's tiny waist, adhering her bottom to the seat.

The plane shimmied, shaking the passengers from side to side. Wendi braced herself with one hand and grabbed her abdomen with the other. *Jesus, I can't handle this right now.* She took hold of her own belt strap and loosened it, letting out a sigh of relief. As Faith looked around inspecting the shifting environment, a flight attendant rushed down the aisle. Faith leaned over against her mother's enlarged womb, curious where the attendant was rushing off to.

"*Ugh.* Faith, you can't lean on Mommy's belly like that. I need you to sit still."

"Sorrwee, Mommy. Id da baby okay?" Faith asked as she gently rested her head against her mother's abdomen to listen.

Yes, Angel, the baby is fine, but Mommy won't be if you keep pressing on her tummy. Now please sit up." The flight attendant scurried back up the aisle, catching Faith's attention. Instinctively she pushed against her mother's stomach, raising herself up.

"Faith!" Wendi snapped, grabbing and repositioning her in the seat. "Do *not* lean on Mommy's belly." She shifted, letting out a moan. "One child on my bladder is enough." She tilted her head back and sighed. She knew the importance of Pete's new job and understood needing to make a good impression, but this was a mistake. *Your pregnant wife is more important than some damn annual meeting. God, could the timing of this move be any worse?*

The plane jerked forward. Wendi braced herself, gripping the armrests. Her loose belt still managed to do its job, locking around her. Another moan pierced her mouth. She reached down, loosening the belt further. The baby shifted, putting even more pressure on her bladder.

"No, Mommy. We haf to keep da baby safe! Dat's my whittle sista." Faith reached over, grabbing a loose end of her mother's belt and pulling.

"Faith, stop!" Wendi swiftly yanked Faith's tiny hands away. Startled, silence washed over her. "Sorry, Angel. Mommy is just *very* uncomfortable and can't handle it right now. You don't want the belt to squish Mommy's bladder and make me pee all over the plane, do you?" Faith's eyes widened as she shook her head at the messy thought.

"Neither do I," she agreed as the plane shuttered again. Wendi flinched as a hand gently touched her shoulder. "Is everything okay, ma'am?" the flight attendant asked, alternating her gaze among Faith, Wendi, and her pregnant belly.

A sarcastic laugh was Wendi's initial response. "You mean other than my daughter driving me crazy, my husband not being here, moving four states away, being pregnant on a bumpy plane, and needing to pee?"

"Oh, my. Well, I'm very sorry about all that. Where are y'all moving to?" The attendant asked, trying to divert the conversation.

"Just outside of High Point. A little place called Trinity, to be specific. I honestly never heard of either."

"Well, I'll be. I grew up around those parts. You'll love it. And I hope it turns out to be the high point of your life," she added, trying to lighten the mood. "Well, we'll do what we can to keep you comfortable during the flight, but unfortunately, you'll have to wait to use the lavatory until the captain turns off the seat belt sign."

"Well, if these bumps continue," disputed Wendi, "I'll either be using it regardless or peeing all over this plane. And none of us want the second option!"

"Well, let's hope *that* doesn't happen." Despite her best effort, the smile drained from the flight attendant's face. "Trying to use the restroom during turbulence can be *very* dangerous, especially for someone in your condition. Now, I must insist you stay seated to keep you and your baby safe." She loomed over Wendi, holding her gaze, patiently waiting for Wendi to comply.

"Of course," Wendi hesitantly replied.

The flight attendant regained her smile, gave an appreciative nod, and looked over at Faith. "And how old are you, Angel?"

"I'm fife!" she said, holding up her five tiny fingers in the air. "My birt-day is today and I get cake!"

"Well, happy birthday to ya! I hope you get everything you wish for, precious. And you are being such a very brave little girl. Do you want to do something very important for me?"

Faith nodded.

"Will you share some of that bravery with your mom? And if she needs help, you call me. Can you do that?"

"Yup yup!"

The plane dipped, quickly followed by the sound of the intercom. "This is your captain again." This time his voice was coated with a hint of unease. "I apologize for the bumpy ride. We're hitting some choppy weather due to an oncoming storm that we're doing our best to avoid. Please remain in your seats until it's safe to move about the cabin. Thank you."

The flight attendant gently rubbed Wendi's shoulder. "You two be safe, stay seated, and I'll check again on ya in a bit." She nodded, turned, and hurried up the aisle.

Wendi carefully shifted, facing her daughter, and pointed out the window. "Let's stare at the clouds for a bit, Angel. Aren't they beautiful?"

Faith agreed and silently gazed out the window, mesmerized by the fluffy shapes stretching out as far as the eye could see. Wendi was happy to see her daughter sharing the same awe and wonder she used to. As a little girl, the window seat was Wendi's favorite place to be. Flying above the clouds was a heavenly playground in the sky. A place she could play, sing, and dance with the Angels. Forgetting her physical discomfort for a moment, calm washed over Wendi as she watched the tranquil landscape float by.

A gust of wind jolted the plane, jogging her out of her serenity. "UGH," she griped as the seat belt pressed against her midsection. Fully present, she was aware again of her teeming bladder. She cautiously reached down and unbuckled. Darkness swallowed the white panorama as dimness crept across the passengers.

Faith's delight drained away, swallowed by fear. "Mommy, I don't wike dis anymore. I want to get off da pwane now. I wantta go home."

"So do I, Angel. So do I." Rain began to beat against the window. The plane jolted again, hard. Wendi shut her eyes, tightening her grip on the armrest. It was quickly becoming an unbearable journey. *Jesus, my bladder's not going to make it. However you have to, make it stop.*

~ ~ ~ O ~ ~ ~

thud!

Bobby snapped out of the daydream to the sound of his books hitting the floor. He looked up from his seat to see Seth lingering above him.

"Be careful. You dropped your books, Booby," Seth huffed before taking his seat, trying to contain his laughter.

The sudden noise got everyone's attention, and all eyes turned to Bobby, except for his teacher. Mr. Wacher was busy writing something on the blackboard. He paused, peered over his shoulder just in time to see Seth sitting back down, and continued writing.

Bobby's jaw tightened as his fists clenched. He inched his way out of his seat, keeping his gaze at the floor, desperately avoiding the stares piercing him like needles. He knelt down and began gathering his scattered books and papers from the floor. He desperately fought his instinct to react, wanting to hurl a book at Seth's head.

As he gathered his things, a gentle hand reached out, lifted his sketchbook off the floor, and handed it to him. He timidly looked up. His gaze was met by a pair of beautiful blue eyes. Trying to keep his hands from shaking, he accepted the gift by swiftly yanking it out of her hand and averted his attention back to the floor. "Tha—thanks," he stammered shyly, still avoiding eye contact.

He grabbed the last of his strewn papers and awkwardly slid back into his seat. *She thinks I'm an idiot.* Being tormented wasn't the way he wanted to get noticed by Sara. It felt like every time he got picked on, she was there to witness it. He could feel her eyes still focused on him, along with the rest of the class. He swallowed hard, too embarrassed to acknowledge Sara's smile, and too angry to look away from Seth.

Seth sat one row over and three seats up. His cronies were still snickering along with him, laughing at Bobby. Bobby hated all of them. His thoughts flooded with all the hurtful ways he could get revenge, all extreme, some even bloody. He was tired of being bullied. He was tired of Seth Baynes.

His emotions were like wildfire, raging in every direction. He did what he always did to keep himself from exploding; he forced his feelings down and began to draw. A quick outline was all he needed to get started, then he quickly began shading his dark creation. His hand feverishly scribbled back and forth as he pushed harder and harder until the point of his pencil snapped off.

Mr. Wacher finished writing on the blackboard, gently set down the chalk, and turned around. "Okay, class," he announced, peering around the room. "Before we begin, I want to thank Sara for helping Bobby with his things. Books are precious. Let's all be a bit more careful to avoid such accidents." Bobby was momentarily surprised that Mr. Wacher even saw Sara helping, then shook his head. *Accident, my ass. You're clueless.* Bobby loved Mr. Wacher for his understanding and patient demeanor with kids, but had little confidence that any of the school staff really knew what happened behind their backs. Mr. Wacher continued. "Seth," he called out in a commanding yet gentle voice, "anything you wish to add?"

"No, sir, your honor, sir," he mocked, causing his companions to laugh again.

"Then next time someone's things *accidentally* fall in your presence, I ask that you help pick them up. Understood?"

"Of course not, your honor," he mocked again.

Mr. Wacher said nothing, but his gaze subtly changed as he maintained eye contact with Seth. Without so much as a blink, he patiently waited. Seth's smile dissolved as he lowered his head, defeated. "Yes, sir." This time, his reply was genuine.

~~~ O ~~~

The rain continued to beat down against the plane with no signs of letting up. A constant jitter took hold as everyone began showing signs of concern. "Could I have your attention again," the Captain begged. "We're trying our best to get out of this storm, but it will be a little longer than expected. We'll get through it soon enough, but we'll have a bumpy ride until we do. Keep your seat belts fastened, stay seated, and I ask you not to use the lavatory until we're through this last leg of the storm. Thank you."

Just as the static of the intercom silenced, a flash lit up the cabin as the plane jerked forward.

BOOM!

All the passengers flinched at the defining crash of thunder that followed. Faith looked up at her mom. "Make it top, Mommy. Make it top. I want da sun and fwuffy cwouds back."

"So do I, Angel. Mommy's praying real hard that it will be over soon." *God, we really—*

Another jolt rocked the plane, and a cry belted out from a woman a few seats up. "Oh, God! Jesus save us!" the woman yelled. Without hesitation, the flight attendant rushed down the aisle to comfort her.

"Calm down, ma'am. The captain has everything under control," the flight attendant insisted. "We've flown through worse storms before. We'll be fine."

"I can't just sit here and be silent any longer!" she raged. "Something terrible is going to happen. I can feel it! Christ Almighty! Jesus save us! Please, Lord Jesus, save us! I can feel it," she stammered, grabbing the flight attendant's arm.

The scene overwhelmed Faith. "Mommy, I want to get off da plane," she cried. Her brow pressed together, wrinkled in worry. Tears began rolling down her soft cheeks.

Wendi pulled her daughter in as best as she could. "Just keep praying, Sweetie. It will be over soon." The pressure on Wendi's bladder was unbearable. An uneasy fetus tossed and kicked inside her. She had never felt such physical and mental stress all at once. The world around her was consumed in darkness, pierced by flashes of lightning. The hysterical woman ranted on, now occupying two attendants. *God, get us off this plane.*

BOOM!

Faith screamed. She grabbed her mom. "Make it top, Mommy," she pleaded. Tears continued to stream down her face as she leaned against Wendi's abdomen. The plane rattled as the passengers held on, all praying for it to end.

A few rows up, the staff desperately tried to calm the woman down. "Stop saying everything will be okay! YOU CAN'T PROMISE ME THAT!" she screamed. "You *cannot* tell me what I feel! Last time I had this feeling, my husband passed. It's the feeling of death. God, help us all!"

Wendi couldn't bear it anymore. Every emotion surged within her. *God, make it all stop. The storm, the woman, my daughter, my bladder—Make it all stop!* She lost it. She leaned into the aisle and screamed out, "Lady, you are panicking my daughter and everyone else on this plane. We heard you the first 20 times. Now if you don't shut your mouth, God help me, you're going to be the one who's dead!" She took a deep breath. "Goddamn it, I have to pee. Get us out of this storm already!" A flash illuminated the plane.

BOOM!

Wendi's fingers tensed, digging into the armrests, and she felt the warm sensation of urine trickle out. Clenching her muscles, she looked up at the seat belt sign, peered over at the flight attendants with the woman, then turned and looked at the bathroom. Unoccupied. *I can't wait. I just can't!*

She turned to Faith. "Angel, listen to mommy. I know you're scared, but I need you to be very, very brave and stay here while Mommy goes to the bathroom. I will be back before you know it."

"No, Mommy, don't leave me," she pleaded, breaking Wendi's heart.

"I can't take you with me. It's too dangerous. You have to stay here." The plane shook as another squirt of pee forced itself out. "Look at me. I am sorry, but Mommy is going to pee all over the plane, and we don't want that, do we? I will be right back." She nodded and rolled herself into the aisle before Faith could reply again.

Faith grabbed Wendi's hand. "Wait, Mommy!"

Wendi yanked her arm away. "Stay here, Faith! It's an emergency. STAY HERE!"

The two flight attendants attending to the hysterical woman quickly took notice of the new commotion.

"Ma'am, stay seated!" they shouted in unison.

The attendant closest to Wendi lunged toward her, but the hysterical woman grabbed her arm. "God has chosen!"

The flight attendant broke free of the woman and ran toward Wendi. "MA'AM! You can't use the facilities right now. It's too dangerous of a situation!"

Wendi was already halfway into the bathroom. "*This* is a dangerous situation," she yelled, pointing at her wet crotch. The bathroom door slammed and locked before the flight attendant could get there. Her bladder released a flood of urine as her eyes released an avalanche of tears. Every ounce of emotion came gushing out. On the other side of the door, the muffled voice of the flight attendant fell on deaf ears as Wendi let the world outside fade away.

Why are you doing this to me? Why? I lit a candle in church and prayed for a safe trip, and this is what I get? Where are you when I need you most, God? Sitting there with an empty bladder, the emotions kept pouring out. She buried her face, sobbing wildly, shaking her head. *What kind of mother leaves her scared, crying, five-year-old daughter alone on a plane in the middle of a thunderstorm?*

bang bang bang

BANG! BANG! BANG!

Wendi snapped back to the present as the muted voice made its way in. "You need to respond, ma'am. Ma'am? We need you to open the door *immediately!*"

She wiped away the tears and pulled herself to her feet. The plane shuttered as she awkwardly tried to pull her underwear back up, yanking with one hand, steadying herself with the other.

A swift jolt rocked the plane, causing her to lose her balance.

bang!

Wendi's head slammed against the mirror. She let out a scream as she fell back onto the toilet. Holding her head, she slowly stood back up, confused. A pounding sound echoed outside her head. It was the flight attendant banging on the door, harder by the second.

"Ma'am, are you all right? I heard you scream. Open the door or we will force it open for your own safety. Ma'am? Do you hear me? We are coming in!" On the other side of the door, the flight attendant motioned to the other, who was still attending to the hysterical woman.

"Stop your pounding," Wendi finally responded. "I'm done." Still holding her head with one hand, she managed to slide open the door with the other. Staring her in the face was an angry flight attendant. Another jolt rocked the plane, and the flight attendant fell forward onto Wendi, knocking her back into the bathroom. A few rows up, sitting next to Wendi's empty seat, Faith cried out for her mother.

Still disoriented, Wendi shoved the attendant back into the aisle. Despite her training, the flight attendant snapped. "That's it! I'm not even supposed to be up in weather like this. A woman in your condition certainly shouldn't be!" She braced herself and seized Wendi's arm. Clenching down, she pulled Wendi into the aisle. "Ma'am, get back to your seat *immediately* so we can assess your head before you jeopardize yourself or the life of your baby any further. Not to mention the child you left behind!"

Wendi exploded, releasing every ounce of pent-up rage. "Who the hell are you to talk to me that way? Should I have pissed all over your goddamn plane? Do you think I even want to be in this death trap? Now let go!" Still holding her head, she forcefully recoiled her other arm, losing her balance. Her hands flailed, desperately trying to catch her balance, revealing the bloody gash across her forehead. She fell against the seat behind her. One hand pushed back on the seat while the other blood-stained hand reached up, pushing against the storage bin above her.

The plane dipped, and the flight attendant tumbled backwards. At the same time, Wendi's ankle twisted, along with her body, launching her to the ground. She crashed face down, landing on her baby. Crying and hysterical, Faith screamed, and looked away. All she saw was darkness outside her once bright window.

With one hand holding her abdomen, Wendi managed to roll herself over and onto her back. Everyone stared in shock. A passenger's hand stretched out, grabbing onto Wendi, attempting to pull her up.

BOOM!

The plane jolted again, harder. The passenger lost his grip as the plane tossed him away from Wendi. The overhead bin snapped open, revealing a small but heavy suitcase. The plane rocked as unforgiving gravity took hold of the suitcase, pulling it down. It crashed down hard onto Wendi's stomach, snapping her head upward. Her blood-soaked forehead slammed into an armrest, knocking her unconscious.

Among the myriad of screams that followed, Faith's ears were only attuned to one—the horrifying outcry of her mother's pain. Faith clenched her eyes as tight as she could and covered her ears, trying to drown out the horror, but her mom's cries continued to echo in her mind.

The plane steadied itself as it broke through the storm.

A ray of light pierced the darkness, shining through the plane window. It illuminated Faith's tear soaked face, and a warmth enveloped her. She slowly opened her eyes, welcoming a burst of light. The world around her went silent, the commotion and hysteria faded, and everything dissolved as she was embraced by the light.

~ ~ ~

That was the last time Faith had spoken. The horrific incident silenced her innocent voice, creating a void in her most impressionable years.

And even though he had not witnessed it, Bobby was never the same. Guilt rattled his mind for not being there to comfort his little sister on her first flight. Ever since, he had appointed himself guardian of his silent sibling, putting himself in harm's way to protect her, and leaving his innocence behind. Not knowing how to cope with the incident or deal with his parents' resentment of each other, he became temperamental.

Along with her unborn child, a vast part of Wendi died that day. She blamed Pete for not being there, forever scorned, constantly reminding him of the choice he made to not be on that flight. Every passing plane or thought of flying became a reminder of the child she lost, jolting her being to its core.

In turn, Pete placed a mountain of blame upon himself, struggling every day to release the guilt. He was the one who had insisted on the move after searching for a new job for months, without any luck. Wendi held hope that he would find the right job just in time, but Pete was the practical one. His unemployment benefits were coming to an end, and he refused to gamble with his family's security. The offer had been too good to pass up, and he convinced Wendi that they would regret it if they didn't jump at the opportunity.

The move broke their spirits; their family was eroding away. Between all that was lost because of it and the friends and family whom Wendi had left behind, everything she loved was gone.

Only a shell remained. She lost her unborn baby, her chatty daughter, her innocent son, her jolly husband, and most importantly, her immovable faith.

~ ~ ~

"Everything all right, Deary?"

A soft, familiar voice snapped Wendi back into the present moment. Looking up, she focused her eyes on Angie, still shaken and confused.

"Ya look like ya just seen your own death. I felt it from across the room. Had to make sure you were still with us. You're as pale as a ghost! But much quieter than one. Lemme tell ya, *they can they talk,*" she added with a hoot. "But seriously, Deary, you okay in there?"

"I'm—I'm fine," Wendi stammered, struggling to be fully present. "Who can talk? Did—did you just say something about ghosts?"

"It's just a silly expression, Deary. But the spirits do love to talk, and they're definitely not pale. People oughtta say you're as pale as a cadaver. But don't you pay me no mind. I'm just jibber-jabberin'. You sure you're okay, Dear?"

"That sound," Wendi questioned, feeling in even more of a haze listening to Angie. "Did you hear it, too, or am I going mad?"

"And what sound would that be, dear? There's a whole lot o' interestin' sounds 'round this place," she chuckled.

bong

"*That* sound," Wendi acknowledged, pointing to the ceiling.

"This is your captain again," came the sound of her boss over the intercom. "I'd like you all to meet me in the break room for a special surprise. Over and out."

"My lord," exclaimed Angie. "I hope he isn't going to use that crazy thing every gosh darn hour. We'll all go mad! But the good news is, you're not crazy."

"Well, if he keeps that bong and flight announcement nonsense going, I will be."

"Well, I truly believe even the crazy ones aren't so crazy, but we'll save that talk for another time. Come on, now. Let's go see what the boss has in store. Hopefully somethin' that will brighten you up, Deary."

~ o ~

Chapter 3:

Glimmers
of Hope

*"Until you invite them into your life
with an open heart, they're limited
in how much they can interfere."*

~ o ~

Wendi leaned forward, peering over the kitchen counter. Faith sat in the corner of the family room, enthralled with her tea party and those in attendance. The TV was on, but she was ignoring it. Misty, the cat, sat quietly next to her, observing. Her blanket was sprawled on the floor, decorated with four place settings. The first three were for her; Bunny, her oldest and dearest stuffed animal; and Dolly, her newest doll. The last space was empty, occupied by her invisible friend, Nobody.

Wendi was always fascinated watching Faith play. She was amazed at the depths of her daughter's imagination, and it reminded her very much of herself. As a little girl, Wendi was always creating, imagining, and playing something new. Role-playing with dolls and stuffed animals was nothing out of the ordinary to Wendi, but she still wasn't sure how to handle the addition of Nobody.

The psychiatrist said it was a healthy outlet for her, since she was no longer comfortable talking to people, but to keep an eye on her interactions for signs of dependency. If she became too comfortable with her imaginary friend, it could create a bigger divide among the real people in her life, and worsen her condition.

Wendi would, on rare occasions, hear Faith having conversations with Nobody. The psychiatrist was pleased by this as well, showing that Faith still had her physical ability to speak. Having conversations, even at a whisper, would continually help in developing her speech.

Wendi paused her dinner preparation and rested the mixer against the bowl. She cautiously attempted to tune into the pre-dinner party happening before her, but she was no match for the "people alarm." Faith would instinctively stop anytime she felt someone tuning in to her conversation and wait for them to go on about their business. It was a sixth sense she had developed along with the "appearance" of her friend.

As Faith sat with her back to the kitchen, serving her friends, she immediately stopped and lifted her head, peering over her shoulder at her mother. Wendi, caught again in the act of eavesdropping, smiled and waved. Faith waved back, and with a keen eye, waited to make sure her mother was again preoccupied with making dinner. She then resumed her secret tea party, whispering as quietly as she could.

"For you, Bunny," she replied to her battered and faithful rabbit, as she placed an imaginary object on his plate. She turned to her next guest and asked, "Wanta stone wit your tea, Dolly?" She suddenly turned her head toward the empty place setting, giggled, and turned back to her doll. "I sorry, Dolly," she softly apologized. "Nobody says *scone*, not stone." Faith smiled and reached into the center of the table, grabbed another imaginary scone, and placed it on Dolly's plate.

Turning to her left, Faith smiled and offered the same to her final guest. "Wanta scone?" she asked, emphasizing the "k" sound in scone. Faith nodded, reaching for the last invisible scone.

Still watching, Misty's tail swooshed from side to side as she observed the amusing scene. Turning her furry head and keen ears toward Faith, then to the empty space, back to Faith, and so on, as if she was watching a tennis match.

"Yup, just baked," Faith whispered as she gently placed the imaginary refreshment in front of her invisible friend. "You said ta have fresh scones wit teatime," she giggled, then quickly clasped both hands over her mouth, muzzling the sound. She looked toward the kitchen, but Wendi hadn't noticed over the noise of the stovetop fan and boiling water. Faith continued her conversation, returning to a whisper. "More tea?"

~~~ O ~~~

Wendi rinsed off her toothbrush and stepped out of the bathroom. "Peter, I'm worried about Faith."

"Well, that's nothing new. She'll be fine," he affirmed as he unhooked his watch and rested it on his night table. "It feels like a long time to us, but she'll talk when she's ready to talk. You know what the doctors said."

"Yeah, they said it could be years. I'm not going to wait years to hear my baby girl's voice again," she insisted as she stepped over to the bed. "I just can't."

"And what are we going to do about it? Force her to talk?"

"It's not the silence I'm worried about," she admitted. "There's more concerning things happening."

"Yes, there are plenty of concerning things happening. Let's be honest. You're not happy. I'm not happy. The kids aren't happy. I don't blame her for not talking yet. She may be the sanest one around here."

"Nice. Real nice. Father of the year."

"I'm sorry, but it's true," rebutted Peter. "She's traumatized. She's still coping with it. We all are."

"It's not like she *can't* talk. She is *choosing* not to talk. I catch her whispering during her little tea parties, to her dolls and uh … well, to other … guests."

"That's called make-believe, Hun. She talks to her dolls and stuffed animals. Every little girl does. It's fine. At least she's talking to somebody, even if it's not a human."

"That's just it. She's talking to Nobody."

Peter hesitated. "Isn't that what I just said? She's talking to no one."

"No, she is literally talking to Nobody. Her imaginary friend? She calls him Nobody."

"Oh, *that* Nobody," he smirked. "They said having an imaginary friend is perfectly normal, and it's better than not talking *at all*."

"Peter, it's diff—"

"It's nothing," Peter interrupted. "We've talked about this over and over. It means her cognitive functions are still healthy and developing." Sighing, he sat down on the edge of the bed. "I'm sorry I interrupted. I just don't understand why we're talking about this again. You had an imaginary friend growing up, right? So what's the difference?"

"It's just different. It's like whomever she is talking to … is talking back."

"Yes, Deary, that's how conversations work, even the imaginary ones."

"Don't be such a—wait, why did you call me Deary? You never call me that. Only Angie does."

"Oh? And who's this Angie you're so *deary* with? Anyone I should know about?" he jested.

"She's just this crazy woman at work who spouts out weird random things," Wendi uttered as she fluffed her pillow and slid into bed, recalling her last interaction with Angie. *Lemme tell ya, they can talk.*

"Like what?" questioned Pete as he rolled back his side of the covers and slid in next to his wife.

Laying there on her back, she mentally prepared herself. "Okay, I know this will sound crazy, but maybe Nobody *is* somebody." She took a breath, and continued, "Maybe Nobody is, well, … a ghost."

"Oh boy. Here we go."

"Don't patronize me," Wendi snapped. "It sounds crazy, yes," she paused, doubting her own words. "Even when I say it out loud, I know how it sounds. Dead people just walking around talking to little girls … It sounds completely insane, but it's also the *only thing* that makes sense. Maybe Angie is onto something."

"Maybe you shouldn't take advice from the crazy woman at work! Your words, by the way." He shook his head, bringing his palms together in front of his chin. "Jesus, help me. My wife is trying to convince me our daughter is having tea parties with a ghost. Who is it, Lewis Carroll? After all, it sounds like she's in Wonderland, having tea parties with rabbits and all. Look, she's an imaginative child. She always was."

"This isn't imagination, hers or mine. She knows things. Things she shouldn't. You don't hear her, Pete. I do. I hear the conversations and they're not normal."

"She probably gets it from TV. She still hears, you know," he jabbed.

"Real nice, smart-ass. No. She's not just hearing things on TV. She knows things about you and me. Things we haven't told her."

"Once again, she's not deaf, dumb, and blind. She probably overhears us on the phone, or talking to each other." He paused, as a concerned look washed across his face. He cautiously approached the closed bedroom door and whispered, "Maybe she's standing outside right now eavesdropping, just like you do to her." He reached out for the doorknob and quickly spun it. Yanking the door open, an empty hallway greeted them. "Darn it! I really thought I was going to bust her whole charade," he chuckled.

"That's not funny," she snarled.

"Oh, yes it is! You're spying on our daughter, and now you think she's having conversations with ghosts? Maybe we should have you checked out."

"Screw you!"

"Later. Now's not the time to sway me with sex. And I'll tell you one more thing … If *you* start hearing voices, I'm sending you to the nut house … or getting you exorcised. Whichever costs less. I'll probably go with the priest."

"Oh, here's one more thing … Go to hell! I'm tired of you not caring. I am worried about our daughter, and you just *have to* make stupid jokes. Always with your goddamn jokes at the worst time. Listen, as crazy as it sounds, her talking to a ghost is the only thing that makes sense."

"Does it? Does it really? Okay. You want me to be serious? Let's be serious," he offered, stepping closer to her. Staring her down with his cold eyes, he took his stand. "The only thing that makes sense is that our daughter is traumatized, and may be for," he stammered, clenching back his emotions. "And may be for the rest of her life," he stammered as his voice trailed off, choking back the tears.

"There's nothing okay with us or with this family," he continued. "Every day, I either want to kill myself, or *you* want to kill me. And our kids will likely be fucked up for the rest of their lives. So you'll have to excuse me if the one thing that makes life bearable, my sense of humor, bothers you. It's the one thing that keeps me sane and keeps me from falling apart."

The hate in Wendi's eyes faded into sorry as her husband's words pierced her cold heart. Her shaking hands reached out for her husband, then dropped to her side. "I—I thought you were in a much better place than me. I didn't realize—you don't talk about—"

"That's just it. We don't talk. Not unless it's about all the problems our kids have. And it's okay. I get it. But it's hard enough as is, and now you seriously want me to believe our child is talking to a ghost? It's too much, Wendi. I can't. I can't take any more. This conversation is over. And I *am* being serious."

"Fine, but I'm telling you, this is no ordinary imaginary friend."

"And I'm telling you—I'll be the one who's a ghost if you keep this up! THERE IS *NO* GHOST HAVING TEA WITH OUR DAUGHTER! I don't want to hear another word about ghosts unless you're talking about the Halloween decorations. Now turn off the bathroom light. I'm going to bed" He ripped off the covers and slid into bed.

Wendi stormed to the bathroom, shut off the light, and got in bed. Pete yanked the sheet over, turning his back to his wife. Laying there in the darkness only three inches from her husband, she felt the abyss between them deepening. As crazy as it seemed, she felt she was onto something, and Pete offered no support. Wendi knew what she had to do.

glub glub glub

Angie always got a chuckle from the sound of the water cooler. She gleefully watched the giant bubbles scurry up while she filled her water bottle. Lingering in the break room behind her, Patty,

Terry, and Alice were catching up on their weekly gossip, peering at Angie out of the corners of their eyes.

Terry leaned in and uttered under her breath, "Have you ever seen anyone so happy to just fill up a water bottle? That woman definitely has a screw loose."

"Just a screw? More like a bucket of 'em," Patty murmured.

Angie tightened her lid and turned to face them. "Well good morning to ya, ladies! How y'all doin' on this lovely day? Is everyone cheery?"

They looked at each other, hesitant to respond. Terry rolled her eyes. Alice chimed in. "Now we've barely had a sip of our coffee, Angie, so I'm not sure any of us are cheery just yet."

Patty jumped in. "Tell us what little secret makes your morning so delightful? We're all ears."

"I know you are, Deary, and I'm glad ya asked. The sun is shinin' and God is smilin, and that's all we ever need to have ourselves a wondrous day!"

"Well, I beg to differ," rebutted Terry, "but I need a little more than sunshine to make me smile in the mornin' … like finding a job, or a man, that's going to give me some lasting security!" They all chuckled.

"Oh my," retorted Angie. "Well Dear, that may be the very root of your predicament, but there's always hope," replied Angie without missing a beat. "Nothing outside of yourself is ever going to give you lasting happiness inside. True happiness has to come from within, not from without. Now you ladies enjoy your coffee, and have a wondrous day." She smiled and serenely strolled out of the break room.

Anxiously sitting in her cubicle, Wendi desperately tried to think up a way to approach Angie. *How do I start a conversation about my child having conversations with ghosts? Wonderful weather today. I hear the ghosts love it, too. That's what my mute daughter tells me.* She buried her face in her hands. *Jesus, I sound like an idiot.* Despite their cubicle proximity, Angie worked in a different department, so there was no breaking the ice with work-related questions. But there was another concern weighing on Wendi. She'd have to deal with the backlash of questions and gossip from the chatty trifecta: Patty, Terry, and Alice. Terry was the worst of them, and Patty was unquestionably the nosiest woman in the office. If Wendi initiated a conversation with Angie, Patty wouldn't let up until she knew every detail of it.

If there was anyone close to being an authority on ghosts, it's Angie. Come on Wendi, the hell with those catty ladies. Wendi's hands were shaking as she quickly finished her coffee. An empty cup was a great excuse to head back to the kitchen and pass by Angie's desk. She stood up and awkwardly stepped over. Her body tensed up as she approached Angie's cubicle. Slowing down, she glanced out of the corner of her eye to see what Angie was doing, but was welcomed by an empty seat.

Wendi's eyes darted every which way as she took in the extravaganza that was Angie's desk. Adorned with all kinds of whimsical creatures, it was covered in figurines, magazines, drawings, and even topped off with a Faeries of the Maiden Mist calendar. *She's certainly the right woman for the job, but maybe this is a bad idea.*

"I admit, me being as neighborly as I am," Patty rambled on, "I've tried to stir up a pleasant conversation with that woman, and the strangest things come out of her mouth."

"Tell me about it," Terry interjected. "I swear she's from a different planet."

"Ladies, come on now," pleaded Alice, "Maybe she's just a zealous Christian delighted by life."

"Well, whatever Kool-Aid she's drinking, it ain't Holy Water because that woman is *not* a Christian," Terry insisted. "I hear she practices witchcraft. Swear to the Lord, I am *not* making it up!"

"Wiccan is actually the proper term, Terry Dear," came Angie's voice from around the corner. "And I hate to disappoint ya, but I can't say I practice it. I just happen to know about it, is all," Angie offered as she meandered past her co-workers. "I apologize for inerruptin' your chat like this. I just forgot to add a slice of lemon to my water."

She grabbed a slice of lemon from a small container on the counter, squeezed it into her water bottle, screwed on the lid, and meandered past the ladies one last time.

Terry watched, barely able to hold her tongue as Angie rounded the corner. "She probably dropped some eye of newt in that water, too."

"Honestly, Terry, you're going straight to hell if you keep talkin' 'bout her like that," exclaimed Alice. "Strange as she is, she's never said a bad word to anyone."

"All right, Alice, don't go gettin' your panties in a bunch, now. I'm just teasin' is all," rebutted Terry. "Now if you don't mind, I gotta pretend to get some work done, ladies. And remember, it's Halloween. Angie will be flyin' home on her broomstick!" She and Patty chuckled again.

"You're too much, Terry," Patti commented as they scampered out of the break room.

~~~ O ~~~

Seth clenched his freshly sharpened pencil. He headed back to his seat, zig-zagging between desks, like a hunter stalking his prey. Bobby's hand paused from shading his newly sketched character. It was one of his best drawings yet, and he had been working on it periodically for days. He looked up at Seth, wondering what he was up to as he cut over to Bobby's row. As Seth passed by, he threw his weight into Bobby's desk. Bobby's hand slid, causing a dark streak across the drawing, ruining it. "Excuse me," blurted out Seth sarcastically as he took a step away.

Bobby slammed down his pencil, and without missing a beat, jutted his foot out, catching Seth's leg. Seth came crashing down, grabbing at a nearby desk. His left hand landed on a pile of books, which all slid off the desk, throwing him to the floor. His right hand, which was balled in a fist still grasping his newly sharpened pencil, hit the ground, with the pencil point sticking straight up. Seth's face came slamming down, his eye missing the point by less than an inch. As his head lunged down, the point caught the top of his ear, piercing the cartilage.

The commotion startled everyone in the room, including Mr. Wacher. Not realizing Seth had been injured, Bobby whispered under his breath, "Have a nice trip?" echoing Seth's words from the prior day.

Among the mess of strewn books and papers, Seth struggled to get up, still clutching his ear, still pierced with a pencil. "You're dead, you little sh—"

"That's enough!" boomed Mr. Wacher's voice as he rushed over.

"Yeah, that's enough, Seth," Bobby whispered under his breath, still not realizing the extent Seth had been injured.

"Bobby," Mr. Wacher called out in a rigid tone, staring straight at him, "I was talking to you. This is a serious injury." Bobby stared back, speechless and motionless, like a deer in headlights.

Mr. Wacher helped Seth to his feet, examining his ear. "Whatever you do, don't pull the pencil out, Seth. We'll get you straight to the nurse, and let her handle this." Mr. Wacher informed him. "Fortunately, you'll live, and we may even send you home with a new earring," he said jokingly, hoping to lighten the dark mood of the class.

"Mr. Baynes, I'll walk you to the nurse myself. Class," he called out. I will be back soon. I expect you all know how to behave for the next five to ten minutes while I'm taking care of this. I am serious when I say I want everyone to remain in their seats until I get back. One injury a day is more than enough." He steadied Seth, then turned to Bobby. "Mr. Farfalla, you're coming with us, but I'll be dropping you off at a different office."

Even though Bobby knew better, he attempted to play dumb. "Me? But Seth tripped. Why am I in trouble?"

Mr. Wacher rarely lost his temper and had several ways of putting students in their place. The first warning was addressing kids by their last name. The second was "the look". He had mastered a stare colder than Medusa's. And when a student was called by their last name and got the look, that's when he was at his limit—but he always remained calm.

Mr. Wacher carefully led Seth to the door, and without another word, he shot Bobby the look. Bobby understood, and followed, closing the classroom door behind him.

~~~ O ~~~

Wendi had just taken a few steps away from Angie's cubicle when she realized she was still holding an empty mug. *I may as well get a refill. I have a feeling I'll need it.* She turned back around, startled by an unexpected greeting.

"Why, hello! And good morning to ya, Miss Wendi!" Angie exclaimed before even looking up from her desk.

"Goodness, Angie, I didn't see you— I was just—where did you—"

"I'm always right where I need to be, when I need to be there, Deary," Angie reassured as she observed Wendi collecting her thoughts. "Somethin' botherin' ya this lovely mornin', Deary? Is it anything I can help ya with?"

It was an uncanny knack Angie had, like she could read minds, even sense someone just looking her way. Wendi felt transparent—naked. It was one of the reasons people felt so uncomfortable around Angie. It wasn't as much about being uncomfortable around her; they were uncomfortable with themselves. "Um, well, yes, actually. If you don't mind. I wanted to ask about, uh, well, something a bit odd."

"Well, lucky for you, odd is my speciality. Ask away, Dear. I don't mind the questions as long as you don't mind the answers," she blurted out with a giggle, as if she already knew the question.

"It's about my daughter."

"Of course, such an Angel, and what a strong spirit she is. How's Faith doing these days? Has the dear little girl found her voice yet?"

"Oh, uh, no, not quite." Wendi stammered. "I'm surprised you remembered."

"Now, how could I forget a thing like that? I can't imagine what it's like for y'all. My heart goes out to ya. But you said you had somethin' *odd* to talk about. Now, I know you're not callin' that sweet little Angel odd."

"Oh no, of course not," spouted out Wendi, with a nervous laugh. "What I'm saying is that there's definitely something odd happening with her. She's still not talking directly to me or Pete, or anyone for that matter. At least, not anyone real. Apparently, she *can* find her voice, but only to talk to her dolls, and um, well —her imaginary friend."

"Well, isn't that somethin'," Angie responded with a smile. "Bet the doctors love that, her whisperin' to an imaginary friend. I'm sure they say she'll grow out of it, and she's just makin' it all up to cope with the trauma."

Wendi was taken aback. Angie's knack for knowing things was remarkable. "Yes, actually, that's exactly what the doctors have said. And, well, it does make sense."

"Does it now? Because I'm feeling like something else must make sense if you're standin' here talkin' to me, Dear. So what do you *really* think is goin' on?"

Wendi took a deep breath. "Well...she's a kid, and has a wonderful and vivid imagination..." She fidgeted with her empty mug as she tried to find her words and conviction. "Well, nothing else makes sense. But this is crazy. It just seems like ... I ... I'm sorry. I'm crazy for even considering it."

"Sorry about what, Deary? About believing doctors don't have all the answers? Believing that something a little more unexplainable and a little less believable is happening?" Angie gently rested her hand atop Wendi's. "My dear, there's no such thing as crazy 'long as you're standin' in my cubicle. Your heart knows the truth and can only be ignored for so long. Now go on and spit it out."

Wendi took a breath as a look washed over her expression as if she were about to give someone bad news. "Okay, okay ... I think her invisible friend is real, not just her imagination. Whatever she's talking to is something or *someone* real. Not a real person, obviously, but was, well is ..." She peered around the office, then continued in a soft tone. "... is a ghost." Wendi exhaled, allowing her tension to disperse. "God, there it is. You *do* believe in ghosts, don't you, Angie?"

"Sure as sunshine, Deary," stated Angie, strong and proud. "But I prefer to call 'em spirits. So much more considerate that way. There's such a negative connotation around the word ghosts. People act like there has to be some tragic or horrifying death involved when they mention ghosts. All those horror movies paint such ugly pictures in people's heads, especially around Halloween. Don't be watchin' them and filling your head with nonsense." She shook her head. "But I'm gettin' off track. So, my dear, you believe little Faith has got herself a spirited friend she's been chattin' with?" asked Angie.

"Yes, well, I've noticed some peculiar conversations, to say the least...and it just doesn't feel like she's talking to herself. It's the *way* she's talking...some of the things she repeats back...It just seems too, well, too *adult*. And she seems to know things she couldn't possibly have overheard. Pete thinks I'm off my rocker," she remarked, rolling her eyes. "But if it *is* a ghost—sorry—a spirit, well, *could* it be a bad one? You said it's just in the movies, but there *are* bad spirits, aren't there? What if it's trying to get her to do something, to do, well, God knows what! You gotta help me, Angie. I'm losing my mind," she admitted, a little embarrassed.

"Oh my," began Angie, looking quite serious. "It's too late."

Wendi's body tensed as a look of horror overcame her. "What's too late? Please don't tell me that, Angie. There has to be something—"

Wendi's fearful plea was interrupted by one of Angie's boisterous cackles. "It's too late because Hollywood's already brainwashed ya!" She chuckled again. "Now I know tomorrow is Halloween, Wendi Dear, but don't be gettin' yourself all worked up thinkin' ya got an evil spirit hauntin' your little Angel. All these shows and movies love to portray scary, demonic ghosts runnin' around possessin' people to get revenge. Oh, what a hoot!" She slapped her knee, snickering like a schoolgirl. "And people have the nerve to say fairy tales are all made up. We need more movies about ghosts we can appreciate. Like a spirit staying behind out of love instead of fear and hate. That would be lovely," she added, drifting off for a moment. "Oh my, there I go rantin' again," she said with a smile, accompanied by her endearing chuckle.

"But I'll never lie to ya, Deary. Yes, negative spirits and entities exist, but it's not as common as Hollywood tries to get ya to believe. Now, here are some better questions to ask," continued Angie. "Do you have a bad feeling about it? Are there any signs of negativity or malice? Has Faith done or said anything harmful?"

"No, goodness no. She's actually quite happy," Wendi delightfully responded. "And to be perfectly honest, she seems to enjoy their little conversations." Wendi's eyes glazed over as a smile crept across her face. "And bless her little heart. She always leaves a place for Nobody at her tea parties. Oh, that's his name … her name … its name? I don't even know. This is all so new to me," she sighed.

"Well, there you have it! And don't worry about any pronouns just yet. There's no gender to our souls, Dear," she stated matter-of-factly. "I'd say Faith has a beautiful being by her side. Did you notice how you lit up when you were talking about her tea parties? And just a few minutes ago, your mind wanted to believe it was an evil spirit. So give yourself some credit. Your heart knows she's safe and happy."

Wendi blushed, shaking her head again. "Yes, well, if her imaginary friend isn't so imaginary, how is that supposed to make me feel better about all this? Even if it's a happy ghost—I mean, spirit—it's still dead! Is that okay?"

"Let me put this another way for you, Deary. Spirits are more alive and awake than most people I know. And yes, I said it was a beautiful being, but not all unseen beings are ghosts, as you like to call them."

"Then what the hell is it?"

"Not hell, Dear." Angie responded. Rather than answering the question directly, she shifted her gaze from Wendi's eyes, giving a nod to the edge of her desk.

Wendi curiously followed Angie's gaze past images of fairies, gnomes, rainbows, and unicorns. There, at the end of her desk, stood a gracefully sculpted figurine with praying hands pressed together over its heart—a beautiful, winged Angel.

Wendi held her gaze on the figure as she unconsciously raised her hand, laying it upon her heart. "My God, Angie, you can't be serious. You're trying to tell me my little girl is having conversations with a doll, a bunny, … and an Angel?" An unexplainable sense of comfort blanketed Wendi. Her body shuddered as a warm tingle traveled up her spine. Her heart called out, but her mind overtook her emotions as she struggled to rationalize the thought of Angels existing in some sort of "real" form. "Angie, Angels don't have conversations with people. And they certainly don't attend tea parties with little girls," she exclaimed with an odd laugh, trying to lighten her growing concern. "I'm sorry, but the ghost was more believable."

"Are you so sure about that, Deary?"

"Look Angie, I was raised Catholic, so I've been taught about Angels my entire life. They watch over us from a distance. They don't practice ABCs and attend tea parties with five-year-olds!"

"And why not? Just as media and society have ruined the image of ghosts, they've done the same to Angels." Angie's energy shifted slightly as a more serious demeanor embraced her. "Wendi, there are many beings from other realms, seen and unseen, that are just as real as you and I, Dear" she asserted, "and much more evolved, for that matter. But don't think for a moment that means we have to distance ourselves from them. They love us. And if loving Faith means havin' an imaginary tea party with her, so be it. What would an Angel loving you look like?"

A somber force took hold of Wendi as she tightened her grip around her mug. "If Angels are so real, where were they when I needed them?" Her trembling hands gripped the mug tighter. "Where were God's damn Angels when I lost my—" She released her grip as her mug crashed to the floor, sending shards scattering across the office floor. A quivering hand rose to her mouth. "I'm sorry. I—" Wendi pulled herself back together as she crouched down to pick up the fragments of her cup, certain the entire office was staring at her. She sniffled and wiped away a renegade tear.

Angie softly laid a hand on Wendi's shoulder. "It's quite all right, Deary," reassured Angie in a serene tone. Wendi paused her frantic gathering and looked up at Angie, whose eyes were patiently waiting to connect with Wendi's. "You have every right to your emotions, even the ones you'd rather not face. What happened on that plane is a tragedy, my dear, plain and simple. And while we don't always understand the purpose of such events when they're happening, I promise there's a greater plan the Universe is unfolding for you to discover."

Angie's words touched a place in Wendi's soul that had been walled off since the accident. "I speak my truth, always, Dear. It's your choice to accept it or leave it. But I'm feeling it's time for you to start believing in more than you can see with your own eyes."

Wendi's hands were shaking as she resumed picking up the shattered pieces, focusing on the ground and away from Angie's compelling gaze. "It was a stretch coming to terms with the thought of a ghost, but it made some sense. You hear ghost stories all the time. There are no Angel stories. People might talk to their Angels, but the Angels aren't talking back, Angie."

"Sure they are," Angie admitted with a look of certainty. "You just have to learn to hear them … and learn to see. Hang around the right people, and you'll hear all the Angels stories you need, Deary." Angie spoke softly but with a confidence that left little room for doubt.

Wendi didn't know what to say. "Oh" was the only word that could escape her mouth as her mind tried to process it all. She tried to think of a graceful way to bow out of the conversation. *Maybe the girls are right about Angie.* Wendi looked up from the broken pieces still scattered on the floor, past the menagerie on Angie's desk, and looked deep into Angie's eyes. *How can she have so much belief in something so far from reality?*

Angie reaffirmed her knowing. "Angels are very real, my dear. Your little girl is very special. There's no doubt about that. We all are. What makes the difference is accepting it. Children know they are special, so they see and do special things. Unfortunately, the world tries to teach us differently because it's afraid to change, afraid to grow. And because children try so hard to be just like their parents, if their parents haven't accepted that they themselves are special, the child loses that belief. Your daughter's silence is a defense mechanism, but not to protect her from the memory of a tragedy. She's protecting herself from the world of doubt that surrounds her. She needs to protect her own innocence and beliefs, and she is doing everything she can—even if it means closing herself off from the people she loves most. Your daughter is not conversing with a ghost, Wendi. Faith is communing with her Guardian Angel. *Your* Angel."

Wendi stood there in silence, battling the apprehension in her mind. She needed an excuse to leave before the conversation overwhelmed her completely.

Her eyes focused on the large clock ticking away on the wall. "Oh my. I didn't realize how long we had been talking, Angie. I really need to get back to my desk. I have a lot of work I must do."

Her reaction was no stranger to Angie who had witnessed it a hundred times and expected it a thousand more. "Of course, Deary. I understand."

"Okay, then. Tha—Thank you, Angie," Wendi blurted out nervously.

"Anytime. I'm always here for you, Dear," Angie reassured her.

Some people fight change their whole life, others simply accept it, and some need to be gently chiseled away at over time to let it sink in. Angie could always sense each type. She could see it in Wendi's eyes. Despite her reaction, a door had opened for Wendi that would not be easily closed.

Wendi returned to her cubicle as swiftly as she could. She ducked in, but before her bottom even hit the seat, a familiar face popped up on the other side.

"What in the dickens just happened?" came the first of a myriad of questions from Patty.

Wendi looked up at her nosey neighbor. Exhausted, only one thought ran across her mind. *Shit.*

"Come on, now. Spill it, Darling."

Wendi just stared, still processing everything that just occurred. The last thing she felt like doing was trying to explain it all to Patty.

"Come on, now, Hun. I ain't got all day. We're leaving early for Halloween. That reminds me. What are your darling kids dressing up as?

"Bobby wanted to be a Ghostbuster, and Faith is being the most adorable ..." Wendi paused as the coincidence sunk in, "... Angel."

The tension was unbearable, even for Mr. Wacher, as he escorted the boys down the hallway. Filling his lungs with air, Mr. Wacher took three deep breaths, pushing the air out fully each time. Feeling centered, he broke the awkward silence.

"As a teacher, I've learned accidents in school aren't always accidents. Bobby, I could have easily pointed out that it was your foot that Seth tripped over, but I felt no need to embarrass or reproach you, meaning scold, in front of the class." Mr. Wacher was famous for speaking with big words that were far above an elementary school level, but always adding in the meaning in a way the children understood. Even during a hallway lecture, he couldn't stop teaching.

"This was not an accident, Bobby," he said in a stern voice, "and that pencil almost went through Seth's eye. You are *very* lucky it's only his ear." Mr. Wacher stopped in front of the nurse's door, looking directly at Bobby. "I'm not trying to make you feel worse than you probably already do, but I need you to understand how serious this could have been."

"That's right, you little—"

"Seth," Mr. Wacher interrupted, "while you are obviously upset *and* in pain, from what I gather, Bobby's fall the other day wasn't an accident either. It left him with several bad scrapes on his hands, and as you can see, on his face." He took another deep breath, eyeing the two of them. "So listen to me, both of you, when I say you two are now even. Next time, one of you could be seriously injured. I won't allow that on my watch. This is enough. And I mean *enough*. Do you understand?" He asked in his stern tone as he held his gaze dead in their eyes awaiting acknowledgment.

They reluctantly agreed. "I want you to wait right here, Bobby, while I explain the situation to the nurse," Mr. Wacher instructed. He wasted no time with the nurse and promptly returned. "Now, for our next stop." He gently placed a hand on Bobby's shoulder. "I know you're dealing with a lot at home," he began, softening his tone. "And I'm not going to pretend to know what your life is like. I just wish you could let go of all this anger you have. Talk to the school counselor before it's too late. Before you do something you might regret. Understood?"

Bobby nodded. "Good," Mr. Wacher acknowledged. "Now let's get you to the principal again. I know this won't go over well, but it's much too serious for me to let slide."

The concern overtaking Bobby's face had much less to do with the principal, and much more to do with facing his father over another violent incident. *Kill me now.*

~~~ O ~~~

For the rest of the day, Wendi couldn't concentrate on her work. Her mind was racing with thoughts, questioning everything. *Are Angels really real? I mean, I believe in Jesus, but the Jesus up there. If Angie told me Faith was literally having tea parties with him, and Jesus was talking back, I'd say she was crazy. Faith can't actually be talking to a Guardian Angel, can she? This is crazy. Peter went ape-shit over a ghost. Any chance he'd react better about an Angel? He'll think Angie's crazy. He'll think I'm crazy!* Wendi was so caught up that she forgot about her excitement for Halloween. They were heading home at 4:00 today. She snapped out of her thoughts, glancing at the clock. 3:33 p.m. *AGAIN with the triple digits?*

Her inner dialogue was interrupted by a voice that was quickly becoming too familiar to her. "How are ya, Deary?" Angie asked, examining Wendi's worried expression. "I wanted to check in on ya before you go scooting' off for the evenin'. Did I mention how much I love Halloween? And I wanted to remind ya to pay a little more attention to Faith's conversations," she advised, before leaning in. "Oh, and maybe try talkin' to your Angel yourself."

"I don't know, Angie. It's all a bit much," responded Wendi, still fighting her uneasiness. "First, you tell me Faith is talking to an Angel, which honestly sounds nuts. And now you want *me* to talk to it? What do I do? Sit down at the imaginary tea party with my daughter and just join the conversation?"

"Why not, Dear! *Anyone* can talk to an Angel. It's not like they discriminate who they respond to. They don't pick and choose who is or isn't worthy of havin' a conversation with. Only people do such nonsense."

"I'm sorry, Angie. You're crazy if you think I can talk to Angels."

"Well, you might be right, Dear. You can't talk to somethin' you don't believe in; so maybe start with that. Just believe," she urged and continued on.

"And here's the thing, Deary. Even if ya don't believe your daughter is speakin' to an Angel, *she does*. That's what matters. She believes in something you don't. That's what keeps her separate from you. That's what keeps her silent. When children are little, everyone tries to teach them to believe in magical things they can't see, like unicorns, fairies, and even Santa Clause. Then the children grow up, and the same people teach them *not* to believe in those very same things. Adults are such walkin' contradictions."

Angie's words made a lot of sense. A calm washed over Wendi. Maybe she needed to be more open-minded."

"I tell ya what, Deary," continued Angie, as if she were reading Wendi's mind. "Let me get your Halloween started early. I'm gonna give ya a little treat right now. It's an Angel intention prayer." Angie grabbed a piece of paper, picked up a pen, and began writing something.

"A what now?" Wendi asked, not having the slightest clue where this was going.

"An Angel intention prayer, Dear. Angels are always with us, but you have to call them if you expect an answer. It's important, Dear," Angie affirmed as she continued writing.

"Call them?"

"Yes, Dear. If you want their help, you have to call and ask for it," she said with a subtle nod. "Until you invite them in with an open heart, Angels are limited in how much they can interfere in your life."

"Hold the phone, Angie. Just how many Angels do I need?"

"Well, for simplicity's sake, let's just start you off with one, Dear. I want you to intentionally connect with your Guardian Angel, the one already with your family. It's always been with you, protecting and watching over you from the outside, and now it's time to let it in. Any time you call, it will lovingly oblige." Angie tore off the piece of paper, folded it in half, and then half again. Tenderly, she took Wendi's hand and gently placed the note in her palm, wrapping her fingers around it.

"When you're feelin' ready, ask, and you shall receive, Dear. I'm giving you a very simple, easy, and powerful prayer," continued Angie. "And feel free to change it to whatever your heart tells you to. Angel prayers don't have to be complicated, and they don't have to be long. However you want to pray, just make sure it comes from the heart. Oh, and they don't have to rhyme. That's just how I like my prayers—makes sayin' them so much more fun!" she added with her signature giggle.

A whirlwind of emotions flowed through Wendi, from doubt and concern to gratitude and wonder. "Why do I feel like you just gave me an incantation? I guess it's appropriate enough for the holiday," she chuckled, trying to ease her tension. "And what will this do?"

"It's a way to open the door to your Angel, and allow it into your life. From now on, it's your job to keep your heart, your eyes, and your ears open. Angels are always sending us signs, whether we know it or not, and whether we acknowledge them or not. Heck, you've probably already seen a few. And I promise you this, Dear: when you ask for a sign, it is always given. You just have to learn how to see it. But we'll get to that another time." Angie paused for a moment, giving Wendi a chance to speak.

Wendi looked down at Angie's hand, still atop hers. She tightened her grip around the paper and stared into Angie's comforting gaze, not sure how to respond.

"Just tuck that into your pocket and save it," advised Angie. "When the need for an Angel arises, recite it with all your heart, Dear. And every little thing will be all right." Angie smiled, her eyes gently peering through Wendi's, touching her soul. For the first time, Wendi felt that her world really would be okay again.

Pete's forehead rested in the palms of his hands, pressing his elbows into the desk. In front of him, a blank screen dimly illuminated his distraught face as he sat alone, lost in thought and memories. Images of his little brother flashed through his mind. He shuttered.

His mother's words echoed in his head. "It was an accident, Pete. Stop allowing this to haunt you. You'll always be brothers."

The dreadful image of their teenage scuffle replayed in Pete's mind. He was taunting his brother, Georgie, as usual. Georgie had tried to run away, but Pete was too quick. He cut Georgie off in the dining room, and took him to the ground. They rolled around, knocking into chairs, and Pete pinned his brother to the floor under the corner of the dining room table. Pete's body weighed down on Georgie. He struggled to break free, jerking himself forward, harder and harder, trying to counter Pete's brute force. Pete, thinking it humorous, shifted his weight, rolling off just as his brother thrust himself forward with all his strength. The force of Georgie's momentum threw his head forward toward the corner of the dining room table—

Pete's fist slammed down, shaking the whole desk. His stomach churned with guilt as he buried his face into his hands again, trying to shake off the vivid and traumatic memory.

"Ya look like ya just saw a ghost," a voice echoed from the doorway.

Caught off-guard, Pete's whole body jerked back, startled by Allen's presence. "Jesus!" Pete exclaimed.

"My beard's not quite that long," Allen chuckled. "But I'll take the compliment. I guess I picked the wrong Halloween costume." Allen always knew how to lighten the atmosphere.

"Hey there, Allen," Pete nervously chuckled as he regained his composure. "How are you, bud?"

"I'm fine, but I'm not so sure I can say the same for you, my friend. What's weighing on your mind so heavily?" Before Pete could answer, Allen answered. "Let me take a wild guess … family matters?"

"You know me too well, Allen," Pete replied, wheeling himself back to his desk and attempting to regain his composure.

"I just found out Bobby was in trouble at school—again. He almost took it too far this time."

"What happened now?" Asked Allen as he stepped into the office, genuinely concerned.

Pete inhaled, breathing out hard. "Bobby tripped someone, and the other kid fell and got a pencil through his ear. The school said the other boy's fine, but was lucky. An inch away ..." Pete struggled to swallow as his throat closed up. "Another inch and ... and they said he would have lost an eye."

"Lord almighty. I'm so sorry," Allen responded, stepping around the desk to Pete's side. "It's okay. You said the boy was okay. You seem to be taking it a bit hard," remarked Allen as he reached out, rubbing Pete's shoulder and upper back.

"It's just ..." Pete swallowed, choking back his watery eyes. "Sorry. It's, um, it's more than that. This seems to be an ongoing skirmish with some local bully, the same kid from last time when I had to leave early to get Bobby. And rather than leave it alone and report him to the teachers, he's retaliating and now getting himself into even more trouble. That boy needs to learn how to control his temper before it's too late."

"Well, I'll keep praying for him. And all of you. I wish I could do more for ya. You be sure to let me know if I can."

"Thank you, Allen. Your friendship means a lot. Now let's bust outta this joint," he said, rising from his chair. "You got the notice that we can leave early, right? It's a Halloween miracle."

"I'm not sure that's a thing, Pete."

"It is now, Allen," Pete assured him as they walked toward the door. He needed all the miracles he could get right now.

~ o ~

·

Chapter 4:

Wishful Thinking

*"God is where all
real magic comes from."*

~ o ~

ding dong

Wendi dropped her fork, jumped up from the dinner table, and excitedly announced, "We have our first trick-or-treater! I feel like they're starting earlier every year." She glanced at the clock. 5:55. *Triple digits again? This is becoming a strange pattern.* She shook her head, feeling a bit lost in the twilight zone.

ding dong

She hurried to the door, grabbing her witch hat along the way. Reaching for the bowl of goodies with one hand, her other swung open the door, excited to see what sort of creature would be awaiting her.

"Well, hello there! Don't you look wonderful," she exclaimed with a look of delight upon seeing a little alien and fairy upon her doorstep.

"I'm takin' over da Earth to eat all da candy," said the little alien boy. "Hand it over, Eart-ling," demanded the exuberant little boy, pointing his raygun at Wendi and making laser sounds.

"Timmy!" his mother shouted, "That's not how we talk to people, even if you are an alien. I'm so sorry, Wendi"

"That's quite all right, Sandy. He's just having fun."

"Still, manners are manners, even on Halloween. Go on, Timmy, what do you say if you'd like some candy from Mrs. Farfalla?"

The little boy's head drooped as he lowered his gun, and he held out his plastic pumpkin, already half full of treats. "Twick or tweat," he uttered in a somber tone. "I wasn't really gonna distinter-gate you."

"Well, thank you," Wendi chuckled. "I appreciate you letting me live. Here, you can take two for being so kind," acknowledged Wendi, tilting the bowl downward so his small hands could easily reach inside.

Next to Timmy, adorned with an adorable fairy outfit, was his even smaller sister. Wendi stared at the delightful girl, recalling fond memories of her own childhood.

~ ~ ~

As a little girl, Wendi loved wearing costumes any time of the year. She insisted that her fairy costume always be within reach for "magic emergencies." She loved casting spells left and right. Anytime she was feeling fun and fanciful, she would grab her fairy dress, complete with wings, and get to work.

Little Wendi would cast spells on anything she thought needed her help. Her favorite was a love spell for the pets. She always tried to get Jeeves, the dog, to fall in love with Mr. Fluffles, the cat. She would wave her little wand in the air, spinning it in circles, and say, "Abawa-cadabawa, you know what we're afta! You wuv each other, dog and cat, you wuv each other just like dat!" and on the "dat," she would flick her wand, releasing the magic.

Despite her many failed attempts, she believed her spells simply needed a little tweaking. She would try again and again, using different words and rhymes. As much as the dog and cat seemed to get along, little Wendi just couldn't get them to lay down and cuddle with each other.

One evening in early December, they were decorating for Christmas. Wendi was in her favorite fairy outfit running about, casting nature spells over the house plants. "Abawa-cadabawa. I'm da fairy queen. Be heal-ty and green," she commanded, waving her wand over the bamboo.

As she scurried over to bless the Christmas tree, she tripped and fell, snapping her magic wand in half. Devastated, tears poured down her precious cheeks. Her father dropped the tinsel and darted to the rescue. He sat her up and snatched the pieces of her broken wand. "It's okay, Sweetie, Daddy will fix your wand for you." In his typical dad fashion—and some duct tape—he wrapped it up from top to bottom and handed it to her.

"There you are. It's as good as new," he attested as he handed a much bulkier wand back to his sobbing little girl. "And now it's a silver wand, too. Did you know silver wands are even more magical?"

Half convinced of her father's words, she wiped her eyes, grabbed her bandaged wand, and began to wave it around. She flicked her wrist to dispense her magic, and the wand limped over. Little Wendi looked at her crippled wand, now with a right angle in it, then looked at her dad. Her mouth trembled as the tears began to flow again.

Her dad lifted up the wand from her tiny fingers and said, "You have to be more delicate with a good wand, Sweetie. We'll just put a little more tape on there, and it will be fine."

"I have a better idea," came the soothing voice of reason. Her mom was the saving grace of the family. Her dad was a gritty, armed service man. He loved his little girls but lacked the nurturing ability of her mom, who always knew how to handle every situation.

Wendi's mom picked a piece of silver garland, then walked to the coat closet, pulled out a white metal hanger, and began bending it. She then walked over to Wendi's father, grabbed the tape and wand out of his hand, opened the trash can, and dropped the wand in.

Little Wendi and her father stood there in shock, mouths open. Her mother winked, entangled the garland around the hanger, taped it in place, and ushered little Wendi over in front of the dining room mirror. Holding it above Wendi's head, she said, "See that, it's a halo! Now you are our little Angel for real!

"But I don't wanna be an Angel," little Wendi pouted. "Dey are not weal."

"They're not?" her mom asked with surprise. "The funny thing is, my love, while I'm sure fairies are real, I never hear any stories about fairies, and I hear stories about Angels all the time! So I'm pretty sure they're real. And guess what the best part about being an Angel is, even better than being a fairy?

"What's dat, mommy?" She asked, sniffling.

"Angels don't need wands to make their magic," she affirmed with a tender smile.

Confusion washed across little Wendi's face. "So where does da magic come from?"

Her mother bent over and softly whispered into her ear, "It comes from God's love," she replied, wiping away Wendi's tears.

"It does?" little Wendi asked, fascinated by the idea.

"Yes. God is where all real magic comes from. And do you know how to call a real Angel?"

"How?" questioned little Wendi, her eyes dry with delight.

"By praying and asking God to send one. And even though God is always listening, he especially grants wishes to good little girls near Christmas to honor the birth of Christ."

Enthralled with the idea, Little Wendi's face lit up. "I godda go," she exclaimed as she started to run off.

"Go to the bathroom?" her dad asked.

"No Daddy, ta say my pwayers and get in bed," she exclaimed before pausing and running back.

"Did you forget something?" her mother asked.

"I forgot ta kiss you and daddy and say I wuv you." She threw her tiny arms around her dad and kissed his cheek, repeating the gestures for her mom.

"Awe, thank you, Angel. I'll finish making your halo so it can attach to your wings. Now get going and say prayers for all the people you love, and pray even harder for the people you don't."

"Okay, Mommy. Can I pray dat Jeeves and Mr. Fluffles will love each other?"

"Yes, Angel," she answered with a laugh. "You can pray for that too, as long as you pray for people to love each other as well. And remember, just because Jeeves and Mr. Fluffles don't cuddle, I think they love each other very much."

"Okay, Mommy. I can't wait ta be an Angel! No one can bwake Angel magic if it's powered by God!" Little Wendi ran off to her bedroom, unable to control her excitement. She was going to have Angel magic.

~ ~ ~

Even though Wendi loved Christmas, Halloween had always been her favorite holiday. Dressing up still held a special place in her heart. There was something about the magic of costumes that even her dark sorrow couldn't hold back.

"Are you all right, Dear," Sandy asked.

"Oh, yes, I was just admiring this beautiful little fairy. It looks just like the costume I had when I was little. Good to see you, Sandy. Now you two adorable kids have yourselves a Happy Halloween!" Wendi called out as they walked away. Closing the door, she returned to the kitchen. The kids had just finished their dinner, still sitting at the table.

"Okay troops, time to get in costume and get out there," Pete exclaimed. "And remember, I get half of everything."

"I don't think so, Dad. Nice try" rebutted Bobby. "Get in a costume and get your own candy."

"Okay, I'll only take twenty percent for being your personal bodyguard for the night, and that's my final offer. And Bobby," Pete beckoned. "I didn't want to bring down the mood tonight by discussing your incident at school. But that doesn't mean you're off the hook. Understand?" he questioned with a stern look."

"Yes, Sir," Bobby replied, knowing now was not the time for sarcasm or a smart-ass reply.

"Okay, then. We'll talk about it tomorrow. And I also want to tell you a story about me and your Uncle Georgie," Pete added hesitantly.

"The one with the weird eye?" asked Bobby.

"Yes, the one with the weird eye," Pete reluctantly answered, choosing not to correct Bobby's choice of words. He swallowed his emotions and changed the subject. "Now the sun is setting, demons and ghosts are on the loose, and I don't know any other team better suited to fend them off than you two," Pete joked, diverting his thoughts. "So get going!" The kids hopped out of their seats and ran upstairs.

Pete smiled at his wife. "Go on up and help Faith get ready. I know you're excited about her costume. I'm glad to see you haven't sworn off Angels along with the big man upstairs," he jested, waiting to see how she'd react.

"Let's just say I'm opening up to various levels of the supernatural and heavenly realms. But I think it's just Halloween getting to me, so don't get too excited," Wendi admitted.

"Too bad. I like hearing you use big sexy words like supernatural and realms. Now go on and help your little Angel get ready. I'll clean up dinner."

Wendi felt her heart soften as a flicker of genuine appreciation for her husband seeped out. "Thank you," she responded, topping it off with a smile. "Make sure you're ready to take some photos when we come down," she called out as she stepped into the hallway.

Wendi knelt down at the base of the stairs, and reached out, stroking Misty's soft fur. "And what are you dressing as, Miss Misty? We'll have to get you a costume next year." As Wendi stood up, the plant on the end table caught her eye. A few leaves were brown, and others were beginning to turn. Recalling her magic nature spell, she reached out, waving her hand over the plant "Abra—"

"Abracadabra," came Pete's voice from the kitchen. "I want to—"

"Pete," Wendi called out from around the corner. "Pete, did you just say Abracadabra?"

"Well, I know my voice isn't exactly pop star material, but I didn't say it. I was singing it," he proudly admitted. Pausing his dinnertime cleanup, he looked up as Wendi emerged from the hallway. "Did you come back because you want me to reach out and grab ya?" he asked hopefully.

"No," she replied, allowing a slight giggle to slip past her lips. "That's not why I'm asking. I was just about to—" embarrassed, she shifted gears. "You were singing?"

"Yeah, Abracadabra by Steve Miller Band. The radio was playing it all day. Guess it's popular on the Halloween playlists."

"Right," acknowledged Wendi. "I know the song, but don't remember the last time I heard it. I was just thinking back to when I was a little girl. Remember I told you how much I loved being a magic fairy and casting spells when I was Faith's age?"

"I sure do, and your mom's mentioned it a hundred times: 'Did I ever tell you Wendi used to dress up and cast spells all over the house, always trying to get the dog and cat to'... hold up, what *were* you trying to get them to do?" he laughed, cracking up at his own humor.

"To fall in love with each other, pervert."

"Well, call it what you want. Anywho, the kids are waiting for you, Hun. Why's it so important?"

"I would always say abracadabra when I cast my spells, and the word was literally coming out of my mouth when I heard you say it. I mean, what are the chances?"

"Ironically, it's been in my head all day, but that's the first time I started singing. Just one of those funny coincidences, is all. Now let me sing and clean, and hurry up and go help your Angel get her wings. Where's my bell?" he cracked himself up again.

Wendi stepped over to her husband, stretched out her arms, and embraced him. Pete melted into his wife, not remembering the last time she allowed a tender moment. He bit his tongue—no jokes, no comments, nothing to spoil the moment. There weren't very many happy days in the Farfalla household, so he made sure to savor every moment of the days that were.

Releasing her husband, Wendi wandered upstairs to check on the kids. Pete happily cleared the table and rinsed off the dishes, all the while humming and singing along to whatever magic was in the air.

Wendi opened the door to Faith's room and stood in the doorway. Faith was looking at herself in the mirror, attempting to affix her halo. Tears welled up in Wendi's eyes as her mind filled with fond memories of her own Angel outfit. The magic of Halloween was in becoming something else, about expressing some part of yourself that wasn't typically allowed to express in the real world, something Wendi wished she never let go of.

There's less room for magic in the life of an adult. As people grow up, the world takes hold, squeezing out the beauty of innocence and the joy of imagination. That's why Wendi wanted a large family; she wanted a reason to keep the magic alive. Watching her daughter allowed Wendi's own inner child to run free once more.

"Look how precious you are. My little Angel," Wendi remarked as she knelt down next to Faith, giving her a hug. Wendi fastened Faith's wings, straightened her halo, and spun her around.

"Look at you! What a perfect little Angel you are. Do you like your costume?"

Faith nodded.

"Do you know that Angels can talk?" Wendi encouraged, but Faith simply smiled, and nodded a silent, affirmative yes. "Now when you get to each door, remember to say trick-or-treat, Okay? It's good manners."

Faith shrugged. *I tried,* Wendi thought as she ushered Faith out of the room, pausing at the next door.

"Bobby, we're ready for pictures."

"*Okay mom,* I'm just getting batteries in my Proton Pack."

Bobby came running down the stairs and flung himself around, pointing the tip of his particle thrower at Misty, who was still lounging on the third step. Bobby made a slew of odd sounds, then yelled, "I got one!"

"I knew the cat was possessed. That explains so much of her behavior," joked Peter. Taking a chance, he leaned in and whispered, "Maybe your mom is possessed, too. That would *also* explain a lot."

"I'm not touching that one," Bobby rebutted with an awkward laugh. They gathered at the bottom of the steps, and Pete directed as Wendi snapped away, photo after photo. Each child posing by themselves, then together, and even some fun poses involving the cat as a prop. She even had Peter set the timer so they could all be in the picture. Happy family photos were rare these days, so both parents were taking advantage of the opportunity.

"Okay mom, can we actually trick-or-treat already or are you going to just keep taking pictures?"

"Okay, okay. You just both look so happy and cute. Grab your pumpkins for your candy."

"Seriously, mom? I'm too old to trick-or-treat with a pumpkin. I'm taking my pillowcase. And I'm not cute. I'm a Ghostbuster."

The neighborhood was abuzz with all types of fantastic beast; a costume runway show illuminated by parents' flashlights.

As much as Wendi wanted to be with the kids, she loved giving out candy and seeing all the neighborhood kid's costumes. It also gave Pete a chance to say hello to the neighbors. It was one of the small saving graces of the move; the people.

After hitting up several houses, they came up to one of Pete's favorite neighbors, Dr. Steven Jones. As Bobby reached out to ring the doorbell, the door swung open, revealing a welcome face. "Hey there, neighbors. Happy Halloween to ya!"

"Trick-or-treat," replied Bobby.

"Ya'll look fantastic. Glad to see everyone has on their happy face this year."

"Thanks, Steve. Hopefully, you mean it," Pete responded.

"Well, why else would I be sayin' somethin' if I didn't mean it, Pete? You northerners crack me up!" he hooted.

"I'm still adjusting to how friendly everyone is down here. When someone asks how you are, they genuinely care to know; they're not being polite."

"Well, that's why Marge and I love the South. We're a little closer to God, down here. And it must be true because I see an Angel," Steve exclaimed, hunching over so Faith could reach the candy bowl. "Don't you look precious, Darlin'. Go on and take as much as you like. You too, Bobby."

"Thank you, Dr. Jones," Bobby politely responded.

"Hey now, call me Indiana," Steve chuckled. "That one never

gets old with me," he added, turning his attention to Pete. "You doin' okay these days, Pete? You look a little flush."

"Doing the best I can, Doc. Ironically, this is me on one of my good nights," Pete added with a laugh.

"Well, we may have to get you in for a checkup sooner rather than later. And how's Wendi doing?"

"Uh, Dad," Bobby interrupted. "Is it okay if we run up to the next house?"

"Sure, bud, I'll be right there."

"Come on, Faith. I'll race you to the corner. Go!"

Bobby and Faith barreled up the sidewalk, quickly reaching the next house. The entrance walkway was facing the far corner and was blocked by tall hedges. As they rounded the bushes, still running, Bobby froze with true terror. He swiftly grabbed Faith's hand, yanking her back. Three large silhouettes were coming toward them, blocking the walkway. They were all in costume: Freddy, Michael, and the biggest out of the three, Jason. Jason, who seemed to be the leader, stopped a few feet in front of Bobby.

"Isn't this a treat!" he bellowed, followed by a blood-curdling laugh. He lifted his mask, revealing an even scarier sight—the face of Seth Baynes.

"Well, look who we have here, boys," Seth spouted with an evil smirk. "Isn't this precious? Where you runnin' to, Booby? Are you tryin' to catch your sister's tongue?" They all laughed. He looked down at Faith. "Now what you doin' with that candy? If you can't ask for it, you don't get to keep it," he asserted. "That's Halloween rules!" Reaching out, he snatched the pumpkin out of her hand.

"Give it back, Seth!" Bobby yelled as he reached for the pumpkin. Seth yanked his arm back, swinging it out of Bobby's reach.

"Hold on," Seth demanded as he drove his plastic machete against Bobby's chest, forcing him to take a step back. "It's Halloween, so I'm in a good mood. All Faith needs to do is say trick-or-treat, and I'll give her candy back." He leaned in, close to her face, and held his other hand up to his ear to listen.

"Well, I don't hear you. All ya have to say is trick-or-treat and you get it back."

"Knock it off, jerk," Bobby demanded. "Go trick-or-treat at the mental hospital where you belong. Now give it back to her right now!"

Seth shifted his gaze from Faith to Bobby. "Or what, dorkbuster? Who you gonna call, your Mummy?" He laughed, peering side to side, waiting for his two sidekicks to join in the laughter.

"I tell you what, Booby, I'll give it back to her if you hand over all your peanut butter cups. Like I said, I'm feelin' nice."

"Fine," Bobby agreed, as his nostrils flared up. He reached into his bag, feeling around for a butter cup. He scooped one up into his hand and clenched as hard as he could. He could feel the shell breaking as its insides oozed out, and flung it at Seth's face.

Seth jerked his head to the side, avoiding the projectile, and flung his machete around, clubbing Bobby on the side of the head. "One more chance, dorkbuster! Your cups, or her candy stays with us."

"You want it? You got it," Bobby yelled, dropping his sack of candy. He reached in, feeling around for the right candy. As his hand emerged, he ripped off the top of the Fun Dip. He threw the powdered sugar into Seth's face, and flung the remains at the other two for good measure. "How's that for a treat, asshole?"

Seth stammered back, dropping Faith's pumpkin to wipe the power from his eyes. Bobby snatched up the pumpkin, grabbed Faith's hand. "Come on Faith, run!" As Bobby took a stride toward the street, he was suddenly jerked backward. Losing his grip on the pumpkin, it fell, scattering Faith's candy across the walkway.

Seth had a hold of Bobby's Proton pack and swung him around. Seth's other arm was raised in the air with a closed fist about to come beating down. "You're dead, you little sh—"

Seth's fist stopped in mid-air as a flash of light blinded his eyes, causing him to flinch.

"WHAT THE HELL IS GOING ON HERE!" came Pete's enraged voice as he swiftly approached.

Seth immediately released Bobby, lowering his hand and stepping away. Pete held the light in Seth's eyes for a moment, noticing the powered candy strewn across his face. He also took note of his bandaged ear. "Enough of this, all of you. Bobby, Halloween is over for you. We are heading straight home. But first, there's going to be an apology."

"Yeah, apologize," repeated Bobby.

Pete turned the flashlight onto Bobby's face. "I meant you, Bobby. This is the boy you tripped in class today and ..." Pete took a breath, shaking his head. He desperately tried to control the rage bubbling inside. "... and got stabbed in the ear by a pencil, isn't it? And I'm guessing he didn't powder himself. So *you* are going to apologize to *him*."

Bobby's eyes lit up in disbelief. Seth, accustomed to being reprimanded by adults, was also shocked by Pete's demand.

"Are you *insane*, Dad? They started this!" Bobby erupted. "No! I'm not apologizing! No way. He asked for it. They took Faith's cand—"

Pete interrupted, shouting even louder, "I don't give a DAMN! I leave you alone for 5 minutes with your sister, and you're getting in a fight? You need to learn when to walk away. When they react, it's their problem. When you react, it's *my* problem. I will handle them, but first, you *will* apologize. It is Halloween, and this is Mr. Peterman's house. This is not the time or place for you to act like this, regardless of *anyone* else's actions and words." Pete's chest tightened as he leaned in toward his son. "Apologize, RIGHT NOW!"

"But—"

"NOW!" Screamed Peter. His whole body tensed up, and his heart was pounding like a snare drum. Standing there gritting his teeth, he impatiently waited for Bobby's reply as the street slowly filled with onlookers. Parents walking up the sidewalk grabbed their children and hurried across to the other side of the street.

Bobby, enraged and humiliated, turned to Seth and mumbled sarcastically, "I'm sorry ... that you're a jerk."

Pete's blood pressure skyrocketed. "ENOUGH!" he yelled, sinking his fingers into Bobby's arm and yanking him away from the others. "I will deal with you at home. Do you understand?"

Bobby nodded, knowing one more word, regardless of what it was, would land him in the kind of trouble he wouldn't be able to get out of. The other boys snickered.

Pete shot them a look, shining his light into their faces. He held the light in their eyes as he peered down at innocent little Faith. Seeing her distraught face, he crouched down and lifted her up in one arm, then turned his gaze back to Seth.

"Just because I asked my son to apologize does not mean you are off the hook," fumed Peter, as his whole body vibrated with anger. "Now, that is my daughter's candy all over the ground, so the three of you have exactly five seconds to gather it back up into her pumpkin, and hand it back ... along with an apology *to her*. Do you understand?" He demanded.

Seth knew his limits when it came to adults. He wasn't afraid to mouth off, but understood this was not the time.

Back at the front door, Mr. Peterman become aware of the commotion around the corner. He handed the bowl of candy to his wife and emerged from around the bushes to see what all the yelling was about.

"Now just what the he—" Mr. Peterman cut himself short. "Oh, Hey Pete. I didn't realize it was you. Everything okay here?"

"It's fine, Jon. Thanks for checking on us. We just had a little problem bumping into these boys, and Faith's candy was spilled. Everything's okay. These boys were just apologizing for bumping into my kids. Isn't that right, boys?"

The three boys swiftly gathered the candy, filling the pumpkin, and Seth gently handed it back to Faith. "Sorry about your candy," he muttered.

"Thank you," Pete responded in a stern voice. "Best you boys head home as well," he insisted, stepping aside to let them pass. Pete nodded at Mr. Peterman, giving him the okay. Jon wanted to be sure everything was all right, but feeling the seriousness of Pete, he took a few steps back.

As Seth was passing Pete, he abruptly grabbed Seth's machete, pulling closer. "I know your type," Pete stated, glaring down at Seth. "Now, nothing excuses what my son did today, and I had half a mind to let you belt him, but what sort of father would that make me?"

"Just like my—"

"I wasn't looking for an answer, Seth" cut in Pete. Seth twitched at hearing his name. "I know who you are. I saw you sitting outside the principal's office when I picked the kids up the other day, and I learned all about you. You seem to be the type who likes to start problems and end them in fights. Now regardless of what started all this between you two, or how long it's been going on, it ends here and now," Pete demanded, his blood still pulsating throughout his veins. "I never want to see you near my kids again. Or even hear your name. I also learned about your parents. I can easily get your step-father's number and explain the situation to him. And I guarantee I will have a very short conversation that will have a very long end for you. AM I CLEAR?"

Seth nodded, showing a twinge of fear. Pete took a breath and let go of the machete. He watched them walk away, then focused on his precious girl. "I'm so sorry, Angel. Tonight started out so well. Are you okay?" He asked. Faith nodded.

"Let's get you home." She nodded again. "Let's go, Bobby." He could feel his heart still pounding. He knew where Bobby got his temper from. It had been a long time since he had lost it like that.

"But we only made it through half the neighborhood! I barely have any—" Pete yanked him onto the sidewalk, cutting off his words.

"You should've thought of that before you got into trouble. Home! NOW, Bobby!" Pete looked up at Mr. Peterman, who was still lingering in the walkway. "I apologize again for any trouble, Jon. He's turning into a teenager too soon."

As Pete continued, Bobby stormed off toward his house. With his head still down, he rounded the corner of the sidewalk, slamming directly into someone, knocking her into the hedges. Startled and embarrassed, he began to scurry off without even looking at his victim.

"Bobby, wait!" a familiar voice called out. "Are you okay?"

Bobby's entire body went into shock as he turned and looked back, realizing who had just knocked over. Silhouetted in the light of the house, translucent butterfly wings spread out behind her with an uncanny glow. There she stood, the features of her face too dark to see against the backlight, but he knew the sound of her voice; his Angel in butterfly wings. It wasn't just any girl he had slammed into, it was Sara.

Hearing her voice was somehow comforting, and yet dreadful, at the same time. A thousand thoughts raced through his mind. *She heard everything. Could this night get any worse? Could my life get any worse?*

"I ... uh ... sorry, Sara. I didn't see you. I ... I gotta go." He ran off without looking back.

~~~ O ~~~

ding dong

Wendi exuberantly opened the door, excited to see the next costumes and wondering if she knew the parents. But as she opened the door, she found herself looking down at two wide-eyed little children, unaccompanied by an adult. Standing there before her, stood a little boy dressed as an Angel and next to him, his even littler sister, in plain clothes. Surprised that such little children were out on their own, she peered past them, checking the driveway and looking up and down the sidewalk. Some parents watched from a distance, but no one else was in sight.

Their soft voices interrupted her concerns. "Trick or treat."

Wendi smiled. "Oh, what a precious little Angel you are. Do you know my little girl is also an Angel?"

"All children are Angels," he replied.

Wendi cocked her head and smiled again, shocked at the reply. "Why, yes. They are," she agreed, shifting her gaze to the little girl. "And where's your costume?"

"I'm an Earth Angel. I look like everyone else," the little girl insisted quite articulately for a child so young.

Wendi was taken aback by the quick and unusual response. "Well, where are your wings and halo?" she asked.

"Only heavenly Angels have halos and wings. That's him," she said, pointing at her brother. "I'm an Earth Angel," she asserted, this time with even more conviction.

"You're an Angel, too," the little boy added with a smile.

Wendi was momentarily speechless. She hadn't expected to hear such commentary from anyone, especially two small children. "Oh, well, thank you, but I don't think I've been much of an Angel to anyone lately."

"Everyone is an Angel to someone," they sang out in unison.

Still dazed by the scene that was unfolding in front of her, Wendi smiled, scratched her head, and looked up the street one more time. "Where are your—"

"God blesses you," the little girl said with a dash of enthusiasm, once again leaving Wendi speechless. The little boy followed suit, saying, "And don't worry, we'll be watching over you and your family!"

Wendi, yet again startled at the remarks, stammered. "Uh, watching over *us*?"

The little boy piped up again, "Of course. What else are Angels for?"

They smiled, abruptly said goodnight, turned, and walked off into the night. Wendi, still shocked and bewildered by the unexpected blessings, stumbled over her words, barely managing to squeak out a "Thank you" and "Happy Halloween" as the kids wandered off. Feeling as if she just had just woken from a daydream, she slowly shut the door and stepped back.

God bless you? We'll watch over you? I am going crazy. Snapping out of her daze, she realized the children didn't even take any candy. She quickly reached for the doorknob, twisted, and pulled. There, standing in the doorway, was Bobby. His arm was stretched out, about to open the door.

"Jesus, where did you come from?" she remarked, startled and confused.

"Nope, not Jesus. Sorry to let you down, too."

"Let me down? What are you talking about? And why are you home so early?" she questioned, wondering if she was caught in a dream. She peeked her head out, peering out past Bobby, looking up and down the street."

"Mom … MOM! What are you doing?"

"Oh, I'm sorry, honey. What are you doing back so soon? Where's your father and Faith?"

He momentarily looked up at her, then his gaze drifted to the floor. "Seth is a jerk, Dad sent me home, and I knocked over Sara." He pushed past her, and ran straight up to his room, slamming the door shut. Wendi watched, even more confused than she was just a few moments prior. She shook her head and turned back to the doorway.

"Jesus!" cried Wendi, jumping back. Silently standing there was Pete, still holding Faith in his arms.

"Nope, just me and an Angel. Sorry to let you down."

Still lost in space, Wendi attempted to reply. "What? Did you … uh … no … I, uh … did you see two little Angels? Well, one little Angel and the other was just, uh—"

"Hun, what the hell are you talking about? This is the only little Angel I've seen. Now can you move?"

"No," she said.

"No, you can't move?"

"No. I mean, yes. I can. No, not that." She sighed. "You had to of seen them. It was the strangest thing."

"Wendi, I don't know what the hell is going on, but none of us are in the mood for games. Please just move so we can get into the *goddamn* house already," he demanded as his heart seized up again.

Wendi stepped aside to let them in, then popped her head back out, taking one last glance. Nothing. She closed the door behind her, turning to face Peter."What happened? Why are you back early, and why is everyone in such a pissy mood?"

"Everyone is not in a pissy mood," Pete responded sarcastically. "Faith is just fine, aren't you, Angel?" he asked, setting her down. She nodded and scurried up to her room with her pumpkin of candy.

"You know what I mean," snapped Wendi.

"Your darling son almost got punched in the face. Maybe I should've just let him get socked in the nose. That boy better change his attitude fast, or I'm going to change it for him." Pete could feel his blood pressure rising again talking about it.

"What happened?"

"Bobby was in another fight with that kid Seth. That's what happened. The same kid he tripped in school today who had to be sent to the nurse."

"How did this happen? Weren't you with him the whole time?"

"No. I let them run ahead. So I suppose this is my fault now?" He added.

"I didn't say that," comforted Wendi.

Pete sighed, shaking his head as a moment of guilt crept in. "I let them run ahead to the next house. I was talking with Dr. Jones, and by the time I got there, they were already fighting."

"So you didn't you see it happen?"

"I saw enough."

"It doesn't sound like it," rebutted Wendi. "I know how you see things. If you weren't there when it started, don't put this all on Bobby. Did you ask him what really happened? Did you hear his side of the story?"

Pete raised his voice. "I said I saw enough! He threw candy sugar right in that kid's face. It could have seriously damaged his eyes. Maybe I shouldn't have interrupted and just let Bobby learn a lesson!" Pete stopped, feeling his chest constricting again.

Blood was rushing to his face as he tried to catch his breath. He stammered back toward the steps and sat down.

"I just want to know what the hell is happening around here. Are you okay?" she asked.

"I'm fine." Pete replied, still breathing hard.

"You don't look fine," she refuted with growing concern. "You're sweating."

"Because I just carried Faith three blocks. I just need to take a shower." Grabbing the banister, he pulled himself to his feet, and slowly climbed the steps.

Wendi was left standing by the door, alone. *What the hell is going on around here? We've all lost our minds.* She opened the door again and looked outside.

Slumped over in the dark, Pete sat on the edge of the bed. His heart was still pounding. He clenched his hand into a fist and drove it into the pillow. Again. And again. *I was too hard on him. He's been through enough.* Pete sighed. *Maybe I overreacted.* He wiped his brow and rested his hand on his chest. It was beating too fast. Taking a deep breath in, he attempted to slow his heartbeat.

His mind wandered back, thinking about his younger brother again. The memory of seeing Georgie come home from the hospital with a patch over his eye still made Pete sick to his stomach. He couldn't look at his brother without being torn apart with an unbearable guilt. Other than forced family gatherings before the move, they no longer spoke.

Wendi had her fill for one night. She turned off the outside lights and locked the front door. It was the first time she ever ended Halloween before the trick-or-treating was done. She followed everyone else's cue and headed upstairs. She knew Bobby needed more time to cool off and checked in on Faith, first.

She was still in her Angel outfit sitting at her little table, which she had dragged out of its corner to the center of the room. All of her candy was piled in the middle of the table, and she was separating it into four piles. She placed a piece of candy in front of herself, one into a pile in front of Bunny, one in front of Dolly, and the last pile formed in front of the empty seat to her right, for Nobody.

"I think we can take off your outfit now, Angel."

Faith looked up, shook her head, and continued sorting.

"Well, you can't go to bed with your wings on!"

Faith looked up again, nodded, and resumed her task.

Wendi stepped over to her little Angel and squatted down beside her. "Were you there with Bobby when he got in trouble?"

Faith nodded.

"Can you tell me what happened?"

Faith shook her head. Wendi gave up. She kissed her little Angel's cheek. As she left, she pulled the door behind her, leaving it slightly ajar. Wendi paused at Bobby's door, about to knock, and thought better of it. *He needs more time.* Bobby sat silently in his room, eating away at his candy as his guilt, shame, and anger ate away at him.

Wendi meandered down the hall toward the bedroom to get out of her witch costume. She was looking forward to some TV time to unwind after all the commotion. As she rounded the corner to the bedroom, she stopped, paralyzed with fear, trying to take in what she was witnessing.

No! Please, God. No!

~ o ~

Chapter 5:

A Prayer
for Help

*"I open my heart and invite you into this space.
Please bless me, Angel, with your grace."*

~ o ~

The light of the hallway silhouetted Wendi's figure against the dim doorway as the horrific scene in front of her sunk in.

Peter was on the floor, struggling to prop himself up against the bed. His shirt was soaked through, and beads of sweat were dripping down his face. Pushing against the floor with one hand, the other clutched his heart. His arm was shaking violently, attempting to find some strength. It gave out, sending his body crashing against the rug. He rolled onto his side, desperately attempting to catch his breath.

Wendi rushed into the bedroom, her feet barely keeping up with her mind. *No! Don't you dare leave this family!* She knelt by her husband's side. A tidal wave of emotions surged over her as dreadful thoughts came crashing down, washing away all hope she had left of returning to a happy life. Sliding her arm around his torso, she desperately hauled him up into a seated position with his back against the side of the bed. She steadied her husband, placing a hand atop his, which still covered his heart. "What's happening? I'm calling an ambulance." He barely had enough energy to lift his head. "PETE, look at me!" she yelled, grabbing his jaw and turning his face toward hers.

He looked up at her terrified eyes. "Now … don't … over … react." His words were slow, taking a breath between each one. "I just… need to … catch … my breath. I'm … okay."

"The hell you are," she exclaimed, looking up at the phone on the nightstand. "I'm calling an ambulance right now." She steadied him with one hand and frantically reached over with the other, knocking the phone to the floor. As she picked up the receiver, he laid his hand atop hers.

"I'll be okay … Honey … just help me … onto the bed." He attempted to push himself up, collapsing back against the bed.

"Peter Farfalla, you are NOT okay!" Her fingers shook as they unsteadily dialed each number: 9-1-1.

"You just keep breathing. You are going to the hospital!" The voice of the operator rang out through the phone. "Nine one one, what's your emergency?" Wendi proceeded to dispense the information they asked for. "Stay calm. An ambulance is on the way, ma'am."

Wendi hung up the phone and sat on the floor, holding her husband. His eyelids were weighing down on him as he struggled to stay conscious. His body started sliding down, and she heaved him back up, holding him tight. She grabbed his face again, slapping his cheek. "Stay with me. You stay here, Peter Farfalla. The ambulance is only eleven minutes away. Stay with me." As Pete sank in and out of consciousness, Wendi laid her head against his, faced with the reality of life without her husband by her side. *Haven't we suffered enough?*

As the tears streamed down, she kept talking, hoping to keep him present. "You need to get through this, Pete. Do you hear me? We need you. I can't do it without you." All felt hopeless. Time was against her, and the only thing she could do was wait for the ambulance to arrive. Wait, hope, and pray. "God, if you take him from me, what's left? You took my baby and left me with a hostile son, a speechless daughter, and a loveless marriage. And now you want to take him? If he's gone, how do I support this family? How do I survive? I can't handle catastrophe upon catastrophe. There'll be nothing left."

Pete looked up at her, and his lips parted, attempting to catch his breath, but no words emerged.

"Don't try to talk, Pete. Just breathe."

Sweat continued to drip down his face, breathing short and shallow. Perhaps for the first time in her life, she saw true fear reflecting in her husband's eyes. "You stay with me. This is no time to go off and die. The ambulance will be here any minute and they're going to fix you up. You hear me," her voice cracked. "They'll fix you right up."

The ambulance had to be close. She didn't want to leave his side, but she also didn't want the children to panic when a wailing siren and flashing lights suddenly pulled into the driveway. She mustered up all the courage she could manage to remain calm and sensible. *I need to reassure the children that Daddy will be fine*, even though she barely believed the thought herself.

She couldn't bear to leave his side a minute too soon. *As soon as I hear the ambulance, I'll gather the children.* With everything that had happened over the last year, he was the one holding the family together. Maybe it was out of guilt, maybe because it was his nature. It didn't matter. She knew she couldn't hold her family together if he was gone.

The dark thoughts in her mind were still breaking through. She kept talking, as much as for herself as for him. "We've lived a good life so far, don't you think? Until it all came crashing down. Is this our punishment for something? What have we done? Are we paying back some sort of bad karma?" She held his hand in hers, gently rocking him like an infant.

His fingers tightened around hers. He looked up at his wife, his desperate eyes straining to connect with hers. His eyes softened as his lips parted, and he took in a breath. Slowly, words began to form again.

"It's ... my ... fault."

"You don't say that. You hear me? I know it's been hard. I know I've been hard on you. Selfish. Angry. Angry at you. Angry at God. But things were just getting better. Tonight was supposed to be better. This is not your fault. Do you hear me? *This is not your fault*...It's mine. I lost myself. I disappeared and left this family with only a shell of a mother and wife."

He shook his head.

"I know things haven't been good," she continued, "but we don't deserve this, do we?"

He took another breath, taking in as much air as his struggling lungs would allow. "Maybe ... you were right ... Maybe ... God ... gave up ... on us." And with that, hope faded from his eyes and within his heart. Those were his last words spoken as he slumped unconsciously into her arms.

"NO! PETER!" Her heart shattered. What hope was there for her if her husband had lost faith? The rock of the family had crumbled.

The dead weight was too much for her to hold up. She strained to gently lay him onto the floor. Her whole body shrunk into a sobbing ball. She laid a hand on his chest, feeling his heart.

thump thump

As long as it was still beating, that was all that mattered. *thump thump* ... Another rush of emotions, images, and thoughts flooded her mind. She thought about the past two days. Seeing the dove ... *thump thump* ... Faith dressed in her adorable little Angel costume ... *thump thump* ... Her childhood joys and magic spells ... *thump thump* ... Her conversation with Angie, *Angels are very real, my dear. Faith is communing with her Guardian Angel. Your Angel* ... *thump thump* ... She even remembered her mysterious little visitors. *God bless you. We'll be watching over you and your family ... thump thump.*

If there was ever a time to truly believe, now was that moment. "Okay. Message received," acknowledged Wendi. A vision flashed in her mind of Angie handing her the piece of paper. She reached into her pocket, revealing Angie's prayer.

> Angel, I call upon you, my divine Guardian of Light.
> I call upon you now, to help me through this night.
> I open my heart and invite you into this space.
> Please bless me with your Grace.

She shook her head, allowing doubt to pull her out of the energy that was culminating inside her. "I feel like I just read an incantation," she blurted out, vocalizing her thoughts. "I'm stuck in the goddamn twilight zone. I'm sorry, Angie," she sighed. "This is *way* too hokey for me." Angie's voice echoed in her mind. *Feel free to change it to whatever your heart tells you to.*

"Okay, let's try something a little more my speed," she whispered as she closed her eyes. She took in a breath and raised a hand to her forehead, down to her heart, and across her chest, making the sign of the cross, and began. "If you're anywhere, God, if you hear my voice, if you have any compassion for our miserable suffering souls down here, we need a legion of Angels to fix this shit show ... but just one will do. If Faith really has an Angel—if *we* have an Angel—send me our Angel. Right now."

She shuddered as she felt a presence enter the room. She looked up, wiping the tears from her eyes, trying to adjust to the dim light. There in the doorway, wings spread, was the silhouette of an Angel. The figure shifted and split in two. Standing before her were her children. Faith, still in her costume, and Bobby behind her. She waved them over, not wanting to leave Pete's side. Their faces were riddled with worry. They slowly inched across the room, staring in shock, remaining at a slight distance. "Daddy will be okay," Wendi assured them. "He fainted, and an ambulance will be here any minute to take him to the hospital." With all her courage, she held back the tears fighting to seep out of her eyes. She had to be strong for her children. "Daddy will be okay," she repeated, reassuring herself.

As the words left her mouth, red and blue flashing lights pierced the window, flooding the room. Peter's chariot had arrived.

"Bobby, I don't want to leave your father. I need you to run down and open the door to let them in. Faith, stay here with us, Honey."

She nodded at the children. Bobby ran down and flung open the door just as the paramedics reached the front step. Wendi waited impatiently, listening for their feet hitting the stairs. It took all her strength to raise herself from the floor and leave her husband's side. She ran to the bedroom doorway, waving the paramedics down the hall.

As they approached, she attempted to explain the situation. "In here, hurry. My husband ... he passed out." Her voice wavered as she continued. "I think he ... he had a heart attack. His heart is still beating ... I don't ... I don't know if ..." She couldn't finish. The tears broke through as pain, sorrow, and fear poured down her face.

They nodded knowingly, also having been briefed by the dispatch. Entering the room, they quickly surveyed the scene.

"It's okay, ma'am. We'll take it from here. We'll do everything we can." They wasted no time, moving precisely and calmly in all their actions. They talked and worked at the same time, asking how long ago the pain started, when he went unconscious, and other simple, yet important questions. Wendi answered any she could. They attached the EKG, checked his pulse and pressure, lifted him to the gurney, and strapped an oxygen mask on.

Outside, a mob had gathered in front of their home. Flashing lights attract plenty of onlookers on a typical night, but Halloween was still in full swing. As Wendi emerged from the front doorway, Ken and Jen, her next-door neighbors, rushed to her side. "Wendi, what happened?" questioned Ken.

She couldn't speak. She knew she would burst into tears again if she tried to answer.

"What happened? Is he going to be okay?" Ken asked again with added concern.

She stared blankly, not knowing how to respond.

"Lord, please have mercy," Jen cried out, "We'll pray for him. We'll all pray for him, Dear."

As the paramedics lifted Pete into the vehicle, one of them turned to Wendi and asked, "Do you have someone to bring you to the hospital, ma'am?"

Somehow, the thought of having to get to the hospital hadn't entered Wendi's fractured mind. As she shook her head, she managed to stammer out a reply. "I … I guess I'll … I can drive myself," she answered hesitantly.

"Are you sure you're okay to drive, ma'am?" The paramedic questioned with a serious regard for her safety.

"We'll take her, if need be," interjected Ken.

The paramedic nodded. "Do you know where the hospital is?"

Wendi nodded, barely able to focus on anything but the thought of her husband surviving. "Please," she whispered. "Take care of him."

"We will, ma'am. We have to go. Just head for the emergency room entrance. And you drive safe, now." With that, the doors closed, the lights twirled, and the tires spun as the ambulance pulled away.

Wendi stood watching as Pete went off with fate to determine whether he would see his family again in this life or the next. She turned around, seeing her children in the front doorway. Bobby was watching the ambulance drive away, holding his little sister in his arms. Seeing how much her son cared and comforted his sister, a glimmer of happiness poked through Wendi's heart. But it quickly faded as she wondered how much more Bobby could handle if Pete didn't return. She looked around, seeing a myriad of concerned faces, then turned to Jen.

"The kids ... would you ..."

"Of course, we can watch them, Dear," Jen interrupted, finishing Wendi's sentence. "Anything you need, you ask, and I mean anything," she added.

Ken gently held Wendi's shoulders, looking her directly in the eyes. "I'll take you to the hospital and Jen will stay with the kids," he insisted. "It's not a problem. I'm concerned about you driving in this condition. We meant what we said. Anything you need; we're here for you. "

With all that had happened with the move, Wendi and Pete had been distant from the neighbors. They always made excuses to avoid barbecues, gatherings, and other social situations, where they'd be asked a lot of questions. They were afraid they wouldn't be able to hide their unhappiness. In that moment, however, Wendi no longer felt like a stranger. She knew that her children were in good hands. A warm feeling of comfort blanketed her as her mind slowed down.

"I think ... I need to just be there alone with Pete," she began.

"No problem. I can drop you off, and—"

She stopped Ken before he could finish. "No. I can drive ... really," she began, finding her voice as she looked at her loving neighbors. A small smile inched across her face. "I know you'd drive back and forth all night if you had to ... and it means the world to me. It does ... Right now, I just need to be alone," she affirmed, nodding and taking in a deep breath. "I'll be okay. You staying here with the kids is enough. Thank you. Come inside and I'll head out."

They both nodded and stepped into the house. A moment later, the garage door opened, and she jumped in the car. While her husband's life hung in the care of the paramedics, and perhaps God, she began her journey into the dark night of the soul.

Only fourteen minutes away, driving to the hospital was the longest ride of her life. As she sped along, she tried to think of anything else to calm her, but dark thoughts kept blanketing her mind. Her life felt like a series of tragedies, and she was bracing herself for another.

Hospitals reminded her of death, disease, and sorrow. After Bobby was born, they had tried for years to conceive and failed. Wendi had three miscarriages before Faith was born. It's why Bobby was so much older than Faith. The last of those miscarriages was the worst of them and landed her in the ER. She shook her head, trying to toss the vision out of her mind. She needed happier thoughts. She thought about her precious Faith. Not all of Wendi's ER visits had ended in tragedy.

Her mind wandered back to the night when it was her in the ambulance, with Pete following behind …

~ ~ ~

She was early. Two months early. The baby was coming, premature, and she knew something was wrong. The pain was unbearable. They hadn't even decided on a name yet.

Sweat rolled down his brow as Peter paced the waiting room for hours, not knowing the condition of his wife and second child. After all the miscarriages, if they lost this one, Wendi would never recover. He wasn't sure if their marriage would either. It hadn't been easy with all she'd been through.

The doors flung open, and the doctors emerged. "I have some good news, and some, well, we'll just say an update," the doctor began. Pete braced himself. "Your wife is okay. It was a little touch and go, but she made it through just fine. The baby is also alive, and she's in intensive care. I don't like to sugarcoat situations like this. We're hopeful the baby will survive. She may very well grow to be a normal, healthy girl, but right now, I can't give you any definitive answers. Your wife is still under the effects of the anesthesia. We'll let you know as soon as you're allowed to see her."

An hour later, he was sitting by his wife's side. The baby remained in the NICU while Wendi was recovering, so she couldn't see her baby girl until she could get up and walk.

The next morning, they were standing at the glass, peering in at their little miracle, still unsure if they'd be bringing a baby sister home to Bobby. She was small, too small, and still very fragile and weak. Uncontrollable tears streamed down Wendi's face. Pete gently placed an arm around her waist, drawing her close.

"Look at me," he said. "She's going to be okay."

"How do you know that?" she asked in a quiet, trembling voice, her tone filled with fear and doubt. "You don't know. What did the doctors say her chances are?"

"Don't worry about what the doctors say. You have a little girl. *We* have a little girl. She's right there," he insisted, pointing to her. "Faith. Just hold onto faith for her."

"Faith doesn't solve everything, Peter." Wendi insisted as she wiped away a tear. "You can't be sure she's coming home."

"She's our little Angel. She's here because God wants her to be here," he said with conviction. "We weren't even sure if you could have another child, remember? We tried and tried for years. The doctors basically told us it was hopeless. That we had little chance of conceiving another child. And then when we did, and they said she may not make it full term. And after all that doubt, here she is. A little early, maybe, but she's here. She's right *here*. This little miracle is God's gift to us. What did I tell you over and over?"

He paused, waiting for a response. "I know you remember? What did I tell you when you wanted to give up time and time again?"

She rolled her eyes. It was the same thing he always told her anytime she doubted they'd be parents to more than one child. "Have faith. God's timing is always better than ours," she recited.

"That's right. I don't believe for a second we made it this far to lose her now. This little soul *wanted* to be here. *God* wanted her to be here. She's special. I can feel it. She was brought to us by an Angel, and she's coming home," Pete professed. "Now, there's only one thing you need to do to make sure that happens…"

She wiped another tear away in awe of her husband's conviction. "And what's that?"

"Have faith. That's all it takes. You just need a little faith."

"Then we should give her a name."

"You said you didn't want to name her until we could hold her in our arms. Until we knew for sure she—"

"I know what I said," Wendi interrupted. "And you said to have faith. So if she's staying, she needs a name. I know we decided on three names to pick from, but standing here now, none of them will do," she insisted, turning to her husband. "She needs a new name."

"Faith," they said in unison.

Wendi nodded. "Her name is Faith."

Tears filled Peter's eyes. "It's perfect. Against the odds, by the grace of God, we have Faith."

~ ~ ~

Wendi grabbed the armrest and decided to have a seat again. Alternating between pacing, sitting, and standing, she didn't know what to do with herself. Every minute felt like an eternity. She stopped, looking at the clock. It only made her more anxious. She wasn't sure how much time had passed, but it seemed like hours.

She may have been physically present in the waiting room, but her thoughts were everywhere else. She didn't know if her husband would survive or if the children would have a father come tomorrow. Her only comfort was that no one had come out to tell her he *didn't* make it. No news was good news. As torturous as waiting was, it meant they were still working on him. It meant he was still alive.

Her mind strayed in a thousand different directions. *What if he doesn't make it? What if he does? What if he has to find a new job? What if he can't work anymore?* Wendi was growing tired of worrying. Tired of thinking. Tired of filling the void with every scenario she could imagine and worrying about how each one would affect the rest of their lives. She was so lost in her mind, she didn't hear the voice calling her.

"Mrs. Farfalla? Ma'am, are you Mrs. Farfalla?" The woman asked again.

Wendi looked up, gaining her bearings. Somehow, the doctor managed to walk right up without her even noticing. An overwhelming sense of horror overcame her as she peered into the doctor's eyes.

She gave an unsteady nod. Wiping away her last tear, she quickly rose to her feet. "Yes, I'm Mrs. Farfalla," she answered reluctantly.

"Mrs. Farfalla," the doctor continued. "I have some good news and some unfortunate news." Wendi took a deep breath as the doctor continued.

"Your husband, Peter, survived, and the heart attack was not as severe as we anticipated."

"Oh thank God," she gasped, collapsing back into her seat as the tears of relief rolled down from the corners of her eyes.

"That's the good news. The unfortunate news," the doctor paused, "is that he is currently in a coma, and we do not know how long it will last. This is not completely uncommon with severe heart attacks like the one your husband has just endured. Typically, it can last for days or even weeks. In some rarer cases, much longer. I'm sorry. He is in good hands, and my best advice is for you to head home and try to get some rest. It is unlikely he will wake up in the next few hours." she announced with a note of compassion in her voice.

Wendi's world collapsed. She had heard too many stories about heart attacks causing brain damage and comas lasting for years, or even permanently, leaving the family with the decision of when to terminate life support. The horrific visions came flooding back into her mind as the doctor rattled off the list of steps they had already taken.

"We did a catheterization … no need for a bypass … lucky to be alive … " Wendi's mind returned to the present conversation.

"It definitely took a lot out of him physically, and there was some damage done from the attack. Hopefully, he'll come out of it soon and make a full recovery."

"Can I see him?"

"Yes, of course. He's being admitted to the ICU, but currently, he's still in the ER. I'll show you to his room, but once they transfer him, I suggest you head home, get some rest, and come back in the morning."

Wendi followed the doctor down the hall and stopped at the open doorway to Pete's room. Despite the wires and beeping machines, he looked quite peaceful laying there with his eyes closed. As terrified as Wendi was, she was grateful to still have a husband. She softly entered the room, stepping to his bedside. She placed a hand over her husband's heart, and placed a warm, loving kiss on his forehead, whispering, "Stay with us. We need you. I need you."

"Faith is sound asleep, and Bobby is still awake, but in his room. I'll let him know you'll be home shortly," informed Jen. Wendi could always take comfort that no matter what was happening, Faith would still fall fast asleep as soon as her head hit the pillow. Bobby, on the other hand, was a different story, allowing his anxiety to keep him up at night. "I agree with the doctor. No sense in being up all night in an uncomfortable chair. Get in your own bed and try to get some rest."

"Thank you, Jen. I appreciate all you've done. I'll head back here in the morning once I get the kids off to school."

"You drive safe, now. You hear me? All of our prayers are with you. We'll see you soon."

"Thank you." As Wendi hung up the phone, the patient transporters came in to wheel Pete away. Wendi said goodbye to her husband and solemnly began her trek home in the dark.

Sitting in the car, she hadn't felt so alone since she had lost the baby. "Why are you doing this to us?" she called out into the silence. "I called your goddamn Angel, and you give me a coma?" Wendi sobbed as her hands tightened around the wheel. Fear, hate, and desperation flooded her consciousness.

"Angie, you're full of shit!" she shouted. The car jittered as she drifted out of the lines into the shoulder. She straightened the wheel and thought about her prayer in the bedroom. *If you have any compassion for our miserable suffering souls down here, we need a legion of Angels to fix this shit show.* Weary and delirious from her long night, a fit of laughter overtook her.

"Maybe not my best prayer," she called out, continuing to laugh. The light ahead turned yellow, catching her attention. Still wrestling with her thoughts, Angie's words sunk in as she coasted to a stop at the red light. *Until you invite them in with an open heart, Angels are limited in how much they can interfere.*

Wendi thought about the paper Angie gave her. *Okay, Angie, you win. Show me how to talk to an Angel.* She shifted, keeping her foot on the brake. She dug into her pocket, pulling out the now crumpled piece of paper. Unfolding it, she held it in front of her, just above the steering wheel. Taking a deep breath, she re-read the prayer, this time with power and conviction.

> Angel, I call upon you, my divine Guardian of Light.
> I call upon you now, to help me through this night.
> I open my heart and invite you into this space.
> Please bless me with your grace.

She closed her eyes, allowing the words to sink deep into her consciousness. She breathed out. As a warm feeling illuminated her heart, calm washed over her. A knowing filled her, a feeling that everything truly was all right.

The light turned green, catching her attention. Just as she looked up, a white bird perched atop the light pole flew off into the night. *It can't be.* As she slowly accelerated through the intersection, she tried to catch another glimpse of her mysterious winged friend, to no avail.

She continued her journey home, strangely at ease with the silence in her mind. Regardless, she felt an urge for some music. Reaching out, she turned on the radio. "I don't know about you, but I've had my fill of Halloween music for the night," announced the DJ. "Let's stray away from the demons and continue our double dose evening with something a little more heavenly. Here's 'How Do You Talk to an Angel,' by The Heights."

Her heart burst open with a feeling of hope. *I guess that's how you talk to an Angel. Thank you, Angie.* She drove along, and as the song faded out, the DJ's voice cut in again. "Our double dose continues with another song coming down from Heaven above." Calming music filled the car. Wendi didn't recognize it at first, but the soothing voice was unmistakable. It was Sarah McLachlan's "Angel."

It provided an eerily comforting soundtrack for the rest of her ride home, as the tears continued. She wondered if her prayers really had been answered. *Maybe Angie was right. Maybe Angels are real.*

~~~ O ~~~

"Really?" Faith asked her ethereal friend as the first rays of morning began to peer into her room. She loved waking up early and beginning her day as usual—morning chats with Nobody.

"Daddy is going ta be okay? Dat's good, because Mommy id very sad. I hope you're wight … Yes, I beweeve you … Dat's what I said, beweeve … be-leeve. Believe. Why do I haf ta keep sayin' words ova and ova? … Okay. I want me to be betta, too … And I wuv you, too."

The sound of a toilet flushing caught Faith's attention. She listened for footsteps in the hall, made sure it was all clear, then resumed her secret conversation. "Weally? ... It's a special day fa everyone? ... I wuv special days ... And we get to have beckfast at da skool? ... And it's a special day fa Bobby, too? ... Oh, wow. Can I help?" she whispered into the air. "Otay. We need a pwan. I like pwans ... p-lans. Plans ... You have one alweady? ... Oooh ... I wike dat pwan, oh, plan. Let's do dat. Bobby's gonna be so happy!" Faith giggled, quickly catching herself.

Outside the door, Wendi strained to hear the conversation, but Faith's whisper was too faint to understand. She shifted her weight, pressing her ear closer. The floor creaked, and she jumped back. Resuming her composure, she knocked, "Faith, are you up? I'm coming in," she announced.

Sitting at her little table, Faith was already dressed and ready for her day. "It's time to get ready for school, Angel," announced Wendi, not realizing how appropriate her term of endearment was for the company.

Wendi stepped over to the small table and knelt down. Her eyes were puffy and bloodshot, and her hair was pulled back in a bun. She had little sleep, and her face was still riddled with worry.

"We're leaving early today. I'm going to drop you and Bobby off at the cafeteria for breakfast at the school so I can get to the hospital as soon as visiting hours start. Is that okay?" Faith nodded and smiled, already knowing the plan.

crunch crunch crunch

Another spoonful of Cheerios hit Bobby's lips as he ate his breakfast. He and Faith sat alone in the corner of the cafeteria. Happily eating her breakfast, she bounced her head around as she crunched each bite, as if creating her own morning symphony.

Bobby, in contrast, welcomed her silence along with his own depression. Luckily, not many kids got to school this early. He wasn't in the mood to talk to anyone. Sitting swirling his spoon in his bowl of milk, he wondered how he could be expected to pay attention in school all day while his father was in a coma.

Without notice, Faith lifted her bowl and slid down to the other end of the bench, distancing herself from her brother. Bobby was used to Faith's oddities and thought nothing of it, as long as she stayed in sight.

He opened up his sketchbook and began to draw as a blinding ray of light hit his face. He flinched, trying to avoid the sunlight reflecting in his eyes. The sparkle moved with him, following him. He shifted repeatedly, trying to dodge whatever was reflecting the sun.

A girl was standing a few feet in front of him, laughing, as Bobby dodged and weaved. She tilted the smooth metallic object back and forth to catch the perfect angle of the sun radiating in from the window. She undoubtedly had his attention.

Bobby raised a hand, attempting to shield his eyes. He looked up to see Sara approaching. His stomach churned, still embarrassed about knocking her over and running away last night.

She stood in front of the table, holding something around her neck that was shining into his eyes. At the end of a silver chain hung a winged pendant. Still glistening in the sunlight, it was difficult for Bobby to see the details. "Is that a bird?" he asked.

"No, silly," she answered, taking a seat across from him. "There are other things that have wings. Look again," she said, lifting it up off her chest so he could get a better look.

Now that it wasn't reflecting the light, Bobby clearly saw the winged being. *An Angel wearing an Angel. Wow, I sound like an idiot.*

"I'm sorry about your dad," Sara expressed in a somber tone. "I hope he's okay. Are you okay?"

"I dunno," he replied awkwardly. "How did you know?"

"My dad told me before school. The neighbors called to tell him. They were all talking about it."

Bobby squirmed in his chair. *Just what I need, another reason for people to talk about us.* "I guess they don't have something better to talk about," he offered sarcastically.

"No. It's not like that. It was for the prayer chain," she clarified with a look of concern.

"The what?"

"They have a prayer chain. If anyone needs prayers, they all call each other to let everyone know who to pray for," answered Sara. "They're all praying for your dad to be okay."

"Oh, wow," he responded, as a spark of hope illuminated his dark thoughts. "Most of them don't even know us." Between Sara taking a liking to him and the thought of a whole community coming together to pray for his dad, something shifted inside him. For the first time since the move, Bobby felt a new possibility—maybe he belonged here.

"You don't have to know someone to pray for them," Sara affirmed as she gently caressed her pendant. "Do you believe in Angels?"

"I, uh, I dunno. My mom, well, uh, nothing."

"I do. I believe in Angels. My Mum Mum gave this to me," she said, holding up the pendant again. "She said I'm always watched over by my Angel. She said that, uh, well, she said an Angel saved me from drowning when I was little. My Mum Mum is psychic and talks to Angels all the time. Last night I couldn't sleep and had the radio on, and the song Angel by Sarah McLachlan came on, and I don't know why, but I thought of you. I prayed that you were okay. Mum Mum says I'm psychic, too. That probably sounds silly." Her eyes drifted off to the side, avoiding contact with Bobby's.

"No. That's cool. And I, uh well, my mom was praying to an Angel to save my dad."

"I pray to my Angel all the time," professed Sara. "We can pray for your dad now if you want?"

Seeing the bewildered look on Bobby's face, she reached her hand out toward his. He jerked it back, too nervous to touch her. "We don't pray anymore," he admitted, feeling slightly ashamed.

"It's okay," she assured him. "I'll say it. And we hold hands when we pray together," she insisted, swiftly grabbing his hand. She bowed her head and began. "Angel, send your love and healing to Bobby's dad, and may he recover quickly. Amen."

Bobby stared at Sara, waiting for her eyes to open. "That's it?" He asked, seeming a little confused.

"Yes, silly. Prayers don't have to be long to work. My dad says simple prayers are the most powerful. Right to the point," she added, flashing a bashful smile.

"Thank you," replied Bobby. A warm sensation filled his cheeks as he noticed they were still holding hands. He pulled away, contrary to his desire to keep holding hers. Reaching for his pencil, he nervously began scribbling back and forth in his sketch pad. "So, what else do you like? Other than Angels?" he asked, still staring down at his drawing.

She paused, thinking about the question. "I like acting. I'm in the 6th-grade Drama Club. I'm going to be in the school extravaganza next week."

"Extravaganza, huh? That sounds fun," Bobby replied, squeezing out an awkward smile.

"Yeah. It is. You should join," she suggested, brushing her hair behind her ear.

"No. I'm not good at acting. Or at much of anything, really."

"That's not true. I've seen your drawings. You're really good," she insisted, giving Bobby an encouraging look. "You don't have to act to be in the club. You can volunteer in lots of ways. Maybe you can help with the sets. I do both, actually. Act and help paint the sets. Mr. Wacher said we need more help making the sets. I think you would be great."

Bobby looked up at her. "Mr. Wacher runs the club?"

"Yeah. He's my favorite teacher. Don't you like him?"

"Well, yeah. I guess. When he's not yelling at me," Bobby replied, still nervously scribbling in his book. "I don't know. I'm not sure I'm good at drawing, either." He looked down at the abstract lines and rough shapes he was creating.

"Yes, you are," she rebutted. "I'll be there this afternoon."

"I can't today. My mom's picking me up from school to go see my dad."

"Of course. I hope he's okay. And I'll tell Mr. Wacher you'll join," she offered, flashing a delightful smile.

"Okay, I guess," he answered casually. Looking up again from his sketchbook into her waiting eyes, he awkwardly held back the excitement he was feeling. If he didn't know any better, she wasn't just inviting him to a school activity, she was asking him to join *with* her.

"Great! You'll like it. I promise. Oh, and about last night," she started, now feeling embarrassed herself. "About Seth. I'm sorry ... He's a jerk ... and, well, he's also my... uh—"

beeeeeep

Sara skittishly hopped up from her seat. "That's the bell. See you in class," she mumbled, scurrying off without finishing her previous statement.

Bobby sat there for a moment, bewildered and wondering what just happened. *Seth is her what? What could he be? Her boyfriend?* His face winced at the thought of it.

He felt a tug at his sleeve and looked down to see Faith waiting and ready to get to class. As he closed the cover of his sketchbook, he paused, looking at his finished doodle. His scribbles had formed two reflecting arches, resembling a pair of wings.

~ o ~

Chapter 6:

Learning
to Believe

*"Simply believe, and the gates of
Heaven themselves open before you."*

~ o ~

Wendi was in shock. She anxiously thanked the nurse, abruptly turned her back, and started running down the hall. She flung open the door to room 222 and paused, processing the scene.

Peter was awake and alert, gazing out the window at a new day. He felt a presence enter the room, assuming it was the nurse again. There, in the doorway, frozen in a moment of disbelief and immense gratitude, stood his wife. Her hands covered her mouth in astonishment at the sight of her husband sitting up in his bed, fully conscious.

It was a new dawn for them in every way. His face lit up with delight as she ran to the bedside and embraced him, trying not to get tangled in the myriad of wires and cords still attached to him. She gently cupped the side of his face and gazed deeply into his eyes. Life together was precious again. Wendi's hate, anger, and resentment melted away with her newfound gratitude for his life.

She held her arms around him, refusing to let go. "You're okay," she whispered into his ear. "I can't believe you're awake. No one told me."

"I guess I woke up from the presence of an Angel," he responded.

Wendi flinched, releasing her embrace. She stared deep into her husband's eyes. "What do you mean? You were actually visited by an Angel? I mean, I prayed, really prayed, and—"

"Hun," Peter tried to interject, but she kept rambling.

"the dove, and the trick-or-treaters, and Angie, and the songs on the radio, and—how—I—"

"Hun!" he called out, giving her a gentle shake. "Hun, I meant you. You're my Angel, get it? I guess you thought the heart attack killed my sense of humor? What in the world are you talking about? Angie? Songs?"

No. It's just—never mind. I'm just really glad you're here," she admitted.

"So am I," he laughed. "The weird thing is—I feel like I've been awake for hours, but I seriously just woke up. I opened my eyes to the sight of the rising sun, then you walked in."

She gazed deep into his eyes again, then softly kissed her husband on his lips, allowing their gaze to linger. A new energy flowed between them, reminiscent of the day they met. She stroked his hair for a few moments before breaking the tender moment with more words.

"You really had us worried," Wendi expressed as her eyes welled up with tears. " I thought I lost you. I couldn't imagine … I don't know what we would do without you."

"Shhh," he interrupted, "Let's not worry about anything like that, at least for today. Can we do that? We've all been through a lot. But we're still here. *I'm* still here. I guess God took one look at me and sent me back," he laughed.

"Stop that," Wendi exclaimed as she smacked his shoulder. "Or maybe you're here because the people down here needed you more than He does."

Peter's heart melted. He took a breath as he gently wiped the falling tears off her cheek. "I haven't helped either …" he paused.

"No, you haven't," Wendi agreed with a playful grin. "But I haven't either. I've been too hard on you for too long. I've been … I've been horrible," she blurted out as her lips quivered. "I probably even wished you were dead at some point." All the tears she had been hiding behind her bitterness came pouring out. "I'm so sorry," she professed, sniffling as the tears fell faster than she could wipe them.

"I'm so sorry for ever allowing such a thought inside my head. We won't make it without you. I won't make it. You hear me? We can't do this without you, Peter Farfalla, so you do whatever you have to do to stay with us." The tears kept pouring down. She grabbed a tissue and wiped her nose, catching her breath. "I can't handle any more crises. I just can't. What does God have against us, anyway?"

He raised his hand, cupping his wife's beautiful face, brushing away her tears with his thumb. "If I'm alive, maybe God is right here with us. Maybe He's always been here." Pete paused, staring lovingly into the depths of his wife's eyes.

"With everything we've been through, I know you feel like He left us," he continued as tears surrounded his eyes. "But maybe it's time to stop blaming God for bad things. Things go well and it's God bless this and God bless that, but as soon as something goes wrong," he paused, shaking his head, "it's suddenly God's fault. We don't have to blame God for everything that goes wrong in our life."

He hesitated, leaning closer to his wife. "It's easy to blame Him for taking away a child, but we have to remember He also allows life to happen, the good and the bad. For whatever reason, bad things happen, and it's up to us to keep faith through all of it. And some things may actually be our own doing, and what does that say about us if we just blame Him for our faults? Maybe we feel at our worst, not because God left us, but because we left Him."

"Wow," Wendi responded with a look of surprise. "One little heart attack, and suddenly my husband is a preacher? Don't get me wrong, I'm grateful you're here. I am," she attested, as her demeanor shifted. "But how is it my fault we lost our child? How is it my fault a suitcase landed on me and crushed ..." Terror filled her eyes as the vivid memory trampled her heart.

"I'm sorry, Pete, but it's not that simple. Why did we move in the first place? I guess it's your fault that you lost your job? I can go back to blaming you for moving us all the way down here, away from everyone we cared about. Is that what you want?" She leaned back, distancing herself from Pete's face. "Thank you, God, for saving my husband, and just screw us for the rest of it?"

"WENDI!" Pete shouted, forcing him to clench his chest.

"Sorry ... Jesus, I'm sorry. Please don't get worked up." She gently laid a hand on his shoulder and guided his body back down against the bed. "I'm ... I'm not ready for all this ... Let's talk about something else."

Pete wouldn't let up. "You really still believe he left us? You stopped going to church, you stopped praying, *you* stopped believing." He squirmed, feeling his chest tightening. "You're happy to damn God for not stopping every tragedy in the world? That's not what he created this experience for." He paused to catch his breath, searching his thoughts. "Look, I'm alive. Maybe this was His way of getting our attention. You just said you were praying your heart out as soon as you thought I was dying, and here I am."

"Well, God really needs to find a better way of getting our attention, unless pain and misery are his calling card," she huffed. "Sounds more like the devil's work."

Peter shook his head and looked toward the window at the morning sun. "Fine. Sure. Maybe you're right. What do I know." He sighed deeply. "Maybe God's not even there, and we made it all up to make ourselves feel better, to blame something bigger so we don't have to take responsibility for life. I mean, why not?" He rambled, completely shifting his thoughts.

"Wow. So now you're actually agreeing with me?" she questioned.

Pushing back with his hand, he straightened himself upright. "Look at what all the Greeks and Romans believed; they thought there was a God for everything—storms, earthquakes, war, love. And the ancient Mayans and Aztecs went around beheading people to sacrifice them to the Gods. And now we have the gall to look back and mock them for having such barbaric beliefs? Living in such a violent society, like we're so enlightened? Aren't we still sacrificing people in the name of God? Aren't we still killing in the name of religion? Just because we do it in the name of a single God rather than many, suddenly we're better and that somehow makes it okay?"

"Hun, seriously, just—"

"I am serious," he continued, ignoring her interruption. "Maybe it's all just bullshit. Maybe future civilizations will be looking back and laughing at us as well. Laughing at us for praying to a God that isn't there. Wouldn't that be something? Maybe the joke is on us, right here, right now. Maybe Angels are actually adolescent, inter-dimensional aliens just f-ing with us.

Or maybe, just maybe, there is no God and we're the only ones, and the only thing, controlling our lives. What then? What if we are the only ones to blame for all the shitty things that happen and for the screwed-up world we live in?" he stopped, clenching his chest again, as his heart pounded away inside.

"Jesus Christ, Pete, calm down," Wendi insisted. "Where the hell is this coming from? God is very real, and so is our Angel," she rebutted, suddenly defending everything she had renounced. "And how do I know? Because I prayed my ass off. I read the prayer Angie gave me, and I called on our Angel, and it saved you. Glory be, hallelujah, and all that jazz. It was an honest to God miracle," she carried on, not even sure where the words were coming from as they left out of her mouth. "I thought Angie was crazy, but I'll tell you this, Peter Farfalla: Whatever God is, whatever Angels are, I really don't care because they're real. If you want to believe our Angel is a goddamn flying alien, go ahead, because praying to it saved your life. That's the only thing I'm sure of this morning."

Pete opened his mouth to interject, but Wendi wasn't done. "It even sang to me on the way home last night. Well, not sang like sang, but through the radio—"

"Wait. What about songs—"

"It sent me songs to acknowledge my prayer was heard. And the white bird was there again."

"Bird? Wha—"

"And Angie thinks it's probably who Faith is talking to."

"Wait, wha—"

"And you believe what you want, but we have a Guardian Angel watching over us." She stopped, wondering how crazy she now sounded.

"HUN! I love you, but what the hell are you talking about?" he insisted, trying to catch his breath. His head was spinning, barely able to keep up with the laundry list his wife had just ran through. "I think we both just need to calm down. Where is this coming from? Did the whole world just go topsy-turvy?" he asked, half sincere, half-mocking. "Suddenly I'm the atheist and you're the faithful one talking about beings sending signs from God as songs?" He paused, just before his expression turned to a look of horror. "I know what's happening!" he announced, pushing himself forward, closer to Wendi. "I figured it out! I woke up in an alternate universe. Maybe my other body died and my consciousness took over this body." He lowered his voice and added, "Welcome to the Twilight Zone. Do-do do-do do-do do-do."

"Oh, my God. We've both lost it," Wendi replied, laughing. She took his hand in hers. "As you can imagine, I barely had any sleep, and apparently you were off visiting alternate dimensions in your coma," she chuckled again. "Jesus, what a pair we are."

"A pair of nuts, maybe. You brought me to the wrong kind of hospital," he joked, as they both let out another laugh. "I don't know what the hell I'm ranting about. Almost sounded like I knew what I was talking about, though, right?" Pete mockingly questioned. He was hoping for some acknowledgment but was left looking like a dog waiting for a treat.

Wendi shook her head. "Sure, Hun. Start writing it down for your groundbreaking novel," she replied, joining in on the fun. "Look, I took the day off," she said, inching closer and resting a hand on his. "I'm staying right here by your side until the kids get home, so go on and rant away. For all we know, you took a little trip to the other side while you were out." She gently caressed his hand. "Just remember to take a few breaths between sentences, will ya? Don't give them any reason to keep you longer than necessary. You're coming home with me, mister," she insisted. She flashed a tender smile, but her eyes gave way to how serious she was.

"Okay. Okay. Let's slow down. We have plenty of time to talk. And somewhere in there, I want to know why you keep mentioning this Angie woman at work. What's *that* about?"

Wendi wasn't sure how to explain it all, or how well it would be received. "Well, I think it's easiest to just say she's helping me find my faith. It's a bit of a long story."

"Well, you got somewhere to be? Pull up a chair and let's talk," he insisted, motioning to the chair in the corner. "Look. I almost don't want to say this, but it needs to be said. Losing our baby took your faith away. Now if it took me almost dying to bring it back, I guess that's what had to happen. Right now, I'm here. And you're here. So let's just talk."

"I'd like that," Wendi softly replied.

"It's been much too long. Remember when we used to just lay in bed for hours at night talking about all kinds of random things?" Pete recalled. "I miss that, Wendi. I miss a lot of things. And that's great if Angie is helping you reconnect with your faith. Allen has always been my voice of reason at work. He keeps me sane."

"Yeah. I know how much you love him. I guess she's my Allen. There you go."

"Well, then. That explains it all," he said with a smile.

It was a pleasant evening for the whole family as they gathered around the dinner table, all genuinely happy for the first time since the move. Bobby was actually interested in talking about school and mentioned wanting to join the Drama Club. There was no talk of fights or bullying, and he even admitted to liking a girl named Sara. They finished up their meal and watched some TV together as a family for the first time in weeks. After the kids were in their rooms, Wendi and Pete headed for the bedroom themselves.

In a strange way, Wendi was grateful for the heart attack. Sometimes it takes a strong jolt to knock someone out of their comfort zone, even if that comfort zone is in itself, uncomfortable. It was hard to fathom after the year they've had, but for the first time, Wendi was looking forward to sharing a bed with her husband in their new home. Having a spouse was a joy again, rather than a burden.

"Do you know how scared I was?" she reminded him as she was undressing. Her tone was filled with honest concern.

Pete sat down on the edge of the bed, took his pants off, and turned to meet his wife's teary gaze. "I know. I was scared, too. Our whole life flashed before my eyes, both past and future. I want to see our kids grow up. I want to retire from a job I love and can be proud of. I want to grow old, and sail off into the sunset with you." He leaned across the bed and whispered, "I don't want to leave this world unless you're by my side." A smile stretched across his lips. "And that will be after we've had a long, happy life together and watched our grandchildren grow and flourish."

Tears rolled down both of their smiling faces. He leaned in and kissed his beautiful wife. First, a few soft gentle kisses on the lips, then passionately, as if they were in love for the first time.

She freely allowed a few more tears to gracefully fall to the ground. Her lips fondly caressed his, then paused, looking lovingly into his eyes, and smiled. "That long, happy life begins again tonight. And you better believe you're on a new stress-free diet, mister, along with an actual diet. You'll be a vegan, if that's what it takes."

A look of horror crossed his face. "Vegan? Let's not get crazy. I mean, if we eat all the plants, what's left for the animals?" he quipped with a chuckle.

"Let's be clear. If you don't start eating healthy," she insisted, "and that means what *I approve* as healthy, then this body is going to be off the menu again."

"One serving of grass, coming right up!" he wholeheartedly agreed.

"I guess I found your motivation," she added as her longing eyes locked with his. They kissed again. Pete's hand slipped around her thigh, slowly moving up, caressing her hips, and sliding around her waist, pulling her close. She gently put her hand on top of his, intertwining their fingers together as she gripped his hand firmly. They kissed passionately as blood surged throughout their bodies. She gently eased away from his lips, allowing her fingers to slide free, grabbing his firm thighs. As he slowly caressed her curves, she overlapped his hand again. She guided it around her thigh, off her body, and onto his own. She pulled away and gave him a pat on the heart.

"Not so fast, Loverboy. You just got home and the doctor specifically said not to do *anything* to get yourself worked up for the next few days. Believe me, holding off is just as hard for me.

"Oh, I'm pretty sure it's harder for me. Here, I'll show you," he insisted, grabbing her hand.

"No need for proof," she answered, quickly moving her hand. "Seriously, Love. You just got home from a massive heart attack and have a wonderful list of things for you to do and not do, especially anything stressful or strenuous, and that includes intimacy," she reminded him with a soft nod.

"Okay, you're right," Pete agreed as he shifted his hand off of her hip.

"I am?"

"Yup. I have orders not to do anything *stressful*, so I'll just lay here, and let you do all the work. You know, to eliminate both physical and emotional stress for me," he suggested, rolling over onto his back and tucking his hand behind his head.

She playfully smacked his arm. "You just got home, and you need a good night's rest," she insisted as he rolled his eyes. "Besides," she added with a playful smirk, "you'll need to save your strength for when we *do* resume some stressful activities." She kissed him one last time and rolled over.

He was overjoyed to see such an amazing change in her. Wendi was radiant, passionate, and determined; all the qualities that attracted him to her which he had missed immensely. It almost killed him to bring about such a drastic change, but it worked. Pete wrapped his arms tightly around her, breathing a sigh of relief. He snuggled up, holding his wife close against his body. While a bit disappointed at the lack of physical affection, he was delighted to be able to cuddle with his wife again before drifting off to sleep.

Wendi also felt at peace. A true glimmer of hope and a rush of faith flooded her, and she felt, for the first time in over a year, that things may finally return to the way they were. She exhaled, and quietly thanked God and her Angel for keeping her husband alive as she eased her mind for a good night's sleep.

Something woke Wendi out of her dream. She rolled over and looked at the glowing 4:44 a.m. on the clock. She remembered how upset she had been the past few days waking up at that hour, being jolting her out of a nightmare. This dream was very different. She was flying, but not on a plane. She was soaring through the air, surrounded by butterflies, heading toward a brilliant light. In her dream, she was filled with an amazing sense of peace, and could still feel it.

Seeing the time filled her with an unexpected comfort. She smiled and closed her eyes, hoping to rejoin her peaceful dream. She quickly drifted back asleep.

tap tap tap

Pete nervously drummed his fingers against the kitchen table, shifting in his seat. "I think it would be best if I could tell Mr. Marshall myself," argued Peter, shifting the phone to his other ear. "Well yes, I certainly understand that he's tied up with meetings and asked you to hold all his calls, I just need a few minutes … Yes, but I think this is important enough to tell him myself … Very well, I'll just leave a voicemail, and I appreciate you passing on the message, too … Thank you." Pete waited for the beep at the end of The Marshal's greeting, took a breath, and mustered up all his strength to leave as calm and polite a message as he could.

"Hello, Mr. Marshall. This is Peter Farfalla. I was hoping to talk to you directly, but I understand you are tied up in meetings all day. As you already know, I suffered a heart attack on Halloween night. I was very fortunate not to need surgery, and I'm back home. I'm feeling much better, but the doctors were adamant about me staying home, not working, and relaxing my mind and body for a week. Please don't hesitate to call if you have any questions. Thank you, and have a good day, sir."

Sorry to bother you, prick. Pete slammed down the phone and looked at his wife. "Apparently, my wonderful boss is too busy to take my call."

"Peter Farfalla, mind your stress!" she responded, raising her voice. You're already getting yourself worked up, and that was just a voicemail. You didn't even talk to him."

"Maybe if I drop dead. That would be important enough to get his attention and interrupt his busy day."

"Peter! I don't want to hear you talking like that, not even joking, you hear me?"

"Yes, mistress," he replied, shooting her a mischievous grin.

"This is exactly why you're *not* at work. And no joking about being dead. Your word is your wish. Aren't you the one usually telling *me* that?"

He rolled his eyes, and responded with a sarcastic, "Yes, Dear. And speaking of work, did you already call out?"

"When I spoke to Terry yesterday, I filled her in. And the good part about that, if I want the whole office to know something, all I have to do is tell Terry," she said with a laugh.

"I told her you were all right, but that I'd be staying home another day to take care of you," Wendi continued. "So, that's what I'm doing today, taking care of you mind, body, and spirit. It's time to start some healthy living around here. And I want us all to go to church this Sunday," added Wendi. "We have a lot of gratitude to give."

"Church? I'm not supposed to do anything stressful this weekend. Remember? Doctor's orders," he joked. "Sit. Stand. Kneel. Hard, wood pews. Can't they at least pad the benches with all that money we've given them?"

"Excuse me, weren't you the one who got upset when we stopped going to church?"

"Yeah, well, what can I say? I got used to *not* going. But you're right about one thing," he added with a smile, reaching out his hand to hold hers. "I have a lot to be grateful for." They stared deeply into each other's eyes, enjoying the moment, and a house to themselves for the first time since they moved.

~ ~ ~ O ~ ~ ~

Wendi was bursting with excitement as she pulled up to the office. She didn't have Angie's personal number, and all weekend, the anticipation was building. She had never been so excited to get to work on a Monday morning. Angie was always early to work, so Wendi made it a point to come in early as well. She couldn't wait to tell Angie about everything that had happened.

Sitting alone at a table in the corner of the break room, Angie was enjoying her coffee in peace. Peering her head in, Wendi's eyes lit up at the sight of Angie. She rushed over to her table. A knowing twinkled in Angie's eyes as she flashed a comforting smile.

"Well, good morning to ya, Deary. So nice to see you shinin' and smilin'," welcomed Angie. "And so early in the mornin', too. Feels like everything's well, but you go on and tell me all about it, Angels and all," she requested with a nod.

Wendi choked up for a moment, amazed at Angie's knack for anticipating a conversation before it even occurred. Her anticipation quickly took over as Wendi burst out filling Angie in with every detail of Halloween night—her memories of magic spells and the story behind her own Angel outfit, the abracadabra coincidence, Bobby's fight, and Peter's heart attack. She even mentioned her shit show prayer, followed by earnestly reading Angie's prayer, the songs on the radio, and how amazing things had been since Pete had returned from the hospital.

"I so desperately wanted to call from home and tell you everything, but I just felt like I needed to tell you in person."

"Of course, Dear. I knew you'd be comin' 'round when the time was right. And I'm so glad you gave that prayer a second chance. After all, they wrote that just for you, Dear."

"You mean *you* wrote it just for me," corrected Wendi.

"My goodness, no," Angie giggled. She reached out and softly took Wendi's hand in hers. "My Dear, you needed help, and while I've been doin' this a long time and have plenty of my own wisdom, when it comes to someone genuinely needin' help, I call it in. I asked them to give me a divine prayer for your highest good, and that's what I wrote for ya. *Their* words, not mine."

The look of excitement on Wendi's face swiftly shifted to one of bewilderment as she listened to Angie speak. "They?" Wendi questioned, her eyebrows raising with curiosity.

"Angels. Guides. Spirit. The Universe. It's all the same, really. The divine creative consciousness takes many forms, and we give it many names. Sometimes 'they' is the simplest way to refer to 'em. But let's not get ahead of ourselves, Dear. You only cracked the door and peaked in. You haven't quite opened it just yet."

Wendi's palms began to sweat. She felt the urge to pull away, but curiosity won her over. "And how do I do that?" Wendi asked, somewhat reluctantly.

"There are a lot of ways, Dear, but I always start with the most basic. Simply believe, and the gates of Heaven themselves open before you."

"Just like that, huh?"

"Yes, Deary, just like that," Angie affirmed. "Of course, it sure does help if ya do it with all your heart, mind, and soul. But you already learned that lesson in the car. Prayers always work best when they come from our hearts, not our minds. And you saw how quickly you were answered, confirmed right through the radio," she chuckled. "I love it when they do that."

"Yes, it was amazing, Angie," Wendi responded delightfully. The words subconsciously flew out of her mouth, recalling the feeling she had in the car. "But what if it was just a weird coincidence?" she questioned, as her mind began churning up doubt. "I mean, coincidences *do* happen. All the time. As amazing as this all is, I also feel schizophrenic. One moment I have the gall to believe I'm summoning Angels by my side, and the next, I think I belong in the nuthouse. What if Peter is just very lucky?"

"And that's why we have lesson number one, Dear: Believe. Even the smallest thing happens for a reason. Every aspect of life is created and synchronized by our energy comminglin' with the energy of the Universe. But in times you still have doubt, not to worry, Deary, your Angel will keep sending you signs until you receive the message loud and clear. Didn't you say you heard two Angel songs playin' in a row?"

"Well, yes, but that's because it was some special double song thing. They were playing a series of two related songs back-to-back. It's not uncommon," Wendi argued.

"Maybe it's just a funny coincidence, is all," Angie laughed. "So when was the last time you turned on the radio and heard one of these double song thing-a-ma-bobs?"

"Well, just, ah, well, I'm not sure," Wendi stammered, "but I've definitely heard them before."

"Okay, Dear. And when was the last time you heard two Angel songs in a row?" Angie asked.

"Well, ah, well, I'm not sure I *ever* heard two Angel songs in a row, but I haven't always paid attention. Maybe they—"

"Maybe," Angie interrupted, "but for whatever reason, even if it *did* happen before, Dear, your awareness had no need to pick up on it. Halloween night, however, you were *very* aware of what was on the radio. And when was the last time you heard even one of those two songs played by themselves?"

"Those songs play all the time, Angie. They're very popular," Wendi affirmed, trying hard to convince herself.

"All the time you say, Deary? When did *you* last hear them?" asked Angie.

"I think I heard the one recently," Wendi began, "and the other, well ... I guess it has been quite a while, now that I think about it," she confessed.

"And that's how it works, Dear. The mind is a powerful deterrent, constantly causing us to doubt ourselves and our experiences. That is why belief is so important. In fact, it's lesson number one."

"How many lessons are there?" Wendi asked, curious and a bit hesitant to know the answer.

Angie let out her signature chuckle. "Just three, Dear. I sure can talk a lot, but universal truths are always simple," she admitted.

Angie held up a finger. "First, *believe*. Believe you are not alone. Believe you have help. And most importantly, believe you are worthy."

She raised a second finger, continuing, "Then *ask*. Ask for whatever you want, Dear. From saving a life to finding your car keys, simply ask. But if you don't believe first, askin' won't do ya a bit of good."

She held up a third and final finger. "And number three, *trust*. Trust that your prayer is answered. Trust in God. Trust in the Universe. Trust in your Angel. And don't allow your mind to cast a shadow over your belief." Angie said with full conviction. Wendi listened intently, hypnotized by the power of such simple, pure truth. Angie's knowledge and insight seemed to have no bounds.

"And trust their timing, not yours," she added. "Sometimes it's instant, and sometimes it's hours, or days, or longer. Your life is not just your own. It affects those you love and countless other lives you touch. Sometimes impatience causes more harm than not asking at all. And if you can do those three things," she continued, "the final lesson isn't a lesson at all. *Receive*. Receive the thing you asked for. Receive the blessing. Receive the miracle."

Wendi wanted to interject, to question, to ask, but bit her tongue. Something inside her was stronger than her doubts, and Angie could sense it.

"I want ya to do me a quick favor, Deary. Close your eyes for a moment," she requested. Wendi obliged, and Angie continued. "Imagine that moment in the car heading home from the hospital. What you were doin' and what you were feelin' that made you want to start prayin' again?"

Under her eyelids, Wendi's eyes fluttered, moving back and forth, as she searched and recalled her memory. Her brow cringed with worry and concern, as anxiety overtook her.

"Now, what did you *feel* after you prayed? And when you immediately heard the songs after, how did *that* make you feel?" Angie asked as she gently guided Wendi through re-living her experience.

Wendi's entire energy shifted as she recalled the Angel songs playing on the radio. Her anxiety dissolved as the same feelings of lightness and bliss she felt that night filled her, here and now. Not a word was needed as Angie sat calmly, allowing Wendi the space to fully re-experience the feelings of that magical moment. *How does it feel just as strong now as it did the other night?* Wendi slowly opened her eyes, breathing in the peace that was surging throughout her body.

"And *that* is what it means to trust your feelings, Deary," Angie affirmed. "Trust that Angels are real. Trust that the signs are real. Trust your feelings over your thoughts. When an Angel sends a sign, you receive it with your heart, not your mind."

"That was amazing, Angie. Thank you."

"It's part of the blessing. You're now attuned to the frequency of bliss. You can recall this feeling and memory anytime you need to."

"I think you're going to fry my brain, Angie. Every time I think you've pushed me beyond my limits, it's only the tip of the iceberg. I was struggling to believe my daughter was talking to a spirit just a few days ago, and now you have me talking to an Angel," Wendi responded in disbelief. "And you're telling me this is just a crack? I can't imagine what an open doorway looks like."

"Well, that's just the thing, Deary. Imagine it, first. See it in your mind, and feel it in your heart, and you'll manifest it into your life. From what I've gathered, ever since you moved here, since the accident, you've given up askin' for help. You've given up your Faith. And if you don't *ask* for help, Dear, it won't be given."

Angie paused and glanced to the side, as if someone were calling her name, then returned her gaze to meet Wendi's. "But let's take one thing at a time so we don't overwhelm you, Deary. We'll chat more about all this at lunchtime," she said, flashing Wendi a gentle smile and rising to her feet. "It's nine o'clock and time to get workin'."

Wendi abruptly popped to her feet, oblivious to how long they had been talking. As she was following Angie out of the break room, she looked up at the clock above the break room door. *How did she know what time it was? She didn't even look at the clock.*

Returning to her cubical, Wendi took a seat at her desk, ready to begin her work day.

On the other side of the wall, Patty was ready to begin her Monday morning gossip. She looked at the time, grabbed the phone, and dialed extension thirteen. Terry picked up, and in a not-so-low whisper, Patty began, "It's me … Yeah, she just got back. Who knows how long they've been at it, and God knows what they were chattin' about … *Right?* Can you *believe* the first person she runs to after all that happened is *her?* … I *know!* Now I'm serious when I say we may have to have one of those interconventions …"

~ ~ ~ O ~ ~ ~

ringggggggg

The kids flooded the playground as recess began. Faith plopped herself on the edge of the blacktop, sitting with her legs crossed. She looked to her right, smiled, and whispered, "Weally? Anodder special sur-pize fa Bobby? … And fa Sara?" She stared into the silence. "What is it," she quietly asked. "It's a sur-pize fa me, too?" She asked in quiet exuberance. She nodded, took out her bouncy ball, and waited.

Bobby didn't have many friends, and he was happy keeping it that way. He was content spending time watching over his sister. It gave him purpose, along with some peace. He stepped out onto the pavement, surveying the playground. There were only a handful of spots Faith liked to be. If she wasn't on the swings, she was typically sitting on the edge of the blacktop, near the four square.

"Hi, Faith," he said, greeting his sister as he walked over. "Having fun?" he asked, as he watched her bounce the small yellow-green ball.

She nodded and smiled.

"Do you want me to spend recess with you?

She looked off to the side and paused. Turning back to her brother, she nodded again, answering his question.

Bobby sat down and folded his legs, facing his precious little sister. She had a rubber ball in her hand she had been rolling around. She began to bounce it gently, attempting to catch it each time in her little hand. Bobby sat there watching, enthralled by the simple peace and joy his sister had. He admired that part of her and often wondered what her secret was. He wished he could be the same way, living without a constant feeling of worry and rage. In the moments he spent with her, his volcano became dormant, and he was able to share in her peace.

He would often talk to Faith when they were alone together. Even though she never responded, he knew she listened. It was his way of venting about life, school, and constant fights between their parents. She created the space for his own private psychotherapy session, but without a doctor trying to analyze everything he said. Other times, he would just sit and watch her in silence. In a way, it would ease his soul.

He sat watching as Faith bounced and caught her little rubber sphere. In-between bounces, she would look to her right, as if looking at something. Then she'd stare into the group of kids ahead, scanning them from side to side, as if she were looking for something or someone. She would occasionally look at Bobby with her warm smile and bounce the ball to him. He caught it and bounced it back. She continued looking past him, occasionally pausing and turning again to whatever was to her right. She looked ahead again, and as she began to bounce the ball back over to Bobby, she raised her hand up a bit higher than usual, and brought it down with extra force, bouncing the ball over Bobby's head, off toward the crown of kids behind him.

"Faith! What'd ya go and do that for!" He scrambled to his feet, racing after the ball before it was lost in the sea of recess madness. She shrugged her shoulders, looked to the side, and whispered, "Why did I do dat?" She paused, staring silently, then smiled.

Bobby reappeared in front of Faith, slightly out of breath, much quicker than she anticipated. He sat back down and asked again, "What was that about? You almost lost the ball."

She simply stared back and began bouncing the ball to her brother again. She caught it, refusing to bounce it back as she watched someone approaching behind him. Standing behind Bobby, facing Faith, the figure raised a hand. She extended a finger upward and placed it in front of her lips—an unnecessary, but playful, gesture to a girl who can't speak. Bobby saw the change of expression on Faith's face, but before he could turn around, a pair of hands covered his eyes.

"Guess who?" came a soft, gentle voice.

Bobby tensed up, too nervous to respond.

"If you can't at least guess, I'll just stand here and you'll have to be blind all day," joked the shadowy figure.

Bobby knew her voice by heart. He didn't need his eyes to know who it was. "Hi Sara," he answered, hoping she didn't sense the nervousness in his voice.

"How did you know it was me?" she asked, gently removing her hands.

"Lucky guess, I guess," Bobby shrugged, still staring at Faith, hoping Sara couldn't see him blushing from from where she stood behind him.

She smiled at Faith and took a seat next to Bobby. "I saw you go running after her bouncy ball. I think it's really sweet that you keep her company. The other boys I know don't want anything to do with their little sisters" She turned toward Faith. "I'm Sara," she said, extending out her hand for a proper introduction.

Faith simply smiled back and returned the honor of a handshake, minus the proper verbal introduction.

"This is my sister, Faith. Don't worry, it's not you. She doesn't talk to anyone. Not even me."

"I heard. What happened?" Sara questioned, mixing her true concern with polite curiosity.

An awkwardness fell across Bobby's face. He was never really sure how to explain it, especially without creating more questions he didn't want to answer. "She, well, she's been like this for a while. There was ... a ... well ..."

Bobby was saved from the unpleasantness of having to finish his answer. He was distracted by Faith, who quickly turned to her right, then looked up toward the sky. She pursued it, turned back to the side, then back up into the sky.

Bobby and Sara both followed Faith's eyes as she looked up in the sky and back again. Sara, puzzled by this, kept her eyes on the sky while leaning into Bobby and whispered, "What's she doing? What's she looking at?"

Bobby only saw an overcast sky. He had no idea what Faith was looking for in the sky, but he was used to her gaze drifting off quite often. Before he could figure out an answer, Faith jumped to her feet and stepped between them. She bent down, grabbed each of their hands, and eagerly tried pulling them to their feet.

"Oh, okay. Where are we going?" Sara asked, directing the question at Faith, but looking at Bobby for an answer.

"She's in her own world. Just to go with it," Bobby replied, as the two of them stood up, still holding onto Faith's hands. Faith lead them forward, staring up into the cloudy sky as they walked. She stopped, still looking up, scanning the sky ahead. Bobby and Sara stood there, staring up as well, bewildered and wondering if she saw something they didn't. Faith looked around, a little confused, then suddenly spun, swinging them around with her. There she remained, transfixed on a large mass of clouds with a faint glow.

"Faith," Bobby asked, "What are we looking at? It's just dark clouds. And it's going to rain. Mom said so." As he finished his words, a cool breeze raced across his body. Still holding onto each of their hands, Faith looked up at her brother. She shook her head and returned her gaze to the sky. The dark mass of clouds began shifting and thinning, revealing a dim light behind them. The clouds slowly parted as a single ray of light pierced through. Drifting further, the center void expanded, revealing a brilliant sun. A shower of golden rays poured through, causing Bobby to flinch.

He looked down at Faith. "Great, Faith. Now I'm blind. What's so important about a hole in the clouds?" he asked, waiting for the spots in his eyes to dissipate. He looked over at Sara, and feeling slightly embarrassed, he began to apologize. "Sorry, she's—"

"Bobby," Sara interrupted, still transfixed on the shifting sky, "Look."

"Look at what, the blinding sun?" he responded, still transfixed on her face.

She turned, meeting his eyes. "Bobby, look again," she insisted, pointing up.

Bobby obliged, turning his gaze to the sky again. As embarrassment and wonder overtook his expression, he suddenly understood. "Oh! Faith, did you ... How? ... Wow."

Above the three of them, the pillowy blanket of dark clouds had parted, leaving a void in the shape of a perfect heart—a glowing, radiating, unmistakable heart. Faith slowly brought their hands together, putting Sara's hand onto Bobby's, and let go. Her mission was accomplished. She quietly snuck back to her corner and began bouncing her ball again.

Bobby, flustered at the touch of Sara's hand, quickly pulled it away, apologizing. "Oh, huh, sorry. She—"

"It's okay," Sara interrupted, as she shyly brushed her hair behind her ear. She looked sideways at Bobby, somewhat smitten, and quickly looked up again. "It's beautiful," she said, as she allowed her fingers to graze against Bobby's. He took a breath and gently clasped his hand around hers. They stood watching as their radiating heart matched the sight above their heads. The clouds continued to drift apart until all that was left was the radiating sun.

"I saw a heart cloud once, but never anything like that. How … how did she know? Like she made it for … uh … us."

A wide grin filled Bobby's face. "Yeah, that was really cool. She's … She's special." he said, glancing at his sister. *She really is.*

Sara looked at Bobby. "I like special," she replied, her beaming smile radiating as bright as the sun.

Bobby was glowing too, barely able to contain his awkward pre-teen emotions, but something deep down was keeping him from fully enjoying the moment. Bobby looked down, then up at the sky again, then finally gathered enough courage to look Sara in the eye.

"Hey … uh … the other morning, in the cafeteria. You said you and … uh…"

She gave his hand a gentle and unexpected, yet welcome, squeeze. "It's okay. Seth is my cousin."

"Oh," replied Bobby with a huff of relief and a floundering laugh. "Your cousin. Yeah, I knew that," he said, puffing his chest out a bit.

"No you didn't, liar," she playfully called him out. "I don't like anyone to know because he's … because he's such a jerk to everyone," she admitted, scrunching her face in disgust.

Then why did you tell me?" he bashfully asked.

"Because you're not just anyone," she softly replied, trying to hide her blushing face. They stood for a moment, still hand in hand, awkwardly attempting to enjoy a tender moment. Swiftly becoming too much for Bobby, he broke the silence.

"This sounds weird, but, uh, do you want to play with me and my little sister?"

"I'd love to," she said, gleefully accepting his offer.

They sat down next to each other, facing Faith, still hand in hand. The sun was still shining brightly overhead. For the first time since he could recall, he had no thoughts of Seth, his parents fighting, or any of the happenings from the past year. For once, Bobby felt true peace.

~ o ~

Chapter 7:

Opening
the Doorway

*"We are God's children,
and they are our guardians.
They help us because they love us."*

~ o ~

Wendi was impatiently staring at the clock, counting down the minutes until her lunch break. Every conversation with Angie had her more intrigued, diminishing her concerns about Patty and the office gossip girls. Regardless, part of Wendi was still questioning her own sanity. A few days ago, she couldn't handle or process half of what was coming out of Angie's mouth. Now she was looking forward to every mysterious teaching Angie had up her sleeve. As the clock struck 12:30, Wendi flew out of her cubical like a prize racehorse.

She rounded the corner, bursting with anticipation. "Hey Angie, ready for lunch? I'm looking forw—"

"I sure am, Deary. But how's that precious husband of yours doin'? Feelin' better, I hope." Angie interrupted, always showing genuine concern for personal matters above all.

"Oh, yes," Wendi responded, now questioning her lack of concern. "He's doing great. Happier than a pig in shit, to be honest," she laughed.

"Well, that certainly answers that question," Angie replied, joining Wendi's laughter.

"Seriously, though," clarified Wendi. "He's loving every minute of having the house all to himself with an official medical excuse to not do a drop of work. I offered to stay home with him for a couple more days, but he didn't want me to use up my time off. He said we were long overdue for a family vacation. I agreed. Sorry. I should have mentioned Pete first," added Wendi, feeling a bit self-conscious. "I guess I was a little too excited to continue our conversation."

"No need for apologies, Deary. I'm glad he's happy at home. One less thing to weigh on your mind. Now let's get to it, shall we?"

They meandered down the hall to the break room to grab their lunches. Wendi had a peanut butter and raisin sandwich, a bag of Doritos, and a can of soda. Angie opened the fridge, revealing an amazing homemade salad. It was a blend of kale and spinach topped with shredded carrots, cabbage, and a blend of healthy seeds. Along with it was a homemade orange ginger vinaigrette. She filled up her water bottle, topping it off with a lemon slice, and they sat at the corner table.

"Let's start with callin' in your Angel every day and acknowledgin' the answer," Angie began. "How's that sound?"

"Is that necessary?" Wendi questioned with a look of surprise. "We've had enough tragedies and ER visits to last a lifetime. I hope we never have to call on an Angel again," she nervously chuckled. "And you want me to call my Angel *every day*? For what?"

"For anything, Deary," Angie answered without hesitation. "Angels offer us their help unconditionally, and they always answer a callin' to be by our side. That includes simply sendin' us signs to show us that they're here," Angie stated matter-of-factly. "So I'd like to start with you callin' on your Angel, asking for, and acknowledgin' their signs. It will help build your trust and belief in your Heavenly Guardian."

Wendi slowly leaned back in her seat. "I'm supposed to just ask that my Angel proves itself to me? I don't know, Angie. It just —"

"It's just like a toddler wantin' to live his life freely," she asserted. "But needin' to know his mom is in sight. And mom will reassure her child anyway she needs to." Angie took a bite of her salad. "They see us as children. And in many ways, we are."

"Angie, these are the most revered beings in Heaven. I can't just call on them for something trivial."

"You sure can," she answered, as a perfect smile zipped across her face. "Angels take pleasure in helpin' us with *anything*, Dear. They don't discriminate a task based on its size or our preconceived worth." She paused, taking a sip of her water. "The little things in life affect us so much more than we realize. It's amazin' how the smallest tasks can trigger such immense stress in people. Like findin' a parking space at the mall at Christmas, dealin' with traffic, or just findin' something misplaced."

Wendi sat there, shaking her head. "I still don't believe it. You have them reserving parking spaces for you, and you want me to ask my Angel to find misplaced objects?" she asked, still struggling. "These are the messengers of God. They came down to announce the birth of Jesus, for Christ's sake. They'll announce the Apocalypse. Things of that magnitude. They obviously have more important things to do. We're talking about *Angels*, Angie, not dogs playing fetch. You can't be serious."

"I tell it like I know it, Deary," Angie replied. Regardless of her big smile, or how often she chuckled, there was something about Angie that made it seem like she was spouting out divine truths of the cosmos. No matter how farfetched something seemed or how impossible it sounded, one thing was for sure: if Angie was talking about it, she fully believed in it. And it was her unwavering belief that made Wendi question everything.

Angie took another bite and chattered along. "They want to help us with anything we feel we can't do on our own. That's truly what stress is—feelin' powerless because we believe we can't change what is. And honestly, sometimes we shouldn't. Some things are meant to be, even what we consider bad things." Angie paused, allowing Wendi a moment to take it all in. "Even when it's life and death, they want you to understand that your soul's highest plan takes precedence. It's important you remember that, Deary."

Wendi was riddled with disbelief, yet her heart was in awe. "Angie, please slow down," she begged. "You've got my head spinning!"

"So sorry, Dear. Bless my ramblin' heart. I just keep goin', don't I?" She laughed. No one enjoyed Angie's rants more than she herself did. "And don't worry 'bout processing it all, Deary. Just allow your ears to hear it and your heart to receive it. And speaking of findin' and fetchin' things," added Angie. "Just the other day, I asked them to help me find my car keys." She took another bite of her salad, allowing Wendi a chance to respond.

"You must be joking," Wendi uttered, staring in disbelief. *An Angel helped her find her car keys?*

"Honest as Abe," Angie continued, as if she heard Wendi's thought. "Strangest thing. No idea why it happened, but it's never my place to question such things. I just ask for help and let go of the outcome. Why does that surprise you, Dear?"

"I lost my car key the day we met. That's how I scraped my hand." Wendi blurted out in amazement. "This is too crazy of a coincidence. Although my situation turned out a bit different," she giggled, "because the *cat* was the one to find it. Not an Angel."

"Well, how 'bout that? I must've lost my keys just to share the experience with ya. And here we are talkin' 'bout asking our Angels to help us with the little things. So, no, Dear. It's *not* a coincidence," she interjected. "It's a *synchronicity*. And just so ya know, animals can see, hear, and sense much more than your average human does. So, it's easier for Angels to nudge animals than humans. People can just be so stubborn and ignorant, and I'm not sayin' it that way to be rude." Angie continued to enjoy her salad while Wendi slowly nibbled at her chips, too enthralled to even take a bite of her sandwich.

"I'm guessin' you scratched your hand *before* you asked for help findin' your key," Angie affirmed. "Most people get their britches in stitches, practically givin' themselves a heart attack, instead of calming their minds and askin' for help."

"But that's just it, Angie. I didn't ask for help," Wendi insisted, looking down at the scratch on her hand, now almost fully healed. "I think the cat was just lucky."

Angie chuckled again. "Life is so much more miraculous than luck and coincidences, Deary," she affirmed as she took another forkful of greens. Her eyes wandered off to the side for a moment, then reconnected with Wendi's. "You asked your husband to help find the key. And he called on a different kind of help …"

Without questioning Angie's knowing, Wendi was thrown back into the memory of that hectic morning. She hadn't yet fully realized it, but that day, everything changed. It felt so long ago, even though it had only been a week. Sitting there with Angie, she felt like a completely different person. She was amazed at the amount of anger she had held on to and how ridiculous the argument with Pete that morning now sounded. She was cursing and screaming at him like a deranged maniac. He was complaining about her language. She was angry at his bad jokes. *Let's call in an angelic locksmith. Hello? Car key Angels, we can use some help down here.* She shook her head, laughing to herself. *How the hell did Angie know—*

"Now you're gettin' it, Deary," Angie interjected as she patiently watched the revelation clicking in Wendi's mind. "What's your cat's name again, Dear?"

"Misty. Wh—"

"And would you save Misty's life if you could?" Angie asked, cutting Wendi short.

"Without a doubt," Wendi responded without hesitation, wondering where these questions were going. "Why—"

"And if you found Misty needin' help," interrupted Angie again, "stuck or hurt, would you watch her struggle, or would you help her?"

"I would help immediately, of course. Who wouldn't? I would do anything without question for—" This time Wendi interrupted herself as a light went off.

"Exactly, Dear," Angie affirmed. "And she's a cat. A completely different species. You can't even communicate directly with her, and yet you would still do anything for her. And if your kids, at any age, lost somethin' as important as a car key, wouldn't you drop everything to help them find it?"

A smile stretched across Wendi's face as she fully appreciated the correlation. "Of course," she nodded. "I would do anything for my cat, my husband, and especially for my children."

Memories flashed through her head of the myriad times she helped her children in infinite ways. As babies and toddlers, she saw how much attention and care she gave them and how her deep love was in every moment they needed her. Even now, with all the pain in her life, no matter what they needed, she was there for them, without question. Her thoughts jumped ahead. She imagined them as teenagers, learning to drive and misplacing their car keys, and struggling with the challenges of life. She jumped ahead even further, helping them through their own struggles with marriage, and being there for her grandkids. Tears welled up in her eyes. She couldn't imagine *not* doing anything for her children, no matter how small or menial.

Angie wasn't just a well of unexpected wisdom; she was a jackhammer of truth. Each point chipped away at the stigmas and preconceived notions Wendi had until all the hard edges were removed.

"You would do anything for them because you love them," Angie affirmed. "That's what we are to Angels. We are God's children, and they are our guardians. They help us because they love us."

As tears ran down Wendi's cheeks, she nodded in recognition. Angie's words continued to illuminate Wendi. Like a piece of ice in the sun, moment by moment, Wendi's heart was melting.

"And they do so much more," Angie continued. "Angels are amazin' healers. And not just physical healin', but emotionally as well. They can help calm our minds and bring us peace. Whenever I feel a bit lost or unsure of how to handle a situation, they're the first ones I call for guidance," she admitted.

"I can't imagine you needing help from anyone or anything. You seem to always have the answer."

"Well, where do you think the answers come from, Deary?" chuckled Angie, as if tickled by her own words. "No matter how much I think I know, I just don't have all the answers. It's a grand cosmos out there, and there's always somethin' new to learn, even for me. And I'll tell ya this," she added. "The secret to the Universe isn't really a secret, Deary. It's love." She paused, staring into Wendi's eyes.

"Now, let's get back to where we started, shall we?" she chuckled. "Even what you might consider a mundane task is an opportunity to welcome your Angel into your life. They are humble beings and receive immense joy in assisting us in any way they can. They even make a little game out of getting our attention and sending us signs." Angie paused to take the last bite of her salad.

"So this is your homework, Dear. When you get in your car to head home, ask your Angel for a sign—a remarkable, unforgettable sign. And be *aware*," she continued, "but don't go tryin' too hard to find the signs, mind you. They'll find you."

"They'll find me?" Wendi repeated.

"Sure as sugar, Deary." Angie assured, pushing together the remaining bits of her salad.

"But what if I just think something's a sign, and it's not?" Wendi questioned. "Or maybe it's a sign for someone else? Or—"

"You're already overthinkin' it, Deary. Signs come in many ways. Don't you worry about how or when. Your job isn't to constantly look for them. No, no. Your job is to *not* dismiss them when they come." She took the last bite of her lunch and rested her fork on the table. "If a sign is meant for you, Dear, it'll get your attention all right. Sometimes people are so stubborn about gettin' the message that their Angels have to take human form. That's when you really know they mean business," Angie chuckled.

Wendi sat there, wide-eyed, as another piece of the puzzle fell into place. *I forgot to tell her about the Angel children on Halloween. I can't believe it. I just can't believe it.* "I can't believe it," Wendi blurted out as her thoughts became too loud to contain.

"Well, Deary, they'll just have to do somethin' about *that*," Angie chuckled again.

<p align="center">~~~ O ~~~</p>

Bobby stood at the side door of the auditorium, second-guessing his decision to join the Drama Club. He didn't care about after-school activities and didn't want to make friends. It was simply a reason to spend more time with Sara. *I hope this is worth it.* He reached for the door and paused, sighing. *I really don't care enough about Drama Club to be here.*

He turned his back and paused again, battling his urge to leave with the prospect of spending time with Sara. He heard the doorknob turn and looked back. The door swung open.

"Hi, Bobby," came the shy and hopeful voice of Sara. "I'm glad you're here."

"Oh, hi, Sara. Where are you going?"

"I was hoping you'd come today," she said, fiddling with a dry paintbrush in her hand. "I had a feeling you were here, so I was looking for you … and here you are," she confirmed, giving him a hopeful smile. "Come on," she insisted. "Let's tell Mr. Wacher you're here."

Before Bobby could change his mind again, Sara had already grabbed his hand and was leading him through the door. Bobby trailed along, questioning every step. *What am I getting myself into?*

They wandered over to where all the other kids were backstage, peering around for the sign of an adult. There was all manner of props, decorations, and half-painted stage sets. Several kids were standing around, waiting for direction from Mrs. B., the art teacher. A few kids were standing on the stage holding scripts, talking to Mr. Wacher.

Sara tugged Bobby's hand, dragging him over. "Hi, Mr. Wacher. I found Bobby. He can help with the sets and whatever non-acting things you need."

Mr. Wacher thanked the other kids for their patience and told them he'd be right with them, turning his attention to Bobby. "I'm so glad you're here with us," he said earnestly. "I think this environment will be really healthy for you. We need more help, and I've seen some of your sketches. Some can be a little dark," he chuckled with a smile, "but talent is talent. And you're very good."

"Oh, ah, thank you," Bobby replied shyly.

A large boy approached Bobby from behind, looking down at a broken prop in his hands. "Uh, Mr. Wacher? We have a problem with the—" he looked up, suddenly recognizing Bobby standing next to his cousin, Sara, who was still holding Bobby's hand.

Hearing the voice of his nemesis, Bobby flung around to face Seth without having a clue how to react. *What the F is he doing here?* Bobby looked at Sara with a concerned face. "You didn't … Why would I … I can't—"

"Bobby," interrupted Mr.Wacher. "It's okay. I made Seth aware you'd be joining our club. Seth is here because, well, because he has to be. But it's also good for him. It's good for both of you. Right, Seth?" Mr. Wacher questioned, looking sternly at Seth.

"Yeah, sure," Seth replied. Mr. Wacher nodded at Seth, as if giving him the go-ahead. Seth froze for a moment, then nervously looked at Bobby. For the first time, Bobby saw something different reflecting in his eyes. "I'm sorry for pickin' on your little sister the other night," Seth simpered as his eyes danced back and forth among Mr. Wacher, Sara, then focusing again on Bobby. "And I'm, uh, sorry about your dad. I heard he's okay."

Bobby was amazed and dumbfounded. *Seth is apologizing to me?* He was truly speechless. All he could summon from his lips was a faint, "Yeah." Mr. Wacher spared him the agony and offered a reply on his behalf.

"Thank you, Seth," Mr. Wacher responded. "Why don't you find the black duct tape, and see if you can repair that for us? I'm sure you'll make it look as good as new," he encouraged.

Seth nodded and walked off. Bobby, still stunned by the exchange, watched Seth disappear backstage. He looked over at Sara, then back to Mr. Wacher.

"Bobby, with everything happening between you two, and with what you've been through with your family, I took it upon myself to have a very sincere talk with Seth. And we came to an understanding. He won't be starting any more trouble with you. And if he does, let me know immediately. And I need you to agree not to start any trouble with him. Understand?"

"Yes, sir," answered Bobby.

"I need to hear you repeat it for me," Mr. Wacher insisted. "Your word is your bond."

"I won't start any trouble."

"Wonderful," replied Mr. Wacher. "then let's get busy. The show must—"

ding ding

From behind the stage, someone rang a bell, interrupting his train of thought. "You know what that means, don't you?" Mr. Wacher asked, not finishing his previous sentence. "Teacher says, every time a bell rings …" He deliberately paused, raising a brow and waiting for Bobby to fill in the sentence.

"Huh? Sorry, I don't know what you mean." Bobby answered meekly. He leaned in toward Sara and whispered, "What's he talking about? What happens when a bell rings?"

~~~ O ~~~

Wendi sat in her car outside the office. *Okay, ask for a sign. Just think it, or say it? Angie didn't say. Maybe it will be more powerful if I say it out loud.* She peered around the parking lot to see if anyone was hopping in a car near her. The coast was clear. *Here goes nothing.* She closed her eyes and in a low voice, began, "Angel, heavenly friend—" *Ugh, that sounds so stupid.* "Heavenly Guardian, I welcome you into my life. Please send me a sign to show me that you are with me. Thank you." *Okay, I guess that's it.* "Oh, Amen. Thanks." She looked around one more time, turned the key, and headed home.

Driving along, she glanced around at passing delivery trucks and bumper stickers, trying to read them as fast as she could. *I wonder what kind of sign it will be. Angie didn't say how quickly the signs come.*

She stayed alert for a few more blocks before realizing she was trying too hard. She allowed her mind to drift off and enjoyed a peaceful ride home. Around the corner from her neighborhood, she coasted to a stop as the traffic light turned red. Patiently waiting for the light to change, she watched the clouds drift by.

The sun was setting directly overhead. As it lowered itself into view, an intense glare blinded her sight of the traffic light. She turned away instinctively, reaching up to pull down the visor. Just as her hand grasped it, the glare dimmed, and her eyes adjusted to a lone cloud drifting by. It crept across the sun, shading its brilliance. It was a typical cloud, big and round, with several puffs sticking out on all sides. She watched curiously as the cloud stretched and morphed itself into something new.

A large portion in the middle stretched out to the left as the bottom thinned out. A smaller piece stretched out toward the right. Thinking about all the animals and fun creatures she would imagine in the clouds as a child, she watched eagerly. As she stared, the section spreading to the left tapered to a point. *Could that be a wing? Maybe it's a dragon.*

She continued to watch, wondering what fanciful shape might materialize. The piece on the left took the clear form of a wing. The ripples flowing along it even gave it the appearance of feathers. *It's a bird!* she excitedly thought, as if she had just solved a puzzle on Wheel of Fortune. Slowly and certainly, a distinct shape emerged. Her eyes widened as her mouth slowly opened. *It's an Angel!*

A distinguishable head and face took form. Its large wings brushed out to the left as an arm reached out to the right. The flowing bottom curved and tapered off into the horizon, giving the illusion of a translucent dress. The sun was directly centered, illuminating a heart of gold. Rays of light shot in all directions, giving the shape an aura. The contrast of the cloud against the sunlight pronounced the shape even more against the colorful sky. It was brilliant, beautiful, and miraculous. No words could accurately describe the beauty she was witnessing. *My God* was all she thought as a warmth grew inside her heart.

She watched as the arm to the right tapered even more into what looked like a hand with a pointing finger. The Angel was facing and gently gliding to the right, and a soft inner voice echoed inside her, *You're moving in the right direction.*

Wendi's whole being shivered, then sank into a deep peace she had never known before. At that moment, nothing mattered. All her cares were washed away, and she was completely present with her angelic vision. A tear of joy gently rolled down her smiling cheek. She couldn't believe that a sign would come so easily, quickly, and magnificently.

The cloud slowly descended, allowing a piece of the sun to peek out of the top. Brilliant rays of light streamed out in directions around its head, creating a vibrant halo. The illuminated cloud was enough to stir wonder in anyone seeing it.

Awestruck over the heavenly vision, she looked around to see if other people were watching the spectacle. To her right, the turn lane curved around into the other road, allowing drivers to just slow down before continuing on. In her rearview mirror, she could see a man in the car behind her looking down at something. She wished someone, anyone else, was sharing this angelic vision with her. But it was meant for her eyes only. It was her own magical moment.

Still glancing into her rearview mirror, the man behind her looked up and started honking his horn. Wendi shifted her focus from the mirror back to the sky and flinched. The cloud had already floated off to the right and shifted into an unrecognizable shape. The sun was now directly in front of her. Pulling down her visor, she could just barely see the green light, and continued her journey home.

dink dink dink

Peter gently hit the spoon against his plate, forcing the mashed potatoes to slide off. "You're in a good mood this evening, Honey," he noted as he passed her the potatoes.

Wendi couldn't contain herself. She had been holding in her excitement since she arrived home. She desperately wanted to tell everyone about the Angel cloud. She was even excited about telling Pete all the details of her discussion with Angie. She thought better of the latter idea, but talking about an Angel cloud seemed safe enough. *Everyone sees shapes in clouds, right?* She wanted to blurt it out as soon as she walked in the door, but thought it best to casually mention it over dinner.

Wendi grabbed the bowl of potatoes from Pete and put a heaping scoop on her plate. "You'll never guess what happened on the way home from work today," she taunted with a glowing smile, glancing around at each family member. Wendi hesitated, expecting them to jump in with just as much enthusiasm as she had. She scanned the table again, impatiently waiting for someone to respond. They all paused and looked up. Waiting for the answer that wasn't given, they continued to shovel down their meals.

"I saw an Angel!" Wendi enthusiastically burst out.

Bobby and Pete froze. Their jaws stopped chewing, and their forks, filled with the next bite, halted halfway to their mouths. They glanced at one another, then back at Wendi. Bobby's eyebrows raised, as if waiting for a punch line. Faith just smiled, and Pete swallowed down this food and let out the only thought coming to mind. "You saw what, now?"

"You heard me," Wendi said.

"Um, that's what I'm afraid of," he responded, letting out a sigh. "And things have been going so well lately," he chuckled.

"Well, maybe it wasn't a *real* Angel."

"Oh, no?" Pete replied sarcastically. "Well, at least I feel a little saner now. Fine, I'll bite," he said, shoveling another forkful of dinner into his mouth. "What kind of Angel was it?" he mumbled as he chewed.

"I saw an Angel in the clouds. It was amazing! Okay, well, I didn't see an Angel *in* the clouds. I saw an Angel cloud," she clarified, losing some of the excitement in her voice.

The stares persisted as silence lingered in the air. "You know, like a cloud *shaped* like an Angel. It was unmistakable. It formed right in front of me while I was stopped at a light." Excitement pulsed through her again. As she recalled the immaculate vision, her words got faster and faster as she blurted them out. "The sun was behind it, shining out from all sides, and it looked glorious and radiant, like a Renaissance painting but real, and the wings looked like feathers, and I've never seen anything like it before, and it was clearly a sign because I had just asked our Angel for one, and it was pointing right, and I heard this voice and—" Wendi stopped, seeing the concern growing again in Pete's face. Her excitement got the better of her as she realized she had revealed too much.

Faith's eyes looked up to the right, as if she were thinking. She paused, looking off into the distance, and smiled. She then grabbed her spoon and began playing with her mashed potatoes. Bobby, recalling the glowing heart that appeared through the clouds at lunch, was lost between curiosity and concern. Feeling awkward about his strange lunchtime experience, he simply let out an "Uh huh. Sounds cool, Mom." Pete chuckled, nodding in approval of Bobby's answer, and turned to Wendi.

"Uh, it sounds beautiful, Hun. Really … but you say it was a sign from our Angel and you heard voices?" he questioned, lowering his fork.

Wendi sat there, staring blankly at Pete, not knowing whether to defend herself or not.

"And how often are you hearing these voices? Maybe you should come with me to my next doctor's appointment."

"I'm not crazy!" she blurted out. "Am I not allowed to believe in Angels? Suddenly you're all a bunch of atheists?" She looked at each family member. "Except you, Angel," she added, looking at Faith.

Faith, still playing with her mashed potatoes, looked up at her mother and smiled. Resuming her work of art, she continued pushing and molding her potatoes with her spoon.

"At least the heart attack didn't kill my sense of humor," remarked Pete. He felt himself approaching the edge and throttled off the joke pedal. "Sorry, Hun. I'm glad your newfound faith is finding … interesting ways to shine through. I'm all for asking Heaven for help down here, but—" He thought better of his next statement and shifted gears. "Anything else interesting happen at work?"

"Well—" Wendi also stopped herself. *He doesn't get it. And he certainly won't understand my talk with Angie.* "Boring day as usual. Anyway, the cloud was a beautiful sight. I just wanted to share it with you. I wish you had all been there to see it with me."

"I'm sure I would have loved it," he replied with a genuine smile. "Sorry that we're not sharing your enthusiasm. Too bad you couldn't take a photo of it."

"No. I didn't get a photo. Even if I could have, it all happened so fast."

"Maybe next time," encouraged Pete. "I was just surprised how much this affected you. Last week, I don't think you would have been pointing out glorious Angel clouds to us. Just demon clouds. They have wings, too," he laughed and resumed eating his dinner.

Wendi sat and watched as Bobby and Pete chomped down their food, not giving the cloud another thought. Words couldn't accurately describe the wondrous sight she beheld. They could neither understand nor truly share her enthusiasm. The visual spectacle, and especially the feeling it inspired, was deeply personal and solely meant for her.

Pete was right, though. A week ago, it probably would have been just a cloud blocking the sun. *What a week.* She laughed to herself, realizing how much had changed in such a short period. No one else had noticed her eyes tearing up. *Thank you, Angel, for such a glorious gift. I welcome you into our life and our home, and eagerly await your next sign.*

Feeling in a lighter mood, she threw in her own little jab. "One more thing, dear husband of mine."

Pete paused and looked at his wife. "If I look up on my way home tomorrow and see four clouds that look like horsemen, I'm telling them they made a mistake and to come back for you!"

Pete let out a loud laugh, followed by Bobby chuckling, as small bits of food flew out of his mouth. "Bring 'em on, Hun. I ain't afraid of no apocalypse," he replied, winking at Bobby, hoping he caught his Ghostbuster pun. "Bobby, did you see any fun clouds today?"

Surprised at his father's question, he stuttered, "No … uh … not exactly. But Faith … uh … well, me, Faith, and Sara … We all saw a hole in the clouds that looked like a heart." He looked around, trying to gauge the reaction. A part of him wanted to blurt out all the details, including Faith leading them around and staring at the sky before it formed. But after his dad's reaction to his mom, he was too embarrassed to offer any more than a simple shape.

Wendi stopped herself from taking the next forkful of food. *Two distinct shapes in the clouds in one day? Could that be a synchronicity?* she questioned, recalling Angie's earlier correction of the word coincidence.

Pete quickly responded. "A heart? That sounds neat. Well, looks like I'm the only one not spending enough time staring at clouds," he amused.

Wendi smiled at Bobby with a look of recognition and kept eating. *I don't want to put him on the spot.* She was content with her vision, seeing her husband in a good mood, and knowing her children also received a sign, whether they knew it or not.

She looked across the table at Faith, not taking any notice of her creation. "Faith, please stop playing with your food and eat it. Thank you."

Bobby glanced over at her plate. She had molded her mashed potatoes into a distinct shape. It was a figure in a dress with wings stretching out to left, and an arm pointing to the right. His eyes lit up, but before any words could come out of his mouth, she dragged her spoon across the middle of it, taking a giant bite of potatoes. It scooped the hand and most of the wings away, leaving two halves of an unrecognizable shape.

Bobby stared in amazement. Faith looked over and flashed her happy, innocent smile. Maybe Faith had paid attention to

Wendi's description, but he doubted it. She was in her own little world the whole time. He had another thought. *Somehow, she knew what the cloud looked like.*

~~~ O ~~~

A brilliant, warm, and welcoming light surrounded Wendi. It felt alive, as if it was somehow embracing her. Unlike staring at the sun, the brighter the light became, the easier she could look at it. A beautiful peace permeated from the dream into her awareness as she slowly opened her eyes. Surrounded by darkness, she looked over at the clock. *4:44.* No longer feeling resentful of her 4:44 awakenings, she finally accepted them as a sign. *Today feels special.* She smiled. Something had shifted within her. Despite waking up so early, she felt awake and alive.

She cautiously pulled back the covers and eased out of bed. Avoiding the squeaky floorboards, she tip-toed out of the bedroom, down to the kitchen, and brewed some coffee. It was the first time she embraced the chance to enjoy the quiet moments of the world before dawn.

As she sat enjoying the calm, sipping her coffee, she felt her stomach rumble. *I'm never up this early. Pete won't be awake for another hour. Maybe I'll surprise everyone and run out for breakfast.*

"One cinnamon raisin and one everything bagel. And then I'll have two glazed with jimmies, two pumpkin spice, and a Boston cream doughnut." Wendi typically prepared four bowls of cereal for breakfast, occasionally with a side of toast. This morning, she felt they all deserved a treat.

As she waited for the employee to fulfill her order, she glanced to the side. The lottery ticket sign caught her eye. Wendi didn't typically play the lottery. She had never won more than a few dollars, and over the past few years, she figured they had too much bad luck to win, anyway.

"Will that be all, ma'am?" the employee asked.

"Yes, thank you," Wendi answered.

The song playing in the background faded out. The tune beginning caught her attention. It was an older song, something from the 50s or 60s. She immediately began singing along, quietly, without even realizing it. "Earth Angel …"

She quickly paused as the words immediately sank into her awareness. *You're kidding. Another Angel song.*

"That's $7.77, ma'am."

Wendi heard the cashier, but she was lost in thought. The numbers triggered something within her. *$7.77. How's that for some lucky numbers? And triple digits again. 4, 44 and now 7, 77.* She glanced at the lottery machine again, as Earth Angel continued playing in the background.

"You're supposed to play the lottery!" came an unexpected voice from a man to her right.

Wendi flinched with surprise, thinking the stranger was talking to her. Her attention quickly shifted from paying her bill to the other register. She looked over, about to ask the man if he was talking to her when she noticed he was speaking to his friend.

"Don't you know a sign when you see one, Will? You're supposed to buy a lottery ticket." The man nudged his friend aside, and looking at the cashier, declared, "We'll take a Pick-6!"

"Ma'am? If there's nothing else, that'll be $7.77."

Wendi shook her head, snapping back to the present. "Yes. I mean, no. Nothing else." Wendi thanked the cashier and handed her a ten-dollar bill.

The man's words repeated in her mind. *Don't you know a sign when you see one? You're supposed to buy a lottery ticket.* The cash register drawer popped open as the cashier collected Wendi's change. *But I only have four numbers. It's a Pick-6.* Angie's voice echoed next. *Your job is simply not to dismiss them when they come.* Wendi felt a tingle inside her. She shuddered as a chill ran up her spine. *Okay, okay. But If you want me to play the lottery, then what are the other numbers?*

"Three thirty-three."

"What did you just say?" asked Wendi, trying to make sense of the next Twilight Zone episode unfolding before her.

"Your change, ma'am. $3.33," the cashier repeated, wiggling her hand to get Wendi's attention.

Wendi took the change and stared at the girl for another moment. "I'm sorry. There *is* something else. Could I get a Pick-6 as well?" she asked.

"Sure. Would you like a quick pick?" she asked.

"No," Wendi politely replied. "I'd like to pick my own numbers." The cashier nodded and Wendi repeated each of the numbers flashing in her mind. "3, 4, 7, 33, 44, and 77."

The girl punched in the numbers and handed the ticket back to Wendi. "Good luck," she said.

"Thank you," replied Wendi, promptly putting the lottery ticket and change in her purse. She grabbed her bagels and doughnuts from the counter and headed out. As she approached the exit, it swung open. The other man who played the lottery was holding the door open, allowing her to pass.

"Thank you," Wendi said graciously.

"You're quite welcome. And good luck to ya. Today feels like a special day."

"It sure does," Wendi agreed with a smile as she stepped out of the bakery into the rising morning light.

~ o ~

Chapter 8:

Making the
Connection

*"If you truly want to live a life in communion
with these beautiful beings, nurture
a stronger connection with them."*

~ o ~

beep beep beep

Faith quickly reached over and turned off her 6 a.m. alarm. She had awoken five minutes prior and had been laying there in bed, waiting for it to go off. She popped up, sitting on her bed, and greeted her morning companion. "Good mornin', Nobody ... Weally? Anodder special day? We're having lots of special days! Who's it special fa dis time? ... Bobby *and* Mommy? Yay!" she whispered excitedly. Tapping her hands together in a clapping motion, she silently applauded. "Is Mommy goin' ta see anodder cloud? ... Even betta?" She softly clapped again, excited for another day as a silent witness to the miracles unfolding.

"Is it time fa me ta tell Bobby about you? ... Oh. He don't under-tand yet? ... He will soon? Yay! ... How soon? ... Very soon? Like tomor-woa soon? ... Fine. Wheneva soon is," she reluctantly agreed, scrunching her face. "I hope my soon and your soon will hurry up and be da same."

~~~ O ~~~

Bobby and Faith waved goodbye to their mom as the bus drove away. As always, Faith sat by the window and Bobby on the end, guarding her against anyone walking by. The bus pulled up to the next stop, and the kids shuffled in. Sara was the first one on. She eagerly looked around, and immediately took the seat across from Bobby and Faith.

"Hi Bobby," she greeted him enthusiastically. "Hi Faith," she added peering around Bobby. Faith looked, smiled, and returned her gaze out the window watching the rising sun.

"Hi Sara," Bobby replied with a considerable grin.

"I have an idea," Sara began. "I was talking to Mr. Wacher, and he said we need more snowflakes for the finale tomorrow night."

"Okay," Bobby replied. "They're easy to make."

"No, silly," she giggled. "Didn't you see the costumes? We always have some non-speaking parts to let kids be on stage. The kids are the snowflakes. We need more. You can be a snowflake, and then you get to be on stage with me."

Bobby looked at her with a blank stare. "Uh, you want me to wear a snowflake costume and spin around on stage? Are you nuts? Are you looking for more reasons for Seth to bully me?"

"Don't worry about Seth. My, uh, Mr. Wacher said he had a talk with Seth."

"That won't stop him. I think I'm okay staying behind the scenes."

"Please," she pleaded with her best puppy dog eyes. "It would really mean a lot. I'm nervous and having you on stage would make me happy." She flashed an irresistible smile, and Bobby melted. He felt a tug on his shirt and turned. Faith was staring up at him with a big grin, nodding her head.

"Okay, okay. I'll be a stupid snowflake. That means I have to stay after school tomorrow. I just have to check with my parents."

"Mr. Wacher said he could bring me home. I'm sure he wouldn't mind dropping you off, too," Sara offered.

"Why is Mr. Wacher driving you home?" Asked Bobby.

"Oh, ah, my mom can't be there and he lives right by us. We're just … ah, close. He's my favorite teacher," she added with a smile. Her reply sufficed, and Bobby wondered what his parents would think of him being a snowflake in the school extravaganza. *This is going to be so embarrassing.*

"Angie! Good morning," Wendi exclaimed enthusiastically as she saw Angie flying by. "I've been looking for you all morning!"

Angie stopped, flashing her contagious smile. "And a blessed morning to ya, Deary. Sorry I've been MIA. I've been tied up in

meetings all mornin' and gotta bunch of notes to type up ASAP,"
she informed Wendi in her typical whimsical tone, beginning to
step away.

"Angie, I *have* to talk to you," Wendi insisted. "You're not
going to believe what happened when I left here yesterday and all
the crazy things happening this morning."

"Oh, I have a feelin' I'll believe every word of it, Deary.
And there's nothing crazy about it, I'm sure. Sounds like you
have plenty to tell, but it'll just have to wait for lunchtime." She
responded without even a hint of curiosity and strolled off to her
desk.

A familiar redhead popped up over the cubicle wall. "For the
record, I'm beginning to think *you're* crazy!" exclaimed Patty.
"What the dickens has been goin' on with you two lately? Now, I
don't mind you goin' and gettin' all religious on us now that your
husband is saved, but I still don't trust that woman. I don't get
greeted with half as much of the pleasantry as you do." Patty
looked across the room to make sure Angie was at her cubicle and
lowered her voice. "And I still say she's a witch."

"She's actually a very wise woman who has just has a …
well, a different take on things."

"I'll say. She'll take your soul!" she said in a joking manner,
with wide eyes and raised brows and all, but Wendi could tell she
still meant it. Patty continued along without missing a beat.

"And how is it ya have such exciting news to tell Angie, and
ya haven't mentioned a darn thing to *me* about it? We're cubicle
buddies, for goodness' sake. It's your job to tell me everything!"
she declared, moving along like a freight train without stops. "So,
what happened when ya left yesterday? And what happened this
mornin'? And why does Angie need to know? And what have you
two been talkin' about at lunch?"

Patty paused for a moment to allow a thought in. She
peered around the office, acting like a covert agent, and
lowered her voice again. "Does it involve a man? You had your
eye on someone, didn't ya? And feel guilty about it now that
your husband had a heart attack? I totally understand. I see the

way John flirts with ya over by the copier. I have a sixth sense about these things, ya know," she proudly admitted and continued.

A look of shock overcame Patty as she mouthed the words "Oh, my God". She leaned in closer to Wendi and began again in a whisper, "Have you takin' a liking to the ladies? *That's* why you're spendin' so much time with Angie. Go on, you can tell me anything, girl. You know me. I'm not one to judge or gossip ... So give me every last dirty detail!"

"Patty! Honestly," Wendi rebutted. "*No*, it does not involve another man or another *woman*. Things have been wonderful with Pete. His heart attack made us both look at life differently. And Angie has been helping me with that ... with looking at things differently. I really think we have a chance of pulling our family back together."

"Well, okay then," Patty remarked with a look of disappointment as she leaned back. "I'll be very happy for y'all if things work out, really. You keep me posted, now. See what happens when ya *don't* tell me things? Rumors start flyin'," she stated with a nod of her big curly hair.

Without waiting for Wendi to respond, she continued. "So, on ta more important things, Love. What in the world *have* y'all been talkin' about? You and Angie. Ya musta been over at her cubicle half a dozen times in the last week. Not that I'm countin' or anything."

Wendi knew she needed to offer a believable story, or at least a partial truth. Patty's sixth sense wasn't quite on par, but she was like a bloodhound when it came to smelling bullshit and lies. "Well lately, we've had more, uh, religious types of talks with Pete surviving his heart attacks and all. But it all started because I needed some advice on Faith. She's been acting weird, and I figured Angie was the go-to person for weird behavior."

"Mmm hmm. You can say that again. But still, I just don't know about any advice that woman would give. You woulda been better off comin' ta me, Love," Patty suggested. "So, what's this strange behavior? And what did her crystal ball tell ya?"

"Angie just has some interesting points of view. Nothing worth mentioning."

"Now I know there's more to it than that, but you go have your little secrets. I'll find out eventually." With that, her red topped head sank back into its gopher hole, then suddenly sprang back up. "Oh, how *is* Pete doin'? Is he still milking it at home, or did ya send his behind back to the grind?"

~~~ O ~~~

knock knock

Allen stood at the door to Pete's office with a beaming smile and a look of gratitude glistening in his eyes. "Peter Farfalla ... Now, I know you shouldn't be back here already, but it *is* good to see you. You don't know how hard it is to get through a day here without my cellmate," he chuckled. "Don't even think about abandoning this Earth and leaving me stuck in this place with The Marshal!"

"You're safe for now, Allen. I'm not dying on you, but that doesn't mean I'm not leaving this place the second I get the chance," Pete laughed.

"So, how are you feeling, my friend?" Allen asked.

"I feel great, actually. Better than I have in years, if you can believe it. But don't tell The Marshal that. I have a doctor's note, and I mean to use it!" They both laughed, and Pete continued, "I really appreciate you stopping by to see me in the hospital the other day. You didn't have to give up your lunch hour to come see me."

"Of course I didn't *have* to, Pete. That's the difference between friends and family. When a friend shows up, you know they actually *want* to see you." They laughed again. "And if you really thought you'd end up in the hospital without me stopping by, you'd better get your head checked again. Our friendship means a lot to me, Pete."

"Thank you, Allen. It means a lot to hear you say that. You are my saving grace."

"You are very welcome. So tell me, how are you *really* feeling, Pete? And I don't mean physically. How are you handling all this? How are things at home with all this going on? I know sometimes a real scare, as horrible as it is, can help bring families together and re-prioritize the important things in life."

"Well said. And you're right, actually. Things have really turned around since the heart attack. I have a new perspective on life and Wendi almost seems like a different person. Kind of strange after all these months of turmoil, but seeing me keeled over about to die triggered something in her. It brought her back to God and she was praying up a storm," Pete added, as he twirled his hands in the air. He hesitated for a moment before continuing his thoughts. "Only thing is, I think she swung a little too far in the other direction. She's getting *too* religious on me."

"That is quite the shift. But facing death, even though not her own, can do that to a person. She's seen the light, my friend, and there's no turning back."

"You're right as usual, Allen," Pete agreed. "What am I complaining about? I'll take it any day over the fights we were having just a week ago. Which reminds me … Now that I'm not living in a war zone at home, we'll have to have you and the misses over for a bite sometime soon. How are things at home? You can always have yourself a little brush with death—does wonders for the marriage!" Pete laughed, and Allen joined right in with a good chuckle.

"You're too much. Good to see you haven't lost your sense of humor, Pete. Things could always be a little better at home with me and the misses, but I think I'll stick to the good old-fashioned approach. Although your way does sound tempting. Let's see … heart attack, almost dying, and being in the hospital vs. talking through our issues heart to heart … a real toss-up," Allen jested, bouncing his hands up and down like a scale weighing the options. "Yeah, I think I'll stick to my way." They both laughed again.

"Now I'll let you get to it, but don't work too hard. Wendi may be looking out for you at home, but I'm keeping an eye on you while you're here. I'll be popping in to tell you a joke every hour to keep your stress down."

"Well, if there's one thing you're good at, it's making me laugh. Now stop stalling and go get some work done before someone alerts The Marshal that you're keeping me from my life-or-death job."

"See now, that one's *not* funny. Better leave the comedy to me and don't quit your day job," he added with a wink.

"Damn it. That was the only thing I had on my to-do list for today!" They both laughed.

~~~ O ~~~

"Angie, I still can't believe you're not the least bit surprised after everything I've told you!" Wendi responded in astonishment, looking at the time. She was on her morning break and only had a few minutes to spare.

"To me, there's nothing surprisin' about it. But don't mistake that in any sort of negative way. I'm thrilled on high that you've come so far, so quickly, Deary."

"Are you saying this is normal, Angie? Angel clouds, Angel songs, triple numbers all day long—what are the chances? These are some really *crazy* coincidences!"

"They are s*ynchronicities,* Dear, and signs. And there is nothing crazy about them. It means you're on the right track. But let me take that back. The Angels manage to delight and surprise me all the time, even though I'm used to it. They're much more clever than I am. Always coming up with new and fun ways to get my attention," she giggled, delighted by her own words.

"When you learn to live in awareness," Angie continued, "you quickly realize how many people are living with their eyes, ears, and hearts closed to God's wonders. And there's much more to come, Deary. So keep all your senses open."

"More? I don't know how much more I can take," she replied with a concerned smile. "And Pete just didn't understand. We've been doing so well since he got out of the hospital, and now I feel this disconnect from him. It was like we finally got over the mountain … Well, more like a volcano, actually," she chuckled, "and a new valley is in the way."

"That'll happen, Deary. It's can be a bit of a blessin' and a curse for newcomers. You'll learn how to navigate the world of sleepin' humans. And unfortunately, many a spouse has fallen into the latter category. He'll either come around, or you'll learn who it's okay and not okay to share your experiences with. Many experiences will truly be for you alone to witness. Others don't always understand. Even when they do, they can't always appreciate your experience because, well, it was yours, Dear," she explained with a loving sparkle in her eye.

"Yeah, I learned that lesson already," Wendi mentioned, rolling her eyes.

"You've only just cracked the door open, Deary. If you truly want to live a life in communion with these beautiful beings, nurture a stronger connection with them. The miracles have only just begun," she added with a wink.

"What kind of connection? How do I connect with an Angel?"

"I'm so glad you asked, Deary, because that's your next lesson for today: strengthening your connection to your Angel."

"You mean by praying more and acknowledging the signs, right?"

Angie chuckled. "That's child's play, Dear. That's what everyone should be doin' every day without needing me to tell 'em," she insisted, flashing her bright smile.

"There's other ways to connect," she began. "We gravitate toward the people we know or feel a connection with. The same principle holds true with your Angels. As you make a stronger connection, you are literally gravitating closer to each other, closing the gap between our realities."

"Come on, now, Angie. If I walk into a room full of people, I can just go over and talk to them. Get to know them. Find things we have in common. What do I possibly have in common with an Angel?"

"Well, that's easy, Deary. Love! All of life is bound together by Love. When we love something, we feel connected to it, and when we fall out of love, it's because we lose that connection. When we feel disconnected, we feel unhappy, afraid, and alone. You've been struggling for a long time because you lost your connection to your kids, your husband, and to God. And look at how quickly things have changed now that you have been reconnecting with all of them." Angie leaned back, allowing Wendi space to process it all.

Wendi started in astonishment. It was one lightbulb illuminating after another every time she spoke with Angie. She felt the runway lighting up for her takeoff. But she wasn't sure of her bearing just yet, nor did she have a clue where she would land when the journey was over. "Where were you a year ago, Angie!" was all she could blurt out.

"Ya weren't ready for me then, or ya would have found me, Deary," she assured Wendi, gently patting her hand. "You reconnected to God by asking for an Angel. You re-connected with your husband because he survived his heart attack. And all of it has prompted a shift in your son. And don't forget this all started when you came to me to understand what was happening with your daughter. In your heart, you are giving love another chance. God has sent you an Angel to piece your life back together and open yourself to a new way of living ... Not to mention He sent me as well. I'm a temp. I'm sent where I'm most needed."

Angie looked deep into Wendi's eyes, yet her smile remained gentle. "Now tell me, Dear, are you ready to open another door?"

Sitting there listening to Angie, Wendi felt like a little girl being told a whimsical bedtime story, wondering what could possibly come next. Overwhelmed with anticipation, she answered with hesitation. "Yes! Yes, I am. I want to keep opening all the doors," she affirmed, feeling her heart lifting.

"Good. Then let's start with the door straight through to your heart. It's time you connected directly with your Angel. Come find me at lunchtime."

Wendi was dumbfounded. "We're going to do this here?"

"Yes, Dear. Well, goodness, no, not standing right here!" she chuckled. "We'll find a quiet place for you to sit down without any interruptions. I know the perfect spot."

~~~ O ~~~

Mr. Wacher glanced at the time as he leaned back against his desk. "I think we can stop here for today. You have about five minutes before the lunch bell. Feel free to socialize or get a jump on your homework," he announced. Mr. Wacher held his gaze on Bobby, waiting to grab his attention. "Bobby, could I have a quick word?" He asked, motioning Bobby to his desk.

Bobby hesitantly approached, wondering if he was in trouble for something he didn't realize. "Yes, Mr. Wacher?"

"I want to have a lengthier conversation to discuss you and Seth. I was hoping to sit down with you after the pencil incident, but after what happened with your dad on Halloween, I wanted to give you some time before bringing it up again. I'd appreciate it if you could hang back at lunch so we can have a private conversation." He leaned a bit closer to Bobby. "You're *not* in trouble ... for once," he added, flashing a smile to let Bobby know he was kidding. "I apologize in advance for taking time away from your lunch. Will that be okay?" he asked politely.

Bobby answered in a cautious tone. "Sure."

"Great. Take your seat and we'll chat soon." Mr. Wacher threw in a wink, and Bobby took his seat. Bobby's experience to date since he moved was that even good conversations with teachers often meant bad news. *If I'm not in trouble, why do we need to talk about it?*

ringgggg

Lunchtime. Bobby remained seated as the students around him popped up and shuffled out the door like cattle. Sara paused as she walked by, smiled, and asked, "Are you coming to lunch?"

"In a bit. Mr. Wacher wants to talk to me about something," Bobby answered as his voice cracked with concern.

Sara leaned in and whispered softly, "It'll be okay," and continued out the door. Her words were a welcome breath of air to his nervous ears, but only slightly eased his discomfort. *Did something happen with Seth? Or to my dad? Or Faith? Why do we need to talk?* As the last student left the room, his eyes turned back to Mr. Wacher, trying to get an inkling of what the talk might be about.

Bobby could feel the emptiness of the classroom; it was just him and Mr. Wacher. He motioned Bobby to the front desk. Bobby stood up and reluctantly approached. Mr. Wacher also stood and swung his chair around to the front of the desk. He stretched out an open hand, offering Bobby his seat. Bobby sat, keeping his head down, still uneasy about the situation.

Mr. Wacher sat on the edge of his desk and sighed. "Bobby," he began in a serious tone, waiting for Bobby to look up so their eyes could connect. Bobby looked up, his eyes filled with a mild terror as sweat began to drip down the side of his face.

Mr. Wacher belted out a laugh, and grabbed Bobby's shoulder, giving it a jiggle. "It's okay, Bobby. I apologize if you're concerned. And while I do have something serious to discuss and talk about, you're not in trouble. No one is. Everything is fine. In fact, I first wanted to ask: How's your father doing?"

A feeling of relief filled Bobby as he sunk into the chair. "Oh, ah, he's good, actually."

"Wonderful. And your mom? How's she been through all this? How are they both, is really what I'm asking."

"Good. They're good," Bobby replied, nodding in agreement with his statement.

"That's wonderful to hear," Mr. Wacher responded with a smile before shifting to a more serious tone. "Bobby, I've learned from being a teacher, and from life, that things aren't always what they seem. And because of that, I do my best not to judge students or jump to conclusions. I've seen a lot of good kids do bad things. And I've learned that in many cases, it's just a cry for attention and acceptance. You're a good kid, Bobby, and some bad things have happened to you. And I don't want to see you create any more bad situations because of it. And do you know what? The same thing is true for the 'bad kids'," he said, making air quotes. "I've found that even though they may treat others badly, they just want attention, and deep down, they want to be accepted and loved, too."

He paused, shifting his weight. "Do you know what compels me, what drives me, the most about being a teacher?"

Bobby looked up and shook his head, remaining silent. It felt more like a therapy session than listening to his teacher. Even before the accident, he wasn't sure his parents had conversations with him like this. So he kept listening, wondering where it was all going.

"The belief that all kids are good kids. That's what drives me. And I believe that even the 'bad kids' are good kids who have been treated badly. I have a soft spot when it comes to those kids because I truly believe they need someone to care about them and it will make all the difference. Because chances are, they don't get that care at home if they are acting out in school. *That* is what compels me to come to class every day, to make a difference, and to help change the lives of my students in a positive way. To add some love and care to the lives of those who may not find it anywhere else." He shifted again, leaning closer.

"I'll say it again: I know you're a good kid, Bobby. And I know you've had some bad things happen since your move. For a while, it seemed like you were letting them get the best of you. Once anger starts leading your life, it can be a tough road to turn back from ... But you did it," he added as a big smile stretched across his face. "You're turning your life around. Things are getting better for you at home, and I see that you and Sara have a special connection. It's making a difference in your life. Wouldn't you agree?"

Bobby, surprised at the unexpected direction of the conversation, took an honest moment to think about it. He returned a smile and nodded in agreement, squeezing out a "yeah".

Mr. Wacher took a quick look around, stood, and grabbed one of the small chairs against the wall. He placed it down and sat facing Bobby, now eye level with him. "You may not think I notice all my students, but I see everything going on here. I see you're an amazing brother. I see how you stand up for your sister. You're like a Guardian Angel to her."

I'm a Guardian Angel? Bobby echoed in his mind.

"I know it's why you get into a lot of fights with Seth. He knows she's your trigger, your weak spot, and uses her against you. And that's why I had a talk with him the other day. That's why he was being polite to you at Drama Club. And that's why I wanted to talk to you today as well. I'm really hoping we can finally put an end to all this, and let you enter Middle School on a high note, not with a record high of principal office visits," he offered with another laugh, hoping to put Bobby more at ease.

"Your last fight with Seth—the pencil incident—was a close call. As you're aware, Seth honestly could have lost an eye. Now, I know it was a culmination, the last straw, if you will, of several incidents. And I'm not here to beat a dead horse. We talked a bit when it happened, and a lot has changed since then." Mr. Wacher paused and drew in a deep breath, keeping an eye on Bobby to see if he was still following along.

"He's just a big—" Bobby stopped himself, shaking his head. Mr. Wacher had good intentions, and Bobby didn't want to dig himself an unnecessary hole. "It's not fair how he treats everyone. He should be expelled."

"Maybe you're right. Maybe it would be better for the other kids, for you, if he wasn't here. But I don't believe that's the answer. And I don't believe it would do Seth any good. In fact, it could make his life worse."

"Good," Bobby mumbled.

"Ahhh, there it is. And that's why I'm talking to you now. Turning our backs on people, even the ones we don't like, doesn't solve any problems. I know Seth has hurt you physically and emotionally, and in order for it to really end, you have to let go of any resentment, any hate, you have for him. I know that's a tall order, and I'm here to help in any way I can. Do you understand what I'm asking of you? It's not something a teacher typically asks of a student, but I think you're mature enough to understand. That's why I'm speaking to you like I would anyone else, not just as a kid."

Bobby nodded. He still wasn't sure exactly what Mr. Wacher expected of him, but he understood the direction the conversation was going.

Mr. Wacher continued. "I know how Seth can be. I know firsthand, actually. I also know Seth is capable of being a good kid. I have to believe that."

"But—" Bobby stopped himself again. He still wasn't sure where the lengthy speech was heading, but it seemed to be someplace not entirely bad. He held his thought and allowed Mr. Wacher to continue.

Still sensing Bobby's struggle with Seth, Mr. Wacher shifted the conversation. "Bobby, do you believe in Angels?"

Bobby was stunned. *Why is he asking me about Angels?* His eyes drifted off to the side as he recalled the myriad of ways which Angels had worked their way into his life in the past week. *Faith's Angel costume. Sara's Angel necklace, and her talking about Angels. Mom's Angel cloud. This is crazy.*

"Is that a no? It's okay if you don't," Mr. Wacher offered, unsure about Bobby's silence.

"I … I guess I should," Bobby mumbled. He looked directly at Mr. Wacher. "Sure … I guess so. It seems to be a new thing in my life," Bobby added with a hint of a smile. "Wh … why?"

Mr. Wacher paused, then smiled back. "Well, that certainly sounds interesting. I'd honestly love to hear more about what you've been experiencing lately, but let's finish this conversation first. Is that okay?"

"Oh, okay," Bobby reluctantly agreed, even more confused about where this was going.

"The reason I ask about Angels, Bobby, is because I believe everyone needs a Guardian Angel, *and* I believe everyone has one." He paused again as Bobby listened in awe of the direction the talk was now taking.

"Sara is a big believer in Angels, if you didn't already know. And sometimes the Angels are up there," he said, looking up, "and sometimes they're right here," he added, motioning his finger between him and Bobby. "I know that one of my roles here, on this Earth, is to be a human Angel to the kids who need guidance. Kids like you, and especially kids like Seth. Now I doubt Seth is calling down any heavenly guardians to help him with his struggles, so I'm here to do what I can for him. And since you seem to be tangled up in it all, I wanted to try and heartfully explain why Seth is the way he is, and why I have so much compassion for him."

Bobby nodded and cautiously replied, "Uh, okay."

Mr. Wacher took a breath and continued. "I've sort of become a Guardian Angel to Seth. That's the phrase my sister uses for me, since she seems to have appointed me the task." He paused and shifted again, looking slightly uneasy with what he was about to say. "I mentioned my sister because she is Seth's mother. He's my nephew.

Seeing the look on Bobby's face, Mr. Wacher paused, giving Bobby a moment to process it all. *Seth is Sara's cousin. Seth is Mr. Wacher's nephew. So—*

"And Sara is my daughter," he added, as if he was reading Bobby's mind. "I thought you should know that, too. Her mom and I aren't married, *yet*. That's why she doesn't have my last name. Sara didn't really like the idea of calling me Dad in class, plus she has no desire to tell people Seth is her cousin. So, we do our best to keep our family tree out of school. She calls me

Mr. Wacher and doesn't tell anyone that Seth is her cousin …
Except for a few special people in her life."

A smirk crept across Bobby's mouth. *I guess I'm special.*

Mr. Wacher held his gaze on Bobby. "I know this isn't a
typical teacher student conversation, but I like to follow my
intuition, and I felt that it was important for you to hear all this
directly from me. I believe knowing the connections we share will
help. And simply to respect Sara, I ask that you to keep this
information to yourself … please. Do you agree?"

Once again, the conversation had turned in another
unexpected direction. *We started with Seth. Then Angels. Now he's
Sara's dad and Seth's uncle? What's next?* Bobby still didn't
know where it was all going, but he wanted to continue down this
road. Still a little nervous and confused, he gave Mr. Wacher a
heartfelt nod.

"Sara talks to me about any issues she has at school. She's
mentioned you numerous times. The last time we spoke, she
asked me if I felt it was okay if she told you more about Seth. She
hoped it would help you understand, but not excuse, his behavior.
I told her that I felt it was better coming from me. That's really
what this talk is about," Mr. Wacher remarked.

"You see, Bobby," he continued, "not everyone has a loving
family to go home to each day like you do. Some kids go home to
very hard, and even dangerous, situations. So, let's just say that
Seth's home may not be as comfortable as yours." He paused.
"Do you see what I'm getting at here, Bobby?"

Bobby nodded again. He appreciated his teacher being so
candid. It helped ease his worries about Seth. Bobby also
appreciated the time Mr. Wacher took to make sure students
understood what he was explaining. *Divulge*—Mr. Wacher's
signature move—expanding kids' vocabularies by using a word
and defining it in the same breath so that its meaning was grasped.

Bobby swallowed the lump forming in his throat. He did
understand. Seth was probably physically or emotionally abused,
maybe both, maybe worse, by his stepfather. Something shifted
inside Bobby, and a sudden wave of compassion swept

throughout him. *Maybe my life isn't that bad.* Even through all his parents' fights, the added stress Bobby was creating through his conflicts, and as much of a hard time as his own father gave him, deep inside, Bobby knew he was loved.

They were wading through the toughest months of their lives. And even though Bobby would rarely admit it to himself, he knew they were trying as hard as they could to remain a family. Gratitude washed over him. Regardless of how dysfunctional his family was, he couldn't imagine going home to a parent who hated and beat him. Bobby choked back his tears. He was beginning to understand a larger piece of life and how interconnected people are.

Mr. Wacher didn't need a verbal answer. Bobby's expression and nod were enough. "I know how often Seth gets yelled at in his own home, so I try to manage him the best I can here at school. I keep my eye on him while trying to keep him in line, trying not to be too hard on him, and trying not to show favoritism. It's not always easy to balance all that."

Bobby tried as subtlety as he could to wipe a tear making its way down his face. Mr. Wacher pretended not to notice and continued. "I think you can see a little more of the bigger picture. Everything in life can change quicker than any of us can imagine. Sometimes for the worse, sometimes for the better. It's how we react to it, and handle it, that matters most. That's what shows who we truly are, Bobby. How we treat others." Mr. Wacher paused again, taking a breath, and letting Bobby soak it all in. He had a growing concern that it all might be too much for Bobby to process, but he kept feeling the nudge to continue.

"Even though it may seem like it, Seth doesn't hate you. He hates his life right now, and you happened to become his new target. You were the new kid. And having a sister who doesn't speak makes it even easier for Seth to push your buttons. When you react to him the way you do, it fuels his fire."

"I want to be clear," Mr. Wacher emphasized, "that none of what I'm saying *excuses* Seth's behavior. I'm hoping to help you *understand* his behavior. And I'm doing what I can to guide him. I don't want you caught up in his pain. What I mentioned at Drama

Club still stands: if he does happen to start anything, please do your best not to react. Let me know as quickly as you can, and I will handle it. What do you say?"

Bobby said nothing. Still too choked up to allow any words out, he kept to his simple nods.

"Now, if you ever want to talk about what's going on in your life, or tell me about your Angels, I'm here to listen. And I hope this talk brings some understanding of Seth and his actions." Mr. Wacher stopped and waited for Bobby to respond.

Bobby wiped away another tear and looked into his teacher's eyes, exchanging an untold understanding. "Th … Thank you." Bobby managed in a whisper. He wanted to say so much more. He wanted to grab ahold of Mr. Wacher, hug him, and cry. He wanted to tell him everything that had happened over the past year, about the plane, and losing a sibling, and why Faith didn't speak, and spill out all the pent-up emotions he had, but it was all too much. It was easier to keep it inside, and he didn't know if he was even allowed to hug his teacher, let alone cry on his shoulder.

Mr. Wacher nodded, intuitively picking up on Bobby's struggle with his emotions. "You're very welcome, Robert. Remember, anytime you want to talk, I'm here for you. And I would like to highly recommend that you meet with your counselor here at school. Her job is literally to listen to you and help you process your emotions." Bobby nodded again and managed to push a smile through his dripping tears. Mr. Wacher stood up. "Oh, and one more thing, Bobby."

Bobby raised a brow, wondering what could possibly follow all that talk.

"I always keep an eye on Sara. So watch yourself," he insisted, switching to a more serious tone.

Bobby froze, afraid of how to respond.

A large smile graced Mr. Wacher's face, relieving Bobby's worry. "I'm just kidding. I wanted to lighten things up a bit before I left. I see this has been a lot for you, so I'm going to leave you here in the classroom, in case you need a few minutes alone. And I do want to hear about your Angels next time we talk. Okay?"

"Okay," Bobby responded. Mr. Wacher walked out the door, looking back at Bobby one more time with a caring smile, and disappeared into the hallway as the door shut behind him.

Bobby sat alone with his feelings and thoughts and cried like he had never cried before. Every emotion, every bit of anger and hate, every bit of fear and worry, all poured out. He finally felt free.

~ ~ ~ O ~ ~ ~

Wendi followed Angie down the hallway. *Where is she taking me?* She wasn't sure where she was being led, but she trusted Angie. They walked past another row of cubicles and around the corner, stopping at a well-lit room. The sign next to the door read Conference Room A. Inside was a large table and eight comfy chairs. A cascade of light flooded the room through the wall of glass covering the opposite wall. They stepped through the door, pausing to take in the majestic view. Angie walked over to the windows, breathed in the beautiful scenery one more time, and closed the blinds.

The room darkened except for a few slivers of light piercing the edges of the blinds, giving off a faint glow. Angie pulled two chairs away from the conference table and set them facing each other.

"We're going to do a meditation to open your heart and connect you directly with your Guardian Angel," she said matter-of-factly.

"Um, meditate?" Wendi asked nervously, looking at the chairs. "I've never meditated in my life. I don't think I even know anyone who meditates."

"Well, you're about to learn, Deary." Angie chuckled. "You sit your little bottom down right here," she said, patting the chair and taking a seat across from her.

A look of hesitation still weighed on Wendi's face. "Aren't meditations for monks hiding in Tibetan mountains or people who do yoga and tai chi and stuff like that? You don't strike me as someone who does yoga, Angie. No offense."

"Yoga? Goodness, no!" She giggled. "Certainly no offense taken. This body isn't meant for yoga," she chuckled again. "But anyone can meditate, Dear. It's for everybody, no matter what age, sex, race, or even religion they are. God doesn't reserve his peace for monks in temples away from the rest of the world. His peace can be found at any time, regardless of where you are or what is happening around you. Meditation is a tool for connecting with things beyond our immediate third-dimensional minds."

"Well, when you put it that way," Wendi shifted in her seat, still a bit nervous. "I guess if you think I'm ready, I'll trust you."

"Yes," Angie replied. "You're more than ready, and that's why we're using meditation as a tool to open your heart and connect with your Angel, among other beings."

Other beings? Wendi didn't even want to go there. She had enough on her plate trying to grasp how she could possibly clear her cluttered mind. She was constantly thinking about the kids, Peter, work, whatever else she had to do for the day, and all the things that have gone wrong along the way. How could she connect with her Angel with all *that* going on in her mind?

"It's fine, dear. Just follow my lead, and I'll help guide you to where your heart wants to be."

"Okay. This just seems silly. So I'm supposed to close my eyes, and my Angel will just fly right up and say hello?"

Angie chuckled again. "Don't worry about a thing, Deary. There's nothing silly or difficult about what we're doing. I'll be guiding your mind to keep it preoccupied for you. You just close your eyes, listen to my voice, and follow my guidance. You'll manage just fine, Dear," she said in her usual sweet demeanor.

"I'll do my best."

"Well, that's perfect. The world would be a wonderful place if all we ever wanted of each other was for our best, without expecting any more or any less. You'll have the experience you are meant to have. I have complete faith in you."

Such simple words, and yet so extraordinarily powerful. Chills ran through Wendi's body. Her eyes glazed over and a warm smile graced her. *She hardly knows me, and yet she has more faith in me than I do in myself.* It touched Wendi to her core. It had been a long time since anyone believed in her, including herself.

"Thank you, Angie. Although I don't know why you believe in me so much. I'm no one special."

"Ah, but you are, Deary. You are very special. And that is what makes it so easy. Because despite the place you think you were stuck in, you don't want to be there anymore. I can see how tired you are of the life you have accepted over the past year. And I see how ready you are for change. *That* is why you already have."

Wendi sighed as her heart yearned for peace. Angie had a magical way of seeing through the walls people create for themselves. It was as if she could hear a person's soul whispering its deepest fears and accepted them fully. Overwhelmed by a release of emotions, Wendi reached out and grabbed Angie. Wrapping her arms around Angie's soft body, she sank in, sobbing. Wendi couldn't remember the last time she felt this safe, and for possibly the first time, she felt truly acknowledged.

She held on for what seemed like several minutes, much longer than expected. A wave of relief washed over her, and she eventually leaned back into her chair. Wiping her tears away, she smiled and offered her appreciation. "I'm sorry. I don't know what came over me. Thank you, Angie, for everything. I guess I really needed that."

"No need to ever be sorry for feeling, Dear. And it is *always* my pleasure. Take your time. We'll start when you're ready."

Wendi wiped away the remaining tears. "I'm okay. I'm ready," she replied with a little more conviction.

"Then let's get started. Close your eyes and relax."

Wendi shut her eyes and took a deep breath.

"Perfect, Dear, you're already ahead of me. Always good to start off with a few long, deep breaths to get you centered, present, and at ease. Breathe in again, slowly. Nice and deep, then slowly exhale."

Her voice subtly changed, coming down a few octaves from her peppy, cheery voice to a steady, slow, soothing tone. "Good. That's good. Continue to breathe slow and deep. Relax your body. Relax your toes, your legs, and your hips. Relax your torso and arms all the way to your fingertips. Relax your shoulders, your neck, and head. Now center yourself. Let your mind wander into the center of your being."

Wendi sank into the chair, allowing her body to be at peace with itself as she relaxed.

"Feel your heartbeat," Angie continued. "Connect with your own pulse, the life force within you. Feel the beat of your heart, and of your soul. Breathe in. Breathe out."

Sinking into a state of ease, Wendi let go of her worries and expectations and followed Angie's soothing voice. She took another long breath and slowly exhaled.

"Good. Now think about all the goodness in your life, all that you have to be grateful for. Feel it in your soul. Truly allow the feeling of gratitude to fill you up completely." Angie paused, also taking a deep breath, and continued.

"What can you be thankful for here and now? Your family? Your job? Your home? Your friends? Anything you can be grateful for, do so now. Think about those who have so little. No matter how little they own, they are still grateful for what they *do* have in their life. As long as you are breathing, you have something to be grateful for. Everything else is simply one more gift you have." She paused again, allowing Wendi time to bring in her gratitude.

Wendi let her mind drift away into her feelings. She felt happy. She felt calm. She felt thankful. She thought about her family. She was grateful for her children. She was grateful Bobby was shifting his attitude, grateful Faith was healthy, even if she didn't talk, and especially grateful for Peter, for still having his life. She felt like it was a second chance—for all of them. For that, she was truly, deeply, grateful. She breathed it all in, slowly. Deeply. Soulfully.

"Good. Very good, Dear," Angie continued. "Now I want you to go beyond your immediate self. What else can you feel thankful for? The air you breathe? The ground you walk on? The sky? The trees? Allow that feeling to grow. Allow the humility of gratitude to fill your heart, your chest, and your whole body. Allow that energy to expand out; beyond yourself; beyond me; beyond this room; beyond this building; and keep continuing outward." Wendi took another deep breath, and she expanded her consciousness outward. She felt herself floating away past the Earth, past the solar system, and melting into the grandness of the cosmos.

"Extend your gratitude again, giving thanks to Mother Earth for sustaining all life; for sharing herself with you. Now, share yourself with her. Feel yourself as part of her and she as part of you. Hear all of nature's sounds. Feel all of nature's love."

Wendi drifted off into a deeper state of being, completely detached from the office that her body sat inside. Her mind was far away from all the worries of her life. She saw herself in a clear meadow, with a big tree in the center. In the distance, a forest surrounded her. There were butterflies and dragonflies all around, and white doves flying overhead. She breathed it all in. She was at peace, grateful for her life, grateful to Mother Earth for all that she provided for humanity.

"Now voyage deep into the heart of Earth. Feel her pulse, her life force. Feel your heart beating in unison with hers. Imagine yourself connected to her, as one life." Angie stopped, allowing Wendi the space to connect and merge with the life-force of the Earth.

"We have journeyed inward, to the heart of physical life. Now we'll journey outward, into the source of all life. See yourself looking up at the stars. Feel the vastness and wonder of the Universe. Reach out to it. Thank it for holding and sustaining your home and your life. Expand your very essence outward from your own heart into the Universe. Expand your feeling of gratitude and wholeness beyond the Earth; beyond the moon; beyond the sun in all its radiance and life-giving energy. Expand beyond all the planets, past our solar system. Go beyond our galaxy, allowing it to fade away into clusters of infinite galaxies. Continue beyond, past all space, all time, outward, expanding into the infinite, until everything fades into a bright, pure white light." Bliss filled Wendi's mind. She was completely detached from her body, floating inside the nothingness that everything is part of.

"This is the source of the infinite where all things are created; where all is love in unmanifested expression. This is the highest realm, the source of the Creator, of Heaven, and of the Angels. Feel its radiance and beauty. Feel its Love. Feel the warmth of the light surrounding you and embracing you. It is part of you and you are part of it. Realize how much you are loved for being a part of all life. You are one with the light, one with the Infinite."

Wendi's consciousness traveled out beyond all that she knew and all she was. She was engulfed by a brilliant, pure white light. It was soothing to her eyes, vast and infinite. She felt all of existence surrounding her. She was at home.

"Now call out to your Angel. Ask your loving guardian to bless you with its presence. Feel its loving essence. Hear its soft whisper as it approaches."

Light surround Wendi, yet within the center of that light an even brighter light emerged. It moved toward her, slowly taking form. She felt a warmth in her heart and knew it was her Angel.

"Thank it for watching over you," Angie continued. "For loving you. Thank it for being in your life, even when you were not aware. Welcome it into your heart and into your being. You share the same spirit, the same love, the same life force."

Still following Angie's voice, Wendi watched as the light in front of her took a loose humanoid form. From the center of its chest, where its heart would be, a ray of light shot out, connecting their hearts together.

As if Angie could see what Wendi was experiencing, her words mirrored Wendi's vision. "Feel its love for you and allow yourself to be connected in love, heart to heart. Feel yourself breathing in unison, sharing each other's energy; each other's light; each other's love. You are now connected beyond the physical, through bonds of unconditional love. Set an intention to stay connected to your Angel, always. Give it permission to enter your earthly life to guide and protect you; to help and to love you. The loving chord of light connecting you will always remain." Angie sat there quietly for a moment, empathically connected to what Wendi was experiencing.

Angie gave her a few more moments, then eased her back. "You may thank your Angel, and take your leave. You may begin your journey back to your body. Allow the light to fade away and feel yourself floating back ... back through the stars ... back into our solar system ... floating back to the Earth ... into this building ... into this chair ... and into your body. Breath in the air around you and allow it to fill your cells, feeling each inch of your physical body. Wiggle your fingers and toes. Roll your shoulders. And once you feel completely present, gently open your eyes."

Angie gracefully opened her eyes as well, awaiting Wendi to open hers. Angie could sense Wendi's humility and peace, her face filled with an expression of gratitude. Wendi slowly opened her eyes, now bright and radiating with love.

"Welcome back," Angie greeted. "You did wonderful, Dear. Take a few deep breaths to get you back to the present."

Wendi gently breathed in and out, grounding herself back into her body. Still overwhelmed with emotion, she couldn't begin to express what she was feeling. Tears filled the corners of her eyes and an indescribable feeling radiated from her being.

"There's no need to talk, Deary. Just hold onto the feeling. It's a beautiful, sunny day. I think the best thing you could do for yourself right now is to get some fresh air and a little nature. Take your lunch with you, go for a short drive, and find a nice spot to let this all sink into your consciousness."

"Wh ... where am I supposed to go?" Wendi asked quietly, not quite feeling like her voice was her own.

"Learn to trust, Dear. Trust yourself. Trust your instincts. Trust your intuition. Now not another word. Stay with the feeling. As quietly as you can, grab your lunch, and go spend some time alone, away from all this chaotic work energy. Things are going to be happening fast for you, now, Deary. I can feel it. It's important that you take even just small moments of time to let yourself integrate your experiences and feelings into your consciousness. You've spent a lot of years closed down, and suddenly opening up can come as a shock to the system. But you'll be fine, Sweetie. You'll be just fine."

You'll be just fine, Sweetie. That was the first time Angie used a term of endearment other than Dear or Deary. It was the same term Wendi's father always said to her when she was upset, and he was always right. He still says it now, but ever since the plane, she stopped believing him. When Angie said it, though, Wendi knew she was right. She'd be just fine.

As Wendi stood up, she almost fell over. She felt weightless, still on a high from the meditation. It was like nothing she had experienced before. She felt like she was about to float away. She hugged Angie, thanked her, and headed to the break room to grab her lunch. The catty three were so enthralled with themselves that they didn't even notice Wendi until she was halfway out the door. She got into her car and turned the key. She didn't have much time left on her lunch break, so wherever she was going, it had to be close.

I'm supposed to find a place, eat lunch, and get back in time? She turned the car key, still having no idea where she was headed or how she was supposed to get there.

Trust. Angie said to trust. She took a breath and put the car in Drive. *Okay. I'm trusting. Angel, guide me to where I'm going!* She took her foot off the brake and headed out in faith.

~ o ~

Chapter 9:

Accepting the Signs

*"Keep an open mind and
never be afraid to follow your heart."*

~ o ~

Do I just drive around in circles? Wendi didn't know where to go, nor did she feel like eating her sandwich by the side of the road. She wasn't familiar with the immediate area, especially if it wasn't something she passed going to and from work. She felt a nudge to turn right out of the parking lot, the opposite direction of her home. As Wendi approached the next intersection, she wasn't getting any other nudges. She pulled up to the stop sign at the end of the road. *Well? Now what? I could use a sign, Angel.*

She looked both ways, noticing an orange road-closed sign on the left. A breeze blew through, shaking a tree branch across the road in front of her. The waving branch caught her attention, as she suddenly noticed a detour sign. Her only option was to go right. *Great. Now I'll really be lost.* She turned, following the detour. At the next corner, the detour had her turning again. *Angie, this can't be what you meant by following signs!* She sat at the intersection for a moment, shaking her head. *Okay, Angie. I'm literally following the signs.* She laughed to herself and turned the corner, still following the detour.

Wendi pulled up to a red light and stopped. *Where am I?* She looked to her right and noticed a park with a little sign at the entrance that read: Serenity Park. She laughed. *Are you kidding? Well, this certainly seems like an appropriate after-meditation lunch spot.* Wendi turned in, parked the car, and stepped into the warm sunlight. The park was scarce of people except for a few mothers with their toddlers on the swings in the playground. Picking at some crumbs, several pigeons roamed the grassy area and picnic benches in front of her.

Among the myriad of gray feathers pecking around, something caught her eye. It stood out like a ray of light piercing through a cloudy sky. It was a single white bird. *It can't be.* Wendi stepped closer. She had never seen a pure white pigeon before. As she stepped closer, all the gray pigeons scattered. The white bird stayed where it was, even as Wendi got closer. Wendi didn't know much about birds, but something deep inside her knew exactly what it was. This was the same white dove she saw flying into the sun when she hit Pete's car; the same one she saw again on her drive home from the hospital.

She took another step closer, and it stretched its wings out and took off soaring through the air. A voice on the wind whispered, *Follow.*

The span of white feathers hooked around some evergreens and out of sight. Wendi hurried along, following her albino friend to the wall of trees. As she stepped around to the other side, she stopped in her tracks. She gently placed her hand over her heart and stood there, staring. She wanted to speak, but no words emerged, only feelings of awe and disbelief. *Am I on Candid Camera? How is this possibly here? How am I possibly here?*

Wendi stepped into the clearing. It was surrounded by a ring of trees, and green grass encircled an object in the center. There, perched on top of a raised hand was her noble white dove. Basking in the sunlight, it stood—a magnificent winged Angel in the center of a fountain. The statue's head was held high, looking toward the heavens. Its arms were outstretched and raised up, reaching for the sky. And behind it, big beautiful wings stretched out over the water. The sun shone down brightly, reflecting off of the water and gently caressing the surface of the Angel. Ripples of light danced up the flowing dress and along its wings. The light brought them to life, as if it had magical feathers fluttering in the breeze. It was truly a sight to behold.

Wendi walked closer, shuddering in amazement. Still floating on high from her meditation, she felt as if she had fallen into a dream. *Detour signs, my white dove, and now I'm standing in front of a magical Angel fountain? How is this possibly happening? I'm either blessed or batshit crazy,* she laughed to herself.

Approaching the statue, she gazed up at its face. Her little white friend, still perched atop it, looked down at her. The glare of the afternoon sun peeked out from behind the wings of the Angel, blinding her view. "Jesus," she blurted out, flinching. She shielded her eyes and stepped forward, trying to avoid the glare. She tripped, stubbing her toe on something. "What the?" She looked down to see what she tripped over, and there at her feet was a plaque with something written on it.

She leaned in and read the inscription: *For he shall give his Angels charge over thee, to keep thee in all thy ways. They shall bear thee up in their hands, lest thou dash thy foot against a stone. ~ Psalm 91:11-12*

"Are you kidding?" she cried out loud, followed by a laugh, as the throbbing in her toe subsided. *Apparently, Angels have a sense of humor along with their incredible gift of irony.* "Who stubs their toe on a plaque that says that!" She laughed again, shaking her head in disbelief at the entire string of events that had just unfolded.

Mesmerized by the gentle wind creating soft ripples in the water, Wendi stepped around the plaque, moving closer to the edge of the fountain. As she watched the reflection of the Angel in the water, her own reflection came into view, overlapping it. The duel reflections created the appearance that she herself, had wings. She looked down, seeing an angelic vision of herself staring back.

"This isn't some coincidence or accident," she began, talking to herself. "Getting a flat tire from a pothole is an accident. Doing an Angel meditation, then going for a drive and following a detour to Serenity Park, then following a white dove to a fountain that has a statue of an Angel, and then seeing this ... It's a miracle ... It really is."

As she stood there taking it all in, overwhelming feelings of awe, wonder, and gratitude filled her heart. Her body shuddered as a tear escaped, blessing her cheek.   Out of the corner of her eye, she noticed a bench next to the fountain. She took a seat and peacefully ate her lunch in the presence of her Angel.

It was a perfect day. The meditation was amazing. The park was beautiful. The statue was magnificent. Even stubbing her toe on the plaque was perfect. Wendi wasn't sure if she could handle a more perfect day without some tragedy occurring just to balance it out. It all seemed too strange and coincidental, which is why she knew it had to be real.

Her eyes continued to water as the gratitude within blossomed. *It's perfect. Everything is perfect. Thank you, God. Thank you, Angel.*

As she took the last bite of her sandwich, she heard a flutter. Looking up just in time, she caught a glimpse of her little angelic friend flying off, ascending into the sunlight.

~~~ O ~~~

A presence stood in the doorway. Pete reluctantly looked up to find The Marshal guarding his office. *Wow, only took half the day for him to come see me. He really seems to care.*

"Peter, good to see you're feeling well and finally back in action again," came an unwanted but inevitable greeting. "I was afraid we might have to replace you. With a temp, of course."

"Of course. It's good to be back, sir," Pete spat out, trying not to choke on his words. *Is this guy for real? My first day back, and he doesn't even ask how I am?*

"I'm just joking. But if you were going to be out much longer, I would've needed to reallocate your workload, and neither of us wants to go through that. It's so much better that you came back to work early to take care of things yourself. It's appreciated and doesn't go unnoticed."

"The doctors wanted me home a full seven days, but ..." Peter thought cautiously about how to respond, keeping his thoughts to himself. *But you'd rather work me to death, literally.* "But as you said, I feel better doing the work myself instead of you needing to hand it off to someone else who will probably just botch it up and come back to me anyway."

"See, you understand these things. You may be manager material someday after all," he topped off with a slight laugh. "I'll be honest. It was very discouraging to hear the news, but I was relieved to hear you were okay."

So you didn't have to scurry to find a replacement, you mean.

"I'm sure you understand why I couldn't speak to you directly. Always meeting about something around here. Am I right?" He said with a laugh, hoping Pete would join in. "There's a lot more responsibility at my level than yours, obviously. Maybe if you ever become a manager, you'll understand. So, how are you feeling?"

Pete swallowed, trying hard to keep his level of annoyance in check. *There it is. Maybe he has a soul after all.* "I'm doing surprisingly well. The doctors said I was lucky to come out of my coma as quickly as I did with no real damage. Thank you for asking."

"Well, of course. I like to know how my people are doing," he offered with a nod. "I knew you had a heart attack, but you didn't mention the coma when you left me your message. Looks like we're all fortunate that it didn't last. Anyway, good to hear you're well. I know you have a lot to do, and Lord knows I'd love for you to be here all night catching up, but we want you to take it easy now. The lawyers said so," he joked, laughing again. "I'm just joking with you. Apparently, I've been so serious around here, it nearly killed you," he added, still snickering.

Pete just smiled, keeping his comments to himself as he thought about how true to life The Marshal's words really were.

"Well, you have a good day. Take as many breaks as you need, and I'll stop back later to check in on you again." With that, The Marshal turned, stepped out of the doorway, and marched down the hall.

"Thanks for caring, Mr. Marshall," Pete mumbled sarcastically to himself as his boss walked off. *Prick.*

"Wendi, I was looking *all* over for ya, and I got the eyes of a hawk," Patty burst out. "Where on Earth were ya for lunch?"

Wendi thought about the meditation and the irony of the question. *Where on Earth was I, indeed.* "I'm not even sure. Out of my mind, I guess you could say." She couldn't help but smile at her own little inside joke. "I needed some fresh air, went for a drive, and had a lovely lunch at this amazing park just around the corner."

"Mmm hmm. I'm getting worried about ya. You've been spendin' quite a bit of time with Angie, and now you're driving off to sit alone in parks like an old person. Somethin' funny's goin' on with y'all." She stopped, quickly raising her hand to her mouth. "*Oh. My. God.* Are you joinin' her cult?"

"No. Nothing like that, Patty. We're just fine. You can stop worrying about us. Angie has been a great support, really. I feel like things are really changing at home and changing for myself, too ... Even if I may be questioning my sanity," Wendi chuckled, making a joke of it.

"Mmm hmm, well that makes two of us, Darlin'! Well, if she starts making you cut off chicken heads, ya better start runnin' and come see me straight away!"

"Patty, I appreciate your concern, but you may want to try getting to know someone instead of just believing rumors about them. Especially the rumors you're starting." Wendi laughed again.

"Well, I'll be. I would take offense to that .. if it weren't just a little bit true," she laughed. It was good to see Patty didn't take herself too seriously.

"Angie is nothing like what you think," Wendi refuted. "She's very kind, and you're more likely to catch her talking to Angels than killing chickens. You should have a serious conversation with her. You may be surprised. She's an amazing woman."

"Mmm hmm. There's that Kool-Aid talkin' again. So she's one of those re-birthed Christians, talkin' to Angels, is she? That may be even worse than those Hairy Krishnas!"

"They're called Born Again Christians, Patty. And I believe it's Hare Krishna."

"Yeah, one of those, too."

"A lot of people believe in Angels. You're Christian, Patty. Don't you believe in Angels?"

"Sure, I do. And I believe in the Lord Jesus as well, but it don't mean I sit around havin' full-on conversations with the man. He's busy savin' all the sinners. I say my prayers and leave it at that. I don't never hear any voices talkin' back to me. Lord help me if I did! I go about my business and they take care of things from up there ... Assuming they see me worthy, which I'm sure they do, of course. Anyway, enough about our Lord and Savior. I gotta get some work done. Just wanted to make sure you were doin' all right, Darlin'." With that, she nodded and sunk back below the wall. Wendi turned to face her desk, but before she was even halfway around, Patty's head popped back up.

"Goodness me, I almost forgot. Are you and Pete still gettin' along? Didn't you mention havin' a lovely evnin' with him the other night? Mmmmm, hmmmmm! I know what that means, no details needed here—unless you want to provide them, of course!"

"We're doing just fine. Thank you. And no details. Sorry. Goodbye, Patty," Wendi said, turning back to her monitor.

Patty began to sink back down, popping right up again like a girl on a pogo-stick. "So where's this amazin' park that's got ya all excited?"

ca-clink ca-clink ca-clink

"Whatcha stirring up there, Pete?" Allen asked. "I'm sure it wouldn't be a cup o' Joe, now would it? And with a morning doughnut next to it as well? Now, I'm no doctor, but I'm guessing you oughta stay off caffeine and sugar, at least while you're recovering. Not good for your ticker, my friend."

"For crap's sake, not you, too, Allen," Pete blurted out. "Can't a guy enjoy a cup of coffee? I get enough of that now at home."

"Well then, it's a dandy good thing I'm here to keep you in line at work. Can't a guy enjoy his life and still sacrifice a few amenities? It's not worth it. Not for a crappy cup of coffee."

"I'm pretty sure the jury is still out on the effects of caffeine, but we'll save that debate for another time," Pete insisted. "You always have to be the voice of reason, don't you, Allen?"

"Well, someone has to be around here! Nice to know you're being kept in line at home. Speaking of which, it sounded like Wendi's getting back to her old self, but did you mention something about her feeling the Spirit? You want to tell me more about what's happening with her? You seemed a little concerned."

"Yeah," Pete shook his head. "Don't get me wrong, things are better than they've been in a *long* time. But she's just been acting a little strange. She even started up about ... well, she said she saw a ... ah, don't worry about it. I just know things are the best they've been since the move, so that's all that matters, right?"

"Well, that's good to hear, but come on, now. You know you can talk about anything with me. Spill it. And I don't mean the coffee ... Well, actually, I do," he chuckled. "Now, what's going on with the wife?"

"It's nothing, really. She just had this thing about seeing an Angel-shaped cloud, but it's not a big deal, really."

"Well, that sounds just marvelous, Pete!" Allen burst out, to Pete's surprise. "I mean it, now. That's something special. We've all seen shapes in the clouds, you and me both, but I don't think I've ever seen one shaped like an Angel. What a blessing for her!"

"I have to admit it, Allen, I'm a little surprised by your response. Not that there's anything wrong with it. I just had a ... *different* reaction. I wish I could see the world through your eyes," Pete remarked, now questioning his attitude about it. *Maybe I was too hard on her.*

"It's just a matter of perspective, Pete. I tell ya, it makes all the difference in life. If more people would change their view on situations instead of getting all worked up about the little things, there'd be a lot more happy people in the world. Now, you told me she lost her faith after that horrible accident. And now it sounds like she's finally embracing it again after all that's happened. If it's true, that's something you ought to encourage, not reject. I tell ya, God's always looking out for us, Pete, even when we're not looking out for Him."

Pete took a moment, reflecting on Allen's words. "You're right again, Allen. Thanks for always being the voice of reason. She says her prayers saved me. She thinks God sent down an Angel for us."

"And don't you doubt it for a second, my friend. God can do wondrous things. He created us, He can destroy us, and He certainly has the power to save us."

"I'm just worried about her swinging too far to the other side."

"Pete, do I really hear what you're saying correctly? Your wife prayed to God to save your life, and you're standing here before me, alive and well, complaining?"

"You're right, Allen. *Again.* I just … well … No, you're right."

"Come on now, Pete. Let me take a step back. Yes, I feel like you might be overreacting a bit, but there's something about it that's bothering you, and *that* is worth talking through. Why's it got you so off kilter?"

Pete hesitated, feeling the genuine concern Allen had for him. "It's more than her just praying when I had my heart attack. Along with seeing Angels in the clouds, she was going on about hearing songs, and magical birds, and I swear I heard her mention something about our mute daughter talking to an Angel—which I guess is better than her first guess—a ghost. I didn't even touch that one. And it seems to be coming from this woman at work, and Wendi got real defensive about it all."

"And who's this woman?" asked Allen.

"If I'm remembering correctly, her name is Angie. Apparently, she's a new temp at Wendi's work, filling her head with a little too much nonsense for my taste. We talked about her a little, but if I didn't know better, I'd think the woman is running a cult. I'm just worried if this keeps up, I'm going to have a wife that's not one of God's spiritual fruits, but another religious nut!" Pete chuckled to himself.

"Well, maybe you should find out a little more about this Angie. Perhaps even meet her for yourself. Honestly, if things are getting better with Wendi, and if this woman is so important to your wife, invite Angie over for dinner. Get to know her yourself before your gavel of judgment comes raining down on the poor woman. And a word of caution … Even if she's a little too far out there, if it's a positive change, you may want to pick your battles."

"Ding ding ding—we have a winner!" Pete enthusiastically called out. "That's the *third* time in this short conversation that you've been my voice of reason. You are right *again*, my friend. I don't know what I would do without you. I will absolutely take that advice with the greatest consideration. But honestly, I think she's over the worst of it. I mean, she's just a temp at work who Wendi hardly knows or sees. Maybe I'm overreacting. After all, how much more influence could this Angie really have over her in just a few days?"

~~~ O ~~~

"I want to spend every minute I have with you, Angie," Wendi vowed. "My life has become a non-stop wonder. It's like I'm living in a dream. I still can't believe it." Wendi expressed as she filled her mug with hot water, submerging a bag of herbal tea. She stared in a daze as feelings of awe sent shivers up her spine.

Angie smiled, letting out one of her jovial laughs as she poured some honey into her mug. She loved her afternoon tea breaks. The flavor of the day was chamomile ginger, which she was delighted to share with Wendi. "You may want to start telling yourself you *do* believe it," she advised.

"It's funny," Wendi realized, "just how much negative language has become commonplace. I need to pay more attention to my words," she added with a nod, releasing the red handle of the hot water.

A joyous smile swept across Angie's lips. "I'm so proud of you, Deary. Just look at how quickly you've accepted all this. And with such an open heart. And now that you've created a stronger, more personal connection to your Angel, the gap between Heaven and Earth is one step closer for ya." she attested.

"Remember," Angie continued, "Angels are on a much higher plane of existence than we are, but they consciously bring themselves down to our vibration to enter our lives. That's *really* how an Angel comes down from Heaven. It's our belief that creates the portal bridgin' the gap among realities, dimensions, and realms. The energy behind our free will is one of the greatest powers in the Universe. So maintain a strong connection with your Angel, Dear, and the miracles will continue to flow," she insisted, taking a cautious sip of her tea.

Wendi listened intently as she watched the stream of honey slowly fill her spoon. She was amazed, as always, at Angie's knowledge on a subject that was rarely discussed among regular people.

"I've been at this for a long time," Angie went on, "and every day the Universe still surprises me. You've only seen the tip of the iceberg. There's always more to learn, Dear. So much more, that you'll be right back to tellin' me you don't believe it!"

"How much more do I really need to know? You've already taught me so much."

Angie chuckled, flashing her contagious smile. "We live in an infinite universe, Dear, so there's no end to our evolution, as impossible as that may sound."

"I can't imagine—oh, sorry," Wendi caught herself. "I *can* imagine how much more there is to come," she laughed as she stirred in the honey. "It feels so surreal, Angie. Part of me thinks I'm making it up. Like maybe I'm seeing things and making connections in my head that aren't really there," Wendi replied, lifting her mug up and pausing just before it hit her lips. "The only thing keeping me sane is that it all *feels* so right. The meditation was the most amazing thing I ever felt … Well, aside from the chills and feeling I got when I saw the Angel cloud. Oh, and in the car on the ride home from the hospital. Wow, I guess this is becoming a regular feeling," she said with a beaming smile.

Just as fast as she lit up, her demeanor shifted as she looked off into the distance. "I wonder what Pete's going to think about all this. I don't even know if I can tell him," she admitted, saying it more to herself than to Angie. She looked back at Angie and her energy shifted again. "And the park ... I had chills running through my whole body all the way back to the office. I'm still feeling it now," she attested, looking down at the goosebumps on her arm. "And my heart feels like it wants to fly away."

"How perfect. Life is *supposed* to feel good, Deary. It means you're on the right path," affirmed Angie as she took another sip of her tea.

"Yes, but then the next minute, I feel absolutely *crazy*, Angie. Questioning everything!"

"That's perfect, too, Dear. Only by questioning can we find the answers that are true to us. You're feelin' truth and having experiences you were meant to have and feel your entire life ... but they've been shielded from you by a world that prefers to stay asleep."

Angie caressed Wendi's shoulder, gently rubbing it. "All of what you're feelin', the good and the bad, is a good feelin' to have, Deary. It's part of the process. You need to question everything, includin' yourself, and the Universe will continue to confirm the *right* path for you. The truth of all things lies within our own hearts. If it *feels* right, then it *is* right ... for you. Maybe Peter won't understand, and maybe he will, and maybe he needs time and experiences of his own. Open him up a little at a time, Deary. When people open too fast, many of them will reject it as a natural defense mechanism. People are afraid of change. They are afraid of things they don't understand. They want to stay safe in their ignorant bubbles. And I mean no offense by that, Dear."

"All of life," she continued, "is a matter of perspective. The truth of the Universe is that even the truth is relative. We can all listen to the same story, and yet we will only hear the part that calls to us, the part that is meant for our ears. And even *that* is filtered through our perspective and beliefs. Even a single word can have drastically different meanings and invoke different feelin's and responses from different people. We each truly live in our own world. Everyone else is just peerin' in from afar."

Angie's expression changed slightly as she held a deep connection to Wendi. "It's very important you only believe what feels right in *your* heart. Don't just believe somthin' because someone else says it … Not even if it's coming from me, Deary."

Wendi stared in shock. *Why would she say that?* About to take her first sip of tea, she lowered the mug. "What are you talking about, Angie? Every word you utter amazes me. I *am* going to listen to everything you say. Before I met you, the only thing I knew about Angels was from Bible stories."

"Well, Dear, there are plenty of stories and beliefs out there about Angels, but even the Bible doesn't really give light to the true relationships we're capable of havin' with God, Angels, or even with our own divinity. In my heart, I don't believe Angels would ever bring death and destruction," Angie went on. "They deliver the same message they always have: that all creation is love and that *we* are the divine, magical beings. Heck, even God wouldn't deliver the wrath of God—He's too loving!" She chuckled again.

"Most of the stories that feel truest to me come from folklore and myths. But any story, no matter how true, is still a story. It's a tale passed down from generation to generation and meant to entertain as well as teach. They're always embellished, and always have some truth to them. Even Jesus told his wisdom in parables, never givin' outright answers. That's one of the qualities of a true master. Truth is meant to be learned and experienced for ourselves, not just taken as fact because someone else experienced somethin'," she insisted, taking another sip of her soothing tea.

"Oh my! Here I am veering off course again," Angie chuckled. "Gettin' back to what I said. Trust yourself, even over me. And I mean that, now. One day, you may find a truth beyond, or even contradictory, to what I'm telling you, and that's okay. Every truth is true until another truth comes along, Dear. The Universe gives us the truths we can handle at the moment. As we evolve, so does the truth."

Still holding her full cup of tea, Wendi stood in amazement and awe once again at the wisdom of Angie. "Well, right now my heart tells me to keep listening to your stories, Angie. Tangents, rambles, and all." Wendi offered a humble smile and a nod of respect and recognition to her angelic guru.

"Thank you, Deary. And it's my pleasure. Just keep an open mind and never be afraid to follow your heart. It's the only way you'll continue to grow. Your story will be yours alone. And even those you share it with will see it differently than you do. But that, Dear, is part of the absolute beauty and wonder of this existence. One simple moment of life can have a thousand meanings, a thousand significances, and ignite a thousand emotions—all different, all beautiful, and all right."

Wendi stood there listening, still holding her mug halfway to her mouth.

"Now, I know you love hearing me yap away, Deary. God bless ya for that, but let's get a little work done, shall we?" she questioned, motioning to the door.

A look of disappointment crossed Wendi's face as they shuffled out of the break room. "How can I concentrate on work with all these miracles happening around me? This is the only work that feels important right now, Angie."

"You don't know how true those words are, Deary," Angie agreed. She stepped into her cubicle and took a seat at her whimsically decorated desk. "But until we collectively manifest Heaven on Earth, we still have bills to pay. Now get goin' and drink your tea before it gets cold, Dear," she advised with a friendly wink, setting her half-empty mug on the desk next to a white feather.

Wendi looked at her mug, still full, and took a sip, noticing the feather. "Why do you have a feather on your desk?"

"It's a gift from my Angel, that's why. I get them in the darnedest ways. Just like any angelic sign, I'll find them when I least expect it, in the most unlikely places," Angie divulged. "You won't believe how I got this one ... or maybe you will," she added with a smile.

~~~ O ~~~

Wendi turned the key, feeling the low rumble of the engine starting. Her ride home was never very long, but it had been enough time to manifest a miraculous and radiant cloud yesterday.

She took a deep breath and whispered to herself, "Okay, Angel, let's keep the blessings and signs coming so I know I'm not just making all this up. Please send me another sign that you're with me. And I know you're supposed to do it on your own time, but for my own sanity, please send it by the time I walk into my house. Thank you. Amen."

The entire ride home, Wendi's gaze was fixated on the sky. She was desperately searching for another cloud and occasionally glancing at passing road signs for some deeper meaning. She almost went the wrong way to follow a detour sign for a road she wasn't taking, then thought better of it. *Nothing.* The closer she got to home, the greater her feeling of disappointment grew. She turned into the driveway and pulled into the garage with a disjointed heart. She put the car in Park and turned the key. She sat there in the silence, feeling abandoned, questioning her sanity.

I guess this isn't how it works. Maybe I'm asking for too much. Did I miss it? Could I have driven by a sign and not seen it? She shook it off, trying to center herself. She opened the door and stepped out, pausing for a moment to recall the amazing day she had.

Maybe I'm being greedy. I had a mind-blowing meditation, was visited by my white dove, and saw my reflection as an Angel in the Angel fountain. What more could I ask for in one day? I can't wait to share it all with Pete. As she headed down the driveway to grab the mail, she had second thoughts. *I may have to keep it to myself. Especially after all the crap I got over a cloud!*

Wendi strolled up the driveway with the mail in her hand, shuffling through it all. *Junk. Bill. Bill. Junk—*

Out of the corner of her eye, she thought she saw a flicker of light. *Is that the sign?* She looked up toward the front door but saw nothing. Then her ear picked up a flutter of wings overhead. *Is that the sign?* She looked up at the sky, thinking her little white friend from the park was back, but saw nothing. She surveyed the trees, the roof, and the sky. *Nothing.* That was all. No Angel children at her door. No white dove above. No other birds; no animals; not even a squirrel. Nothing but calm.

Feeling like she missed something, she looked around again, but saw and heard nothing. Her heart sank again.

She continued her walk toward the house, flipping through the last few pieces of mail. *Junk. Junk. And more Jun—*

She stopped. As she was shifting the last piece of junk mail to the back of the pile, something caught her eye. She shifted the envelope back to the top of the pile. In the corner was a white bird flying into rays of sunlight. It was eerily similar to the first time she saw her little angelic friend. It was from the Church of Jesus Christ of Latter-day Saints. Across the front of the envelope were the words: Looking for a Sign? Look Inside…

You've got to be kidding. She flipped it over, ripped open the flap, and took out the pamphlet inside. The heading read: Looking for a sign? You found one.

Wendi let out a loud laugh. *I see your sense of humor is still shining through, my Angel.* She looked up, hoping her dove was back, but was only greeted by a beautiful blue sky. Even though she was disappointed not to have a grander sign after the spectacle she had witnessed the day prior, she still accepted the flyer as an answer to her request—she had her sign.

Suddenly, the front door swung open, catching her off guard. Startled, she flinched, dropping the mail. Bobby stood in the front doorway, questionably looking at his mother. "Mom, what are you doing? And what are you looking at? And what was so funny? I heard your laugh through the door."

She looked up at her son with a blank stare, not knowing how to explain it. "Oh, I just found a piece of junk mail amusing," she answered as she gathered the strewn mail off the ground. The envelope from the Latter-day Saints was just out of reach, laying on the doorstep. She stepped closer, noticing something sticking out from under the corner with the image of the bird. *It can't be.* She lifted the envelope, and there, lying on the doorstep, gently rocking in the breeze, was a brilliant white feather.

She looked up at Bobby, who was still standing in the doorway, then down at the feather again, as if to contest her own eyes. *I knew I heard the sound of wings,* she thought as she reached over and picked it up. It was the softest, lightest feather she had ever felt. It had an opalescent glow as it shimmered in the light. Somehow, it contained a hint of every color of the rainbow reflecting in its purity, and yet it was the brightest white she had ever seen. She caressed it gently in her palm, then shifted her eyes up to the front door. Bobby was still standing there with a look of concern.

"You see this, right?" she asked her son, holding up the feather.

The expression of bewilderment on his face stayed the same, other than his eyebrows raising a little higher. "Uh, yeah, mom, I see it. It's just a feather."

"Don't be so sure it's *just* a feather," she responded with a smile. Bobby gave a half-hearted smile in return. "Sure, Mom," he replied, nodded, and walked off into the house. He pushed the door closed behind him but didn't use enough force, leaving the door slightly ajar.

It's okay. It's not for him. And it's probably not for Pete, either. I'll just keep it to myself, she thought, trying not to allow his response to diminish her amazement. She looked left and then right, seeing if any of the neighbors were out. The neighborhood was empty. Slowly, she held the feather up to her face and allowed its silky texture to softly caress her cheek. *It's an Angel feather. It has to be.* She melted in its gentle touch and whispered,

"Thank you." Still enthralled in the feeling, she began running it through her fingers and—

honk!

Wendi jumped, dropping the mail again.

A moment prior, Pete was rounding the corner, about to pull into the driveway. *Maybe he's right,* Pete thought as he rehashed his conversation with Allen in his mind. *Maybe I shouldn't look a gift horse in the mouth. A wife who literally believes in Angels is better than a wife who doesn't believe in anything.*

Lost in thought, he slowly pulled into the driveway. As he reached up to hit the garage door button, he paused, hitting the brake as well. The scene in front of him was mind-boggling. The front door was partially ajar, and standing in front of the doorstep was his wife. She was holding a scattered pile of mail in one hand, and an empty envelope was blowing through the yard. Her eyes were closed, and if he didn't know any better, she was experiencing some sort of bliss. *How did she not hear the car pull up?* She was just standing there. And with her other hand, she was caressing her face with a white feather. *What the fu—*

honk!

Wendi looked over, shocked out of her bliss and also quite embarrassed, and gathered up the mail. Pete pulled into the garage. Still not sure what he had just witnessed, he closed the garage door behind him, assuming his wife would be entering through the front door, which was still open, inviting flies inside.

"I'm home!" Pete shouted, despite there being no reply these days. He used to love announcing himself upon arriving home from work. In the early days, Wendi would greet him with a kiss. Once the kids came along, they took first place, running ahead of Wendi to give him a big hug and yap about something menial that was extremely exciting to them.

Those days were gone. Bobby was too old for such affection from his father, and although he might occasionally still get a warm hug from his little Angel, there was no more shouting, laughing, or warm greetings from her. He had given up on receiving kisses from his wife after the move. And although things had changed with her, this evening he had obviously been replaced by a feather.

He put down his briefcase and rounded the corner, hoping to see his smiling little girl. He was greeted, but by an awkward smile from his wife instead.

"Hello, Darling," Wendi nervously blurted out as she placed the mail on the counter. In her other hand, she still held the Latter-day flyer, and behind it, the feather. *I have to tell him.* "It's not what you think … or maybe it is." *I mean TWO signs? Maybe he'll finally get it.* "Okay. You're going to think I'm crazy." she blurted out as her nervous tone began changing to one of excitement. "I can't even begin to explain my day, but I feel like I've been guided and receiving signs from our Angel all day!"

"Oh, have you?" Pete asked doubtfully, trying to retain his composure. *Remember what Allen said.* "Did you see another cloud?" he asked, trying to support his wife's enthusiasm.

"No, no more clouds," she replied. But I saw this," she said, handing him the flyer, while she hid the feather behind her back in her other hand.

"Uh, and what's this?" he asked, taking it from her. "Is Angie a Latter-day Saint? Does she want us to convert or something?" he asked, afraid of the answer.

"No, don't be silly, Hun."

Thank God. Yeah, silly me.

"Read it," she exclaimed, pointing to the headline. "It says, Looking for a sign? You found one. I mean, come on. Even you can't refute that."

Squinting his face in an expression of doubt, he answered with a nod. "I'm pretty sure I can. It's a piece of junk mail, Hun.

We get them all the time. Probably once a month. It's just a coincidence. A cloud is one thing, but I'm not sure this really counts as a sign from Heaven."

"It's not just junk. It literally says we found a *sign*."

"Well, it literally says: You found one," he responded sarcastically, trying to lighten his own concerns. "I'm sorry," he apologized, catching himself. "I shouldn't be joking right now." *Okay, Pete. What would Allen say?* "But ... I can understand why you'd be excited about it."

"Okay. Fine. I thought the paper alone wouldn't win you over. So then how do you explain this?" she asked, raising up her arm and revealing her single, white feather.

Pete took a step back, distancing himself from the feather waving in his face. "Ah, okay. What am I missing?" he asked, scratching his head. *Allen, I need you, buddy.* Pete racked his brain, trying to come up with a reason to share his wife's excitement. She held the feather up, waiting for some divine revelation to strike her husband. *Okay. It's her journey. Try to be understanding.* "Oh, I get it."

"You do?" Wendi asked with a burst of excitement.

"Yes. Last week, when we had the little ... accident in the driveway ... You said it was because you saw a white bird. See, I pay attention," he said proudly. "So you're excited about the feather because it's from the white bird ... from a week ago." *Which wouldn't still be on our doorstep, or even in our neighborhood, a week later.*

"Well, yes. No. Maybe." *At least he's catching on. Maybe he'll get it.* "I *swear* I heard the flutter of wings, but I looked around and didn't see a bird *anywhere*. But I also don't think the bird is really a bird. I mean, it's like a messenger," she paused, realizing she was on the edge of sounding crazy again. "Anyway, have you ever seen anything so beautiful? I still can't believe it. It appeared out of nowhere." She was filled with so much excitement, her words were leaping off her lips. She looked up with her best puppy dog eyes, deep into her husband's questioning gaze.

"This is *way* beyond a bunch of coincidences. I need to explain the full chain of events, so you'll understand it all. So first I meditated with Angie today—"

"Wait, what? *You* meditated?"

"Yeah, it was amazing, but just let me tell you everything first," she insisted, taking a deep breath. "So I *meditated*, and then went for a drive and followed the detours, and saw the white bird, and found this amazing Angel statue, and stubbed my toe on the Angel plaque," she began, rambling on with building enthusiasm. "and then asked for a sign on the way home, and got here, and still didn't have a sign, and got the mail, and there was an image of *white dove* flying into the sun on the corner of the envelope, I mean, what are the chances, and the envelope *literally* asked if I was looking for a sign, and I opened it, and it *literally* said I found one, and then Bobby opened the door, and I dropped the mail, and there was nothing on the doorstep where it landed, and Bobby will tell you that because he was right there when I dropped it, and then when I picked up the flyer—that had fallen on the doorstep with nothing on it— under the flyer ... was *this* white feather. It *literally* appeared out of nowhere. Can you believe it?"

Pete stared for a moment, trying to find the words. "Uh, no ... I mean, yes, I can't believe it," he joked. *Allen, I need YOU to appear out of nowhere.* "Well, wherever it came from, I can tell you're excited about it." *Remember, spiritual nut is better than nothing. Hold it together, Pete.*

"Come on. After all that and you're not amazed? It's not an accident. It's not a coincidence. It's not just a feather. It's a—" she stopped herself, thinking better than to continue with what she was going to say. "It's just special ... *to me.* That's all."

"I bet it is," he exclaimed, not being able to hold back anymore. "I saw the way you were rubbing it all over your face. Did you think a genie was about to pop out?" Feeling the sudden shift in her energy, he quickly backed off. "Sorry. I can't help it. Mr. Funnyman, remember? Not even a near-death experience can kill my sense of humor. Anyway, I know this is all part of your

Angel thing … with Angie … So I guess I'm supposed to believe this is an Angel feather?

"Yes!" Wendi screamed with excitement. *He gets it!* "It's an *Angel* feather, Pete! I just *know* it!"

I don't get it. "I'm not sure we're on the same page with this one, Hun," he began, struggling to support her train of thought. "It's more likely a feather from Faith's Angel costume from Halloween, or from any Angel costume for that matter. And even *that* seems unlikely to still be blowing around, but it's possible. But I get it. Ask and receive. You asked for a sign and got a message in the mail and found the feather."

"You're not getting it, Pete," she desperately pleaded. "You're trying to rationalize it away. It's not from a costume. This is a *real* feather! Look at it!"

"Okay, okay. yes, it's real. From an albino pigeon or a dove, both being highly unlikely to be flying around here. So *yes*, it is special."

"*Yes!* That's the point," she pleaded again. "Angie was right. She said she finds them in places and in ways that a feather wouldn't just appear. *That's* how you know. It's from our *Angel*, Pete. I asked to see a sign before I got home, and I almost gave up, and I realized I didn't ask for the sign before I got home, but before I stepped *inside*. And there it was on the front doorstep. And I heard it, too. I heard wings, but there was no bird. Just the sound of wings and a single feather. I actually *heard* it, Peter, I heard our An—"

"Whoa! I can't!" he called out as his heart began beating faster. "I just can't. I'm trying, Honey. I really am. And I can believe I was saved by the grace of God. No problem. And you prayed to an Angel, sure. I'm with you. But please don't tell me an actual bird-winged being is flying over our house!"

"Well, no. That sounds silly."

"Yes! Thank you."

"I admit, I was going back and forth in my mind, wondering if I was crazy all day … That's why I asked for another sign, and I got a *real* feather that was *sent* from our Ange—"

"Woohoo! Earth to Wendi—come back to reality!" Pete lost it and began waving his hands, criss-crossing them in front of her face. "What are you doing with this Angie woman? If you want to have renewed faith, *fine*. If you want the flyer to mean something, *fine*. If you want the feather to mean something, that's fine, too. All that is *fine*."

He rolled his eyes and took a breath, trying to slow his heart rate. He shook his head from side to side and continued. "But just like you said, it is a real feather. That's it. Birds lose them all the time. You happened to find one. It didn't manifest out of thin air! Come on, Honey, come back to me. After all we've been through, things were just getting better. Don't ruin it. Having faith is one thing, but this … this is …" He paused, seeing the anguish of his words overcoming his wife's face.

Wendi stood there as all her joy and exuberance drained away. "Ruin it?" she questioned, her voice slowly rising. "Yes, things *are* getting better, and *this* is why. Because we have help. Because God is on our side, again. Because we have an *Angel* on our side. I'm not about to lose my faith again because you don't want to believe Angels are *real*."

She looked down at her feather. Her voice softened. She swallowed the lump of sadness gathering in her throat. "I'm not crazy. I know what I've seen. I know what this is."

"I know what it is, too, Honey," debated Pete, stubbornly refusing to let it go. "It's a feather. From a bird. It didn't magically appear," he said with a sigh. Wendi's smile had faded, and as far as he was concerned, so had her sanity.

Her expression shifted. "Just because you've lost faith, don't put that on anyone else. I'm *not* crazy. If you don't want to believe, then don't. And regardless of where this feather came from, I *know* we have a real Angel, straight from Heaven, sent by God, to watch over and protect us."

Wendi was at a loss. Other than Angie, whom she didn't even talk to two weeks ago, who else talked about Angels, signs, and feathers being gifts from Heaven? Who else was seeing clouds and statues of Angels? She was alone in this battle, with little proof, and no real evidence other than a white feather that was on their doorstep. A silent tear rolled down her cheek. She allowed it to fall, landing softly on the floor.

Pete continued to shake his head in disapproval. His heart began pounding harder and harder inside his chest. He stopped to take another breath, and a small figure caught his eye. Shifted his head, he glanced around Wendi. In the next room was his own little Angel. She was standing there in the background, listening and watching it all with tears in her eyes.

Faith rarely showed emotion, other than an occasional smile, but she had a look Peter had never witnessed before. It was more than just a look of worry. For the first time since the move, despite all the fighting and arguments she had witnessed, Faith looked scared. Pete pulled himself together, looked at Wendi, and nodded toward their daughter.

He shifted to the side, refocusing his gaze on Faith. Raising his voice a few octaves higher, he attempted to lighten the mood. "I guess Mommy is right. We *do* have an Angel watching us!" he smiled. "You, Sweetie," he said, pointing at her, "You are the only Angel we need, and you are certainly the most beautiful Angel I've ever seen. Come here, Angel. It's okay. We're not going to fight anymore." He waved her over. "It's okay, Angel, come on over."

Faith slowly inched closer to her parents.

Pete was great at changing the mood of a conversation when he needed to. It was like a perfect sleight of hand, diverting attention away from the thing he didn't want you to see. Faith was the perfect diversion. He took another breath, calming himself, and waved her even closer.

"Maybe Mommy is right. Maybe this *is* an Angel feather. Is this *your* feather, little Angel? Did you lose a feather from your Halloween Angel costume?"

Wendi wasn't going to let Pete off the hook that easily. "She agrees with me that it's a *real* Angel feather, don't you, Sweetie?" Wendi asked, looking down at her precious, scared daughter.

Faith looked up at her dad. Staring with big, bright blue eyes, she shook her head, answering no to his question about her costume. She then shifted her gaze to her mom. Their eyes met briefly. She glanced at the feather, then back at Wendi, and let a little smile slip out as if to agree.

"See that, even Faith knows. You don't have to be such a cynic, Pete. Don't you see what's happening here? Angie said our belief draws our Angel to us and opens a portal, allowing it into our lives. We just have to ask and give them permission. We just have to believe."

"Open a portal? Give them permission? What kind of nonsense is this Angie putting in your head?" Peter questioned.

Wendi immediately defended her mentor. "If you knew Angie, you'd know nothing she says is nonsense. She's amazing. And she's very wise."

Allen's advice echoed in Pete's mind. *Get to know her yourself before you judge her.*

"I thought you said she was just a temp. What makes her so special?" Pete asked. "Honestly."

"I can't even explain it to you. She knows more than you or I can dream about, for starters. She's the most positive person I know, and she has this quality ... I can't explain it ... She just makes life seem more ..." Wendi looked up, searching for the perfect word. "More magical."

Pete paused, feeling a bit guilty about his growing skepticism of Angie. But he still couldn't fathom how his wife believed a feather manifested out of thin air as a gift from a "real" Angel. A faint noise coming from outside caught his attention. He looked up, listening intently as it grew louder. "Do you hear that?" he asked.

She cocked her head, straining to hear what Pete was listening to. "Is that geese honking? Is that what's so important?"

"It's fall. They fly by all the time," he pointed out. "Probably every day. Don't you think it's possible one of them could have a white feather? It could have easily fallen off a goose's butt and landed on our doorstep. And even if you tried to convince me it's from your white dove, they aren't even native to North America. Just saying."

"Jesus, Pete. Really? Don't you understand what's happening to me? To *us*?" questioned Wendi. "Isn't God real, even if you don't see Him? So why wouldn't His Angels be real, even if you don't see them? Angels exist, whether you believe they do or not. They just can't do their job if you don't let them. So maybe you should open your mind just a little wider."

"Listen. I don't want to fight. We've had enough of that over the last year to last us a lifetime," he insisted. "After I woke up in the hospital, I thought I finally had the woman I married back ... but I'm not sure I know who the woman is now standing in front of me."

"Good, because that woman, the one you married, disappeared a long time ago. And honestly, I don't want her back. I prefer the woman you're looking at. Even I don't know who I'm becoming. But I'll tell you one thing ... I'm not looking back. This woman," she said, pointing at herself, "This is the one who knows we are blessed with an Angel that is literally right here with us," she said, holding up the feather again. She looked down at Faith. "Our Angel is with us. Isn't it, Sweetie?"

She looked up, glanced over at her dad, then back to Wendi, and nodded in agreement.

"There you have it. Sometimes you have to open your heart, instead of shutting it down, to make the impossible possible. Open your heart, Pete, while you still have one beating." She patted him on the chest, leaving her hand there.

Pete stood there, motionless. *Open your heart? How does my wife turn from Satan's sidekick to Mother Teresa overnight?* He felt his heart pounding, anxious and agitated.

"Hun, I'm not going to keep having this argument with you," Pete insisted, trying to slow his racing heart. "Even if we have our own Guardian Angel right here with us, what makes you think they actually have wings? It's a personification of something grander than us that we can't wrap our little Homo sapien brains around. I mean, they fly, so we gave them bird wings. They radiate light, so we gave them a gold ring floating above their head and called it a halo. I'm telling you, God is *not* some old guy with a long white beard, and Angels are *not* humans with big bird wings, and so that is *not* a *real* Angel feather."

"Well then, Mr. Wizard, what *do* Angels really look like if they're not flying humans with wings?"

"How should I know? I've never seen one. And I don't plan on seeing one until I'm dead. I'll come back from the other side just to tell you all about it. Come on, Honey. These are God's creations we're talking about. They're heavenly beings. They're probably, well, heavenly."

"Is that the best you can do? They're heavenly? *Really?*"

"Yeah. I think it's better than slapping a pair of wings on some smooth-skinned, baby-faced teenager or a little baby for Christ's sake. Yes, they're heavenly. They're probably radiating with light ... blinding, beautiful, heavenly light. Like looking at the sun. That's probably why no one has seen one. We'd literally be blinded by their radiance. That makes a lot more sense to me than flying babies or bird people."

"Fine. That ... well, that actually makes sense," she reluctantly agreed. "But even if this feather didn't come directly from an Angel's wing, it doesn't mean it wasn't *sent* by an Angel."

"Fine," he said, shaking his head. "So," he asked, "what's for dinner?" Attempting once again to deflect the conversation.

"Unbelievable. Fine, change the subject. But I'm telling you, I don't care if this is a feather from a goose's butt or from an albino flying pig. It was sent here, as a *sign,* for *me,* by *our* Angel. *That,* I am sure of. And speaking of flying pigs ... We're having pork chops," she said with a huff and dashed off to the kitchen.

Bobby stood at the top of the stairs, clutching the railing. He had heard every word of the argument. *I thought things had changed.* A tear rolled down as he headed back to his room. He sat on his bed, feeling lost. *Who am I kidding? I'm an idiot for thinking everything was better.*

~ o ~

Chapter 10:

Standing at the Precipice

*"Even if you believe in something with
all your heart, if you allow your mind
to rationalize it away, you block the miracle."*

~ o ~

Faith sat in her room, scrunching her brow. Scared and confused, tension riddled her face. She stared out her window at the setting sun, watching the light fade away as brilliant colors filled the sky. Her stuffed friends were of little comfort, but as usual, Nobody was by her side.

"You said today was special," she whispered, pouting her lip. "You lied … Yes, you did … If id was special, why are mommy and daddy fighting? Dat's not special. Dat's how it always is … I don't care. Go away. I'm not talkin' to you anymore." Tears collected on the table in front of her, and for the first time since the move, Faith felt hopeless.

~~~ O ~~~

*bu*zzzzzzzz

Wendi pulled the pan out of the oven and gathered the pork chops one by one. Pete sat in the other room, distracting himself with the evening news. He barely acknowledged the oven timer going off but refused to move from the couch. Even though Wendi preferred to run the kitchen herself, she would often ask Pete to chop vegetables for her. Tonight, she preferred to be in the kitchen alone, not that Pete had offered to help. The tension was still high, and it felt like they were right back to where they were a week ago.

Wendi placed the meat and sides on the table one by one and announced that dinner was ready. With heavy hearts, they each took their seats for their family meal.

Bobby carefully watched his parents slowly dishing out food, passing plates back and forth, cordially avoiding one another in silence. He looked across the table at his sister. Her glowing smile at dinner typically lightened the weight of his day, but tonight something was different; something was wrong.

He smiled at her, but there was no smile in return. "Are you okay?" he asked his sister, hoping to at least receive a nod in return.

Wendi and Pete stopped as all eyes turned to Faith. She shook her head from side to side, choking back her tiny tears. Bobby's heart shattered. For the past year, he had grown accustomed to arguments at home and dreadful days at school. His only solace was in seeing the joy of his little sister, whom he fought so hard to defend. If her light was extinguished, faith was truly gone.

Bobby was at a loss. For the first time, he felt powerless to help his sister. "I thought you were okay now. What happened?" he hesitantly asked, awaiting an answer from either parent.

"Ask your mother," was the only response from Pete.

"It's fine, Bobby. Your father is just having some issues believing in Angels," she said, shooting a sly glance at her husband. Seeing the anguish in her son's face, she leaned in and lowered her voice. "Don't worry; he'll figure it out one way or another."

An awkward silence filled the air. Bobby took the chance to change the subject, remembering that he was invited to be a snowflake in the Fall/Winter Extravaganza. "Um, so … Mom, Dad? You know how I'm helping with Drama Club?"

"Yes," Wendi answered. "You said you help with sets, right? Isn't there some event tomorrow evening?"

"Yeah," Bobby replied. *Invite them*, a soft voice echoed in his mind.

Pete looked up with a bit of confusion. "What event?"

Wendi shook her head. "The event he's been helping with and staying after school for. I see you still don't pay attention," she jabbed.

"Gimme a break," responded Pete. "I had a heart attack. Isn't that a good enough excuse?"

"It would be a good excuse if that had anything to do with you not paying action," she answered, then turned back to her son. "I'm so sorry, Sweetie. With everything happening lately, I didn't even ask if you wanted to go. What's it called again?"

"It's a Fall/Winter Extravaganza. And yeah, um, about that. So, Sara said they need more extras, and she asked me to be in it."

"That's great, Bud," added Peter, still not fully paying attention. He took a bite of his meal and stopped chewing halfway. "Be in what?"

Wendi glanced over at him with a scowl, then looked back at Bobby. "You're going to be *part* of the performance?" she asked.

"I'm just an extra," Bobby replied. "They need, uh, more kids to be … snowflakes. During the finale … because it's fall and winter," he clarified. As his eyes darted from side to side between his parents, he heard another subtle nudge: *Invite them.* Feeling that it was some kind of inner voice or intuition, he went with it. "So, uh, I think it would be really great if all of you could be there … as a family event … for my big performance," he awkwardly chuckled. He added a big smile, then turned to Faith and nodded, acknowledging her as well.

"Oh," Wendi and Pete said in unison. "Well, what time is it?" Wendi asked.

"Seating starts at 5:00, and they said it starts at 5:30."

"So I have to leave work early? Don't you think a little more notice would have been appropriate?" Peter asked.

"Well, yes. But I just found out this morning. And Dad, you're not supposed to be working full days," he looked at his parents again, hoping something as ridiculous as him being a twirling snowflake would bring some joy back to them, Faith included. "I just thought I'd ask. I thought it would be nice … and if you come, you get to see the set pieces I worked on … and … well, you get to meet Sara."

"OHHH," Wendi and Pete echoed in unison.

"Now that's a different story," exclaimed Pete. "It all makes sense now," he chuckled.

"I don't know why they make these things so early," Wendi chimed in. "How are families supposed to have time to eat before it starts?"

"Not to mention expecting parents to leave work early," added Pete, rolling his eyes.

"Yeah, and, uh, there's one more thing," Bobby reluctantly mentioned. "The auditorium has a leak, and it's supposed to rain tomorrow. So now they have to move it to the high school. Mr. Wacher said if we get permission from our parents, we can stay after school, help get the sets in place at the high school, and then be there for the performance. He said they'll order pizza for anyone helping."

"Well, that's a lot going on all in one evening. I don't even know where the high school is," Wendi said jokingly, but quite seriously.

"I know, Mom. It's just that, well, it wasn't a big deal when I joined, but everything's been going so well at school lately ... and Sara wants me to be there ... and, well, I just thought it would be nice for all of us to be there. That's all," he said humbly.

Wendi's eyes teared up. Bobby was right. They hadn't done anything as a family in a long time. "Okay. I'll see what I can do," she promised and turned toward Peter. "And it's about time to cash in your doctor's note. You're not even supposed to be back to work yet, and you were specifically told not to put in full days for at least two weeks. You've put in too much time this week already."

"Easy for you to say," Pete replied.

"And easy for you to do. You tell that warden of yours that your health and your family come first."

"Marshal, but close enough," Pete laughed.

"Fine. You tell *The Marshal* that you'll be having a discussion with HR if he has an issue. I know how these big corporations work. You take anything to HR and they make sure things are done by the book. They may not care about you, but they certainly care about a lawsuit!"

Pete hesitated as he looked around at his family. Things got a little heated today, and he had no intention of going back to the way they were before. Even Faith had perked up, and her infectious smile had returned. He smiled and nodded at Bobby, then looked at his wife and replied, "As you wish."

Reaching across the table, Wendi grabbed Pete's hand, giving it a loving squeeze. She turned back to Bobby and said, "Well then, that's settled. I'll call the school first thing in the morning to give permission. Bobby, you'll stay after school, and we'll see you at the event. Faith, Mommy will pick you up so you won't have to be on the bus alone, okay?" Faith smiled and nodded and Wendi looked at Pete. "And Daddy will be leaving early, *right?*"

"Right," Pete agreed. "Leaving early for my son's first school play."

"It's not a play, Dad. There's orchestra and choir, too. That's why it's an extravaganza."

"I stand corrected," admitted Pete. "Leaving early for my son's first *extravaganza*. It's settled then. Tomorrow night is Family Night, and God better have a good reason if something gets in the way!"

~ ~ ~ O ~ ~ ~

Wendi closed the bathroom door behind her. But instead of using the toilet, she stood there, looking at herself in the mirror. Despite things going well at dinner and Bobby saving the day, she still felt self-conscious about praying in front of Peter. After everything that happened earlier, she didn't want to ruffle any feathers, literally. The bathroom was the one place where she could have a private moment to herself, even if it wasn't the most glorious atmosphere. She had such a miraculous morning, and even though they stumbled, she wanted to make sure her family stayed on the path they were headed.

Quietly, she began to pray, keeping her voice just below a whisper. "Angel, thank you for all you have shown me today. Thank you for your signs and your presence, and for being by my side through these challenging days. And thank you most of all for putting up with this crazy family." She smiled, assuming Angels appreciate a little humor, and continued. "I hope you love them as much as I do."

"I ask for your ongoing guidance, protection, and help," she prayed. "I am grateful for your love, and I promise to continue to follow your signs with an open heart." She paused, taking a deep breath.

"And Angel, thank you for all the changes we've seen in Bobby. I ask that you continue to do what you can for him, to bring him peace and happiness again. And Angel, I know it's an even bigger request, but please help Faith find her voice. Whatever needs to happen for my little girl to talk again, please do so." She paused once more and added a final request. "And this may be your biggest challenge yet, but if there is a way to get my husband to believe you are real, please do whatever it takes to help him see with his heart, instead of his mind. Thank you."

As the morning rays illuminated the house, Pete straightened his tie and grabbed his briefcase, ready to head out to the office. He hopped in the car, started the ignition, and slowly backed out of the garage. About halfway into the driveway, he stopped. There was something on his windshield flapping in the breeze. *I don't believe this.* He rolled his window down and reached out, grabbing at it, but couldn't reach. His annoyance level kicked up a few degrees. "She really won't let it go," he mumbled to himself, shaking his head as he got out of the car. He walked around the door, grabbed it, and got back in, slamming the door shut. Pete sat in his car for a moment, staring at a single, brilliant white feather.

How is putting this feather on my windshield going to change my mind? He threw it on the passenger seat, put the car in Reverse, and recklessly backed out of the driveway. He headed off to work, occasionally glancing over at the feather.

The morning was dragging on. At least The Marshal had seemed a bit more relaxed the past two days about Pete's workload, or him leaving a bit early. Pete figured The Marshal was more concerned with the legality of the situation than actually caring, but Pete would take it. He looked at the clock.

11:11 a.m.

Pete's emotions wavered as his mind wandered. He thought about Wendi and the argument over the feather, wondered if Faith would ever speak again, and hoped Bobby was really on a new path. There hadn't been any mention of Seth or more altercations at school, and that was a relief. He thought about the excitement and nervousness in Bobby's voice when he was talking about Sara. A smile crept across his face. *My boy's first girlfriend. Maybe things aren't so bad. And who knows, Angie is a temp. It's probably just a phase Wendi is going through.* He shook it off, trying to refocus himself on work.

ahem

His thoughts halted, realizing who was standing in his doorway. The Marshal didn't even have to speak for Pete to recognize his presence.

"Good morning, Marshal. Ah, sorry, *Mr.* Marshall. What can I do for you?"

"I'm sure you're aware of this big project we've all been working on. I didn't want to replace you while you were out, and I know you're taking it easy, but it's left a gap in the workflow and we need to get this done. I believe you have one final report that needs to be run and analyzed. This is coming from the top, so I need you to jump right on that and get it to me by the end of the day. I'm coming in early tomorrow morning to have time to incorporate it into my presentation before handing it off to the head honcho for final approval."

Pete bit his tongue. "Yes, I'm working on it right now, sir, but this one's a doozy. And it's probably the most important report. I don't want to rush it. It will probably take a full day or more to double-check the numbers. I will do my absolute best to get it done for you today, but to be honest, I'm already not feeling well. I had an argument with my wife, and tonight is Family Nigh—"

"Pete, maybe you're not understanding me. This needs to be finished *today*. Do you think I want to come in early tomorrow? No, but that's what a manager does. We do what we need to do to get the job done. And I need my employees to have the same work ethic."

"Yes, well sir, maybe I can come in early tomorrow and get it to you by noon. When is the meeting this is being presented at?"

"That's not your concern. I was told by the president to have it to him tomorrow *before* noon. So, the only thing you need to concern yourself with is getting this to me by the end of the day— *today*. It's not your job to worry about anything else other than what I'm telling you. Understand?"

Pete could tell he was treading into dangerous water and chose not to continue arguing. "Like I said, sir, I'll do my best."

"Your best? Look, Pete. I don't care what it takes. Skip your lunch break, skip your dinner, too, if you have to, but your best better consist of a report being on my desk *before* you leave. That's your only task for the day, no matter how long it takes. Is that clear?"

"But my son is—"

"Why am I repeating myself, Pete? *Before* you leave. Thanks."

Pete clenched his teeth and felt his heart rate quickening. He took a breath and nodded. "Yes, sir. Will do."

Marshall shot Pete one last stern look, nodding back to Pete, and walked out. Pete clenched his fist and stared out the window, trying to calm himself. *If he doesn't kill me first, I'm going to get a gun and shoot the son of a—*

ahem

Jesus! Now what? Pete looked up, bracing himself for what The Marshal had come back to say. To Pete's surprise, it was a welcome face.

"Hey there, Pete. I just passed The Marshal as I was coming to check on you, and he did not look happy. I hope he isn't going to give you another heart attack before the end of the day. I'm here for you, Buddy. Your friendly neighborhood lifeline." Allen was great at his daily sanity checks.

"I know you're kidding, Allen, but you don't know how true that is. I'm supposed to be taking it easy this week, even you know that. The Marshal just put me on lockdown for the day. You know about this final report I'm working on, right?"

"I sure do, and it's a doozy. I'm glad it's your job and not mine," he added with a chuckle.

Pete shook his head with a glimmer of concern reflecting in his eyes. "That ..." Pete lowered his voice, clenching his fist again, "That bastard just gave me a bunch of crap about not leaving today until this report is done. It could take all night, and we decided to make tonight Family Night because Bobby is in the Fall/Winter Extravaganza at school. If I have to skip lunch, fine. But I'm expected to skip dinner *and* miss my son's event? This guy is a real piece of—"

"Whoa! Slow down there, bud. You're getting me worked up!"

"Sorry, I'm just really stressed about all this, and if I don't get it done today, The Marshal will have my ass."

"Okay, let's put this in perspective, Buddy. Tonight is important for your son, right?"

"Right."

"Things are much better at home with Wendi, regardless of her going a little off the spiritual deep end, right?"

"Right."

"So, let me get this straight. Bobby, instead of trying to get dragged out of school, is now dragging you to school. Your wife is looking forward to spending a night with you and the family. The Marshal just told you about this deadline this morning. And you have a medical excuse to do less work and leave early."

"Right." Pete knew exactly which direction Allen was heading, but the fear of losing his job was weighing too heavily on Pete.

"So, things have finally changed for the better for you, and you want to jeopardize it all, including your health, over a report? Your health *and* your family are on the line. If you ask me, this is a no-brainer, Pete. Thank God for how quickly things have changed, and get your butt to that school!" A strange look overcame Allen's face as he stepped closer to Pete's desk, looking under it.

"Um, watcha looking for down there, good buddy? Checking out my sexy legs again?" Pete joked.

Allen belted out a good laugh. He bent down and grabbed something off of Pete's briefcase, which was tucked along the side of the desk. "Speaking of sexy legs, are you moonlighting again?" He asked, lifting up his hand, revealing a pure white feather. "Something you want to tell me? I'm guessing this little beauty is from your costume!"

"I'll be damned. How the hell did *that* get in *here*?"

"You tell me," Allen replied.

"Oh, yeah, sorry. So you know Wendi is on this Angel kick. Well, she found this feather on the doorstep last night. Claims it's an Angel feather, manifested out of thin air, mind you, and then somehow leaves it on my windshield this morning without me noticing. It was her way of messing with me because I told her it was from a bird, not an Angel." Pete paused, contemplating the situation again. Allen simply nodded, taking it in, waiting for Pete to finish.

"You believe in Angels, don't you, Allen?"

"Sure do. What good Christian doesn't? Don't you believe in them?" He asked, but continued before receiving an answer. "I'm not quite understanding why this Angel thing has got ya so knotted up."

"Well, sure, I believe in Angels, but this is different," argued Pete. "She's taking it to this whole new level, swearing this feather literally came from an Angel's wing. Just because we depict Angels as bird-winged people, it doesn't mean they literally have wings. I really think this Angie is messing with her head. Something doesn't feel right to me," he added, shaking his head.

"So, seriously, Allen. Do you think we all have our own Guardian Angels? I understand the Biblical Angels delivering messages for God and all, but she's talking about us having our *own* personal Angel. Like it's a case worker or something."

"Honestly, I think there's a lot of Angels up there watching out for all of us down here. So, why wouldn't we have our own Angel watching out for each of us? And I feel that our loved ones become Guardian Angels for us, too. I'm sure my grandmom is watching over me. We were really close when I was growing up. Heck, she may be right here with us."

"It sounds like there's a lot on your mind, my friend. I'm glad you're asking me about all this, but I have a feeling this is a discussion we need to have over a proper meal, not in your office. And I'm not just talking about our lunch break."

Pete managed a smile, but the worried look on his face was still inching through. "Thank you, Allen. Really. And I agree. Let's grab some dinner and continue this. But right now, I need to get on this report."

"How about we run out for a bite right after work tomorrow?"

"Sounds like a plan. Thanks, Allen. Thanks for everything," Pete earnestly replied.

"It's a date. Now stop your chit-chatting already and get to work, you slacker!" They laughed, and Allen took his leave.

~~~ O ~~~

"Hi, Bobby," came the sweet voice of Sara out of a sea of screaming children at morning recess. "I'm really glad you'll be at the extravaganza tonight."

"Yeah, it was cool helping out. And I, uh, like hanging out with you."

"I like hanging out with you, too. That reminds me. I wanted to give you something ... for tonight."

"Oh? Now?"

"Yeah, but it's a secret, so you need to come with me," she said in a shy tone as she took his hand. She led him around to the side of the school, facing away from the playground. As they turned the corner, she quickly turned, stepped closer, and kissed him on the cheek.

His face turned red with embarrassment. "That was—"

"Disgusting," came a very unwanted interruption. "Oh, were you in the middle of something?" Seth asked.

Bobby was horrified. The last thing he expected was a kiss from Sara, and only in his worst nightmare would Seth be there to see it. Seth was told to stay away from him, but the look in Seth's eyes said differently.

"Didn't I tell you to stay away from Sara, Booby?" Seth asked, stepping closer to them.

"And didn't Mr. Wacher tell you to leave me alone?" Bobby pulled Sara behind him as he puffed out his chest. "So, if you have a problem with that, go talk to your Uncle Wacher about it."

Seth was thrown off for a moment, but didn't care that Bobby knew about his family connection. If he was hanging around with Sara, he was bound to find out eventually. "Just because I agreed to something to get my uncle off my back, doesn't mean I'm going to let you keep hanging around my cousin. Don't kid yourself, Boo-by. She doesn't really like you. She just feels bad because your family is so screwed up."

Bobby's fingers clenched together into a fist. As he stepped toward Seth, Sara laid a hand on his shoulder, stopping him. She pulled Bobby back and shifted in front of him. "Stop it, Seth. Bobby is really sweet, and so is his sister. Don't forget how much your stepdad likes to use his belt. So back off, or I promise he'll be using it on you after the show."

"If you think that's going to save you every time, think again," he snapped. He shifted his glance to Bobby.

"Good thing your girlfriend was here to save you," Seth mocked. "She won't always be there. Watch your back, Booby."

~~~ O ~~~

"Well, good day to ya, Deary."

It was nice to hear Angie's voice. Wendi actually looked forward to her daily dose of Angie Insight, as she now referred to it. To Wendi, it had become the soothing sound of clarity and encouragement. She no longer felt embarrassed if anyone else overheard her talking about Angels, nor did she care about petty office gossip. She was following her own internal desire to do what was right for herself and her family.

"Angie, I have to show you something. You won't believe what I found yesterday. It's so exciting!" Wendi announced, barely able to contain herself. "I asked for another sign when I left work, and right before I got in the house, on the doorstep, was the most amazing ... beautiful ..." she paused, looking around her cubicle.

"—white feather," Angie added, finishing the statement.

"Yes!" exclaimed Wendi, looking up. "I found a white feather. How ... how did you know?"

"Because I found one myself yesterday, and an image of you popped into my mind when I picked it up."

Wendi stared in disbelief. "Wait. You found an Angel feather, too, and thought of me?"

"Sure did. I told ya that I find them all the time. Sometimes they're specifically for me, but sometimes they're sent with a message for someone else. I thought I was supposed to give it to ya, but I guess it was just to confirm that yours is real, too."

Wendi's eyes lit up. "So, it really is an Angel feather? I'm not crazy? Can you call my husband and let him know?" she asked, scanning the floor.

Angie laughed. "Yes, Deary, it's really an Angel feather. I know one when I see one," she confirmed. "Or I should say, when I feel one."

"Right!" Wendi enthusiastically agreed. "They feel *wonderful*, don't they?" Wendi interjected as she continued her search, peering around under her desk. "I couldn't help but rub it on my cheek. That's when—"

Angie laughed again, interrupting Wendi's thought. "I didn't mean feel it with my hands, Deary. Although I agree. They do feel wonderful. I mean, I can feel it, energetically."

"Oh," Wendi paused, looking up at Angie again. "You'll have to teach me more about feeling things. That's a whole different world we haven't even gotten into. But …"

"One step at a time," they said in unison.

Finding what she was searching for, Wendi reached under her desk and grabbed her purse. "I wanted to show you," she insisted, anxiously rummaging through it. "Where is it?"

"It's quite all right, Deary. I don't need to see it to believe it."

"It's just … I know I took it to work with me. And it's not in my purse. Maybe it fell out," she said, scanning the floor again.

"Wendi, Dear," Angie said in a soft voice, "Just as these things find us when the time is right, sometimes they leave us when the time is also right."

With a look of disappointment, Wendi stopped her search. "Okay. It's just that … well, Pete didn't believe it was real. I guess I'm not surprised. I was going to keep it to myself, but he caught me in the act when I found it. We got into a big argument about it. He even gave me a whole speech about how Angels don't really have bird wings," she said.

"Well, he's right, Deary. Angels aren't human … Although they *can* appear to us that way."

Wendi slowly set her purse down. Her eyebrows cringed as her look of disappointment deepened. "You mean it's *not* a real Angel feather? It could be *any* feather?"

Angie unexpectedly knelt down, putting herself eye to eye with Wendi. "You're missin' the point, Deary. I honestly don't know *where* they come from. But what I do know is that when I say it's an Angel feather, I mean it's *sent* by an Angel. It could have come out of thin air, or it could have fallen right off of a goose's bottom for all I know," she giggled.

"You're shitting me, Angie. Did you seriously just say off a goose's bottom? Of all the phrases, why would you—"

"It's what popped into my mind for ya, Dear," she interrupted. "I don't question it. I just say it. And by your reaction, it sounds like it was exactly the right thing for you to hear ... whether ya wanted to or not," she chuckled. "I don't let myself get caught up in the whys or the details. Particulars are for the mind, not the heart, Deary."

"People start going crazy looking too hard for answers," Angie continued. "Not all questions need answering. Just let things be what they are, Dear. What somethin' means to you can mean somethin' completely different for someone else." She paused, allowing the words to sink in. "As long as you know somethin' is sent from your Angel, then simply trust that it is. That's all that matters. Save yourself the trouble later and understand that piece of wisdom now."

Wendi wasn't sure how to reply to first. Talking to Angie would often leave Wendi feeling like she was juggling. But Angie would toss so many new ideas to her at once that she was forced to drop all the thoughts she previously had to keep the new ones in the air. "Let's back up. So Angels don't have wings?"

"They probably do, in a sense. But like I said, they're not human, or bird, or anything we know in this dense reality. They are beings of pure divine light and energy. The mind has trouble conceiving somethin' it doesn't know. That's why we want to make Angel wings look like bird wings. It brings the thing closer to our own reality so our mind accepts it. Don't allow your mind to trip you up tryin' to figure out what somethin' is *supposed* to look like. It really doesn't matter what anything looks like. What matters is how you *feel* when you experience it."

As usual, Wendi listened intently. She tried her best not to interrupt with a million questions that would prevent the lessons from sinking into her deeper awareness.

"Most miracles aren't somethin' as grand as walking on water," Angie explained. "The best miracles are the subtle ones. The ones where the timing is just right to bring two things together that are meant to be together, at the perfect moment.

Maybe it lasts forever or just a single instant, but in that instant, the world is changed forever."

"There are many layers to truth, Deary," she continued. "There is the obvious truth, the subtle truth, and the deeper truth to all things. The obvious truth is that you found a feather. A year ago, your conscious mind may not have even seen it, and you would have walked right by. Even if you had picked it up and admired it, it wouldn't have even crossed your mind that it came from an Angel. And if someone told you it was sent from an Angel, you would have thought it as ridiculous as your husband did. It's our own perspective that is the lens we see the truth through." She chuckled at the irony. "But you didn't pass it by, and it's not just a feather to you now, is it? To you, it's a sign. To your husband, it's a feather. When a sign is for you, share it or don't share. It doesn't matter, as long as you don't allow others' perspectives to diminish your miracle. Miracles are very personal, Dear. Do you understand?"

"Yes. Thank you, Angie. I don't know how you do it, but you speak about the craziest, far-fetched things, and yet it all makes perfect sense. It all *feels* so right."

"Because I speak from the heart, Dear. From the spirit. Sometimes I don't even know if they're my own words," she chuckled. "Most days I'm just as impressed as you!" she chuckled again. "But I don't get caught up in trying to figure it out. I just accept that this world is more than what I comprehend it to be, and little by little they show me more, so I can understand a little more. One step at a time."

"And all this sharing constantly has me going off on the wildest tangents. God bless ya for listening to it all, Deary. I'll tell ya one thing about the feathers, though. Sometimes they do seem to appear out of thin air, but even if some scientist could prove it's just a feather from a bird, I'd like to see him explain how it got in my kitchen!"

"You found a feather in your kitchen?"

"Sure as sugar. I told ya the other day most of my feathers show up in the craziest places. And sometimes a feather isn't even a feather, Dear. I might find a painting of a feather, or someone walkin' by grabs my attention, and low and behold, the pattern on their shirt is all feathers! It makes it so much more fun that way and keeps you on your toes. I imagine it compares to us seeing a child's delight during an Easter egg hunt. You know how kids get, knowing there is something to be found and not knowing exactly where it is. They can't wait to discover it. They just run around, keeping their eyes open, waiting for something to catch their attention, and when they find an egg ... Oh, the delight on their little precious faces!" She giggled again, like a delighted child herself. "We're the children, and our Angels are constantly hiding Easter eggs for us to find. It makes life so much fun," she chuckled again.

"Like I keep tellin' ya, Deary, this is only the beginning. Clouds and feathers are child's play to an Angel. It doesn't matter how big or small a miracle is to them. Those are human concepts. Could you imagine the world we would live in if more people believed?" she asked, taking a moment to feel it for herself, and her face lit up with delight.

"And honestly," she went on, "it's not just because people don't ask. There aren't more miracles in the world because not enough people believe! You'd be surprised how many people feel unworthy of receiving a miracle, or more to the point, of receiving love. After all, that's what miracles are, Dear. They are the Universe, the Angels, and God showing us love. That's why miracles are so natural for Angels. It's what Angels *are*, Dear. Love and miracles."

"So, let me get this straight," Wendi clarified. "If I have enough belief and faith, you're telling me anything is possible?"

"All that is possible already exists, Deary. It's just waiting for us. Technology is proof. Things that technology does today were impossible yesterday. And things we say are impossible today, technology will find a way to do tomorrow. Light bulbs exist not because a man created one, but because a man believed he could. Everything is *already* possible, Dear. It doesn't matter if you believe it or not, but we turn what's possible into reality by believing."

"And I just have to believe? It sounds too much like a fairy tale. That sounds way too easy, Angie!"

"We are very powerful beings, Dear. We just haven't been trained to use our power. Or even believe we have it, for that matter," Angie replied. "But to answer you more directly, it most certainly is easy, and it most certainly is not. You can tell your mind to believe, but if deep in your heart you doubt, you block the miracle from manifesting. And the same goes for the mind. Even if you believe in something with all your heart, if you allow your mind to rationalize it away, you block the miracle again. You have to believe it deep within your heart *and* accept it with your mind." She paused. "So try to go easy on your husband with all this. It's no one's fault he hasn't learned what's possible. So when he calls, Dear, try to be understanding. I'll grab a cup of tea in the meantime." And with that, Angie stood and quickly disappeared down the aisle.

"What? Wait, Angie, what are you talking about?" Wendi cried out, popping up from her seat. "When is he calling? And why wouldn't I go easy on him?"

As Wendi stood there in disbelief, a familiar head popped up over the cubicle wall.

"I'm not even going to say it, Hun. Whatever is going on between you two is way beyond my comprehension ... and honestly, it's too confusin' to even gossip about." And with that, Patty sank back into her hole.

Wendi waited a moment before sitting back down, and as expected, the redhead popped back up again. "But I still don't trust that woman," added Patty.

"Patty," said Wendi, making sure she had her attention. "You really need to lighten up."

~~~ O ~~~

The afternoon felt like it would never end. Pete skipped his lunch break to continue working on the report, but it wasn't enough. He knew the report wouldn't be finished anytime soon. Even if he were to stay all night, it was a daunting task to finish. He also knew going back to The Marshal wouldn't help. He had to make a decision. His entire body tensed up as he dialed the phone.

ring ring

"Hello?" Wendi answered.

"Hi, Hun. It's me."

"This is a surprise." *How did Angie know?* "Are you leaving work this early?"

"No. Not quite."

"What's going on? Something is wrong, isn't it?" she asked.

"The Marshal barged in this morning demanding I get a huge report done before I leave. He needs to review it in the morning and get it to the president by noon. I'm sorry. I'm working my hardest. I skipped lunch, but there's no way I'll have it done anytime soon. I'm going to be here most of the evening. This presentation is a huge deal."

"Us being together tonight is a huge deal!"

"I know, Honey. I know. Things have been bad enough around here with me trying to catch up on work and not putting in full days. This is for the president. It's not coming from the Marshal. If I don't get this to him today, who knows what will happen. He'll probably get me canned. I told The Marshal I had to leave early. It didn't register in his stone heart. I really hate that guy. I really do. I can't get out early. I just can't."

"Pete, we talked about this already, and I am dead serious. You march yourself straight to HR, and then you leave for the day. They can't *make* you stay."

"Trust me, it's not that simple," he replied, rubbing his chest as the tightness set in.

"It *is* that simple," Wendi demanded. "You listen to me, Peter Farfalla. You're still recovering and shouldn't be working this hard, *regardless* of any family obligations. And on top of that, I've got a bad feeling about this. Something doesn't sit right about going without you tonight. Now, you find a way to get it done and get home to your family, or just don't finish the damn report! Make your family more important than your work for once."

"How can you say that?"

"Easily!"

"That's not fair."

"What's not fair is you not showing up tonight." She took a breath, centered herself, and calmed her voice. "Listen to me. It's just a report, and it's just a job. I know you think I've been acting crazy lately, and maybe a silly school performance doesn't sound like a big deal, but it is to Bobby. And it is to me, too." Her stomach tightened as a ball of unease grew inside her. "Something doesn't feel right, Pete. Are you okay? This *has to* be stressing you out because it's stressing me out."

"I'm fine. And I hear you, but he's just an extra. It's not like he has a lead role. It isn't worth me losing my job over. It just isn't."

"*Fine.* Do what you want. I'll pick up Faith, grab some fast food, and head straight to the high school. You know where we'll be if you change your mind."

click

The phone went silent. Pete slowly hung up the receiver as his heart pounded deep within his chest. He sighed and buried his face in his hands.

She's right. What good is money without happiness ... or worse, if I'm not around to enjoy it? But if I get fired over this, then what? God, I don't know what the right thing is to do here. I need some help.

Wendi sat at her desk for several minutes, unable to focus. She wanted to scream.

"Easy, there, Deary. It will be all right," Angie said, appearing as fast as she had left. "That's why I gave ya the heads up."

"But how—"

"When we quiet our minds and tune into the Universe," Angie interrupted, "we realize we already know everything we ever needed to know. Which reminds me, Dear. Didn't you say you were leavin' at 3:30? Just look at the time."

Wendi glanced at the clock. 3:33. "Oh my goodness, I'm sitting here daydreaming and I need to get Faith. She looked at the time again. "Triple digits? Is that seriously the right time?" Wendi asked as she jumped up out of her seat.

"Right or wrong, it's the time you needed to see. And it just happened to be the time when I got a nudge to check on ya. Don't think the signs ever stop showing themselves. Heck, I couldn't get away from them if I tried. After all, my name *is* Angelina."

"Wait, that's your full name?" Wendi stared, awestruck. "You're telling me the woman teaching me about Angels is named Angelina? Your name literally means Angel?"

"Little Angel, actually, Dear. Although the little part may not be so accurate," she said, grabbing her belly. "Now get yourself together and get going. Your Angel is waiting."

Wendi grabbed her purse and paused again. "You mean my little girl who's an Angel, or my Angel, Angel?

"Yes. Now get movin'!" Angie insisted, shuffling Wendi out of her cubicle. "Timing is everything."

~~~ O ~~~

Wendi strapped Faith in, hopped into the front seat, and buckled in. "Did you have a good day?" Wendi asked as she circled out of the parking lot. Faith answered with a nod.

"That's good. We have a little change in plans, though. It seems like Daddy isn't going to be with us," she informed her daughter. Wendi peered at the clock. They had more than enough time to do everything and still be early enough to grab a good seat. "We're going to quickly stop home so Mommy can change, then we'll grab some fast food and we'll be at the high school right on time, just you and me. How does that sound?"

A mixture of sadness and concern washed over Faith's little face. She shook her head, disagreeing with what Wendi was saying.

"I'm sorry, Angel, but Daddy won't make it. Apparently, his work is more important. Now, where do you want to eat?" Wendi knew how to get to all their favorite eateries, but what she wasn't sure about was how to get to the high school from where they would be. She pulled up to the exit and the crossing guard waved her on. She sped off toward home, noticing dark clouds looming in her rearview mirror.

Pete's heart was pounding as he worked as fast as he could. He was stressed enough about the report and knew leaving early would set The Marshal off. But he couldn't get the conversation with Wendi out of his head. Every time he thought about it, his heart seized up. *Why doesn't she understand,* he thought. Allen's words echoed in his mind. *Your health and your family are on the line.* He looked up as a figure appeared in the doorway. Just the sight of The Marshal was enough to raise his blood pressure.

"How's it coming, Pete?"

"Mr. Marshall," Pete began. "Look, I'm sorry. I tried my best, but I can't get this done. I'm stressed enough about the report, and I'm getting even more stressed about missing my son's event at school tonight. I have to get home and rest. I can come in early and hopefully have it to you by noon."

"I know you're not telling me that a school play is more important than a multi-million dollar deal?"

Pete looked up in amazement. "Mr. Marshall, I'm not even supposed to be here. I've told you more than once that I have doctor's orders not to get stressed and to leave work early. Plus, tonight is very important for my son and our whole family. And it's not a play, it's an extravaganza. I really need to be there. I'm sure you can find a way to understand."

"I understand we have a presentation due. Now, if you're not capable of doing your job, I'm happy to find someone who can. So, I advise you to work a *lot* faster if you plan on catching any of your son's play."

Pete clenched his fists under the desk. "Is that supposed to be a threat?"

"Not a threat. A promise. People get paid well here to do the work, including when overtime is needed. They don't get paid to leave early, and they don't get paid to pick up kids from school. We look for reliable, hard-working employees here."

"Well, Mr. Marshall, on any other day, I'd be happy to oblige your ridiculous requests, but not today," Pete asserted as he stood up from his desk. "I'd like to remind you, *for the third time today*, that my doctor told me not to overwork myself and not to get stressed. I will be sure that HR knows how many times I've had to remind you today."

"Is that a threat?" asked The Marshal.

"It's a promise," Pete answered. "And even if I didn't have a doctor's note, I'm making my family a priority. I guess you wouldn't understand that."

He could feel his pressure rising. Pete stepped out from behind his desk and walked toward the door. "You have yourself a wonderful evening, Warden. I'm leaving. Good luck with that presentation."

Mr. Marshall grabbed Pete's arm, looking him dead in the eye. "You don't answer to HR. You answer to me. Now you have yourself a wonderful night, Mr. Farfalla," The Marshal's voice grew steadily louder. "And you'll have plenty of time to recuperate from your heart attack now, since you're out of a job! You won't be coming in tomorrow. YOU'RE FIRED! And don't even think about filing for unemployment!"

"Like I said, I'm making my family a priority," Pete affirmed as his heart raced. "When you can make your family more important than your work, maybe you'll get that stick out of your ass. Which reminds me, how is your wife, Mr. Marshall? I hear rumors you're having some trouble," Pete jabbed, yanking his arm from The Marshal's grip. "Keep your job, keep your hard work ethic, and I'll keep my family. Now goodbye!"

And with that, he pushed past The Marshal as his adrenaline spiked. He walked down the hall, feeling like he was about to collapse. Mustering all his strength, he steadied himself, refusing to show The Marshal any sign of weakness. As he turned the corner, his heart pounded, echoing throughout his body ... *thump thump* ... He headed straight for the reception area, and paused, looking back. *I'll call Allen later and tell him. I need to get out of here* ... *thump thump* ... He stopped, leaning against the front door of the office suite, catching his breath. Janine, the receptionist, stood up behind her desk. "Are you okay, Pete?" she asked with growing concern weighing on her face.

Pete took a deep breath before answering, trying to slow his heart rate ... *thump* ... *thump* ... "I'll be fine. Just catching my breath."

"You don't look fine," she replied as she rushed to his side.

"I'm leaving to go home and get some rest. I just need to be away from here and I'll be A-OK," he added with a wink, trying to mask the pain he was feeling.

"Maybe I should call someone."

Pete straightened himself and reached for the door. "No. It's okay, Janine. I just need to get home." He pushed the door open, stepped through, and looked back to face her. "It's been wonderful working with you. Goodbye, Janine."

She stood there watching Pete slowly make his way to the elevator, wondering about the tone of his goodbye. As the front door closed, she turned and rushed back to her desk. She dialed extension 11, waiting for Mr. Marshall to answer.

As the elevator doors opened, Pete stepped into the empty cube and collapsed against the back wall. He steadied himself on the railing, pressed the lobby button, and held on for his downward descent.

By the time he reached the front doors of the building, he was out of breath. His chest felt like it was being crushed in a vice. Pain raced down his left side. He stopped, leaning against the door frame. His heart was pounding, his chest was tight, and he was desperately trying to catch his breath. *I just need to get out of here, and I'll be okay. No need for another hospital visit, Pete.* He sucked it up and kept moving forward for his triumphant exit. Mustering up his remaining strength, he raised his arm and extended a middle finger to the 13th floor.

He got into his car, started the engine, and took a moment to compose himself. He looked at the time. 4:44. It was too late to meet up with Wendi, but he could still make it to the high school on time.

~ o ~

Chapter 11:

Dark Night
of the Soul

"God, don't do this to us. Not again.
You keep them safe. You hear me?
This time, you keep them safe!"

~ o ~

blink blink blink

Wendi's brow cramped up as she cautiously turned the wheel, following the orange detour sign. Rain steadily began to beat down against the car. *Where is this taking me? Why would I need to get on the highway to get to the high school?* After the move, she had no desire to explore her new surroundings—not Trinity, High Point, or any part of North Carolina—leaving her a stranger in her own backyard. Other than a few key shopping points and local eateries, Wendi had become a hermit. It was just one more way to rebel against her new home, which she now regretted.

Several minutes prior, she and Faith had finished eating and hopped in the car as the dark clouds approached. She turned out of the parking lot, heading for the high school. As she approached the next turn, a large road sign blocked her path. It read: Road Closed. Lightning flashed, illuminating the sky. She nervously turned, following the black arrow of the detour that was pointing her in the other direction. The last detour she took led her to a magnificent winged Angel fountain in the middle of a beautiful park. This time, the pit in her stomach had her believing that the deviation would not lead to such a perfect outcome. She saw the next detour sign up ahead, pointing toward the entrance for the highway. The storm was beginning to resurface her trauma, and the detour was salt on the wound. *The high school shouldn't be far. I'm sure it's only one exit,* she told herself.

Heavy rain began pouring down, thumping on the windshield. She turned her wipers on high. Keeping an eye on the road, she desperately tried to see the detour signs through the voracious swiping of blades and blinding rain.

BOOM!

Wendi shuttered as the ominous clap of thunder shocked her system. Peering into the rearview mirror at her daughter, she tried to hide the growing concern looming deep inside her. *Pete, why aren't you here?* It was the same feeling she had when they moved, and in that moment, she knew her husband was supposed to be by her side—and wasn't.

Barely able to see, she spotted the detour sign just past the North entrance, pointing to the South entrance. Disoriented by the poor visibility of manic wipers and onslaught of water collapsing from the sky, she veered to the right too soon. Wendi was heading North onto the highway in the wrong direction. Barely able to see, she glimpsed an opening to merge into traffic just ahead of a long line of antique cars. She hit the gas, squeezing in just ahead of a vintage Cadillac.

A knot formed inside her stomach. Something was telling her to turn around, but she had already merged into the speeding traffic. *Why is this happening? I just want to be there for my son.* There was no turning back now.

~~~ O ~~~

Peter raced along, focusing on his breath. He was desperately trying to calm his heart and ease his mind. After all the hard work, stress, and late hours without overtime, he had walked out.

His heart thumped as the knot in his stomach grew larger with each passing thought. *Did I make the right choice? I finally stood up to The Marshal, and I put my family first. But where did it get me? Fired, with barely any savings and no income. That jackass better not fight my unemployment.* A tug of war raged within his mind, going back and forth between resentment and pride regarding his actions. *Why did Wendi have to give me so much shit about tonight? Bobby sprung this on us at the last minute. It's not like I'm missing the family vacation. Why couldn't she understand? Now I don't have a job. This is all her fault ... No, Pete. Take responsibility. You did it. You walked out. It's the best decision you've made since moving here.* He grasped his chest and took in a deep breath, trying to ease the tension in his body. *Calm down, Pete. Your health is more important. They need you.*

He coasted to a red light, staring at the impending rainstorm he was heading into. Lightning flashed across the sky as the battle in his mind raged on. *Why did I go there with The Marshal's wife? That was a low blow, Pete ... but it's probably true. Who would stay with a guy like that? She probably loves it when he works late and she doesn't have to see him.*

BOOM!

The delayed sound of thunder snapped him back into the physical pain coursing throughout his body. The tightness in his chest was bordering on unbearable as his heart pumped harder. *I'm glad I left. It's not worth working my life away for that piece of trash. Take your management material and shove it up your—*

honk! honk!

He looked up at the green light and stepped on the gas pedal. Veering off toward the highway entrance, a dreadful feeling overcame him. It was something beyond the distressing feelings he already had. On the phone, Wendi mentioned having a bad feeling. *I'll be there in time,* he kept telling himself. *We'll be there together. Everything will be fine.*

"You hear me?" he called out, looking up at the darkness overtaking the sky. "I'll be there!"

Dark clouds consumed the sun, turning the world to night. *Help us out, God. I don't know if we can survive any more tragedies.*

~~~ O ~~~

Bobby had been on edge since school let out. Seth was coming for him, and their conflict was far from over. Tattling to Mr. Wacher about Seth's threat didn't feel right, but Bobby was tired of fighting. He cautiously moved about backstage, avoiding his nemesis at all costs.

BOOM!

Startled, Bobby jumped as a loud crash echoed behind him. He quickly turned, afraid of what he might find. One of the backdrop scenes had fallen over and landed with a loud thud only a few inches away from him. There, in place of the scene, stood Seth Baynes.

He looked at Bobby with a sinister grin. "Watch your back, Booby. Things are dangerous back here," he assured Bobby and crept back into the shadows. Bobby's heart was racing, but it wasn't just the loud thud or Seth's threats. *Something else* didn't feel right.

Bobby bent down to pick up the fallen set piece, but it was too heavy. As he struggled to lift it, a soft voice whispered, *Everything will be all right.*

Momentarily confused by the words he heard, he looked around but saw no one. Startled by the sound of footsteps quickly approaching behind him, he spun around as a large figure reached for him.

"Are you all right?" Mr. Wacher asked, placing a kind hand on Bobby's shoulder.

"Oh, it's you, Mr. Wacher … Yeah. I'm okay," Bobby hesitantly answered. *I guess I heard him wrong the first time,* Bobby convinced himself. "The scene feel down."

Thunder rumbled outside. As the vibration rattled the entire auditorium, they both scanned their surroundings. Out of the corner of his eye, Bobby caught a glimpse of Seth lurking in the darkness.

"Luckily, we got here before this rain started," commented Mr. Wacher. "It sounds like a doozy. I feel sorry for all the parents driving in this. I've been putting out positive intentions to keep everyone safe. Speaking of which, are you sure you're okay?"

"Yeah," Bobby replied. "I was a few feet away," Bobby lied, still concealing the inevitable confrontation between him and Seth.

"Hopefully, it didn't get scratched up," Mr. Wacher added. "It's my favorite scene. Here, let's lift it together. Just be mindful of the edges. We don't want anyone getting hurt tonight," he cautioned as they lifted the backdrop.

"I know you're new to the Club, Bobby, but you were still a huge asset, a big help," he complimented as they straightened the scene. "Now grab your snowflake costume and practice your twirls. It's almost 5:00, and we want to be ready on time."

"Okay," answered Bobby. "I'd still rather be the snowman."

"Next year," Mr. Wacher promised. As he hurried off to his next task, Bobby scanned the area. There was no sign of Seth. There was no sign of Sara, either. The other person Bobby was keeping an eye out for. *Maybe she's getting her costume on.*

"Uh, hey, Bobby?" A meek voice beckoned from behind. Bobby spun around, hoping to see Sara, but it was only Jesse standing there. Jesse was in a few of his classes, but never spoke much to Bobby. Jesse stared for a moment, awkwardly fiddling with something.

"I ... uh ... I was told to give this to you," Jesse said nervously, holding out a hand. Bobby looked down, accepting a wrinkled piece of paper that was folded several times.

He unfolded the paper, revealing a handwritten note inside. It read: *Meet me at the bathrooms. –Sara.* Bobby looked up, but before he could ask any questions, Jesse had already run off. Bobby was unfamiliar with the high school, and other than the auditorium, the bathroom was the only place the kids were shown when they arrived. *The bathrooms? That's weird. I guess it's the only place to be alone.*

Excited about the thought of being with Sara, Bobby hastily shoved the note in his back pocket. As he ran off, the paper slipped out, falling onto the floor.

~~~ O ~~~

After picking up Faith from school and before leaving for dinner, they had stopped home for Wendi to change. She couldn't wait to get out of her work clothes at the end of the day. The high school was nearby, and she had easily calculated that with over an hour to spare, she could stop home, change, grab a quick bite to eat, and still be at the school just after 5:00—leaving them plenty of time before the event actually started.

As she and Faith were about to leave the house, Wendi's keys were missing—*again*. Misty was perched on the third step, watching. Wendi immediately questioned the cat, to no avail. She then looked under the rug, hoping it was some sort of cosmic joke by her Angel, but the keys weren't there. When she lost the keys the day she scraped her hand, the first place she looked was behind the foyer table, assuming they fell behind it. Remembering the scrape, she cautiously looked behind the table. Luckily, that's exactly where they were this time.

If she hadn't found the keys so quickly, it would have put a serious kink in her perfect timing. She shot Misty a devious look. "I know you had something to do with this. What are you up to?" she asked, half expecting an answer. The cat simply meowed. Wendi grabbed her daughter's hand. "We're still on schedule! Let's get going, Sweetie," she said, heading out the door with Faith by her side.

Wendi was still heading up the highway in the wrong direction. As the thunderous rain poured down, her mind went rampant. *Pete's not here, the keys mysteriously fell behind the table, and to top it off, the road to the school was closed. Angie never told me what to do when all the signs are bad.*

Go back, her inner voice whispered. *This is crazy,* she thought. *Go back where? Back home? Aren't we supposed to be there for Bobby? I don't want to miss his big debut.* After all the changes in Bobby's life lately, and in all their lives, Wendi felt it was pivotal to be there for him—a chance to function as a happy family again. She couldn't imagine a valid reason to bail on her son. *Come on, Angel. Not rain, nor sleet, nor snow. Help me get to my son, so I can see his show!* She chuckled to herself, amused at her little rhyme.

Faith was sitting calmly in her booster seat with her hands tucked into the pockets of her overalls. She stared out the window, watching the raindrops zipping by. Wendi glanced into the rearview mirror, amazed at how easily her little Angel could entertain herself, even in a perverse thunderstorm. Wendi wished she had the courage Faith had.

Wendi held an encouraging smile as she watched her daughter. She hoped a smile would somehow diminish her own uneasiness as well. "It's okay, Sweetie. The rain won't stop us," she said, trying to ease her apprehension. She leaned forward, squinting her eyes, desperately trying to see through the torrent of raindrops pounding the glass. Even with the wipers on high, the world around her was a blur. *Where's the next detour sign? Did I miss it?*

A flash of lightning lit up the sky. She tightened her grip around the wheel and braced herself for the crash of thunder to follow.

BOOM!

Her mind began to panic. Every burst of lightning and crash of thunder triggered a flashback: traveling with Faith on the plane, no husband by their side, a torrential storm. She thought about her panic attack; how angry she was with Peter; how rude she got with the flight attendant; and how upset she was with Faith, leaving her helpless daughter alone while she cried in the airplane bathroom. Lost in the storm of her mind, barely able to see the road, she whipped past the next exit.

Another round of lightning and thunder seized the sky as she recalled her darkest trauma. It was all resurfacing, all the memories, all the fear, all the anger, all the guilt. All of it. Things were better, but she was far from being fully healed.

Reliving it all again, rage bubbled up as she thought about her husband. *He should have been there with us. Why isn't he here now? Because work is more important than his family, again?* It was too much of a coincidence, and the dreadful feeling was overwhelming. *He wasn't supposed to be working tonight. He should be right here with us. I shouldn't be the one driving through this storm. This can't be happening again.*

"Not again!" she burst out. Realizing she said it out loud, she peered into the mirror, looking for Faith's reaction.

Two little blue eyes were staring back as Faith bore witness, yet again, to her mother breaking down. This time, however, Faith was perfectly calm, watching with a blank look on her face, neither concerned nor happy. Wendi began to pray. *Angel, we're lost. We need you. I don't have time for fancy prayers and rhymes. I just need you to help us. Right now!*

Wendi desperately looked for the next detour or exit sign, alternating her eyes between the road and her daughter. Sitting contently in her booster seat, Faith was now intently watching the empty space next to her. She whispered something, then looked ahead, trying to see through the distorted windshield. Leaning forward, she tilted her head, staring at something in the distance. She turned back to the empty seat and nodded. A smirk crept across her face, as if someone had whispered a compliment in her ear.

Looking up again, Faith caught her mother's eye and raised a finger, pointing to something ahead. On occasion, Faith would point to something in response to a question, but would rarely initiate communication. Caught off guard, Wendi's eyes darted back and forth between Faith and straining to see what her daughter was pointing at in the distance. In the moments between windshield wipes, she saw an upcoming billboard for the hospital.

The Road to Recovery, it read.

Confused and curious, Wendi questioned the strange gesture. "Faith, are you pointing to that sign?" Faith looked at her mother and nodded.

Once again, Wendi was caught off guard, and hopes of verbal communication arose in her mind. "What does the sign mean, Faith? Please tell Mommy," Wendi pleaded, wondering if the billboard was a sign from their Angel. "Please, talk to Mommy." She paused, honestly believing an answer was coming.

silence

Despite being unfamiliar with the highway, Wendi knew that she had been driving too long. *I must have missed the detour sign. And I had to have passed the next exit by now.* An odd feeling arose as she tried to recall why the billboard seemed familiar. *Wait. The hospital is on the way to Pete's office. We're going the wrong way!*

~~~ O ~~~

Lightning flashed across the sky as the rain began. Pete turned his windshield wipers on high, battling the onslaught of heavy droplets as he veered onto the South entrance ramp of the highway. A growing concern was building in his mind, escalating his stress.

His thoughts wandered off into the hypnotic pulse of the blades as he searched for answers. If anything happened to Wendi and Faith, he would never forgive himself. He merged onto the highway, still distracted in thought and physical anguish. As he began merging, a car in his blind spot honked.

"Jesus!" He yelled, swerving into the shoulder. His heart tensed up. He grabbed his chest and tightened his grip on the wheel with the other hand, trying to steady the car.

honk! honk!

The driver flipped Pete the middle finger—a pointless gesture in the pouring rain—and sped ahead, distancing himself. Pete took a few deep breaths as he watched the car pull past. Regaining control, he steered off the shoulder into the right lane. "Don't tell me I left work just to crash on the highway. Wouldn't that be some shitty irony!" he blurted out loud.

BOOM!

Thunder crackled, echoing into the distance. *I hope Wendi isn't driving in this.* Their phone conversation replayed in his mind. *Why was she so concerned? Why did she have such a bad feeling?* The last time she had that feeling, she was boarding a plane. She lost their baby, Faith stopped speaking, and their world descended into hell. He shook his head from side to side, trying to deny the thought. He got a glimpse of the time. 5:00. *She loves being early to school events. She's probably already there.*

The ominous feeling grew worse. *But if she got delayed, she'd be on the road right now, driving in this storm. Maybe there was a long line to eat, or she could have been held up because of an accident. Or maybe she was in a—*

His mind flashed with disturbing images of horrible car wrecks. Vehicles flipping. Glass everywhere, and the two most precious girls in his life …

His heart seized up as he swerved halfway into the other lane. Luckily, no one was next to him, but the car behind him began honking. Straightening the wheel, he shook it off, slapping his face to stay present.

This isn't the same. They'll be okay. The voice in his head got louder until he screamed it out. "This isn't the same!"

"IT'S NOT THE SAME!" he yelled out frantically, beginning to panic. His heart seized again and he felt his whole body tighten. "God, don't do this to us. Not again. You keep them safe. YOU HEAR ME? THIS TIME, YOU KEEP THEM SAFE!"

His heart couldn't handle the pain. His mind couldn't handle the anguish. He was scared, angry, and determined. A vast range of emotions came flooding in. He didn't know *how* to feel it all, but the anger was winning. The rain continued to slam down against the windshield as the pit in his stomach grew deeper. Even with the wipers at full speed, they barely managed to keep the view clear for more than a few seconds at a time.

~~~ O ~~~

The bathrooms were in the hall next to the auditorium. Bobby opened the door, peering into an empty hallway. To the left, an exit sign hung over a glass door, leading out to athletic fields behind the school. The rain feverishly pounded against the glass door, echoing down the hallway. To the right were two bathroom doors, one per gender, with a water fountain between them. Bobby stepped into the hallway as a flash of lightning filled the hall.

slam!

He jumped as the heavy stage door closed behind him.

BOOM!

He jumped again as thunder rattled the school, echoing down the empty hallway. Bobby stared for a moment at the torrent of rain coming down, banging on the exit door. He looked right, scanning the hallway. *Maybe she had to use the bathroom?* Stepping over to the restrooms, he leaned against the Girls' door, listening to see if it was in use. He couldn't hear anything over the pounding of rain against the glass door. The noise was drowning out all sounds, including the murmurs of parents entering the main lobby of the school. He looked at the exit door again, watching the ferocious beating it was receiving from the simple act of water falling from the sky.

Behind him, the Boys' bathroom door slowly opened, and a hand reached out, grabbing his shoulder. Bobby winced as the strong fingers dug into his shoulder with crushing strength. Seth yanked Bobby back, forcefully throwing him against the water fountain. The cold metal slammed into his spine, and Bobby collapsed to the ground.

"I told you to watch your back, Booby," Seth taunted. "I can't believe you fell for that stupid note. I told Jesse to give it to you and run, or else. If you think Sara's handwriting is that bad, you're dumber than I thought."

Bobby grabbed the edge of the water fountain and pulled himself to his feet, sending a sharp pain down his spine. "Go to hell, Seth. Wait until your step—"

umph!

Without waiting for Bobby to finish his sentence, Seth's large hands shoved Bobby against the water fountain again, knocking the wind out of him a second time. Seth lifted up his shirt, revealing numerous scars on his body. "You think I give a shit what else my bastard stepdad is going to do to me?"

A glimmer of compassion reflected in Bobby's eyes, as he thought about his talk with Mr. Wacher, and the horrible life Seth must have at home. A flash of light filled the hall as another bolt of lightning streaked across the sky.

~~~ O ~~~

Another flash filled the sky as memories of the past year haunted Wendi's mind. She thought about everything her family had been through over the past year. In the beginning, the anguish was so overwhelming, it was easier to pretend it didn't exist. Depression had turned into her way of life, and she eventually became numb to the pain. Looking back, she had no idea how they had lived the way they did.

BOOM!

She came back to the present moment, recalling the billboard. *The Road to Recovery.* It seems like a lifetime ago that she first talked to Angie and saw the white dove. She thought about how much had changed so quickly. With the help of Angie, and Wendi's newfound faith in her Angel, she really was on the road to recovery. A lightness filled her heart.

Hoping it was time for Faith to break her silence, she tried again. "Faith, why did you point at the billboard, Sweetie? Is it a sign from our Angel?"

Faith nodded. It wasn't a verbal answer, but Wendi had her confirmation. Tears filled her eyes. "Really? The sign is a sign from our Angel?"

Faith smiled and nodded again. She looked off into the distance and pointed toward the next approaching billboard. Wendi recognized the name immediately from the day she had found the feather. It was a billboard for the Church of Jesus Christ for Latter-day Saints, which read in big, bold letters, *Forgiveness Is the Way*.

The pieces of the puzzle fell into place. Wendi had been so bitter for so long, she was blind to the pain she had suppressed, and ignorant to the burden her husband had carried for the family. How long had they pretended they would be fine? How long had she resented him? Even though his heart attack changed everything, they still hadn't spoken about the day they *both* lost their child. *The Road to Recovery. Forgiveness Is the Way.*

Between her newfound mentor and her connection with her Angel, things had drastically changed in her life. But through all of it, a piece of the puzzle was still missing. *Did I move on after the heart attack but not actually forgive my husband?* Even though she was happy now, she hadn't consciously forgiven or let go of the past. It also occurred to her it must be difficult for Pete to understand how much she's changed. Wendi had Angie to guide her, to help her awaken, but Pete didn't have a mentor, other than some occasional advice from Allen. What had she offered her husband? Stories about a dove, a cloud, a fountain, some junk mail, and a feather. He was doing the best he could.

Her hands tightened around the steering wheel as thoughts continued to flash through her mind. Pete always carried immense guilt for everything that happened, and she allowed him to bear it all. She never admitted, even to herself, that it was her choices that led their family into darkness.

It was easy for her to direct her anger at Pete and blame him for not being on the plane. It gave her a reason to suppress her own guilt. Even though her actions seemed justified, she was the one who ignored the seatbelt sign, stood up on an airplane during a thunderstorm, ignored the stewardess, and left her daughter alone—all while carrying their unborn child. How many times had she diverted her own guilt by projecting it onto Peter? Deep down, she knew it was her own anger and emotions that led to the tragedy. She had yet to take responsibility for losing the baby.

I killed him. It was all my fault. How could I have been so selfish? So stupid. It's all my fault. I deserved the pain. I deserved the misery ... but they didn't. Faith, Bobby, and Peter didn't deserve any of this. I had no right to continually punish Pete. She looked up at her daughter. Tears poured down her face as the rain continued to beat against the windows.

Faith looked up at her mother with a bewildered look as she watched her mother's struggle with guilt. Everything that was building up inside of Wendi's heart for the past year was erupting.

Wendi stared deep into her daughter's beautiful blue eyes. She couldn't hold it in any longer. She couldn't hold on to the pain, anger, and guilt suffocating her from within. It was time to release it all. She felt like her heart was going to explode. Unlike a heart attack constricting the heart, this was different. A feeling of built-up pressure was ready to release, like a dam bursting, allowing the waters to flow free once again.

"Faith?" she called, getting her daughter's attention. "Everything that happened on the plane ... It was my fault, Angel. I'm sorry. I'm so sorry. It was all Mommy's fault. Not Daddy's and absolutely not yours." The tears continued to stream down her cheeks. "Look what I did to our family. Look what I did to you. I'm so sorry, my precious love." She paused, staring at her beautiful little Angel through her tears.

"Do you forgive me? Do you forgive Mommy?"

As Faith stared at her mother, droplets gathered in the corners of her eyes. She smiled, then slowly cracked open her little mouth. A soft, precious voice replied, "Yes, Mommy. I fergive you."

~~~ O ~~~

"You keep them safe," Pete repeated, gritting his teeth. The knot in his stomach tightened, fighting for attention over his tightening chest. The only thing louder than the pounding of his heart was the pounding of rain on the car. A tear began to trickle down his cheek. "I didn't leave my family. I left work. I'm on my way. Nothing bad has to happen!" he screamed out, followed by a whisper from the devil inside. *But you left too late.* Sorrow overcame his anger as more visions of crashes and foreboding possibilities stirred in his mind. He winced as a pain shot down his left arm.

Red taillights pierced through the torrent of rain. As the cars ahead stopped, Pete hit the brake pedal, sending his car hydroplaning. He gripped the wheel with both hands, attempting to stay in his lane. His car drifted a few inches into the shoulder just before he regained control.

Another vision flashed into his mind of cars piling up, and his wife and Faith at the center of it. The thought of going through life without them shook him to his core. He and Bobby would be all that was left of their family. They wouldn't make it. Bobby would hate him forever, blaming him again for what happened.

Tears streamed down his face, mixing with the beads of sweat rolling off his forehead. It hurt too much to breathe in fully, and he was desperately trying to get as much air into his lungs as he could. He began to panic as his mind fiercely searched for resolve. Another pain shot through his arm.

"I didn't survive one heart attack to have another in my car in a goddamn rain storm on a goddamn highway on the day I finally walked out of my goddamn job!" he burst out, barely able to hear his own voice over the sound of the rain. "Why'd you bother saving me? What was the goddamn point!" he yelled. Feeling lightheaded, his eyes began to close. He franticly shook his head, slapping his cheeks to stay conscious.

A bright flash of light filled the sky.

BOOM!

He forcefully inhaled and exhaled, trying his hardest to get oxygen flowing through his body. "Help me out here, God. Please," he begged. "What's the point of saving me to kill me now? And I *know* you wouldn't save me to have me live without my wife and daughter. That would be too cruel, even for you. We're better. Aren't we? Maybe Allen is right. That's not so bad —my wife being an Angel fanatic. It's a good thing," Pete agreed, finally conceding to the idea.

"You win, God. I give up," he mumbled. Another pain shot through him. "YOU WIN!" he yelled out, deliriously laughing to himself. "You win, Hun. It was a real Angel feather." He shook his head. "We have an honest-to-God, real-life, Guardian Angel watching over and protecting our family." As he said the words, something within the pain in his heart shifted.

Delirious waves of giddiness continued to wash over him. "Haha! We have an Angel!" he yelled, laughing out loud hysterically. "I admit it," he said, looking over at the bright, emerald green Chevy in the next lane. "My wife is right. We have an Angel!" he exclaimed, nodding his head as if the other driver could hear him. His tears shifted from drops of fear into streams of joy, releasing a torrent of emotion. "WE HAVE AN ANGEL!" He yelled out again, gripping the steering wheel as the car shimmied. He leaned forward, trying to see the road through the rain and the tears.

"Okay, God. Let's see what sort of Guardian you sent us. Angel, do you hear me? Please protect my wife and daughter. Keep them safe. And when I say safe, I mean absolutely safe. *Not a single scratch*. You hear me, Angel? NOT A SCRATCH!" Pete screamed. Another wave of emotion washed over him as the tears continued, obstructing his vision even more. "And if ... *if* you have to take one of us ... take *me*. Do you hear me? If you have to take one of us, TAKE ME!"

He feverishly wiped his tears away, trying to see. "And one more thing, Angel. Please give me a sign telling me they're okay. Don't you dare take me from this world without knowing they're okay. YOU GOT THAT?"

A faint whisper echoed within him. *I am with you.*

Pete sat there in awe, wondering if the voice was real or his delirious imagination. He wiped away the wake of tears streaming down his face and breathed deeply, forcing in whatever air his constricting chest would allow. He breathed out. His heart pounded as the rain poured down. Lightning flashed again, quickly followed by the crash of thunder.

The beating of water against the car was unbearable. Pete cranked up the radio up to drown out the rain. As soon as he heard the song playing, he took his hand off the dial. *I can't believe it.* It had to be a coincidence—it just had to be. Young Michael's voice came through, singing a message that was crystal clear. It was "I'll Be There for You," by The Jackson 5.

As the song played on, the rain eased up, no longer drowning out the music. He turned and looked out the window as the clouds thinned out, just enough to allow a few rays of sunlight to escape. The words struck his heart, putting his mind at ease. As he sang along with the radio, the voice whispered again. *I'll always be there for you.*

Peace washed over his mind, but the strain on his heart and body had already reached its breaking point. Physically, it was too late for Peter Farfalla.

BOOM!

"My stepdad will get his soon enough," Seth promised as thunder echoed through the hall. "And trust me, Booby. If you go running to Mr. Wacher again, you'll be looking over your shoulder every day of every grade," he vowed, inching closer to Bobby's face. "And I'll be watching your sister, too. I'll keep a real close eye on little Fake for you," Seth snickered with an evil grin.

That was Bobby's tipping point. His eyes shifted from compassion to punishment. He lost control and retaliated. Flinging himself into Seth's solid torso, Bobby pushed him back with both hands. As Seth staggered back, he grabbed Bobby's arms. He spun around, and using Bobby's momentum against him, Seth threw him to the ground. Bobby slid across the hallway, slamming into the wall. Before he could rise to his knees, Seth stomped down against his back, shooting pain through his spine. Bobby's body pressed against the unforgiving ground. Before he could retaliate again, Seth was on top of him, forcing his knee into Bobby's back. His mammoth hand crashed down onto Bobby's face, smacking his cheek against the cold, hard floor.

Gathering his rage, Bobby bend his leg and braced a foot against the wall. He pushed off with all his might, sending Seth toppling over. Seth instantly rebounded, leaping back onto Bobby, pinning him against the floor again.

Bobby squirmed an arm free, clawing at Seth's face, but he couldn't reach. Seth grabbed Bobby's arm, twisting it into a chicken wing. Bobby grimaced in pain as Seth pushed his arm higher.

Laying there completely helpless, Bobby felt defeated. Out of the corner of his eye, he saw Seth pull a sharp object out of his pocket. He raised his hand up, revealing the large nail he found backstage. Another bolt of lightning flashed, brighter than the last.

"Payback's a bitch, Booby. Let's see how you look with a nice scar on your face." His hand came thrusting down toward's Bobby's cheek. As the tip of the nail pierced Bobby's skin, Seth dragged it across, leaving a trail of blood.

BOOM!

The deafening crack of thunder masked the sound of the stage door slamming shut. Seth didn't hear the sound of footsteps quickly approaching, either. A pair of hands grabbed his arm, pulling the nail away from Bobby's face. "NO!" she screamed.

Through Seth's fingers, Bobby only got a glimpse of the winged figure who had come to his rescue. Standing behind Seth, trying to counter his brutal strength with all her might, was Sara —fully dressed in her Angel costume. "Stop it, right now, Seth! This is serious," she cried out.

Seth peered over his shoulder at his new opponent. Tensing his muscle, he slowly pulled Sara closer, countering her shameful attempt to stop him. "Awe, are you here to save your weak little boyfriend?" he mocked.

Releasing the tension in his arm, he allowed Sara to pull it back just enough to gain some extra leverage. Using all his strength, he threw his arm forward, sending Sara plummeting to the ground in front of them. He climbed off Bobby, plunging a foot into his gut for good measure, and eyed his cousin.

"You need to learn a lesson, Cuz. I have a good idea," he offered, raising the nail. "I'll give you and Bobby matching scars. Wouldn't that be cute?" he bellowed, lurching toward her.

Sara looked around, desperate for help, but the hall was still empty. She closed her eyes and grabbed her necklace. *Angel, help us.*

~~~ O ~~~

Wendi was in utter shock. For over a year, her daughter's precious voice had been kept from her, hidden away because Wendi's pain and selfishness had separated them. Her mind scrambled for a perfect response, not sure if the silence had been broken for good.

Faith's tiny hand raised, pointing one last time. Wendi followed the direction of her outstretched finger. Through the downpour, she could see the headline of another billboard: *It Begins With You.*

The Road to Recovery. Forgiveness Is the Way. It begins with you. In that moment, her awareness shifted. Something switched deep inside her soul. Wendi truly believed in miracles again. Chills filled her body, and she understood.

Forgiveness was the way. But it wasn't just about her forgiving Pete for not being on the plane or her daughter's forgiveness. The final and most important piece of the puzzle: She had to forgive herself.

The tears continued pouring down as forceful as the rain. Tears of gratitude for her life, her family, and her Angel; *their* Angel. Her soul had been crying out in pain for a year, waiting for her to release it all.

Wendi had kept it all inside, feeling so much guilt and shame for the death of her child. Guilt that she had never admitted to herself, until now. A faint whisper echoed within her. *It was an accident.*

No. She refused to accept the simple truth. She heard it again. *It was an accident.*

Tears kept streaming down. *I didn't mean to panic. I didn't mean to hurt Faith. I didn't mean to ... to kill my baby. I'm sorry, my baby. Oh, my precious baby. I'm so sorry.* Any remnant of unshed grief that had hardened in her heart was melting, allowing emotions she hadn't felt since the accident to flow again. *It WAS an accident.* The sudden revelation and admittance struck her like a lightning bolt from the storm. It had been an accident—terrible and tragic—but an accident, nevertheless. Something moved through her and she was finally able to say the most important words ...

Wendi, I forgive you. A warmth filled her being as she felt her heart expand. She was finally free.

The rain let up, becoming a soft drizzle. She turned the wipers on low and looked at her precious child. She couldn't control the tears.

"It's okay, Mommy," Faith whispered. Wendi stared in disbelief. Her daughter's voice had returned. As Wendi was about to reply, she noticed Faith tracking something just outside the car.

Wendi quickly peered out the window, following her daughter's gaze. There it was again: a white dove. Wendi disbelieved her own eyes and looked back at Faith, who was still following the bird. Wendi looked again, following it as it flew off ahead toward the dark sky. The clouds began thinning, and a few rays of light emerged, illuminating the dove.

As the clouds parted to the right, the full brightness of the setting sun shone through, lighting up the sky. To her left, as the clouds drifted away, a magnificent rainbow arched across the sky.

~~~ O ~~~

The bright rays of sunlight streaked across the wet road, causing a hazardous glare. Pete flinched, holding up a hand to shade his eyes.

Deep within his chest cavity, his heart seized up, sending another sharp pain throughout his body. His left arm tensed up and his fingers clenched around the steering wheel. Reaching for his chest, he moved his other hand, allowing the glare to blind him. As he recoiled, his whole body jolted, jerking his arm and pulling down on the wheel. His car swerved to the left.

Somehow, the green Chevy in the left lane reacted in time and swerved into the shoulder, avoiding a collision. Pete was now riding in the left lane, with the green car alongside him in the shoulder, honking to get his attention. Darkness overcame Pete as his world began to fade out. He shook his head, trying to stay conscious. The red auras of taillights lit up his windshield as the cars in front slowed down. In a manic state, and barely hanging onto consciousness, he pressed the gas pedal. Speeding toward the brake lights, Pete raced ahead of the Chevy, which was still in the shoulder. A shot of adrenaline shocked his system. A moment of clarity shone through as he swiftly approached the braking cars.

The other driver frantically tried to get out of the shoulder and merge back into traffic. Anticipating an accident, the cars behind them were already decelerating. The driver in the green car watched, still honking, as Pete slammed down on the brake pedal, sending his car hydroplaning again.

Spinning a full 180 degrees, Pete's car came to a stop, facing the opposite direction. The Chevy was now heading straight into a head-on collision with Pete. The driver forced his foot down against the brake, losing control.

~~~ O ~~~

As Seth closed in, Sara held her pendant tight, praying for help from her Angel.

"NO!" Bobby howled. Reaching out, he wrapped his fingers around Seth's ankle and yanked as hard as he could. Seth came crashing down, like a giant falling from a beanstalk, knocking his head against the side of the metal water fountain. A loud thud rang out, echoing down the hallway, but the sounds of parents shuffling into the school muffled the noise. The entrance was around the corner, and no one could see the brutal scuffle unfolding.

Seth collapsed onto the hard floor, stunned and in shock. The nail dropped from his hand, rolling under the water fountain, now stained with blood.

Bobby impulsively reacted and sprang to his feet. He was focused on protecting Sara and getting revenge for all the hurt Seth had caused. Channeling every bit of his anger and strength, he sent a foot sailing deep into Seth's stomach. "How do you like it, you piece of shit?"

Frenzy overtook Bobby's mind as he jumped onto Seth. He grabbed Seth's hands, crossed his arms, and pinned them with his knee. Still disoriented, Seth was now the one who was powerless. Bobby's hand pressed Seth's face down with all his weight, smashing it into the cold floor.

"NO!" Sara cried out as she scrambled to stop Bobby, grabbing his arm. "That's enough!"

"No!" Bobby screamed. "He needs to be taught a lesson!" Running on pure adrenaline and blinded with rage, he shoved Sara back.

Horrified, Sara silently screamed again for her Angel to intervene.

Out of the corner of his eye, Bobby saw the nail lying on the ground. Without thinking, he reached over and grabbed it. Raising his arm in the air, his hand came driving down with the tip of the nail heading for Seth's eye.

~~~ O ~~~

"Rainbow," Faith's voice squeaked from the back seat.

Wendi smiled at the sweet sound of her daughter's voice, and stared out the window, mesmerized by the prism of colors. As she admired the huge rainbow, a car coming up in the left lane caught her eye. The antique cars that had followed her through the storm were speeding up, preparing to pass. The Cadillac, which had been directly behind her, was swiftly overtaking her on the left. On the front of its hood, shining like a star in the sunlight, was a unique ornament. It was shaped like a person leaning into the wind, with long, flowing hair blowing in the wind. Where its arms should be were wings, stretched back behind it. The angelic hood ornament glistened in the sunlight, aglow with radiance.

The little heavenly ornament raced on ahead, disappearing from her sight as the Cadillac pulled ahead of them. The next car in line was a Rolls-Royce, adorned with yet another winged ornament. Its body and wings reflected the light, and Wendi watched in amazement. Another glowing Angel was passing by, gifted with the backdrop of what had turned into a double rainbow.

Wendi was in bliss. A warm, safe feeling filled her heart, and she knew without a doubt that she and her daughter were being guarded by their Angel. As she watched the car pass by, she realized the next exit was finally in view. She breathed a sigh of relief and a smile graced her face.

She had forgiven Pete, apologized to her daughter, and forgiven herself. The message was undeniable. She accepted that sometimes circumstances are out of her control and panicking only escalates the probability of a far worse tragedy. Holding onto faith, that was her true saving grace.

She drove along with a calm feeling in her being, finally approaching the exit. She was running behind schedule, but was hopeful that she'd still make it to the high school before the extravaganza began. As she eased into the thought of seeing her son, her expression suddenly changed.

Something was happening ahead on the other side of the highway. Cars began hydroplaning and sliding out of control. A few cars in front of her, a tractor trailer was changing lanes to let the line of antique cars by. The driver eased his foot off the gas, on guard with a front-row seat to the accident unfolding on the other side of the railing.

Before she could react, a horrific scene unfolded.

Pete's heart was pounding, and each beat echoed throughout his body ... *thump thump.* He faded in and out of consciousness. The world around him started to fade away ... *thump thump* ... His eyes refocused on the green Chevy that was heading straight for him. As it lost control, it spun out and hit the guardrail. Pete faded again ... *thump thump* ... His vision re-focused one last time as he witnessed the following car swerve, avoiding the Chevy, and was heading straight for him ... *thump thump* ... Barely aware, a white feather floated down in front of him. It was the same feather he had grabbed off his windshield this morning. He collapsed against his seatbelt as one last thought pushed through his mind: *Angel ... Help ...*

The radio was still blasting, and as his sight began to fade. The vision of a beautiful double rainbow streaking across the sky dissolved as a bright, white light embraced him.

~~~ O ~~~

Sara released her Angel pendant and scrambled, pushing herself up onto her knees. As she straightened herself, light caught her necklace, reflecting across Bobby's face. Seeing the light reflecting in his eyes, he froze, stopping the nail only a few inches away from Seth's eye. He looked down at Seth, who was staring back with true fear in his eyes. Bobby snapped out of his rage and turned to Sara. The Angel pendant around her neck teetered back and forth, hypnotizing Bobby as he stared at the pulsating light.

His hand fell to the side, releasing the nail. As it rolled off his palm, the world faded away as a blinding white light surrounded him.

~~~ O ~~~

The commotion ahead on the other side happened so fast for Wendi, her mind could barely take it all in. After several cars had lost control, and a bright green car slammed into the guardrail, sending pieces sailing across the highway. Its entire hood flung off, piercing the grill of the tractor trailer a few cars ahead of her. The truck began to swerve recklessly from side to side, and the driver slammed on his brakes while desperately trying to maintain control.

Time stopped as everything else happened in slow motion. Wendi watched as it all unfolded, one element at a time. Sliding across the wet road, the truck lost control, and the trailer began spinning around. The cars between the truck and Wendi all reacted at the same time. They had no choice but to slam on their brakes, each praying to be saved from the accident about to occur.

As the front cab veered off into the left lane, the trailer swung toward the right lane. As it spun around, it began to capsize. Three other cars separated Wendi and Faith from the tipping tractor trailer blocking both lanes. There was no avoiding a collision.

Wendi's heart skipped a beat as she watched it play out in a fraction of a second in her head. The trailer would tip over, and both cab and trailer would go tumbling and flipping, blocking both lanes of the highway. The three cars ahead, all out of control, would slide into the trailer, piling up against it. She'd slam on her brakes, too, also sending her car hydroplaning across the road. She and Faith would slam into the pile of wreckage, followed by countless other cars behind her; all trying to stop in time; all colliding with one another; all at the mercy of the slick, wet pavement.

She snapped back to the present moment. If only she had listened to her intuition and turned around, but here she was. But if they hadn't gotten on the highway in the wrong direction, she wouldn't have seen the billboards, received the message, and heard her daughter speak. She wouldn't have forgiven. Despite the terrifying scene unfolding before her eyes, she was still in a space of pure peace, awareness, and bliss. Nothing could change it.

She was done with tragedies. She was done with heartache. She was done with suffering. A single word graced her mind. *No.* She wouldn't accept this as her fate.

She found her faith stronger than ever, never to be lost again. With the accident still unfolding in front of her, her mind and thoughts raced past the speed of light. She knew what she had to do. *Believe. Ask. Trust. And Receive.* The first lesson was now engrained in her soul: *Believe.* But what good was it for her to believe in her own Guardian Angel if she wasn't going to call upon it in her most desperate hour of need? She knew what she must do.

Wendi's world pervaded space and time as her foot slid off the gas pedal, and she took a deep breath. Unlike the first time she called upon her Angel to save her husband from his heart attack, this time, she wasn't calling out in fear. This time, she was calling out in pure faith from a place of her own power and divinity. No fancy poems or rhymes, just a simple, focused intention ... and lesson two: *Ask.*

"Angel, please protect us. NOW!"

The three cars in front of Wendi were all out of control, sliding, skidding, twisting, and turning on the wet road. Even though she felt calm and focused, her survival instinct took over, and her body reacted the same way the other drivers did: she slammed on the brakes, sending her car hydroplaning across the wet road.

She felt completely helpless. As the gap between her and the cars in front of her closed in, her entire body tensed up, and she tightened her grip on the steering wheel. Desperately trying to regain control, the third lesson came into her awareness. *Trust.* She closed her eyes and prayed as hard as she could, one last time. *Angel, I hand our lives to you. Save us.*

Wendi let go of all expectation, fear, and doubt. She released herself completely into the arms of her Angel, liberating her soul. The final step that happens without any further action or thought: *Receive.*

She immediately felt the warmth of a radiating light caressing her face. It was the feeling of warm sunlight breaking through the clouds, but the clouds had already parted. This light wasn't coming from the sky. She instinctively opened her eyes, finding herself being engulfed in a beautiful, pure white light. It had no source and surrounded her, growing more intense by the second. Everything faded from view. No cars. No tractor trailer. No accident or highway. Even Faith disappeared. Only a beautiful, white light remained.

~ o ~

Chapter 12:

Embracing
the Light

"Is this a dream?
Did we die?"

~ o ~

Pete's sight dissolved first.

As the Light engulfed him, everything faded into a pure white radiance of love and harmony. From the center of the Light, a dot appeared, extending into a line, thus splitting the Light. Rays of every color and hue, from red to yellow to indigo, radiated out from the center line. Colors shot out at all angles, fractalizing the white light into prisms of colors beyond the known perception of the human eye.

The sounds of honking horns, screeching tires, and metallic crashes faded. As the song on the radio faded out, a new one began to play. The sound of the radio faintly permeated his awareness, merging with his vision, like the waking world piercing a dream. Some part of his awareness registered the sound of a sweet and familiar song with a melody pure and true: "Three Little Birds" by Bob Marley & The Wailers.

An infinite amount of colors and hues danced in fractals all around him, shifting vibrations and tones to the beat of the song. As the lyrics faded into the background, Bob Marley's message rang clear: somehow, everything was going to be all right. The brilliant prisms of light slowly faded into darkness, and an infinite blackness consumed Peter.

~~~ O ~~~

As Wendi's consciousness faded into infinity, her body was still reacting. Her foot was pressing down on the brake as hard as it could, and her hands were clenched around the steering wheel like a vice. As the Light soaked into her being, a peace overcame her. Every bit of tension dissolved from her body. As she gently eased her grasp on the wheel, her foot released its force off of the pedal.

Her mind succumbed to pure, indescribable bliss as she merged with the Light. A presence of pure unconditional love surrounded her, embracing and caressing her. A split-second became eternity, and Wendi became one with the Light. She was in a place of pure tranquility, everywhere and nowhere.

Some part of her awareness felt the steering wheel turning, as if something had taken control of the vehicle. Her hands simply followed its motion.

The Light subsided, and the world re-materialized. Time began again, and the slow-motion tragedy that played in her mind now gained full momentum, moving faster than life. There was no avoiding what was about to occur.

The massive tractor trailer continued to capsize, now sideways and spanning both lanes. The trailer unhinged from the cab and came crashing down like an avalanche. Landing with an echoing thud, it scraped along the highway, shooting sparks out in all directions from the grinding metal.

Screeches filled the air like a thousand banshees screaming as every car in a quarter-mile radius consecutively slammed on their brakes. The force of the trailer falling broke the hitch and sent the front cab of the truck into a tumble, flipping over and over again. Each of the three drivers in front of Wendi had reacted instinctually out of fear to avoid colliding head-on with the falling trailer.

They were all hydroplaning across the wet road, drifting in different directions. Every driver had lost control of their vehicle as fate took over.

The first car was an SUV, in the right lane ahead of Wendi, and closest to the truck. It had no room or time to stop and was the first to hit. The car spun around almost a full 180 degrees, as the trunk impacted the trailer with near full force, scattering glass across the highway. Since the trailer was still in motion, the trailer and SUV continued to slide together, connected by the impact, until the friction of the trailer overcame its momentum, bringing them to a halt.

The two other vintage cars followed, the Cadillac and the Rolls-Royce, and Wendi behind them. Since the line of antique cars had pulled into the left lane to pass Wendi, there was some extra space between her and the next vehicle behind her. Luckily, the antique car that was behind the Rolls-Royce hadn't caught up, leaving space in the left lane next to Wendi. As her car hydroplaned and began to spin, there was no immediate danger around her, but there was little room between her and the three other cars in front. There was no way to stop in time.

The Cadillac was next. Its back slid into a tailspin, swinging it around. The car drifted sideways, and the passenger side slammed against the bottom of the capsized trailer.

The third car, the Rolls-Royce, followed closely behind. The driver had attempted to swerve to the right, trying to avoid the Cadillac, his foot instinctively glued to the brake pedal. The car left a trail of smoke as its braking tires eroded against the asphalt. It shot off to the right, heading toward the backward SUV. The driver yanked the wheel to the left, flipping the car around. If an impact was imminent, his trunk, instead of his engine, would hit the front of the SUV—now pinned against the unforgiving size and weight of the trailer.

Momentum kept the Rolls-Royce skidding to the right. Its trunk clipped the front of the SUV, sending it flipping around the SUV, spinning onto the shoulder. The passenger side crashed hard against the guardrail along the side of the road. The passenger window shattered, sending glass flying across the grass. The car flipped up, raising the driver side wheels off the ground, and then collapsed back to the ground.

Wendi and Faith were next. Crashing was the only scenario filling Wendi's brain, but her heart knew different. She was in a state of duality, existing in multiple planes of existence at once. The peace and divinity of the Light still filled every aspect of her being. Regardless of what her eyes were witnessing, she wasn't afraid.

Her Angel had not appeared in any visible, tangible form, but Wendi fully felt its presence surrounding her and Faith. She was also present, witnessing the accident, but no longer felt that she was in her body. She didn't know whether her hand was being guided as she turned the wheel, or if the wheel was guiding her hands. All she knew was some force greater than her, and somehow part of her, was guiding the car. She looked up in the mirror at her daughter. Faith was still buckled in her seat, smiling. Somehow, she was also oddly calm, watching the same tragedy unfold before their eyes.

~~~ O ~~~

silence

The Light enveloped Bobby as Sara, Seth, and the school faded into pure nothingness. He remained there for what seemed like only a moment, and at the same time, an eternity. The Light shifted, and soft colors slowly blended into a visual spectacle. The colors formed images and movies as he began watching his life from a new awareness. In an instant, a deluge of memories and visions flooded in. One by one, Bobby relived his life as if he were witnessing them as an outside observer.

He saw himself as a small, happy baby. He relived the delight of meeting his baby sister for the first time. A kaleidoscope of happy memories and feelings whizzed by of him and his sister as toddlers. Time sped up until after the move. He continued to witness profound moments in his life: Seeing Sara for the first time. Faith connecting his hand with hers. The golden heart in the clouds. Seth's ear getting pierced. His dad blaming him for the scuffle on Halloween. His father laying on the floor in his mother's arms, close to death. Mr. Wacher confiding in him and showing compassion for Seth.

New visions followed as time stood still. He saw his mother, sister, and father caught in a terrifying car accident. Vehicles piled up for miles as sirens and flashing lights followed. He saw images of Seth being beaten by his stepfather and Seth retaliating, knocking him out with a hammer. He saw Seth at his stepfather's funeral, followed by Seth sitting behind bars. Bobby's mind fast-forwarded several years later. Faith was a teenager and speaking to him about something they had witnessed. Sara was with them. She was holding Bobby's hand, and around his neck hung a matching Angel pendant. He looked at it and lifted it in his palm. It caught a ray of sunlight, which reflected into his eyes. He flinched, merging back into the present moment.

The world around him came back into view. He was still in the hallway on top of Seth, but shards of glass were flying all around him as a gust of wind blew through the shattered exit door.

Sara was still a few feet away. She was on her knees, covering her face with her arm. Without thinking, he hopped off of Seth, grabbed Sara, and wrapped his arms around her, shielding her from harm.

~~~ O ~~~

Wendi's hands kept flowing with the turning of the wheel as her eyes took in the surrounding carnage. The trailer had flipped over, sending the front cab tumbling ahead. The SUV spun completely around, smashing its back into the undercarriage of the trailer, followed by the Cadillac, and finally the Rolls-Royce was wedged against the side rail in the right shoulder and the back of the trailer.

Her car was drifting off toward the left shoulder. With the cab unhitched and the angle of the trailer, there was a small space between the trailer and the guardrail separating her and the other side of the highway. She watched in disbelief as they passed by the wreckage, squeezing through an opening on the left, missing the trailer and guardrail by only inches. Suddenly, the wheel turned to the right, and their car fishtailed, swinging its back against the guardrail. The hit ricocheted her car back into the left lane, forcing the wheels to grip the road again, regaining control. They glided past the trailer, safe from colliding with the pile-up.

Wendi stared out of the passenger side window as they passed the fallen trailer and exhaled. They had just avoided a head-on collision by the grace of their Angel. Believing they were clear of danger, her mind took over. She tightened her grip around the wheel with her own conscious force, and straightened out the car.

In the same moment she took the wheel and looked ahead, Wendi also caught Faith's expression in the rearview mirror. The look on her face shifted as she pointed a little finger forward at the same object now fully in Wendi's awareness. Wendi had been so mesmerized by the other collisions and her near miss with the trailer that she wasn't paying attention to what was straight ahead.

Directly in front of them, on its side, was the cab of the truck. It was ravaged with dents, scrapes, and cracked parts from tumbling over itself several times. It was directly in line with her, blocking the shoulder and the entire left lane. It had landed on the driver side with the windshield facing the southbound lanes, and the top facing her. If the driver was still inside, a direct collision could crush him.

Instinctively, she pressed on the brakes, hard. Her attention was now laser-focused on what lay in the road ahead. The realization gripped her that she had lost control of the car, and it was hydroplaning toward the mangled truck. The peace of the Light still pervaded her, but she had fully snapped back into her body and full awareness.

If she hadn't taken back control and slammed the brakes, she could have easily steered around the cab. They were now at the mercy of an out-of-control car.

The vehicle drifted around clockwise, swinging the driver side toward the truck. She held on tight, trying to overcome the force of the steering wheel pulling to the left. Nothing could happen now to avoid a collision. There was no guiding force this time, only the sheer power of momentum.

She only had seconds. A single tear began to fall as she focused on the one option left—prayer. *Angel, we need you one more time. And if you can't save us both, save Faith.*

~~~ O ~~~

As the wind died down, the last shard of glass came skidding to a stop at the far end of the hallway. The rain stopped, and a calm filled the hall. Bobby looked deep into Sara's eyes. Knowing what their future could hold, he allowed his lips to softly press against hers. The kiss lasted only a moment, but felt like a lifetime. New feelings filled Bobby's chest that he could only describe as his heart expanding into the space of true love.

As Seth gained his bearings, he jolted up from the floor. His forehead slammed against the cold metal of the water fountain, knocking him back to the ground. He laid there, holding the back of his head with one hand and his forehead with the other.

A wave of compassion washed over Bobby. "Don't move," he whispered to Sara. He cautiously stepped over to Seth as glass crunched beneath his feet. He stopped by Seth's side, staring at the large boy he once considered his emissary of anguish. Bobby stared for a moment with a look of tenderness and empathy. "Here," Bobby said, reaching out and offering Seth his hand. "Get up slow. You hit your head really hard … And watch out for all the glass," Bobby warned, nodding to the shards encircling them.

Seth hesitated, staring back. As he looked deep into Bobby's eyes, something shifted within him. Regardless of their history, up until a moment ago when a bolt of lightning exploded the exit door, Seth knew Bobby was no longer his prey. Seth reached out, accepting Bobby's hand. Bobby braced himself, helping Seth to his feet, just as the side door flung open.

Mr. Wacher emerged out of the darkness of the auditorium. He quickly observed the scene: Glass strewn across the hallway; Sara on her knees with small cuts on her arms and legs; and Seth and Bobby facing each other, engaged in some kind of arm wrestling match. For the first time, Bobby witnessed panic seize his teacher. "What the hell is going on?"

~ ~ ~ O ~ ~ ~

Wendi didn't know what to do. The wheels were locked up as they continued hydroplaning toward the truck. They couldn't grip enough of the wet road to bring them to a halt. The only thing that would stop her car was a collision.

As the car floated across the pavement, she took her foot off the brake. She hoped to regain control by hitting the brakes again and forcefully turning the wheel. She had to take the chance; an impact at that speed could kill them both.

Wait, came a soft angelic voice, reading her thoughts.

A giggle from the back seat followed, distracting Wendi for a fraction of a second. She quickly peered into the rearview mirror to see her white Angel feather somehow floating in mid-air, gently falling into Faith's lap. She wasn't aware that the feather had slipped out as she grabbed her purse heading into the office.

Wait, the voice came again, as Wendi refocused on the car.

Wait ... Now!

She firmly pressed on the brakes and tensed her arms, using all her strength to steadily steer toward the right. The car went into a spin, tilting up onto the passenger side wheels. It continued to tip, landing on its side with enough ease that the shatterproof windows cracked, but held together.

The car scraped along the road, still sliding on its side with the wheels facing the cab. The back wheels hit first, causing the car to flip around the hitch, sending the car spinning into the right lane. It landed back on all four tires and skidded into the shoulder. The car was still spinning, and swung around as the passenger side slid against the guardrail, finally coming to a halt. The smell of burning rubber scented the air as cars on both sides of the highway all skidded to a halt.

Wendi sat in shock, taking a moment to process it all.

Her ears were ringing, and she felt disoriented. Faith seemed a bit rattled but looked fine. "Are you okay, Angel?" Wendi asked, focusing back on the present moment.

Faith nodded. Wendi unbuckled and flipped around, looking at her daughter, who was perfectly content and unharmed.

A realization dawned. Wendi wasn't in pain. Nothing hurt. She looked down at herself. She flipped each hand over, examining them closely. She closed each one and slowly opened them back up, watching each finger bend with ease. She inspected her arms and legs. *Not a single scratch.* As she allowed the accident to settle in her mind, she processed it again. *How can we be okay? We should be broken. Cut. Bruised. Something. Anything. I'm fine. Faith is fine.*

She inspected herself again, looking for blood, scrapes, anything—some proof that the accident was real. *Is this a dream? Did we die?*

There had to be a nick, or a cut, or even a scratch. There had to be some physical proof on their bodies of what they had just encountered—the worst car crash of their lives. It wasn't possible to come out of such a violent scene and simply stand up and walk away. Her mind fought vigorously to make sense of it, but her heart already knew the answer. As illogical as it seemed, her mind quickly conceded to her heart. *Our Angel saved us.*

Somehow her whole being *knew* she and her daughter were both perfectly okay. It was not a hope or an assumption, nor a prayer or a wish. It was a knowing in her heart, radiating throughout her being, telling her they were safe and completely unharmed. They had just lived through a miracle; they *were* the miracle.

Overwhelming feelings of peace, love, and gratitude overcame Wendi. If she wasn't sitting in a car, she would have fallen to her knees in humility and gratitude for her life, the life of her daughter, and all life. The feelings flooded to every cell and corner of her being. She looked around in wonder, smiled, and laughed as the incredible peace and joy made her giddy on life.

Faith looked up at her, sharing a similar feeling of peace, but something was slightly different. Unlike her mother, Faith wasn't giddy or overwhelmed. She was in the same space she always was. Maybe it was because she had believed ever since the plane.

Believed in the Light. Believed that nothing could harm her. Maybe Faith had believed even before she was asked to. Maybe she was grateful even before she needed to be. Maybe that was her miracle. Maybe that was the key to all miracles.

The accident faded from Wendi's mind, along with the commotion going on outside of the car. All that mattered in that moment was the joy of her and her daughter being alive. The immense feelings surging through her body continued to overwhelm her, and her laughter turned to cleansing tears.

She stared at Faith through her watery eyes, smiling, as the miracle permeated her being. "We're okay! I'm okay. And you're okay. We're really okay, Sweetheart!"

Faith nodded. "Yeah, Mommy. Dat was fun!" she giggled, as if she just stepped off her first roller coaster ride.

Wendi belt out a laugh. She was glowing, lighting up with a childlike joy. She felt like she was going to explode and cover the world in pure happiness. She continued laughing. Slowly at first, and then uncontrollably. "We're okay!" she repeated as her laughter turned to tears. She reached back, unbuckled her daughter, and held her in her arms. Wendi looked her in the eyes, and whispered, "Our Angel saved us."

Faith nodded, smiling back at her mother. "Nobody saved us."

Wendi, slightly confused at the comment, corrected her daughter. "Not nobody, Sweetie. Our Angel. Our Angel saved us."

"Dat's what I said, Mommy. Nobody saved us."

Wendi nodded as the recognition set in. Wendi laughed again at the perfect answer she could give to all the non-believers. "Yes, Sweetie. Nobody saved us."

It's what started it all—Faith talking to their Angel. In the aftermath of the accident, Nobody was the last name on Wendi's mind, but every conversation she had witnessed from afar, and eavesdropped in on, now made perfect sense.

Her mind even traveled back to the days and weeks just after the plane crash. The therapists had asked Faith to draw what happened, hoping that they could get some visual answers, since Faith was non-verbal. Faith kept drawing a bright light next to a plane over and over. The therapists wrote it off as a large sun, but Wendi had noticed on a few drawings that there was a bright light *and* a sun.

Wendi had now shared the same experience. Their Angel had kept Faith safe on the plane, and had been by her side, holding her in the Light, ever since.

~~~ O ~~~

As Mr. Wacher stepped into the hallway, Sara immediately jumped to her feet, responding, "It's okay, Dad. Oh, I mean Mr. Wacher. Lightning shattered the door. It wasn't anyone's fault. Bobby protected me from the glass, and he was just helping Seth up."

Mr. Wacher smiled, looked over at the boys, then back at his daughter, who was standing in a river of glass. He allowed the stage door to close behind him, and peered down the other end of the hall, seeing the shattered frame of the exit door. His panic faded into compassion, realizing what a traumatic experience they had all just witnessed. "First things first. Are you *all* okay?" he asked, watching each one nod in recognition. "Second, I can't continue with the three of you like this."

They each looked at him, concerned about what his next words might be. "Sara, Angel, I can't go on seeing you every day, and not hear you call me Dad. But it's your choice. I respect whatever you decide. But first things first. Let's take a closer look at what happened here, shall we?"

He cautiously stepped closer as glass crackled with each step, stopping next to the boys. With years of practice of being a keen observer, Mr. Wacher caught a glimpse of a very large nail next to Seth's foot. "Bobby, that's a very nasty gash on your check," he said, noticing some remnants of blood on the tip of the nail. "I don't think you'll need stitches, but we need to get all of you to the nurse right away ... Although I'd prefer to sweep the glass out of the way first. Are you sure you're all okay for a few minutes while I grab a broom?"

As Mr. Wacher finished his sentence, the side door slowly opened, revealing two other teachers. "Oh my goodness," Mrs. B. gasped. "We all heard the crash, but didn't know what happened. Looks like you found the scene of the crime. Is everyone okay?"

They all nodded again. She turned to Mr. Smith, laying a hand on his shoulder. "Could you grab the large broom to the right of the stage?" she asked, then turned back to Mr. Wacher. "This is quite a mess. Should we cancel the event?"

"It's just an isolated incident," Mr Wacher replied. "I think we can continue with one less snowflake, and maybe someone else can be our Angel."

"No," Sara chimed in. "I'm your Angel," she insisted. "It's only a few scrapes. I just need some bandaids, and I don't go on until the last act. I'll be fine."

"You're my Angel," Bobby whispered to her in a not-so-low voice.

Seth looked at Bobby, opened his mouth, pointed to the back of his throat, and made a gagging sound. "And you're *my* Angel," he added with a sarcastic voice and laughed.

"And I guess that makes you mine," Sara said to Seth, completing the circle. They all laughed.

"Well, I think we'll be just fine," Mr. Wacher declared. "On with the show!" he exclaimed.

Wendi slowly turned her head, surveying the chaos and destruction around her. Broken glass was everywhere. Pieces of metal and debris were scattered all around, and yet there they sat —in her demolished car—safe, unharmed, and unscathed. She tried opening her door, but it was jammed. She slammed her body against it several times, to no avail.

Wendi looked back at Faith. "Hold on, Sweetie. Mommy will get us out." She looked around, assessing the situation. *Her door is probably jammed, too.* Wendi leaned over, inspecting the passenger side door. The car had skidded into the guardrail, pinning them in. Even if the door worked, it wouldn't open more than a half an inch. The driver side windows were shattered, and she doubted they'd be able to open. If the passenger window still worked, she may be able to climb out. She realized the engine was still running. As she reached for the button to lower the window, she was startled by a noise behind her.

tap tap tap tap tap

Wendi jumped, alarmed by the frantic rapping on the window. She and Faith both turned their heads to see a man standing there, leaning over. The sun was approaching the horizon and shining directly behind him. All that could be seen was a silhouette and rays of light emanating all around him.

He mouthed something, but Wendi's ears were still ringing, and the voice was muffled through the glass.

"ARE YOU OKAY?" he yelled again. Wendi nodded. He looked at Faith and repeated the question. She also nodded and smiled at the angelic figure.

The man wasted no time. "I'm going to try opening Faith's door," he said in a loud voice, nodding and pointing down to her handle. It didn't dawn on Wendi that their savior knew her daughter's name. He grabbed the handle and yanked. With a screeching swing, the door flung open.

As he ducked his head into the car, tears poured down Pete's face as he gazed upon his wife and little Angel. "Thank God you're okay. Thank you, God! You're both really okay?" Pete asked again, looking back and forth between them.

Wendi couldn't believe her eyes. "Pete? ... How? ... Is this real?"

He nodded as the tears continued flowing from his eyes. Choking up, he couldn't squeeze another word out of his mouth.

Pure gratitude overwhelmed him. He was thankful to be alive and thankful his wife and daughter were safe. *Thank you, Angel.*

Pete gingerly lifted Faith out of her car seat and into his arms. "It's okay, Sweetie. I have you," he whispered. As they emerged from the car, he held his precious daughter close to his chest and hugged her tightly.

Gently setting her on her feet, he wiped away his tears. He looked her over in disbelief, sure she had to be injured, but couldn't find a single cut or bruise.

Another wave of gratitude washed over him. After surviving another heart attack and finding his wife and daughter unharmed through a terrifying accident, Pete didn't think it was possible for any more miracles to occur in one day—but the day was far from done.

Faith smiled, staring into her father's eyes with joy and whispered, "I love you, Daddy."

~~~ O ~~~

The teachers and custodians worked together to clear a path through the shattered glass along the hallway. Mrs. B turned to Mr. Wacher and advised, "You get them to the nurse. We'll finish up here." He nodded, and as they turned to walk away, a fluttering noise outside caught their attention.

They spun around, and everyone in the hallway looked toward the shattered exit door. At the foot of the door was a pure white dove, staring back at them. Behind it, spanning the field, stretched an enormous double rainbow. It had to be the brightest rainbow they had ever seen, every color pronounced and glowing against the backdrop of dark clouds that were receding into the distance. The bird cooed, bobbed its head, and flew off into the sunlight.

They all looked at each other, bewildered by the bird, and in awe of the beautiful prism of colors gracing the sky.

Mr. Wacher escorted the three students around a few corners, and as they approached the nurse's office, he turned and addressed them. "Before I leave you with the nurse, I'll give you all one more chance. Now, which one of you wants to tell me what *really* happened?"

Bobby looked at Sara, then Seth, then his teacher. "I need to be honest with you, Mr. Wacher. I'm not sure I can trust Seth to tell you what actually happened," he began. "Because you wouldn't believe it. It turns out he's just a good kid that bad things happen to," Bobby admitted, mirroring his teacher's words back to him. Mr. Wacher appreciated the reflection, smiled, and nodded.

Bobby nodded at Seth and continued. "It was pretty scary. When the lightning hit, and the door shattered, a piece of glass got me real good. It sliced my cheek. The blast knocked Seth against the water fountain. He hit the back of his head pretty hard, then fell and banged his forehead on the floor. He got it pretty good from both ends. I was just helping him up when you opened the door."

"Is that so?" Mr. Wacher asked, alternating his gaze between Seth and Sara.

"No, Bobby is lying," Seth opposed. Bobby and Sara shot Seth a worried look, shaking their heads and hoping he'd take the hint. "I'm the one who saved Sara and was helping Bobby up, but don't make a big deal about me being a hero and all," he said in a cocky voice, throwing a wink and a smile back at Bobby.

"I'm more likely to go with Bobby's version on this one, but nice try, Mr. Baynes," Mr. Wacher admitted. He shifted his look to his daughter. "Do you have another version of this story?" he asked.

Sara looked at her father with a serious face and replied, "I swear on my Angel. Bobby was helping Seth up after he fell." She was proud of her perfect truth, minus several details before the lightning had struck.

Those words were enough for Mr. Wacher to stop his inquisition, despite other questions he had. "Well, if that's the story you're all sticking with, that's what we'll tell the nurse and anyone else who asks. Now, let's get all of you some medical attention," he said, opening the door to the nurse's office.

Seth walked through first, followed by Bobby. As Sara stepped through the doorway, Mr. Wacher stopped her. Reaching into his pocket, he pulled out a crumpled note and handed it to her. "Oh, by the way, Bobby must have dropped your note to him. And we're going to have to work on your handwriting, Angel. It's horrible. In fact, it's as bad as your cousin's," he added with a wink. "We can talk about this later, but if you three are *honestly* good with each other, that's all that matters to me."

"Thank you, Daddy. I love you," she proclaimed, tipping onto her toes and kissing him on the cheek.

~ ~ ~ O ~ ~ ~

"You talked! Oh, my God, you talked!" Pete cheered, embracing his little Angel. For the first time in over a year, he heard his daughter's voice again. "Thank you, God," he repeated, holding on a moment longer as fresh tears returned to his face.

"Hun!" he called out. "Hun, did you hear that? She talked!"

Wrapped up in the moment, Pete realized his wife was still stuck in the wrecked car. "Oh, sorry, Hun! I'm coming!" he hollered, turning his head back and forth between his wife and daughter. He grabbed Faith, shifting her to the side, and popped his head back into the car, then looked back at Faith.

"Faith, stay right there. Don't move. I'm going to help Mommy."

"I can try climbing into the back seat," Wendi suggested.

"Let's try your door one more time, together," Pete responded with a nod. He popped out, grabbed the door handle from outside, and counted. "One … Two … Three!" He yanked on the door as she rammed her shoulder against it from the inside, and the door swung open.

Pete reached out, and Wendi took her husband's hand. He gently guided his beloved wife out of the car. The moment she was out, he threw his arms around her, embracing her with all his love. As sirens wailed around them, tears uncontrollably streamed down their faces.

"Thank you, God. Thank you," was all he could say, whispering it over and over in her ear, as they stood there within their own moment of time. He held her tightly, and they embraced each other, heart to heart.

Staring into each other's eyes, there was a deep recognition that something was different; they were no longer the same people they were this morning. Instead of being shaken up and traumatized by such an atrocious accident, they only felt a joyous peace. Gratitude filled their beings, and a pure love emanated from their hearts. Pete lifted up his daughter, and they embraced Faith, together.

Releasing the hug, Pete stared at his wife and daughter with a look of wonder, still engrossed in the moment. "I … I still can't believe it … I found you," he said, choking back more tears. "I thought … I thought I was going to die … I thought you were going to …" he stammered, overwhelmed with emotion.

"Every-ting's gonna be all wight, Daddy," Faith's adorable voice squeaked out.

There seemed to be no end to the day's synchronicities and miracles. Pete flashed back to the song that was playing as he was engulfed by the Light, and a warmth filled his soul. He smiled and nodded in agreement. "Yes, Angel. Everything's going to be all right."

Looking at his wife, Pete blurted out his story without stopping. "I didn't even see your side of the accident, but I knew you were in it, I *knew*, and I ran across the highway, looking at all the smashed cars, but couldn't find you, and something said to look around the other side of the trailer, so I ran around, and there was your car—smashed, dented, and scraped—but I wasn't panicking," he admitted, finally taking a breath. Wendi was about to interject, but he continued before she could. "And I don't know why, but I was calm, and something kept telling me you were all right, but part of me couldn't believe it, wouldn't believe it, until I saw you with my own eyes. And there you were. *Here* you are," he finished, looking over his wife and daughter one more time. "You're safe. Perfectly safe ..."

"Not a *scratch*," he and Wendi repeated in unison. They looked at each other with a glimmer in their eyes and laughed.

"It's a *miracle*," they declared simultaneously. They laughed again at their coinciding remark. Still in sync, they mimicked each other one last time. "Our Angel saved us."

"What did you just say?" Wendi asked, breaking their harmonic resonance. She also couldn't believe the day held any more surprises. She choked up, forcing the words out. "You ... you believe me now?"

"I do," he answered, his eyes filled with joy and tears. He reached into his shirt pocket, revealing a brilliant, white feather. "And I have *a lot more* to tell you," he added, holding it up.

"You found your own feather!" she exclaimed.

"No," Pete rebutted. "You left yours on the windshield of my car ... before I left for work this morning."

"No. I didn't," she countered.

"Yes. You did," he insisted.

"No, Daddy," interrupted Faith's sweet voice as she tugged on her father's leg. She reached her little hand into the pocket of her overalls and pulled out a beautiful, white feather. "Dis one is Mommy's feadder," she said, holding it up.

Pete stared, amazed yet again at the continuation of miracles. Wendi gently caressed his face, turning his gaze to meet hers. "*That* feather is yours. From *our* Angel. And I have *a lot* to tell you," she added with a glowing grin.

"Wait," she added as a realization dawned on her. "Why did you think you were going to die?" she questioned. "You were *in* the accident? On that side? At the same time?"

A strange look crossed Pete's face, one of humor and guilt mixed together. "I may have *possibly* had another heart attack, *while driving,* and sort of *caused* the accident." He added in a crooked smile for good measure.

"Pete!" Wendi yelled. "*You* caused all this?"

"Easy with the announcement, there," he said, shushing his wife. "It's not like I was *trying* to have a heart attack!"

"Pete, we all could have—"

"But we didn't. We're okay. Look at us. Somehow we're better than okay."

"Yes, we are," Wendi agreed as she began looking around. "But what about everyone else? It was horrible. I saw it all happening right in front of me. The people in the other cars. They couldn't all be as lucky as we were."

Realizing they had been in their own little family bubble the whole time, the magnitude of the accident began soaking into Pete's awareness. Let's find out what's going on with everyone else." He started to turn around, then looked back at his wife. "Wait. Why are you *here?*" he asked. "You're supposed to be at the school!"

~~~ O ~~~

As the nurse cared for Seth's injuries in the back, Bobby and Sara sat up front, waiting by the office door. Mr. Wacher had run off to announce the start of the extravaganza and assured them he would quickly return.

Bobby looked back toward Seth, then peered over at Sara. His mind and heart were split in so many directions. The peace and awe he felt from merging with the Light, along with the future vision of Sara and Faith, filled his heart while replays of the hallway fight and the other concerning visions darkened his thoughts. His mind jumped from his family's horrifying accident, to Seth's violent future, then back to the memory of him driving the nail toward Seth's eye. His whole body shook.

"Are you okay?" Sara asked.

"I don't know," he answered honestly. "I … I'm sorry for pushing you back. You were just trying to stop me. I can't believe … I almost …" Bobby paused.

"It's okay," she said.

"No, it's not. I could have really hurt him. I don't ever want to be that angry again."

She stared at him for a moment, as if searching his soul. "You won't," she promised. She wasn't sure how, but she knew she was telling the truth. She could feel the difference in him and the shift in his relationship with Seth.

"I want to … uh, something …" he stammered, fiddling with his hands as he had second thoughts about sharing his experience. "I, uh, I saw something. When the lightning hit. It sounds weird, but I had visions. Of, uh …" Bobby paused, not sure if he should share everything he saw or how to translate it all into words.

"It's okay," she reassured him. "I have visions all the time."

"You do?" he asked, surprised by her comment.

"Yes. It's, well, it's one of my gifts."

Gifts? She has gifts? I'm seeing the future. A white dove just nodded at me. What's happening? he questioned, debating his sanity.

"It's okay, Bobby. You can tell me anything," she promised

Bobby's eyes lit up, knowing she meant it. Any secret he had would be safe with Sara. "When the lightning hit … something weird happened. I saw some bad things, but then I saw some good things. I saw you and me, older, and Faith was with us, talking," he began."

"Oh my God, Bobby. That's wonderful!" she exclaimed.

"Yeah. It was," he agreed. A smile began to creep across his face, then he winced in pain, raising a hand to his bandaged cheek. "But before that part, I saw my family in a bad car accident," he began.

"Oh no," Sara gasped, shooting a hand over her mouth.

"And then I saw Seth and he, uh…" Bobby paused, afraid to verbalize his vision.

"Saw me what?" Seth's voice rang out as he stepped over.

Sara and Bobby both flinched at the sound of his voice. "Uh, ah, nothing," Bobby replied with a waver in his voice and a concerned look in his eye. A nudge deep inside was telling him that he had to reveal his vision to Sara and Seth, but he was unsure how Seth would react.

"You're next, Angel," the nurse interrupted, looking at Sara, still in her Angel costume. "Looks like you hurt yourself when you fell from Heaven," she chuckled. As a school nurse, she learned it's always best to lighten the mood, even with a bad joke.

As Sara walked off with the nurse, Seth took her seat next to Bobby. "Talkin' about me behind my back already?" he asked. "You know what that means, don't you?"

A new wave of concern overcame Bobby. He really thought things had changed, but maybe he was fooling himself. Before he could reply, Seth kept going.

"It means I don't give a crap," he said with a booming laugh. Seth could feel that something shifted inside him as well, but he had no desire to flaunt it. "You're okay, Booby. Thanks for not being a snitch," Seth admitted as he punched Bobby's shoulder. It was as close to an apology as Bobby would get, and he took it.

"Sure. So we're cool?"

"No. You'll never be cool," Seth bellowed. "But we're good."

"Okay," Bobby replied with relief. "And, uh, maybe you can stop calling me Booby now."

"Okay. That name was getting old, anyway," Seth surprisingly agreed as he examined Bobby's cheek. "With that gash on your face, I think I'll call you BooBoo, instead." He laughed.

It wasn't the best improvement, but being a step up from Booby, Bobby accepted his new name—for now.

As they sat there, Bobby worried about his visions, particularly about Seth's future and what felt like an impending car accident for his family. He wasn't present in those visions and wondered where he would be during them, and how soon they would happen. Faith looked the same age, so it had to be soon. *Everything will be all right*, a voice whispered in his ear.

At the same moment, the door swung open, and Mr. Wacher popped his head in. "Everything all right in here?"

Bobby nodded a "yes", but his mind thought otherwise. *I'm going crazy.*

As soon as Sara was ready, Mr. Wacher escorted her and Bobby back to the auditorium. Seth stayed with the nurse so she could keep an eye on him in case he had a concussion. Bobby said he wanted to be on stage with Sara for the final act and went to get his snowflake costume on. Mr. Wacher agreed, hoping the performance would be a positive replacement for any trauma the incident may have created.

The nurse did a good job with Bobby's cheek, and he didn't want to panic any parents by making an announcement to find Bobby's family. The teachers were asked to keep an eye on the audience, but the Farfallas hadn't been spotted yet.

"We still haven't seen Bobby's parents, but we will keep looking," he said to Sara.

Concerned, she felt a burning need to share Bobby's secret. "Dad," she whispered. "Bobby had a *vision.*"

The word sparked something in Mr. Wacher. His eyebrows raised in concern, offering his full attention. "What did he see?" he asked.

"He said he saw his parents in a car accident," Sara disclosed.

"Do you believe him? Did it *feel* true?"

"Yes," Sara immediately replied.

Mr. Wacher nodded, knowing what he had to do. "Okay, I'll tell the teachers to look for them again in the audience, in case they arrived late, and I'll check with the police for any accidents in the area. It'll be okay," he assured her, not fully believing his own words.

~ o ~

Chapter 13:

Messenger of Heaven

"You are loved more than you know, infinitely and always, without end."

~ o ~

As the impending sirens of police vehicles, ambulances, and fire trucks closed in on the accident, an approaching voice interrupted Wendi and Pete's conversation.

"Is everyone okay?" a man called out from behind, accompanied by the sound of hurried footsteps.

"Yes. We're all okay," responded Peter, spinning around, expecting to see a first responder.

The plainly dressed man halted his jog in front of them and smiled. "You're all really okay, aren't you? After getting out of *this*?" he said, holding back a chuckle and pointing to their partially demolished car. "Let me guess. Not even a scratch?" he commented, almost in jest.

Wendi looked at the man, curious that those were his exact words. He wasn't a first responder, and he certainly didn't look like a victim of the accident. As their eyes connected, she sensed something familiar, something within him that was shining through. He exhibited the same newfound sense of being and pure gratitude to be alive as she and Pete—along with the same radiant smile and glow. She *knew* that he was part of this same horrific, miraculous collision: he survived the crash completely unharmed.

"Not a scratch," Wendi replied. "We're perfectly, absolutely fine. Thank you."

"Amazing!" he bellowed. "I figured as much, but I had to find out. Your car's another story, though," he chuckled, pointing to it.

"I don't mean this to be rude," Pete interjected, "but who are you?" he asked, leery of the cheery man.

"I was driving *that!*" The man said, pointing to the ravaged cab of the truck and laughing. "I don't know how, but I'm perfectly fine. Can you believe it! We should probably all be dead!" he exclaimed, giddy beyond reason.

Pete and Wendi stared at the man's odd behavior, but some part of them understood it. "My mind keeps trying to tell me different," he went on, "I shouldn't be okay, but here I am!

And there you are! It's a *miracle!*" he exclaimed as he burst out in laughter again.

"It certainly is," Wendi replied. "We were saved by our Angel," she humbly admitted.

A look of astonishment replaced the man's giddy smile. He brought his voice down to a humble tone. "I know. Dear God, I know. Thank you, heavenly Angel. Thank you for saving all of us." Tears began rolling down his face, disappearing into his beard. "That hood flew off and hit me, and I lost control. I thought I was going to die, or worse, kill someone else. So I prayed as hard as I could. I prayed to the Angels that everyone would be okay, or at worst, that my life be taken so that everyone else be saved. I asked that they keep us safe, and that we make it through all this unharmed—without a scratch." Pete and Wendi's eyes welled up as they listened to the truck driver's miraculous retelling.

"I … I don't know how this is possible," he continued, "but despite the collisions, the damage, the wreckage—we're okay. And not just me and you—*everyone* survived without a scratch. It's incredible! It's a *miracle!* It really is." He tried wiping away his tears, but he was helpless against them as they continued pouring down.

"Everyone?" Pete and Wendi repeated, falling back into unison. The miracles kept piling up. *Everyone was saved … without a scratch.* They were just beginning to understand the magnitude of it all.

"Yes! Everyone!" he repeated. "They're all okay!" He turned and pointed to several people who were gathered by his truck, now being debriefed by the police. "They all just climbed right out of their cars, walking around without a scratch, thanking God, high on life! My God, the feeling! *It's incredible!*" he burst out, looking up and raising his hands to the sky. "Thank you, God!"

"All of us are feeling it," he continued. "One by one, each of the other drivers met up on the other side of the trailer, sharing their stories, then ran over to see if we were okay. They saw y'all sharing an intimate moment and wanted to give you a minute while they helped me down from the truck. They had just filled me in when I saw the police coming over, and I needed to get to you first. I wanted to find out for myself if it was really true—if y'all also emerged without a scratch—and you did!"

Tears streamed down Wendi and Pete's faces as they listened in amazement to the man's story. The miracle extended beyond their own family and had encompassed so many. Everyone who was part of this collision of vehicles, and of lives, survived—completely unharmed. The true power of Heaven had shown through and encompassed them all.

"Not a scratch," he repeated. "Not a single scratch! Well, not on any of the people, anyway. Our cars are a different story," he said with another burst of laughter.

The swift sound of footsteps interrupted their conversation once again as two officers and an EMT approached. They stopped, and as the first officer was about to speak, he paused, looking over each of them.

Shaking his head with an enormous smile gracing his face and a look of wonder in his eyes, he declared, "Let me guess. Not a scratch?"

~~~ O ~~~

The blessings continued. One of the officers on-site happened to live in the neighborhood and offered to drive Wendi, Peter, and Faith home as soon as he could. They had never met, but the officer, Ed, as he had asked to be called, knew exactly who Pete and Wendi were upon hearing their last name—the family he and his wife had prayed for when they heard about his heart attack on Halloween night.

Ed was able to get through to the school, and Mr. Wacher spoke to Wendi. The Fall/Winter Extravaganza had just ended, and they agreed it was better to meet at the house. He assured her that he would get Bobby home safe.

Shortly after, Officer Ed and his passengers arrived at the Farfalla household. They thanked him profusely, and as Pete, Wendi, and Faith stepped out of the car, Mr. Wacher pulled up. Bobby immediately jumped out and ran to his family. Waterfalls of tears flowed as they embraced each other as a family for the first time in over a year—grateful to God, grateful to be home together.

Sara, having not said a proper goodbye to Bobby, reached for the car door handle, but was stopped by her dad.

"Sara, I know you really want to say goodbye, but don't you think they need this moment to themselves? Maybe it's best we head home, shall we?"

She nodded in agreement and flashed a smile. "Let's go home, Dad." As they pulled away, Sara pressed her hand against the glass, knowing she would see Bobby again soon—and that her life would never be the same.

After experiencing their own tragedies and revelations, Wendi, Peter, Bobby, and Faith congregated together in the comfort of their home. Still filled with the grace of the Light, their hearts emanated a palpable love for each other, and they embraced again, as a family,.

Overwhelmed with the excitement of their individual experiences, each member looked deeply into their family's loving eyes, and a burst of emotion seized them. It all came pouring out in a joyous sharing, and they each took turns rambling off their own journeys, piece by piece.

Sharing together, they wove their words in and out of each other's stories. The details spilled out into one giant loom of interconnected threads, separate and at the same time together. As fast as they all rambled on, all the pieces were fully absorbed and understood, as if they shared one consciousness.

"I walked out without finishing the report, and I got fired, and I had to get to the school to be with you, and I had a bad feeling, and I couldn't understand why ..."

"... and there was this detour, and it was pouring rain, and I couldn't see, and I got on the highway in the wrong direction, and I knew something was wrong ..."

"... and Seth pushed the scene over, and it almost hit me, and I felt like something was wrong, and I got this note from Sara, but it wasn't from Sara ..."

"... and Faith was pointing at billboards, and they were messages for me, and I had to forgive myself, and Faith talked for the first time ..."

"... and I felt another heart attack beginning, and I prayed to our Angel, and if I had to die, I demanded that you and Faith be saved, without a scratch..."

"... and Seth and I were fighting, and he pinned me, and he had this huge nail, and it scraped my cheek, and then Sara tried to stop him, and Seth was going to hurt her, and I tripped him, and he hit his head, and then I had the nail ..."

"... and this voice said, 'I am with you', and then I *did* have a heart attack, and I saw the accident happening, and I passed out, and I heard the song say everything would be all right, and this beautiful light engulfed me ..."

"... and we saw the accident on the other side, and everyone in front of us was crashing, and I prayed to our Angel, and then I was embraced by this loving light ..."

"... and then Sara's Angel was shining in my eye, then I was embraced by this amazing light, and I had visions, and Seth was hurting his step-dad, and Faith was talking ..."

"... and we were heading toward the truck, and I prayed again, and the car was on its side, and our Angel saved us, again, and we were okay ..."

"... and I was alive, and I got out of the car, and saw the dove, and the pile-up across the highway, and I *knew* you were in it ..."

"... and lightning hit the door, and glass was flying everywhere, and I helped Seth up ..."

"… and then Pete tapped on the window, and he got us out of the car …"

"… and then Faith told me she loved me …"

"… and me and Seth are okay now …"

As they rattled off their experiences, their love for each other expanded. Each of their words lifted the others, and as their energy vibrated higher and higher, it filled the entire home.

Their individual, yet collective, story approached its end, and all together, they spoke in unison, "… and it felt like a dream, and we were saved by our Angel … and now we're home."

As silence filled the room, they realized that Faith hadn't shared.

Wendi bent down, eye to eye with her precious daughter. "Faith, Sweetie, don't you want to share? Did you see the Light, too?"

Faith nodded.

Tears came to Wendi's eyes as Faith confirmed what Wendi suspected. "And was it the same light you saw on the plane?"

Faith nodded again.

Wendi brushed Faith's hair behind her ear and gently caressed her daughter's cheek. "What did it look like? Can you tell us, Sweetie? Can you tell us what you saw in the Light?" Wendi asked, eagerly hoping for a response.

Faith shook her head, refusing to answer.

"Sure you can, Sweetie," Pete interjected. "You can talk, and I promise we'll listen."

Faith shook her head again and reinforced her reply with a single word. "No."

She looked up at each of them, her mother, father, and brother, and reached out her hands. She took her mother's hand first, and with her other hand, grabbed Bobby's. Instinctively, Pete reached out and clasped the hands of his wife and his son, completing the circle.

They looked at each other for a moment, feeling an intense yet gentle love pouring out from each of their hearts. Faith closed her eyes, and they each followed suit. As their eyelids closed, the room dimmed for a moment, followed by a sudden burst of light. They instinctively opened their eyes, each witnessing an illuminated sphere of radiant light floating in the center of their family circle.

It was hovering above the ground, level to Pete and Wendi's chests. The Light began to expand, slowly encompassing them. Resonating with the joy and love they were feeling, its warmth infused their hearts. They knew this light. It was the Light of Heaven: the Light of their Angel.

For over a year, Faith had known and felt its presence. And while not as familiar to Bobby, Pete, and Wendi, it was as natural to their souls as being home. The source of the Light grew larger, spreading out in all directions. It was alive, flowing and expanding, becoming something they had never imagined, yet somehow already knew.

The Light surrounded them with its brilliant radiance. The center began glowing even brighter, taking on a life of its own. It was moving, stretching, and materializing into something new, something almost tangible. It was beautiful. Glorious and radiant. Nothing could accurately describe the miracle they were witnessing.

A familiar presence emerged as a radiant Being of Light, their Angel, manifested before their eyes.

Their hearts called out to it, rejoicing at the sight of this being that their souls had known for eons. The highest magnitude of peace, joy, and love filled their beings. A hundred times a hundred and ten thousand times more than the love they thought possible.

An indescribable goodness flowed around their bodies like water in a hot bath, permeating their skin from the outside, and at the same time, coming from within.

Tears formed within each of their eyes as the Light washed away every thought and feeling other than that of pure unconditional love. As the tears gently washed down their cheeks, the Light caressed them, leaving only the soft embrace of Heaven.

Its warm incandescence was divine. A blinding light breaking the darkness. The brilliance of eleven giant suns, yet somehow soft and gentle to their eyes.

As light and energy flowed, rippled, and pierced the room, a torso formed. It stretched out, forming a head, body, and two arms. The arms extended into hand-like shapes, but there were no distinguishable fingers—just rays of light emanating from the tips. Although it seemed to be standing, there were no legs. The lower part of its body tapered into one flowing pillar of radiance, widening again at the bottom and sweeping out along the floor.

Light radiated out from the center of its back, mirroring itself, creating a distinct form that resembled wings. Light arched up and over, coming down like a gentle waterfall forming its wings. There were no feathers to be found, just ripples of soft flowing light which gave an appearance as such. It was a continuous cascade of energy and light, infinitely replenishing itself. Within its pure brilliance, there existed multiple degrees of brightness, like light dispersing into light.

Its heart was floating where the sphere first appeared and seemed to be its source, where all light was emanating from.

Light flared out in all directions from the top of its head, like rays of sunshine reaching for the heavens, creating a crown of light.

Within the center of its head, a face of pure light emerged, vague, yet revealing distinguishable features. Eyes, nose, cheeks, and mouth loosely evolved. Its two eyelids of light slowly opened, revealing blue irises of an even deeper, blue light—the only distinguishable color on the being.

Its eyes resembled human eyes, but had a life unlike nothing they had ever seen. They were big, beautiful, and radiant, slightly larger than they should be, almost disproportionate, yet perfect. The irises were made of pure energy, radiating out from its center. They were an iridescent, brilliant blue. One look into their vastness, and the enormity of the cosmos could be seen in a single focal point.

Looking at the being standing fully in its radiance, the eyes felt like the focal point of its consciousness. They contained all the wisdom of Heaven and only unconditional, forgiving love could be seen within them.

Below its eyes, the light molded itself into a hint of a nose, yet there were no nostrils. Below that, a small curvature formed a mouth. Light flowed along the top and bottom, creating the illusion of lips around it. The edges curved up into a warm, gentle smile that pierced their hearts.

It was genderless, exhibiting slight characteristics of both, radiating masculine and feminine energy at the same time. It was gentle and nurturing, yet powerful and strong.

Pure love radiated from every part of its miraculous being. Its energy carried a vibration, which in turn, carried a sound. Not an auditory sound that they picked up with their ears, but a heavenly vibration their hearts translated into music.

All of time and space stood still. An eternity passed in an instant. They didn't know how long they gazed upon this heavenly being, lost in the depths of its eyes, but what was only a fraction of time was an eternity to their souls.

In a single instant, they knew every curve, every ray of light, and every sparkle of its eyes, forever seared into their hearts. The Light itself was a living being, and the being itself was the living light of Heaven.

No fear, worry, or judgement could exist in its presence, only love. It was infinitely accepting, and love was all that it could be. As Wendi, Pete, Bobby, and Faith gazed upon their Angel, love *for* it and *from* it became one in the same, coexisting in harmony. Love given and received all at once, indistinguishable.

Within that moment, a new sound emerged. It was the voice of their Angel, or possibly a thousand voices in harmony, singing to every one of their senses. "Thank you," the voice said. "Thank you for your courage and your strength, and most of all, thank you for believing."

Its lips did not move, yet every word was a clear tone ringing in their souls. The sound of its voice was the sound of pure joy echoing in their hearts.

"You have never been, nor shall you ever be, alone. We are always with you. You are loved more than you know, infinitely and always, without end."

These were the only auditory words it spoke, but along with them came a deluge of feelings, images, and visions. In a single instant, an infinite knowing was transferred.

An understanding of life pervaded each of them in their own way. All life—all its sorrow, pain, joy, and love—came into focus. They were each shown the infinite possibilities of humanity's potential, evolving into a society of pure peace and love. They saw the vision of a transparent society where people could sense and read each other's energy, along with the energy of all life: plants, animals, and the Earth itself. To cause another pain was instantly felt as harming oneself. There was no more war, no more killing, and no more abuse. Families, couples, friends, and strangers understood and respected each other, communicating their truest emotions and deepest fears with the greatest of ease. Both humanity and the Earth flourished.

Other visions of the future followed, and one by one, each family was shown their path and asked to be a guiding light through the perceived darkness. They were each tasked with sharing their story and helping others to navigate the storm of humanness. People's minds needed guidance to get through the waves of misunderstanding and the false pretenses that caused suffering and led to wars. They were gifted tools and insights to serve humanity as beacons of light guiding others back to their true selves.

As the visions faded away, they were left with one last unified thought: No one is ever truly alone or unloved. The Divine Consciousness of Creation surrounds us, is within us, and is us.

The images faded into the light and only the vision of the Angel remained. It bowed its head, offering its gratitude and respect. The Angel looked at each of them one last time, connecting deeply with their souls. Its light slowly retracted, folding in upon itself, contracting back into a brilliant sphere. Its radiant glow slowly dissipated as the being gently retreated into the single point of light from which it had emerged.

They stood there in magnificent silence, frozen in awe at the day's final miracle that they had just witnessed. Feelings of love continued to course through their bodies, even after their Angel had gone. While its physical glow was no longer present, the room still seemed illuminated by the residual energy of the Angel's presence.

They huddled together on the couch, holding each other tightly. None of them spoke another word for the rest of the night. They didn't need to. No words could describe the miracle their senses had witnessed. They embraced each other as a family, each of them experiencing the same feelings. The hearts and souls of Wendi, Peter, Bobby, and Faith were changed forever.

Wendi laid her head on her husband's shoulder. Faith cozied up between them, resting her head on her father's heart, and Bobby laid down on the other side of his father, his arm stretched out, embracing his sister. Pete, in the middle of his family, embraced them all. They stayed there, and drifted off into a deep, peaceful sleep.

~~~ O ~~~

ring ring ... ring ring

Peter was reluctant to pick up the phone. He was unsure if he could speak to anyone after what they had all experienced the previous night. His heart, however, had other plans. He had a newfound desire to connect with everyone he knew, and a sense of who was calling flashed in his mind. "Hello?" he graciously answered.

"Yes, hello. Is Peter Farfalla there?" a shaky, uncertain, and nervous voice asked from the other end. Peter knew the voice immediately. He knew it well.

"Hello, Mr. Marshall. This is Peter speaking. What can I do for you?" Peter wasn't certain why his former boss was calling, or why he had such a different tone in his voice. Even if he was offering Pete his job back, Pete didn't plan on taking it.

"Yes, ah, of course it's you, Peter. I'm sorry for calling you at home, especially this early. And I'm sure you're still upset about yesterday. I'm sure you don't think favorably of me, and you probably have some choice words you want to share," he commented in a nervous tone. He paused, waiting for Pete to acknowledge or respond, but instead of hearing any sort of backlash or anger, all Frank Marshall heard was what sounded like a smile.

Frank hesitantly continued, "I called because, uh, well, I wanted to tell you something firsthand." He paused again. "As I was finishing up for the day, the company president came into my office to talk. I had already informed him after you left that you would not be returning, and I let him know that I would have someone finish the report in the morning. He sat down and told me he wanted to be frank—like I haven't heard that joke before— except he wasn't smiling when he said it."

Frank Marshall paused again. "He said HR was concerned that there could be a lawsuit against the company for firing a dedicated employee, as he referred to you, who was still recovering from a heart attack, who had direct orders from his doctor to work part-time. And, well, I know you tried to tell me that, and I wasn't listening to you very well. HR was concerned it could become an issue. He told me that they needed to institute some department cutbacks. And so … well … I was the one cut back. Just like that, after 10 years of hard work and dedication. He also said they had received some negative reports about my performance and attitude, and they would use those reports against me if I tried to contest it. So that's it. I no longer have a job due to 'department cutbacks.' I know they plan on contacting you directly to let you know that you still have a job, but I wanted to tell you first," he summed up, his voice still rattled.

Less than twenty-four hours ago, Pete would have had plenty to say in return, but this morning, he was content to simply listen. "Thank you for letting me know, Mr. Marshall."

"Frank. I'm not your boss anymore, so please, call me Frank."

"Okay then. Thank you, Frank. I'll still have to reconsider the job. Was that all?"

"Yes … Well, uh … no, actually. There was one more thing. Do you remember your little comment about my wife?"

Pete sighed, remembering his harsh words. His heart was filled with too much love to wish pain on anyone. "I apologize about that. I was angry, and it was uncalled for."

"Oh, well, thank you," Frank replied, not expecting an apology. "And regardless, I'm sure you'll be happy to know that when I got home, my wife had left me."

Hearing a sigh on the other end of the phone, Pete realized why he had never heard this tone in Frank's voice: Frank Marshall was suffering. He was alone and scared. A wave of forgiveness washed over Pete. Everything this man had ever done or said to Peter dissolved into the past, and all Pete felt in that moment was compassion and love for his ex-boss.

Pete was fully present in the moment, and a quiet inner knowing filled his being. He knew Frank felt that he deserved the suffering. He deserved to lose his job, and he deserved to lose his wife. What Frank Marshall needed most right now was forgiveness and friendship.

"We've had issues for a long time." Frank added. "It's why I put so much time into work, and why I've been such a hard-ass. So I also called because, well … I wanted to apologize." Frank continued, his voice still shaking. "I'm sorry, Pete. Sorry for how I treated you this entire year. You're a good man. I didn't mean to be so hard on you. I just wanted to see you be a more disciplined and dedicated employee. I guess it doesn't really matter now, huh? Look where dedication got me. Nowhere."

"It's okay, Frank. There's no need to apologize. And I'm sorry to hear about your wife. I really am." Pete respectfully responded.

"Oh, uh, did I hear you right, Pete?" Frank said in a bewildered tone, not expecting Pete to accept his apology. "It's okay to be angry with me, Pete. I expected it, and I certainly deserve whatever you have to say."

"It's okay, Frank. You're in pain," was Pete's reply. "And when people are in pain, they treat others with that same pain. You didn't know what else to do with your own. You also did what you thought was best for the company. And honestly, if the company doesn't see what a valuable employee you are, then they don't deserve you. Things happen for a reason. Believe me. Even if it feels like the worst thing at the time, like you're not going to survive it, it's really just God's way of preparing you for a better life. Just take a moment to shed the right light on all this. This is an opportunity for you to move on to something bigger and better in your career, and possibly your relationship. What's most important is that you learn and grow from all this."

Pete paused for a moment. Frank was in such shock, and he didn't know how to take it all in. "I have a feeling you and your wife just need some time apart, and you'll be just fine. And if you need it, I'd be happy to be a referral for you for any companies you interview with."

On the other end, Frank sat with the phone to his ear in complete shock. "Wha ... I don't ... Wow. Pete, I never expected any of this. I'm not sure I even understand, but thank you ... I ... I don't know why you would offer that, but thank you. I may just take you up on it."

"You're quite welcome, Frank. And, well, something happened last night after I left. Something incredible. I really don't want to discuss it just now, especially over the phone. I need to be with my family today, but you have my number, so if you give me a call sometime, I'd be happy to tell you all about it. Maybe we could go out and grab a bite to eat. After all," he chuckled, "we both have plenty of time being unemployed!"

Frank awkwardly laughed along, his voice no longer filled with guilt and fear, but with gratitude. "If you're really serious, Pete, I'd like that. After all the hours together at work, I never took the time to get to know you. You're an honest, genuine guy. I'm sorry again for mistreating you. I don't want to hold you up any longer. You have a wonderful day. Give my best to your family, and we'll get that bite to eat."

"I look forward to it. You'll be fine, Frank. We all will."

As Pete hung up the phone, Wendi walked into the room and noticed the light blinking on the answering machine. "We have a message?" she asked.

"That's odd," Pete replied. "I was talking with Frank Marshall, but I didn't notice anyone calling while I was on with him."

"Mr. Marshall, really? What was that about?"

"Ironically, he lost his job, and I still have mine. He called to tell me and to apologize. I can tell you more about it later. Let's see who the message is from," Pete said as he pressed the button.

beep

"You have one new message. Friday. 5:55 p.m."

"Well, hello, Deary! It's Angie. Somethin' hit me when I got home yesterday. With all the talks we've had, and all my rambles, I'm not sure I ever gave you this piece of advice … When you ask for help from your Angel, it can come in all shapes and sizes. I promise they'll get the job done, but it doesn't always show up the way you expect. So when you pray to your Angel for help, Dear, always ask it be done with *ease and grace*. I hope you enjoyed the school extravaganza and had a magical night. I was getting an odd feeling every time I thought of you, but they kept tellin' me everything was going to be all right. So I thought it was important to call ya at home to tell ya. And there's something else I wanted to tell ya, but I prefer to tell ya in person."

"Last message."

beep

~~~ O ~~~

Wendi finished up in the kitchen and joined the rest of her family. She filled in the gap on the couch between her beautiful son and adoring husband, who, thanks to an Angel, was still alive and well. Pete's heart was pumping strong and healthy, flowing with love. She gave him a kiss and nestled in next to him.

Faith was sitting in front of them on the floor, but still seemed too far away. "Faith, Sweetie," Wendi beckoned, "Why don't you join us on the couch?"

Faith looked back, smiled, and sprang to her feet. "Okay." The couch was only big enough for three, but that didn't stop her. There was always room for Faith. They all cuddled up, watching the news together.

"They're calling it *The Miracle on the Highway*," announced the newscaster. "The massive pile-up along the highway involved multiple collisions. Eleven of the crashes involved extensive damage, leaving those eleven cars completely totaled. Along with subsequent fender-benders as cars failed to stop, sliding into each other. The accident included a total of twenty-two vehicles. All-in-all, drivers and passengers, the accident involved thirty-three individuals: men, women, and children. Just the numbers themselves are miraculous, but that's not the true story here," the newscaster admitted.

"You can see by the aerial footage all the extensive damage to the vehicles involved. First responders expected to fill several ambulances and anticipated a multitude of injuries ranging from cuts to broken bones, possibly even casualties. But that wasn't the case. Miraculously, not a single person needed treatment or help. I'll say it again: no one was hurt in any way, not a single scrape, cut, or bruise. With the amount of glass covering the highway, responders said it was impossible to not have several cuts to patch up, referring to it as a miracle. And the miracles continued. A man who reportedly experienced a heart attack and may have been the cause of the accident, got right out of his car and ran across the highway to get to his wife, who was in the accident on the northbound side."

"We interviewed as many of the victims as we could," he continued, "and they all called it a miracle. They were all smiling, happy, and grateful to God to be alive. Continuing the miracle, they all gave the same report, using the exact same words. Each one of them reported that just before the crash, they prayed to their Guardian Angel to be saved, and to keep everyone safe—not even a scratch. They each ended by saying this angelic accident … was no accident."

Peter sat in the corner with his arm lovingly wrapped around his beautiful wife. He turned to her and smiled, looking deeply into her loving eyes. Leaning over, he gently kissed her lips. She happily accepted, returned the smile, then looked to her left at her son. She reached over, gently caressing his hair, and passed along a kiss to his forehead. He smiled as well, and all three of them looked down at the precious little Angel laying there.

Laying across all three of them, already dozing off, Faith was cuddled in her mother's lap, had her head resting on her father's thigh, and her feet across Bobby's legs. She must have felt their gaze, because she looked up at her family with a glorious smile on her face. Her eyes returned their loving stare, each still radiating with the love and peace of their heavenly encounter.

Faith looked at each one of them and whispered a soft, "I love you."

As the news segment ended, the next announcement caught Wendi's attention. "And here are the winning lottery numbers from last night's Pick-6, in case you missed them. Thank you, and goodnight." The TV flashed the six winning numbers, displaying each pick boldly across the screen.

$$3, 4, 7, 33, 44, 77$$

The jackpot was estimated at $2.22 million.

After everything that had happened since the morning she ran out to the bakery, Wendi had completely forgotten about the lottery ticket tucked inside her purse. The moment she saw the numbers on the screen, she remembered it all. Every detail came rushing back to her. Waking up at 4:44 a.m., the cost of breakfast totaling $7.77, and her change being $3.33. She remembered the song playing in the background, the man at the other register talking about signs, and telling her it felt like a special day as she left. Although she had visited the bakery numerous times, it wasn't until that moment that she realized the name of the store itself was also a sign—Angelo's Bakery.

Faith stared for a moment at the screen, reading the numbers, not even knowing her mom had purchased a ticket. Her eyes shifted away from the TV to her right. She listened, smiled, and nodded, acknowledging the voice of Nobody, who was now somebody to all of them. She looked up at her mom and repeated the words she had just heard.

"We won!"

Wendi let out a boisterous, joyful laugh, looked into her daughter's shining eyes, and replied, "We sure did, Angel. We sure did."

~ o ~

Chapter 14:

Epilogue

"Believe."

~ o ~

I still remember it all as if it happened yesterday. It affected our hearts and lives forever, not just our immediate family, but all the others we've touched along the way.

After our Angel vanished that night, its presence stayed with us, and continues to live within our hearts. That was the only time we *physically* witnessed the Angel, but it is always with us, loving, protecting, and guiding us. We had all been supercharged by the Light and infused with its love. We still feel it radiating out of every cell.

We're different now, closer to how we were created to be, yet part of us remained the same. The amazing feelings we were infused with by our Angel still echo in our hearts. Immense feelings of oneness and harmony have permeated our beings, an interconnectedness with each other and all of life.

We stayed home the day after the accident to process it all, bask in the amazing feelings that were still coursing through our bodies and minds, and to just be together as a family. Pete didn't return to work and instead accepted a very nice severance package. Angie was gone when I got in the following day. Whatever project she was brought in for had abruptly ended. I never saw her again, but she left a note on my desk. It ended with her calling me Deary, of course. As much as I miss her, she taught me what she needed to. There's no real reason to say goodbye to someone you always carry in your heart—plus, I have a feeling that Angie will pop back into our lives if she's ever needed again.

The next week, Bobby told Seth about the visions he had regarding Seth and his stepfather. Typically, Seth would laugh at such comments and reply with something like, "Good. The bastard deserves it." But there was something about *the way* Bobby told Seth, something in Bobby's eyes that surpassed Seth's ego and connected with his heart. Bobby, who once hated this other boy, now genuinely cared about how Seth's life would turn out if the vision came to fruition. Something shifted in Seth at the thought of actually being locked up for murder, and he, Bobby, and Sara—who was now also privy to the vision— asked Mr. Wacher for help. Sara first requested they all pray together. Seth refused at first, then reluctantly agreed. He was willing to try anything to live a life without abuse. The funny thing about it, though, was that by the time they persuaded Seth's mom to finally take action, his stepdad had just picked up and left overnight.

We also had the only jackpot-winning lottery ticket. With extra money and our newfound connection to life, we flew in our families for the holidays, including Pete's brother, Georgie, and his wife and kids. It was a true joy to have the whole family together. There was even talk of them moving down south so we could all be together again. Pete followed his intuition, and with the help of a few signs, made some very wise investments. So while we no longer had to think about money for a long time, the irony was, we didn't care. No amount of, or lack of, money and possessions mattered. All that mattered was the joy we carried in our hearts from that night forward. Just the thought of our Angel, the slightest glimpse in our memory, still fills our hearts with such peace and love that it cannot fully be described in words. It is something that can only be felt; something to be experienced.

We all finally understood what Faith had seen so many years ago outside that plane window. In one form or another, she had been communicating with our Angel since then. We never would have understood or believed her until we witnessed the Angel's full presence and grace for ourselves.

All things have their place and purpose, and if our lives had unfolded any other way, if we hadn't undergone the tragedies we did, our story would no longer be the same and we would not have shared the miracles that we did.

Afterward, we asked Faith why she called the Angel Nobody, and she told us this simple truth, from the mind of a child …

When she first started communicating with the Angel, she asked why she only saw a big blur of light. It told her that it didn't have a body like she did, and that it took a very special connection and a lot of energy to appear in that form. She said she had to name it something, and since it had no body, she named it Nobody. Her Angel respectfully accepted its name, emphasizing that no matter what name she chose, it was always with her.

Apparently, these were some of the typical conversations a little girl has with an Angel. She had many more stories about her conversations, but to our surprise, most of them were simple chats. She didn't ask for the secrets of the Universe or to explain the meaning of God. She didn't want to know her purpose in life, or why we were all here. Most of her questions were simply about how she could help her family find happiness again. That's all that was important to her.

That's why it was easy for her to maintain her connection with Nobody. Her intentions were pure, always coming from her heart with innocence and humility. She had direct access to one of God's glorious, heavenly beings, who held the keys to all the Universe and Heaven itself, and yet she had never asked for any of it. A little girl doesn't need to know the inner workings of the universe or the human mind. She only wants peace, love, and joy in the moment, not even for herself, but for those she loves.

She loved her tea time with Nobody. She enjoyed the simple company, truths, and candidness of her Angel that people typically do not offer to children. She loved that it never treated her like a child, and was always patient, kind, and loving. Soon after, Faith mentioned that another guest had joined her tea parties —her unborn sister—but that's a story for another time.

We all call upon our Guardian of Light often, and it always answers. You may think we spend every day wishing to see it again, but we don't really need to. Part of it now exists inside us, and we know that part of us exists within it. The love of that Celestial Being of Light is forever engrained in our hearts, etched in our souls, and somehow connected to our very being. Not a single day passes in which we do not remember the love it brought to us that night.

The true gift to each of us, even beyond the visions, was the realization of the first words uttered by the Angel when it appeared: *thank you.*

It took time to truly grasp the meaning of those words. The Angel had thanked us. This divine being of love, which had crossed all dimensions of space and time, emerging within our earthly realm to save *us*, appeared before us and thanked *us*. We owed our lives and every ounce of gratitude we had within our hearts to this magnificent being, and yet it was holding *us* in gratitude. It was thanking *us* for believing in it. What had we done to deserve its gratitude? Wasn't it the Angel that created the miracle, and not us?

As Angie said, Angels are always with us, but they can only intervene if we allow them. If we don't *believe, ask,* and *trust,* we'll never *receive.* They will still be standing by our side, loving us and patiently waiting to help, but they won't. The best way I can explain it is this: Imagine the feeling of watching a child suffering, possibly endangering its own life, *knowing* you can help, and not being *allowed* to. It would be heartbreaking.

And even beyond that, we learned that the true miracle was our combined faith. It was *that* power, *our* power, that changed and saved our lives. The Angel simply assisted. It was our love for each other and our belief in our Angel that allowed this messenger of light to step through into our world.

A legion of Angels is patiently waiting to help humanity. An Angel's path always leads to our door, but we are the ones who keep it locked. We hold the key to allow their love in, and our belief is that key. Angels are always there, always watching, waiting, loving, and believing in us, but it is our belief in them that opens the doorway.

The more who doubt, the more difficult it is for Angels to help humanity as a whole, to help us fulfill our purpose. But for every human who opens their heart, a thousand veils are lifted between our worlds. And everyone who shares their story and their faith— not by preaching, judging, or being righteous, but simply by being a loving example—brightens our world and bridges the gap between Heaven and Earth.

We are loved in more ways than we can comprehend. We are part of something much grander, and it is part of us. Inseparable.

And while Angels have the power to create all types of miracles, that is not their true purpose. They exist to guide our minds to our hearts, our hearts to our souls, and our collective being to a new plane of existence. Every Angel's wish is to help us embody unconditional love. They are here to teach us to love ourselves, to love each other, and to love all of creation.

Believe.

Believe in magic and miracles. Believe in yourself, your own divinity, and believe in the divinity in others.

Angels are the Keepers of the Universe, the Teachers of Truth, and the Stewards of the Light. They are pure love, here to love us all, and nothing less. Whenever you feel lost and alone, sad and confused, frustrated and angry, call on your Angel. Ask for its love and grace, its knowledge and wisdom, and its light—and it will be granted. In any situation, no matter how big or small, call and your Angel will answer. It shares as much gratitude to be in your life as you will have for it to be in yours. Your Angel is already with you, watching, waiting, and guiding. It already believes in you. It is simply waiting for you to believe in it, and in yourself.

I felt it. It still lives inside us, calling out to us every day; calling out to you. What the Angel passed on to us that night, we now pass on to you through our story. For every heart that hears it, we wish for them to join us in creating a world of peace and harmony—a world of unconditional love.

Now it's your turn.

Ease your mind and open your heart. Call forth the love within your soul and believe. Believe in something greater. Take a chance, a leap of faith, and believe in the unseen. Create your own experiences, write your own stories, share them, and inspire others.

Your Angel is waiting to share its love and light with you.

Welcome it into your life.

Your story is next. We are waiting to hear it. The world is waiting. And your Angel is waiting for you … *to believe.*

~ o ~

The Guide:
Connecting With Your Angel

"Believe. Ask. Trust. And Receive."

.

~ o ~

Where to Begin

You already have.

Simply by picking up this book, you have set an intention, consciously or unconsciously, to connect deeper with your Angels. And if you finished the story, your mind has already been filled with wisdom, prayers, and even a meditation, to offer you guidance, insight, and tools to create a whole new way of living— in constant connection with the divine. So let's continue your journey...

The concepts and teachings presented in *Angel*, along with this practical guide, will help you in creating or strengthening the connection you have with your own Guardian Angels.

Whether you have never before prayed to Angels for help and guidance, or you already have a strong connection, this book is perfect for you. To those new at connecting to Angels, I welcome you to a miraculous way of living your life. For those who have already cultivated connections with your Angels, allow this book to be a reminder of what you have already learned and a resource to strengthen that bond.

Much of the wisdom within this novel was channeled through me or has become part of my awareness through my own experiences or learning from others' wisdom. The signs that were shown throughout the story—numbers, songs, feathers, and more —were also based on real experiences by myself or others whom I know.

Angels Are Real

They are beings of pure light and love. As messengers, they are the carriers of God's love and the bringers of God's light. As guides, they are here to help us navigate this life and realize our true power, purpose, and connection to divine creation.

I truly believe these words, but if you have any doubts, follow the practices outlined in this book and see for yourself. And as with many other aspects of faith, you may find that life is easier if you believe first, rather than waiting to "see it to believe it". It was clear in writing this book that believing was the most important and powerful aspect of our relationship with our Angels. After I began writing, I had a clear vision of my Angel, which I did my best to describe in Chapter 13: Messenger of Heaven (pp. 314-316).

But that was how the Angel appeared *to me*. While I deeply believe it was a more accurate depiction of a real Angel, Angels can take any form as opposed to the traditional human with feathered wings Pete pokes fun at in Chapter 9: Accepting the Signs (p. 223). I also believe they appear to us in a way that resonates with us and one in which we will recognize them. So for some, that's a plain human form. For others, it includes wings or may appear as a being of light. Even beyond that, it may have no distinct form, or your Angel could be a sound or simply a feeling. I encourage you to let go of any expectation of what your Angel *should* or even *could* look like.

And while my vision of a light being Angel was more of a "portrait" than a true meeting or visceral experience, I know many others who have stood in the presence of Angels and witnessed a living being appear to them. Those experiences were very real to each of them, not just a dream or vision.

I have personally received many signs and nudges from my Angels, including the constant appearance of my "Angel numbers" (recurring numbers associated with Angels). These numbers will come to me so many times a day that coincidence is impossible, and the synchronicities are undeniable.

I also invite you to join the *Angel* novel community on social media or through the website AngelNovel.com to read and share your own Angel stories.

Ways to Strengthen Your Connection

While Angel is a work of metaphysical fiction (or meta-fiction, as I like to call it), it holds many truths. Allow its wisdom and concepts to lay the groundwork for you to connect to your own Angels, here and now, and follow the practices demonstrated within to continue to strengthen that connection. Make praying, meditating, and talking to your Angels as routine as brushing your teeth and checking your mobile phone. Along with giving Wendi a prayer to get her started, Angie talks about the importance of cultivating a stronger connection with Angels in Chapter 8: Making the Connection (pp. 178-179). Let's look at some of the many ways you can connect with your Angels...

Intention: Everything starts with intention. Behind every action, word, and thought, an intention is created by your consciousness (even if you're not aware of it). Typically, if you're calling on your Angel, your intention is to ask for help. So be in that space. Have the humility to ask for help, and be humble enough to receive it. Simply by putting out an intention to connect with your Angel, you have already unlocked the door.

Prayer/Request: Call it what you will: whether you craft a well-sounding prayer, a playful rhyme, or very plainly ask, they all work. Angels do not judge or care *how* we try to communicate with them, they simply wait for us *to* communicate. Just as Angie says in Chapter 3: Glimmers of Hope (p. 74), they cannot interfere in our lives until we give them permission. They respect our free will to choose our own path. In praying and asking for help, we are inviting them into our lives. We typically pray when we are in need, and regardless of how big or small that need is, having that need puts us in a space to be vulnerable, humble, and open our hearts to receiving love, guidance, and support.

If you're new to praying or asking for help, don't get caught up in whether it sounds right or not. It's the simple act *of asking* that matters, and more importantly, *how* you ask (or pray). As Wendi learned in Chapter 5: A Prayer for Help (p. 114), it's coming from an earnest and heartfelt place that makes the difference over the words that are used. And when you come from that place within yourself, you'll be surprised at how the perfect words emerge, almost as if you were channeling the prayer. Know and believe that your prayers are always heard.

If you're not particularly religious, please don't get caught up in the idea of prayer. Praying is a powerful tool, but a simple heartfelt request can still send the same message. So choose to ask in a way that *feels* right to *you*. If you're religious, crafting a prayer in the traditional sense will help you to connect on a deeper level because it's what resonates with you most. For those not-so-religious types, an earnest request is all that's needed. The most important thing to remember when asking is to *feel* it. Regardless of the words, say them with all your heart and soul and pour your love into your request. This is mentioned by Angie as she hands Wendi the prayer in Chapter 3: Glimmers of Hope (pp. 74-75).

Meditation: A wonderful way to connect with your Angel on a deeper level—mentally, spiritually, and emotionally—is through the practice of meditation. Going into a state of meditation literally shifts your brainwaves into a state of deep relaxation and rest. In this state, we can ease the ego, calm the mind, and set aside worries and fears that interfere with our connection to the divine, to ourselves, and to our Angels.

If you've never meditated before, don't fret. Meditation can be one minute of deep breathing, or an hour or more of deep connection. It can be seated with your legs crossed or feet on the floor. You can be alone or with a group, silent or with music, or guided. Even walking through the woods can be a meditative experience. It is your intent to meditate that sets the tone.

As with all things, it takes practice and trusting your own intuition to know what type of meditation works for you, if any. If you're new to meditation, you may find guided meditation works better for you, and it can lead you into a steady practice of meditating silently to allow whatever is needed to enter your consciousness. I have many guided meditations available online that you can discover through the *Angel* website. You can also listen to the exact meditation said by Angie at the end of Chapter 8: Making the Connection (pp. 191-194). This meditation to meet and connect with your Angel has been recorded by my dear friend Wendi Rose (whom Wendi Farfalla was named after as a thank you to the amazing Earth Angel Wendi has been to me), and we have made it available on AngelNovel.com.

***Conversations*:** How do you talk to an Angel? Like you talk to anyone else! Just like in prayer—or when talking to God, Spirit, the Universe, or whichever higher power you believe in—always speak freely and openly, from the heart. It can be a thought in your mind, a whisper, a normal voice, or a shout at the top of your lungs. It makes no difference to them. However you choose to communicate, it is always heard.

And while Angels may be divine heavenly beings existing on a level we probably can't comprehend from down here, don't let that change anything. They want us to communicate with them however we feel most comfortable. Talk to them like they are your dearest friend and your fondest relationship. The more loving of a connection you have with someone, the more of your true self shines through. That's the type of relationship and conversation that your Angels want to have with you.

Remember, just like you don't want a friend whom you only hear from when they need help, you can talk to your Angel without needing help in return. Your Angel loves you and is not just here to answer prayers, but to listen and openly communicate, as demonstrated through the innocence of Faith's conversations throughout the novel.

And with that said, it is truly my hope that you will have such a close and amazing connection with your Angels, that you will not only talk to them daily, but you will hear them *answer*. It takes time and practice, but we're all capable of having open, two-way communication with our Angels—asking *and* receiving. Answers from your Angels don't just come in the form of signs. You are capable of *hearing* the answers to your many questions.

Asking for Help

So now you're ready to communicate with your Angels, and remember, miracles have no size. You can ask for help with anything, from saving someone's life, to something as simple as getting the perfect parking spot. You can review Angie's teaching about this in Chapter 7: Opening the Doorway (pp. 150-153).

Let's delve further into Angie's 4-step process for asking your Angels for help, referenced in Chapter 6: Learning to Believe (p. 138): Believe. Ask. Trust. And Receive.

Believe: While many people will tell you to ask first, then trust, without believing first, I don't feel you can truly trust that help is coming. So start with believing. Believe that you are not alone. Believe that the Universe will rearrange itself to answer your prayer and show that you are loved. And possibly most importantly, believe that you are worthy of being helped.

Ask: Sometimes when we feel stuck, lost, or hopeless, we get so caught up in those feelings, we don't ask for help—not from the physical people in our lives, or for divine help. And some people may feel too proud, or whatever the case may be, to ask for help, wishing to work through things themselves. And that's fine. But if you truly find yourself feeling down and needing help, the only way to get it is to ask. We've also reviewed this in the prayer and conversations section.

Trust: Once you've asked for help, it's important to trust that you have been heard, and trust that guidance is on the way. It's so easy for us to doubt, or feel unworthy, of help. And the longer it takes for a sign or for help to appear, the easier it is to doubt we've been heard. So trust that in one way or another, your prayer has been heard and *already* answered.

How you're answered or helped will come in many ways. Sometimes signs, answers, and guidance come immediately, and sometimes it takes a while. Our desired timing doesn't always match the best timing for our soul's growth. I promise your requests and prayers are always heard, and as much as I'd like to promise you that you'll always be answered and helped, sometimes our soul's grander plan takes precedence.

While I believe help is always here for us in some way, help may be our Angels stepping back so our souls can learn and experience a lesson firsthand, and strengthen ourselves by overcoming it on our own. (But even in those cases, I believe there are subtle ways we are helped behind the scenes.)

Receive: Trusting that a prayer has been answered and receiving the answer really are two different things. We may have been heard, and signs, guidance, or help may have been sent, but we still have to step up and receive them.

So many people may finally ask for help but don't feel they're truly worthy of receiving it. These thoughts and feelings can thwart your Angel's attempt to help and guide you, as Angels respect your free will. And like it or not, our thoughts and feelings are an extension of our free will. You can *say* you want help, but if you don't *feel* worthy of help, you may not receive it. So ask, trust, and be ready to receive!

Acknowledge the signs when they come. *Listen* to the guidance when you hear it (sometimes in the form of another person— someone close or a complete stranger—saying something meant just for us). And finally, *let go* of any expectations and desired outcomes. We're helped in ways that best serve our soul, so receive the help however it comes. And finally...

Surrender and Gratitude: While I didn't include this specifically as one of Angie's steps, it's important that we let go and surrender throughout this entire process of asking and receiving. Set aside fear and ego, step into humility, and you'll become a clear channel to *ask and receive* divine help.

And as with all things, taking on an attitude of gratitude is always the best way to approach life. All of life is a gift, and any help we receive from the other side—from passed loved ones, Guides, Angels, Spirit, God, you name it—is always a gift. Be thankful for the life you have, for any guidance and help that is given (from the physical and non-physical), and even for the struggles. All of it is here to help us grow, evolve, and remember who we really are: divine, powerful, infinite, loving beings!

Signs

Signs are everywhere. They always have been, but if it wasn't in our awareness to be on the lookout, we likely have missed or dismissed them. Now that you've connected to your Angel and asked for help, keep your mind and awareness open.

When we talk about receiving signs from Angels, they come in countless ways for countless reasons. Some are a simple reassurance that you're not alone. Other signs will directly answer questions or confirm an answer or intuition you already have. Some signs will be simple and obvious, and some will be subtle or only mean something to you personally. Some of the more common ways were demonstrated throughout the book and are outlined below.

It's also important that you follow your intuition and *feelings* when receiving a sign. Something that may seem very commonplace, or that you're unsure of as a sign, may spark something inside you that confirms it as a sign: a knowing, a nudge, a whisper in your mind, or a very visceral feeling in your heart. Seeing the sign and acknowledging them can be two different things. Angie talks about signs throughout the book and specifically mentions receiving signs in Chapter 7: Opening the Doorway (p. 154).

Synchronicities: One of my favorite and undeniable ways to receive signs is through synchronicities. It's not just about *getting* the sign, but the timing and way the sign appears make an infinite difference in assuring you that it is beyond coincidence or accident. Let's take feathers, for example. Birds and feathers are everywhere, but how often do you see them on a daily basis, and what are the chances of seeing them at the exact moment, or moments after, talking about Angels or asking for signs? Or you ask a question of the Universe and an obvious and undeniable answer reveals itself. Angie mentions synchronicities in Chapter 8: Making the Connection (p. 177).

Feathers: Because we relate Angels to winged beings, feathers, specifically white feathers, have long been seen as signs from Angels. Since bird feathers can be so common, it's important to pay attention to where, when, and how the feathers appear. I have a friend who wanted reassurance that her Angels and Guides were with her, and she started seeing multitudes of feathers on her daily walks, in obvious places. And remember, it doesn't have to be a real feather. A feather appearing as a sign can be an image of a feather such as art, or on a shirt, poster, etc. Refer to Angie's teaching about how and where feathers can appear in Chapter 10 Standing at the Precipice (pp. 243-244).

Numbers: Numbers are another one of my favorite signs. They will follow you around, appearing so often and in such ways that they are an unmistakable sign. Triple digits have long been associated with the divine and with Angels, but your numbers may be personal to you. I used the example of triple digits right from the start of the book to show that even before Wendi started praying, the Angel was already making itself known (Chapter 1: Seeds of Doubt, p. 3).

My Angel numbers are two specific numbers that meant nothing until I hosted a daylong symposium about Angels. (I'll refrain from mentioning the numbers here to allow your own numbers to appear without influence from mine.) Ever since then, those numbers have been associated with my Angels and have repeated incessantly. My favorite occurrence happened one night as I was streaming a message. I was speaking about my Angel numbers being one of my signs, and at that exact moment, the lights flickered, I looked at the time, and there were the numbers. It was amazing!

My numbers will appear on the clock every night before bed for days on end, or on a phone number that keeps calling, or a bank or credit card statement. I see them most at times when I need reassurance or ask for help, but it's also become so commonplace, I see it as a daily reminder my Angels are with me. My Angel numbers showed up very strongly during the writing of this book. What numbers have been showing up for you? Feel free to share them with us on our social media and website.

Clouds: On any given day, spotting shapes in the clouds are fun to see, but spotting Angel or feather-shaped clouds carry a deep message: Your Angel is with you. While finding bird feathers can be a common occurrence, signs in the form of clouds are a quite rare. A cloud with a distinct, inarguable shape is always a clear sign and to be taken as one. I loved adding the description of the Angel cloud (Chapter 7: Opening the Doorway, pp. 158-159). Soon after I wrote it, a friend of mine shared a photo of her and pointed out the peculiar cloud above her head. It was a small, but unmistakable, Angel-shaped cloud. She had no idea I had just written about clouds, and it was a beautiful confirmation that my Angels were supporting and watching over me during this time.

Songs: Songs are such wonderful ways to receive signs from your Angels. Sometimes it's the name of the song, the chorus, or both, that grab your attention. But that's obvious. Sometimes it's a single line of a song that grabs your attention right after asking a question (even if it's just a thought in your mind) that gives you the perfect answer or reassurance. While songs were also used when Wendi got her lottery ticket, and as Pete was seeing the Light during his accident, my favorite scene was Wendi hearing the songs on her way home from the hospital in Chapter 5: A Prayer for Help (p. 115).

Movies, TV: Along with the radio, all other types of media are perfect for delivering messages to us, especially visual media. Pay special attention to synchronicities when watching movies and TV. It could be the name of a character or place, a number within the movie, or a line mentioned that is just what you need to hear. It could also be something that is a confirmation for you. As a visual and auditory medium, it's a great way for signs to come through.

The internet: In this day and age, we spend a lot of time looking at websites, emails, and social media. Any of these can contain signs and messages for you. There have been many times a "junk email" catches my attention just before I delete it. It will turn out to be an event, or something else, that my Angels want me to attend.

Other types of signs: There are countless ways that signs can appear to us. Angels will use any means they can. In the beginning of the book, a bar of soap gives Pete the answer to his question in Chapter 2: Losing Faith (p. 35). Later on in the book, it's junk mail delivering an answer to Wendi in Chapter 9: Accepting the Signs (p. 213) and of course, she received deep understanding and healing through the messages delivered on the billboards in Chapter 11: Dark Night of the Soul (p262, 266-267, & 273).

The Next Step

While I believe that we're surrounded by this team of divine celestial light beings who will instantly be at our side to help us, they're not a crutch or here to "save" us. Parents who love their children unconditionally will do anything for them, at any time, until their dying day. However, those same parents do not wish to raise a child who is helpless, or who relies on them their entire lives. Nothing would make those parents prouder than to see that child grow up to be strong, wise, loving, and self-sufficient, and even beyond the parents' hopes.

We are the children of an infinite God; we're not here to be saved by something or someone outside of ourselves. Quite the contrary. We are truly here to discover our own power and embrace it fully. We are created to learn, grow, and evolve. We are created to discover our own strength and power and to wield it to create a better experience for us all.

Once you fully embrace your own power and realize the miracles you're capable of creating, you may no longer need to call on your Angel—but it doesn't mean you can't. We begin this journey by asking Angels to help, protect, and guide us. And while they will do so for as long as we wish (they don't live inside time, as we do), they, like any parent, wish for us to realize our worth, embrace our own divinity, and use our *own* power, rather than asking them to use theirs. They are here to show us what is possible and teach us to love and believe in ourselves.

So call on your Angels as often as you wish, for whatever you wish. Just know that they're really here to show you how to call on your own power, use it, and pass that knowledge on to others.

I would love for you to share on the *Angel* website and social media the myriad ways that your Angels and their signs are appearing in your life.

Moving on...

I am immensely grateful that you have taken the time to read this novel and guide. I firmly hope it has brought you insight, wisdom, and most importantly, a closer connection with your own Angels.

It's important that throughout this process of connecting with your Angels, and any process you have for cultivating spiritual growth, you do what feels right to you. Allow this book to guide you—but not be taken as absolute truth. Truth is something for you to discover for yourself, and as you grow and evolve, so will your truths.

~ o ~

Afterword

I hope you enjoyed reading this book as much as I enjoyed writing it. It was an amazing journey from start to finish sharing these characters' lives and transcribing their story for the world to partake in. Much of Angie's wisdom felt channeled and came through me as a stream of consciousness. I truly enjoyed sharing her words and what felt like deep wisdom and truth as to how life is really meant to be lived.

This book has the power to change the world. But it's not the book itself that will do that. It's you. And the best way to change the world is to change yourself. Take the time to connect with, and strengthen your connection with, your own Angel. Pray, meditate, and follow the guidance you receive. Share your experiences with others, if you are called to, and pass on what you have learned and experienced. Learn to trust your inner voice and the quiet voice of knowing, and you will continually change your life for the better. And that, in turn, betters the lives of all those around you. As you change, you change the world.

As each of us evolves our hearts and minds, we collectively grow closer to making the vision of a peaceful, loving humanity a reality. We are never alone. God has sent divine beings of love and light to help and guide us every step of the way through this ever-evolving experience we call life. Through our collective experience, along with the help of the seen and unseen, we can change the world.

If you know someone whose life needs a spark of hope, mention this book, pass on your copy, or gift one to them.

And remember: *Believe, Ask, Trust, and Receive.* But it all starts with that one word ... *Believe.*

~~~ O ~~~

Let the journey continue…

Learn more about this book and the author, read and share Angel stories and experiences, and connect with the *Angel* community at:

AngelNovel.com

~~~ O ~~~

Gregory Campisi is a husband and parent, writer and author, graphic and website designer, speaker and spiritual leader, and founder, president, and director of AWAKEN Center for Human Evolution, a 501(c)(3) non-profit organization.

Learn more about Greg, his other writings, art, and creations at:

GregCampisi.com

Learn more about Greg's first children's book, *The Good Pirate,* at:

TheGoodPirate.org

Learn more about his stepdaughter's book series, *The CueCue's*, at:

CueCues.com

Learn more about AWAKEN Center for Human Evolution at:

AwakenCHE.org